Escape to the Art Café

Books in series:
Summer at the Art Café
Meet Me at the Art Café
Escape to the Art Café
Summer of Hopes and Dreams (June 2021)

Escape to the Art Café

Sue McDonagh

Where heroes are like chocolate – irresistible!

Copyright © 2021 Sue McDonagh

Published 2021 by Choc Lit Limited
Penrose House, Crawley Drive, Camberley, Surrey GU15 2AB, UK
www.choc-lit.com

A CIP catalogue record for this book is available
from the British Library

ISBN 978-1-78189-463-7

Printed and bound in Great Britain
by Clays Ltd, Elcograf S.p.A.

Dedicated to my children, whom I love dearly

Acknowledgements

Huge thanks are due to my dear friend Pamela Jones for her patient explanations and diagrams, and for being on the end of phone with answers when I needed them. If there are any discrepancies with reference to the catering and hotel sections, please know any mistakes are mine alone.

As in my previous novels, I'm deeply indebted to Pippa, who runs fabulous chocolate shop Cocoa and Co in Cowbridge. Pippa has a gift for seeing past the raw manuscript into the characters as real people, and we have spent many hours discussing my characters as if they were real people. (They are really.)

To the Cowbridge Cursors, and the Romantic Novelists Association Cardiff Chapter, thanks for letting me thrash out my plot problems over coffee, coffee and more coffee. With cake.

To my super-fit son Andrew, and his wife Natalie, now Club Captain of the Surf Life Saving Club that I used to help run, thank you for up to date assistance regarding surf rescues.

Lastly but by no means least, thank you to the Choc Lit team, for advice and support, and to my editor, whose persistence enabled me to get this book into shape and for whom I have the utmost respect.

Thanks must also go to the Tasting Panel readers who said 'yes' to this manuscript and made publication possible especially to: Isabelle D, Alan Roberton, Alma Hough, Carole Rowsell, Donna Morgan, Elisabeth Hall, Erin Thorn, Gill Leivers, Janice Butler, Jenny Kinsman, Jo Osborne, Joy Saunders, Lucie Wheatcroft, Mel Appleyard, Ruth Nägele, Shalini G and Yvonne Greene.

Prologue

'This is that biker I've told you about, who's been on the TV.' Flora flipped the double-page spread to show the girls who'd also managed to grab a quick lunch break in the hair salon where they all worked. It featured Flora's hero, Lucy Daumier, co-owner of the Art Café on the glorious South Wales Gower Peninsula, who had completely changed her life after learning to ride the motorbike she won in a raffle. She'd dumped her two-timing husband, found new love and appeared in a television series featuring her as a motorbiking artist.

'I know that area so well. We used to holiday there every year when I was little. My parents owned a cottage right on the beach, years ago. It's beautiful.' She gazed round the walls of the salon, feeling claustrophobic suddenly. Coventry seemed a long way from the sea.

'But – you're nearly thirty – so that's aaaages ago! Haven't you been since?' Karlie, her closest friend there, was straight-faced.

'Oi, cheeky!' Flora shook her head. 'No. Things changed for us and it wasn't the same.'

The receptionist put her head round the door.

'Your cut and colour is here, Flora.'

Lunch was over. But later that night when Flora closed her eyes, her mind floated back to sandy beaches and turquoise seas, rainy days and rock pools, cliff walks and sing-song voices, always kind to her.

Her mum owned the cottage now, part of the divorce settlement. She rented it out as a holiday let, and Flora knew that the long overdue renovations were finally in the process of completion.

It was ridiculous that she hadn't been back there since she was eleven. Her April birthday fell on a weekend this year – what better way of spending it than by the sea in a romantic cottage? And wouldn't it be the perfect place for Spence to propose? He was always so busy but he'd been very secretive lately. Perhaps he was planning it already! She just needed to give him the setting.

Decision made, Flora picked up her phone to call her mum.

Chapter One

Rocks.

Not the glittering kind Flora had hoped to be wearing on the third finger of her left hand this weekend. The dark, jagged rocks emerging from the foaming grey Welsh sea were more the type that Flora Bexton, hairdresser (resigned – definitely not sacked), would like to throw at the head of her boyfriend (dumped – totally, irretrievably dumped), after the not at all nice surprise he'd given her.

The waves washed over her, sending icy cold seawater flooding from collar to crotch through her too big, borrowed wetsuit. Squinting through salt-stung eyes towards the shore, she was shocked and scared to see how far away it was. Her mum's cottage was just a pale blob. Bodyboarding in sea as blue as a duck's egg had been so much fun – until suddenly it wasn't. Elbows propped on the board, she'd started thinking about the day before, and lining up her position with the land was the last thing on her mind. She'd gritted her teeth as her brain tortured her with the first instalment.

Her client for that afternoon had cancelled so she'd offered to shampoo a customer for one of the other girls. Her boss, Rex, was mixing colour on the worktop behind her.

'Do you mind if I push off early, Rex? It's my big birthday weekend and I'm so looking forward to it. The forecast looks amazing.' She glanced at him sidelong as she pumped conditioner from the big container into her palm. 'My client has cancelled, so...'

He ignored her, and she wondered if he'd actually heard her. She massaged the conditioner into the customer's scalp, until she felt him behind her, way too close behind her, pushing himself into her so that she was forced to brace herself against the sink or fall across the customer's face.

'I can do you a little favour, if you do one for me,' he whispered into her ear. Momentarily stunned, she watched as if from afar as he gripped her hands inside his.

Loudly, he said, 'No, Flora, this is how you do a head massage!' while he ground his hardening crotch into her butt.

'Mmm, that's lovely,' said the customer, her eyes shut and a blissful expression on her face. 'Nice and firm, just how I like it.'

Furious and with her hands imprisoned, Flora stamped hard on his foot and jerked her head backwards into his face.

'You fucking pervert!' she yelled, past caring what the customer thought. Rex hopped on one foot, holding his face, his eyes streaming.

'My doze! You 'itch!' His voice was muffled behind his hand. 'You're hired! I bean, you're skacked! Gegg ouk!'

For one hysterical moment, Flora wanted to laugh. She'd totally had it with him and his dirty little jokes and constant brushing past her. This was too much. She was dimly aware of the other girls, their mouths hanging open in shock. They'd discussed his behaviour in secret, tutting and raising their eyebrows, but not one of them spoke up for her now.

'Oh, don't worry, I'm leaving. You can stuff your stupid job. I'm gone!' She stormed into the staff room and threw open the door to her locker, taking furious delight in watching it rebound off the adjacent locker, leaving a dent. She rammed her belongings into her backpack.

'Oh, Flora, no! Don't let him sack you!' It was Karlie. Who'd complained about him in the staff room only the other day.

'He didn't,' said Flora, biting her lip. 'I sacked myself. I'm finding somewhere better, don't you worry!' They hugged briefly. 'Say bye to the girls! Keep in touch.' She'd left – and then things had got even worse. The memory stopped abruptly as she bounced off a rock and slashed her fingers.

If she got out of this, she bargained, watching the rivulets of blood as if they belonged to someone else, she'd be nicer. Nicer to her dad? Maaaybe. Nicer to her half-sister? Never. Scheming, hateful bitch. She would not give Amber the satisfaction of drowning.

She screamed at the rocks, digging into her last reserves of strength. She was fit. She could get out of this.

Couldn't she?

Jake's Australian body clock seemed finally to be resetting to Wales o'clock, and his stomach rumbled at approximately breakfast time for the first time in ages. Grabbing a quick shower, which was mostly tepid as the water took so long to warm up, he pulled on jeans and a T-shirt and headed downstairs, eyeing the pale dawn through the curtains. With a bit of luck, there'd be no guests around this early in the hotel, and he could throw a couple of eggs together with some toast and not be in the way.

Pete, the breakfast chef, was busy laying out bacon rashers in neat rows to be baked in the oven. He lifted his chin at Jake by way of a greeting, and Jake caught sight of the edge of an amateurish looking tattoo rising from his wrist.

'Mind if I just scramble some eggs, mate?' He nodded towards the hob. 'I'll be two secs, and out of your hair, if that's okay? I'll clear up after me.'

Pete narrowed his eyes at him and Jake got the distinct impression that he wanted to say no. He couldn't really blame him. Breakfast was a busy time in even a small hotel like theirs. But being the owners' grandson had to count for something.

'Yeah, whatev,' Pete grunted, eventually. 'Kettle's boiled. Use that pan. Don't get in my way.'

Maybe he just wasn't a morning person, Jake thought with an inner shrug, as he assembled his breakfast, finding that, apart from the new chef, nothing else had changed much in the kitchen since he'd left. Only the deep tan on his forearms reminded him that he'd actually been away, and he still hadn't been able to explain properly to his grandparents the real reason for his return. Instead, he'd allowed himself to be swallowed up by the timeless routines of the hotel that had hardly changed since he'd arrived there as a bewildered little boy.

His gran had told him over her welcoming hugs that he was too thin, and his grandfather had instructed him how to use the shower in his room. The room he'd lived in since he was four.

'It's okay, Gramps. I'm thirty-one,' he'd said with a smile. 'I know how to use a shower.'

If anyone was looking thin, it was his grandad. A tall man, he'd always been full of energy. As Jake piled his eggs onto a plate along with half a dozen slices of buttered toast, his grandfather, Bryn, strolled in, his silver white hair flattened and still damp.

'Bore da!' As his good morning in Welsh boomed round the kitchen, Jake noticed his slight stoop and trawled his memory, wondering whether he'd always had it, or whether it was much worse now. He wasn't that old, was he? Although he had to be seventy, at least. That wasn't old though, not these days.

'Bore da, Gramps!' Jake echoed, putting his plate and coffee onto a tray to take back upstairs to his bedroom. He'd never eaten with the guests, and he didn't want to eat at the kitchen table, with Grumpy Pete the Cook glaring at him. 'I'll bring this lot down when I've finished and give you a hand if you like?' Had he imagined Pete's rolled eyes? His grandad's smile faltered a little, and Jake said, hurriedly, 'Only if you need a hand. I'm not saying you do, I just thought I'd be useful, you know...' His grandfather was hovering at Pete's elbow and seemed to have forgotten that Jake was there. Pete hunched possessively over the tray of cereals he was setting out.

'These are small. Are those our usual croissants?' His grandad's tone was hectoring, and Jake saw Pete blow his cheeks out, head hunched between his shoulders.

'Yes, Mr Thomas.'

'And are you sure that's the local honeys and jams? They look different to me.'

'Yes, they're the same. They've changed the packaging, that's all.'

'Is that bacon burning?'

'No, it's fine. Don't open the oven door, please, you'll let the heat out.'

Frowning, Jake returned to his room, feeling somehow displaced, and homesick for the homes he'd left behind. Both this one, and the one in the scorching Australian heat. He felt that he didn't belong to either.

Breakfast devoured as he watched the sea from his window, he headed back downstairs, wondering whether it was still a bit early for some leftover pastries he could help to 'tidy away'. He met his gran on the landing.

'Good morning, Jake. Sleep okay?'

'More or less.' He stooped to kiss her cheek. At least Gran still seemed the same as ever. His stomach turned over a little as he registered that he'd lived in blissful ignorance about his grandparents' health all the time he'd been away – but now he was back, it was a different matter. They were all he had left, after all.

'Gran, the water wasn't very hot this morning. Do you need me to look at the boiler?'

'You just need to let it run. It's fine.' His gran raised a dismissive hand and turned towards the stairs, and he heard himself blurt, like the child he seemed to have morphed into, what was really on his mind.

'Is Gramps okay?'

'What do you mean? He's perfectly fine.'

'Oh, just that, he... er, didn't seem his usual self this morning. A bit stressy, like. In the kitchen. With the new chef?'

'Oh, him.' His gran tossed her head in irritation. 'He's a bit of a nuisance. Bryn says he forgets things.' She contemplated him and for a moment he was eight years old again. 'So, you've come back and now you're picking holes in everything?'

'Not at all! I was just a bit worried about him, that's all!' Jake shrugged.

'He's fine. He just likes to check that everything is right. Well. I'm busy, darling. Enjoy your day. Whatever it is you're doing.' She sailed down the stairs without a backward glance, leaving Jake feeling as if he'd been admonished for his aimlessness and blocked from being of any use in the hotel.

He followed her down with his tray, and smiled as he heard his grandfather charmingly instructing a table of guests how to use the small cafetière of coffee he'd delivered. But the instructions became word for word identical with each successive guest on each table, and Jake's smile froze as he lurked outside the dining room and spotted the guests raising their eyebrows at each other behind his grandfather's back, and worse, swopping their teapots, quite loudly.

'I've got an Earl Grey – I'll raise you for the English Breakfast!' called one wag, across the room, to much hilarity.

'Pot for one here – anyone got the family pot?'

Whilst Jake had never liked the forced silence of the 'guest house breakfast', he crept away feeling disquieted by the jocularity of the guests at his grandfather's expense. Bryn wasn't usually this, well, potty old bloke, was he? Wouldn't Gran have said something? Or was she in denial. What if Bryn was in the early stages of dementia? He shuddered at the idea of broaching the subject. Perhaps it was just a one-off. He'd keep an eye out. It was a horrible thought.

Restless, out of sorts, and worse, feeling unwanted, Jake went in search of his surfboard and wetsuit, finding them exactly where he'd left them on his last visit, in the outbuilding which also contained his train set, unfinished Airfix kits, books and Lego. He seriously needed to have a clear out.

He nipped back to his room, changing quickly into his wetsuit and loped down to the beach. The early chill was soon dissipated by his jog, although the neoprene of his wetsuit was stiff and unyielding, and he was glad of the smooth rash vest beneath, insulating and protecting him from chafing.

He stood for a few moments on the golden sand, waxing the board for better grip, watching the sea, feeling the offshore wind at his neck. The tide was just about to turn, and the waves were not very big, but this was Wales, and not Australia.

He scanned the beach and then noticed that the big roller shutter doors for the Lifeguard Station were open. He'd been a member of the Surf Life Saving Club here since he was a child. The big trailer carrying the racing surf skis and racing Malibu boards was parked on the forecourt, and he could see adults and children carrying out full black bin bags. So, it must be school holidays, and the start of the spring clear up. That would be fun – he'd go and give them a hand, make himself useful, say hello and find out what had been going on since he'd been away. Maybe pick up some work and local job info.

As he jogged closer, he could see several people pointing out to sea, and his gaze travelled towards the rocky outcrop east of the beach until he spotted something in the water, close to the rocks. Was it a seal, maybe? They'd seen seals before in the bay. He squinted, realising that it was a tiny figure. A child? Alone in the sea? Surely not. He froze, his stomach contracting. Please don't let it be a child.

The small gathering greeted him in brief recognition, relaying the phone message they'd just received. They turned hopeful faces towards him, relieved at his presence. The Aussie Pro Lifeguard. That's what they saw. Not the failure that he was. He couldn't do it. Not a child. He stared at them, seeing their jeans and fleeces. They were parents and helpers, not trained lifeguards.

It took a huge amount of effort to move his legs. Abandoning his surfboard, he selected the familiar yellow rescue Malibu board from the rack, to a chorus of 'Take care!' and 'We're right behind ya!'

Hefting the more substantial board beneath his arm, he ran into the sea, cursing legs gone rubbery. Fighting against his pounding heart, he threw himself onto the board and ducked beneath the waves, surfacing to scan for an adult parent close by. As he closed the gap to the rocks he could see that it wasn't a child and relief flooded over him. A teenager, maybe? Rip currents could tire a swimmer incredibly quickly.

This one looked exhausted, head down on the bodyboard, barely paddling and clearly caught in the pull of the reef. He needed to get there fast. The blood quickened in his veins as he powered towards the stricken surfer. This was what he did best. He could do it. Couldn't he?

Flora clung to the slippery surface of the bodyboard. There was no pain now. Only survival.

This had definitely not been in the plan. A weekend at the cottage to lick her wounds and then – collect her stuff, look for another job, somewhere to live... her mind slid away. None of it was going to happen.

She was going to *die* out here.

Chapter Two

'Alright, mate?'

She heard the voice, ragged on the wind, and thought she must be hallucinating.

'Don't panic, we'll getcha!'

It was definitely a voice. The muscles in her shoulders shrieked in protest as she lifted her head to look. She gaped. Was that someone? Out here, coming towards her? She knuckled saltwater from her eyes and squinted again.

'Lovely day for it, huh?' The shout was much closer and the tip of a yellow surfboard appeared over a mountainous wave, the rider paddling it towards her with reassuringly strong strokes. Surely it couldn't be...

'So you found our famous magnetic rocks! Don't worry, soon have yer outta here.'

Chris Hemsworth? Thor? From the movies?

'Yeaaah, I get that a lot.' He grinned, now alongside her. 'My biceps are bigger than his though.'

Her teeth chattered. Surely she hadn't said that out loud... And was she imagining an Australian accent? Here, in Wales?

The momentary relief of possible rescue loosened her grip and she plummeted beneath the roaring grey sea.

'If you could, just...' the man grunted as he pulled her upwards and across his board in front of him '... lie on the front by there, we'll soon be back.'

'Th-th-tha-nkkkk,' Flora tried, through teeth chattering so hard she thought she might break them. 'So... c-c-cold... sorry...'

'No worries! Right, my name's Jake and I'm gonna paddle us both back. Okay? I don't think we need this any more.'

He reached across and Flora heard the rip of the Velcro

on her wrist as the bodyboard leash was removed. She was newly terrified at the prospect of losing her flotation device as it bobbed away from them.

'Noooo! It's not mine! I can do it. I'll g-get back myself. It'll be f-f-fine.' Her words sounded like the ravings of a madwoman, and she was relieved when her rescuer wisely ignored her.

'Don't worry, it'll get washed in. Or someone will pop out and collect it. It'll be fine. I don't know how you got out all this way on that piece of junk anyway.'

His cheery confidence began to fill her with hope. Until she peeped towards the shore and saw how far out they were. And why was she at the front?

'I don't know how to steer! Shouldn't I be at the back?'

'I'm going to be your engine back here. I'm paddling for both of us. Right?' Jake's voice was calm and steady. 'I want you to hold on tight to those handles there, right by your ears, see them? One on each side.' Flora gripped them, feeling her body positioned further up the board. Her legs spreadeagled, her feet in the fins almost dangling over the sides.

'Don't let go, whatever happens.'

'Ok-k-ka-ay!' She really didn't need to be told to hold on tight. She was *never* letting go.

There was a sudden warm weight on the small of her lower back as Jake lay behind her, and with her head turned to the side, she could see his arms scooping water past, timing his actions to meet the sea as it dipped and rolled. Was, was... his chin on her... on her butt? Was it? It had to be...

There was no time to dwell on it as the next wave tossed them sideways and down. Flora was aware of Jake counterbalancing them, sitting back and leaning one way and then the other.

'Hold tight!' Jake shouted as the board tipped them both into the water. Gripping the handles, Flora saw the yellow board suspended above her as the grey brown surf boiled over them. She was almost surprised as the board flipped over and she found herself lying back on top of it.

'You okay? Sorry about that!' Jake yelled. 'Nearly there now. Always worse this close in. Messy little suckers.'

The beach closed in fast, and Flora saw a little gathering of people at the water's edge, trousers rolled to their knees, wading out to them.

She groaned as she forced her frozen body onto all fours to dismount – and slid off, colliding with Jake's solid body, her face buried in his crotch. She could feel the warmth of his body through the neoprene against her icy skin, and would have quite liked to stay there.

'Oops, I'm sorry,' she gasped, pushing herself away from him with reluctance, 'but it *is* my birthday!' Would she ever learn to engage her brain before her mouth?

'Yeah, and it was nearly your last one!' Pulling her straight up, he sat her on the board facing him, and tugged her flippers off. She clutched her calves, gasping as the muscles cramped. Her toes were icy against the warmth of his hands as he pulled them back and forth.

'Give it a minute,' he said, looking into her face.

Blinking, she stared back at him. Deepset eyes the colour of sea-washed glass in a deeply tanned face, broad mouth, his long sun-streaked blond hair tied at the nape of his neck.

'Alright, we got it now, cheers, Jake, well done, mate.' Arms in Day-Glo yellow reached out to help her off the board, and one of them cloaked a silver blanket around her shoulders. 'Can you walk? Do you need a carry?'

'I'm fine, thanks,' she lied, willing some life into her legs. Was it possible to be this cold and still be alive? She turned to face Jake. 'Th-th-thank y-y-y-you.' It was as much as her clattering jaw could manage.

'No worries.' Jake nodded. Lifting the yellow board

under his substantial bicep, he swivelled his head towards her, his expression intense, his jaw clenched. 'But look – just remember, if you're going out in conditions like this, or any time, come to that, always wear gear that fits you properly, and… did you even think to check the weather forecast?' He swept her with a look that made her cringe. 'No watch. No buoyancy aid.'

'I d-don't need a buoyancy aid with a bodyboard,' Flora said, immediately wishing she'd kept her mouth shut, as his eyebrows lifted.

'Don't tell me. You did it on holiday, right?' She nodded, shrinking into her blanket. 'On nice blue seas, in the sunshine?' She nodded again. 'And now you're an expert.' He shook his head, his mouth a straight line. And even though Flora cringed at her own crassness, she couldn't help noticing what a nice mouth it was. Firm. Lips – just right.

'Typical rookie mistake,' he carried on. 'Not checking the tide, the weather, your gear, not properly kitted out.' He glanced down at her wet suit, which hung in folds around her limbs like one of those Chinese designer dogs. 'And no surfing buddy. Never,' he fixed her with those fathomless eyes, 'ever, surf on your own. Ever. Always go with someone.' His voice was stern.

The blood pounded suddenly in her head. She'd been betrayed by her boyfriend and lost her job and nearly died out there and she did not need to be lectured like a child.

'I don't h-have anyone to go surfing with.' Aghast at the break in her voice, she heard herself sob. 'I d-don't ha-have anyone to do anything with any more…' Covering her face with her hands to block out the sight of Jake's suddenly shocked expression, she stalked stiff legged up the beach between two tall, silent girls wearing huge, high-vis jackets and sympathetic expressions.

Her nose poured with snot and seawater, and she tried to

cuff it, sniffing and shuddering under her blanket. This wasn't the escape she'd thought it would be. She was an idiot. She would get her stuff and leave. She couldn't stay here. Except that she had nowhere to go. Not home. Not back to him. How could he – they – have done that? Fresh tears flowed, and she thought her heart would break.

'Are you okay?' one of the girls asked, after a moment, as her ragged sobs abated. 'That's a little bit of a cut on your hand, we'll sort that out for you now. Is there anyone you'd like us to call? Have you got far to go home? Would you like to go to hospital? Is there anyone to take you? Have you had a tetanus shot recently?'

The questions flowed over Flora and she shook her head to all of them until the last one, which she nodded to. She would be sticking to her motorbike from now on, she decided. And people thought that was dangerous! This was ten times worse. Plus you got to wear more clothes on a bike. She was never going to be warm again.

As she walked up the beach between the girls, she cranked her aching neck over her shoulder, to a sea the colour of mussel shells and a pewter sky. She had been lucky.

'Please thank him again, from me,' she said to the Day-Glo jacket walking alongside. 'I tried, but...'

'Oh, don't worry – that's his job, in Australia,' said one of the girls inside the huge fluorescent jacket. The note of pride in her voice was unmistakeable. 'He's amazing. Everyone talks about him...' She shrugged. 'You were lucky.'

'He gave me a massive bollocking,' said Flora. 'But, really, everything he said was spot on. I won't be going out there again in a hurry. If at all. I'll stick to my motorbike. Less dangerous!' She tried for a laugh but heard it emerge as a hoarse intake of breath instead.

'You're a biker? You'll get on with the girls in the café then. They're all proper into their bikes.'

'The Art Café?' Flora was jolted with excitement, her misery forgotten for a moment. 'Do you know her, the one who runs it? Lucy?'

The girls chuckled. 'Course! Everyone knows Lucy. Our resident TV star. But she's lovely. So nice. Actually, it was someone from the café who rang here to tell us you were in trouble in the sea.'

'Wow. I'll have to go over and say thank you.' Flora swallowed, realising again how lucky she'd been. 'This is my birthday weekend. I saw her on the TV and I was hoping that we'd have afternoon tea there. Me. Not we,' she edited herself, quickly.

'You should definitely pop in and say hi then. They do the best hot chocolate over there. That'd warm you up.' They'd reached the first aid room, and Flora sank onto a chair with the silver blanket round her shoulders, while they inspected the gash on the side of her hand. Once it was washed and dried, it didn't look too bad. With instructions to go directly to Casualty if there were any problems with it, they gave her a waterproof plaster to put over it.

Casualty? Flora was planning to head over to the café as soon as she'd given her details to the pleasant-faced girl lifeguards. 'Are you staying locally?' they'd asked her. 'Is there anyone we can ring?'

Flora shook her head, tightening her lips over the tears threatening once again at how alone she really was there. What a stupid idea this had been. And so typical of her. Rush in, make a mess of everything.

'Do you want a hand getting changed?'

Flora shook her head. 'I haven't got anything on under this,' she told the girls in a rush. Her other woes queued up, ready to spill at the first kind word from either of them.

'Hardcore!' The girls laughed, and Flora's shoulders relaxed.

'It's not my wetsuit,' she began, and the girls laughed again.

'You don't say,' one of them said, her face straight, but her eyes twinkling. Flora looked down at the baggy neoprene and joined in with their laughter.

'And my front door key is in the little pocket at the back here.' She indicated the back of her neck. 'And I'll have to take my wetsuit off to get to it... Outside the front door... with nothing on...'

'No worries. Turn round. You won't be the first.' She felt their warm fingers at the nape of her neck and they handed her the key.

Her conscience pricked her as she gave them a false name and address after they'd been so nice to her but she really didn't want anyone tracking her down to here, not after what she'd done.

The false name had popped into her head after reading it on one of the life-size half torsos stacked in the corner of the first aid room. A resuscitation training device, it was quite creepy really, with that pale face, slightly open mouth and closed eyes.

Thanking them for their help, she plodded back towards Sea-Spray Cottage, holding a flipper in each hand. Although it was only just across the road from the beach, it might as well have been miles to her leaden legs.

She trailed wet sand into the pristine cottage, without the energy to take off the wetsuit booties. When she'd arrived at that front door late the previous evening, she'd steeled herself for a flood of memories from those childhood summers. She still wasn't sure whether to be relieved or disappointed that she remembered nothing of the cottage. Was it the extensive refit? Or her brain, wiping it all out? She'd really thought it would all come back to her, but she felt like a stranger.

It was lovely though. Huge sliding doors looked out over

the beach, and the striped window seat covered in bold floral cushions, was a perfect place to sit and watch the world go by. Flora had exclusive use of it for the weekend, plus her lovely mum had even provided a basket of groceries for her, as a birthday present.

Flora gulped now, close to tears as her eyes rested on the champagne, red and white wines and foil wrapped chocolate hearts, for her 'romantic birthday break'.

Thinking of her mum made her feel even more lonely. She wished she'd asked her to come with her now. But she'd been so prickly – angry and spitting with rage, that no one in their right mind would have wanted to spend any time with her.

She trudged into the bathroom, painted soft white and chalky blue just like the rest of the cottage, turned the shower to hot and stepped under it in her wetsuit as steam billowed into the room. Only after the warm water had poured down between the clammy neoprene and her skin did she struggle out of the clinging wetsuit, kicking it to one side of the shower tray.

Her skin was goose-pimpled and cold as a chilled chicken. She had to force herself to shampoo her short hair and squirt some shower gel into hands that tingled as the blood returned, and then she slid down the wall and sat in the shower tray as the hot water flowed over her.

She could have slept in there. It was a huge effort to switch the shower off and leave it. Wrapping herself in a huge, thick towel and thanking her mum in her head for her ability to choose the best of everything, she patted herself dry without her usual brisk energy, turned up the heating, and pulled the thoughtfully provided bathrobe on. Her cropped hair took moments to finger dry. She thought about making herself a hot drink, but instead, crawled between the sheets of the bed that she'd tossed and turned in all night long, and closed her eyes, desperate for sleep.

Chapter Three

Behind the blankness of her eyelids, yesterday replayed itself again like a film that she didn't want to watch. No matter how much she squeezed her eyes shut, tossed and punched the pillow, it reeled relentlessly until she had no option but to watch it all over again.

She'd been so looking forward to the weekend. The magazine article had planted a tiny seed about returning to visit the beach in Wales where she'd spent so many endless school holidays, and she'd booked the cottage for her and Spence. Just for the weekend. Just for her birthday. Her thirtieth. A bit of a milestone, really, as birthdays went.

They used to be so magical, her birthdays at the cottage when she was little. And then, after that bombshell on her eleventh birthday, well, they weren't so wonderful. Not. At. All. They were a measure each year of just how rubbish her life was. The memory was still bright in her mind, and every now and again she brought it out to assess how much it mattered to her. It was hard to imagine sometimes that it was possible to hold the piercing misery of that day for so many years, but she had.

And what on earth had made them, her parents, think that her birthday was a good time to tell her that the new little girl who'd arrived to join in with her party on the beach was actually her half-sister? A half-sister who seemed only a little younger than she was!

She'd never returned to the cottage since. With the intransigence that only a pre-teen could manage, she utterly refused to go back. She'd closed her mind off to its existence, and never spoke of it, despite her mum's gentle persuasion. Her father, whom she'd adored, had totally betrayed them and Flora hated what he'd done.

The fact that all the adults behaved with polite civility made it worse as far as she was concerned. She wanted her mum to rant and scream, and she never did. She smiled gently, hugged her dad and was nice to the 'other woman', Helen.

Flora made up for all the screaming and ranting, she remembered. Possessed with a pure rage, she vented it on everybody, and they all returned her fury with love and patience. Except Amber. Amber, the new and exceptionally beautiful child at her beach birthday party, who she'd actually quite liked – until she'd found out that she was her little sister – was the perfect mirror to her turbulent emotions. Amber was horrible. Truly horrible. But she knew how to act the part. So where Flora cried and sulked, Amber was sweet and compliant. Her sly and nasty pranks went mostly unpunished, because everyone thought Flora was whining as usual. It was hard to admit to being bullied by a younger sister.

True to form, here was her birthday weekend and like a house of cards, one disaster had crashed into the next. She was in a romantic and beautiful cottage on the beach – on her own.

She jerked upwards and then flung herself back on the pillows, kicking the duvet. This weekend topped all the others though. Nothing had ever been this bad. Squeezing her eyes shut she snarled as the internal film of her disaster weekend began to play again, continuing smoothly on from her biffing her boss and walking out...

Outside the hair salon, in the cool air, she'd gulped in some deep breaths, her hand shaking as she dropped the key to her motorbike lock over and over until she could shriek. She had to calm down; she couldn't ride in the state she was in. The anger that flooded her body had left her nauseous and shaky.

When she felt a bit calmer, she screwed her earplugs in, pulled on her crash helmet and tightened the buckle beneath her chin. As she focused on the ride in quiet traffic and with the sun warming her back, the tension in her stomach eased, and she could hear her optimistic brain making plans to apply to other salons. Stuff Rex and his salon. She could do so much better. One day, she'd have her own hair salon and she'd be a thousand times better at running it than that pervert was.

As she turned into her road, she slowed, pressed the fob, which opened the garage door remotely, watched it roll reliably upwards, then turned the engine off and freewheeled down the steep drive straight into the garage. It always filled her with glee, watching that door slide reliably upwards so that she could just ride straight in.

Unfortunately, there wasn't a remote control to turn her bike around once it was actually inside the garage, and try as she might, she found the space too small to do it herself. It frustrated her that she had to wait for her boyfriend, Spence, to do it for her. He either pushed it backwards into the garage for her, or he swivelled it on its side stand. She couldn't watch when he did either, anxious that he might drop her precious bike.

It wasn't a cool, expensive bike, like his Ducati, but it was hers, it was paid for and it represented her mobility, cheap transport to work and fun to ride. Her precious bright green 300cc Ninja.

She'd let herself in, quietly, as Spence worked from home and often held video calls that she'd once blundered into with a cheery, 'Hello, big boy!' She'd only done that the once. He'd been livid with her.

Dumping her rucksack by the door, she crept upstairs, put her head round the office door and saw his empty chair. Assuming he was in the loo, she pushed open the door to their bedroom to change out of her bike gear. And after what she'd seen, she'd had no choice – she'd fled.

And she'd left her own bike behind...

* * *

She must have slept from sheer exhaustion as she awoke a few hours later to a barrage of pings from WhatsApp, the girls from the salon wishing her a happy birthday. Feeling a little tearful and emotional to be away from everyone her thumbs flew over the little keyboard, thanking them for their messages. There was no news of Rex or what he might be planning to do, and she didn't quite dare to ask. There was a limit to what she could cope with at the moment. And no messages from Spence.

She didn't know what to think about that. Was he worried that she was missing? Had he taken any notice of where they'd been planning to go that weekend? She suspected that he hadn't. She wasn't sure that he'd paid very much attention at all to her excited planning, seeing as he'd had other things on his mind. Had he ever paid any attention to *her*?

Her stomach contracted, sending hot stabs of pain through her chest. She clamped her mouth over the fury of betrayal. Jumping up, she paced the room, twitching with nervous energy.

The girl lifeguard's words floated like a salve into her troubled mind. 'They do the best hot chocolate over there. That'd warm you up.' Her stomach rumbled at the thought of a tall hot chocolate with whipped cream and marshmallows and a flake. And then she'd text the girls and tell them where she was… at the famous Lucy's Art Café. She couldn't just sit there like a loser all weekend.

Dressing, she pulled her bike jacket on over her fleece, and headed back over the road towards the café, shivering in the freshening wind. The flurry of messages from her friends had made her feel homesick, but the two motorbikes parked in the car park and the knowledge that the café belonged to bikers felt familiar and made her feel as if she might belong too. Directly overlooking the beach, the paint was smart and designer sea-greenish grey, the signage arty and trendy, and

Flora knew, from her avid research, that it was also a leading place to buy art, handmade jewellery and ceramics. That was Lucy's responsibility. Her co-partner Richard made the cakes. It seemed to be a partnership made in heaven and she was thrilled to see it in real life.

As she pushed the door open the warm air drew her in, and she stepped inside, sniffing the fresh milled coffee beans and comforting scents of toast and teacakes on the air. It was so similar to the stylish coffee shops she visited back home, that she sat and drank big lattes in with her shithead ex-boyfriend – she couldn't even give his name headroom – and she was astonished to find herself swallowing down a sob and swiping tears from her eyes with the back of her hand. Why had they done this to her?

She needed a friendly, familiar face right now, someone who knew her and would make allowances for her being a bit weird – and these people in the café were just strangers. Her body reflected her indecisions, hesitating, flinching, making for the exit, and she had to make it stay, like a bad dog that never did as she wanted. Why was everything so black and white for her? Such a drama? Running away couldn't always be the answer.

She should have stayed at her mum's – the sofa would have done at a pinch – then gone back home after a few days, talked it over with Spence. As she thought it, she knew she could not have done that. It wasn't how she was made. If she'd gone back, she'd have killed him. And although it was one of those things you say that you don't really mean, at that moment, when she'd seen them, together, her long legs around his clenched butt, she'd had to turn away, not at all responsible for what her body might do without her brain engaged. She didn't want to think about it, about them.

What she *had* done seemed bad enough.

Chapter Four

The lifeguard clubhouse was a hive of industry, swarming with volunteers, plus junior members and their parents, all brought together that day to clean the building and equipment ready for the start of the summer season. It had been lucky for the girl he'd rescued that they'd just opened up. There were no patrols scheduled at this time of the year, so there had been no warning flags out. Not that she would have taken any notice, he suspected.

Several people looked up from their sweeping and gathering rubbish into black bin liners to hail him.

'Alright, Jake – good job out there!'

'Good thing you were here!'

'You should be nominated for an award!'

He acknowledged them all with a smile. An award? They wouldn't be saying that if they knew... He shivered, as the chill caught up with him.

Later, showered and changed, he casually wandered into the first aid room, glancing at the register of details from lost children, those who received first aid attention and people who were plucked out of the sea.

The last line read, 'Annie Rees, Clare Gardens.' As he read it, his eyes travelled around the room, resting on one of the mannequins on which they practised their lifesaving techniques. Clearly printed in big letters on the bag were the words, 'Re-Sussi Annie'. Annie Rees. Bit too much of a coincidence? A false name. Had to be. He frowned to himself and couldn't help wondering why she'd done that. What did she have to hide?

But finding out wasn't actually his job, and he knew it. He was wasting time. Restlessness and guilt crept up on him and he went upstairs into the steamy kitchen, where the helpers and parents were splitting long bread rolls and holding them out to be filled from the vast tureen of hot dog sausages heating on the hob. A line of small children who had been working clearing rubbish off the beach and into bin liners, squirted into the loaded rolls from yellow and red bottles, devouring them enthusiastically.

'Wanna 'dog?' Someone held one out to him, and Jake took it, aware at that moment of his piercing hunger. Three hot dogs later, and his appetite sated for the time being, he waved a goodbye to the club members who were winding down now, munching on hot dogs and discussing the year's competitions, awards and training.

A Lifeguard Club, the members of the charity organisation who arranged lifeguard training and beach patrols, was never at rest for long, there was always a calendar of events to attend to and required a hundred per cent input from everyone. It was what he'd always liked most about it. The feeling of belonging. Jake was not only a local from childhood, he knew that he represented the pinnacle of Surf Life Saving by working as a professional in Australia. And despite assurances from everyone to the contrary, he could not shake off the terrible guilt of the rescue that had gone horribly wrong. It was why he'd come home. He could have stayed, applied for residency. But he just couldn't live with himself right now.

He didn't plan to go far now he was home again. He loved it here. Looking around him at the beach, swept by a chilly breeze and with the sun hiding behind grey clouds, he still thought it knocked socks off the sun scorched Aussie sands. Or maybe it was just that it represented home. Where, if he was honest with himself, he would rather not be but he needed a place to lick his wounds and realised it was time to shoulder his responsibilities and do some growing up. It was easy to throw himself into the sea, an environment he knew and could deal with. His body was trained, his muscles strong. Physical exertion had always come easy to him.

This though – this mental anguish – was much harder to get to grips with than lifting heavy weights.

The café was warm, which was good, and full to bursting, which was not so good. Having acknowledged that she felt the need for company, Flora wasn't at all sure that she actually wanted to talk to anyone. She felt emotional and vulnerable, which wasn't at all like the hard as nails exterior she took care to preserve. Her nickname in school had been 'Cactus', or 'Spike', at odds with her floral name but very in keeping with her personality.

She couldn't avoid thinking that it was all very well having this little holiday by the seaside for a few days, but she had to return to her old life some time, and right now she had no job, no boyfriend, and nowhere to live. Sitting in this nice café overlooking the beach was just another way of holding off the inevitable – life on her mum's sofa.

'Hot chocolate, please,' she said, eyeing up the cabinet full of delicious looking cakes. Her stomach gurgled loudly and the tall, dark-haired girl behind the counter laughed. The name badge on the smart black pinny emblazoned with the Art Café logo of an artists' palette of cakes said her name was Jo.

'With all the toppings?' she asked.

Flora nodded. 'Yes, please – and that cake there.' She pointed at a giant slab of carrot cake, her favourite.

'You want custard with it?'

'Custard? Is that usual?'

'It's a great way to warm up,' Jo said with a smile. 'You look frozen, if you don't mind me saying. And you sound starving.'

'Oh, hell, yeah, go on then.' Flora smiled back at her. 'Right on both counts, as it happens.'

'I'll bring it to your table. Where are you sitting?'

Flora scanned the café. Her heart sank as she saw that the only vacant seat was at a table already occupied by her cantankerous rescuer of that morning, unmistakeable by his long surfer dude tied back hair, deep tan and breadth of shoulder. What had the lifeguard girl said his name was? Jake. He stared gloomily into his cup, and she decided that at least he wouldn't want to make conversation.

'There.' She pointed, and then added impulsively, before her nerve failed, 'Is the manager in today? I wondered if there were any vacancies in the café?'

'Can you call in tomorrow? We open at ten. There'll be someone here then.' Jo smiled and threw a pointed look over Flora's shoulder to indicate that there was a queue behind her, so Flora weaved her way through the tables and sat down opposite Jake.

He looked up briefly, acknowledging her presence with a lift of his chin. Flora opened her mouth to say something and clamped it shut as he returned to nursing his coffee, stirring it into a whirlpool with grim determination. He obviously hadn't recognised her. Well, she was dry, and she had clothes on, and he'd only looked at her long enough to berate her in any case.

'There'll be a distress flare going up in there any minute,' she said, nodding at his cup. He frowned at her.

'Sorry?' He pinned her with his sea green eyes, the chiselled planes of his face sharp, and she sat up straighter, a part of her wishing as she always did, that she'd kept her mouth shut.

'I, er, just wanted to say thank you for rescuing me this morning.' She watched his gaze travel over her face. 'Bodyboard on the magnetic rocks?' His eyebrows shot up. Thick, sun-bleached against his tan. Like his hair. Which she was itching to get her hairdresser's hands on. It seriously needed a decent cut and some conditioner. Those salted locks were almost dreads now.

'Ah.' He nodded, his expression still stern. 'You're "Annie Rees". Apparently.'

Flora could hear the inverted commas around the made up name, which told her that he knew it was fake. She barely knew why she'd done that. She'd have been a hopeless undercover agent.

'Er...' She fidgeted, feeling awkward, looking around for another seat somewhere and seeing none. Her hot chocolate arrived and when she looked back at him, he was still regarding her steadily. She felt as if she was being peeled like an apple.

'Okay, I think I owe you an apology,' he said, throwing her completely.

'Huh? Really? I thought it was me that had the drama queen meltdown.'

He looked taken aback, and Flora watched as a slow smile lifted his face, revealing white teeth and laughter lines radiating from his eyes. He looked like a completely different person in that moment, back to the jokey hero in the surf. 'We all have our troubles, I'm sure. It was the wrong time to be lecturing you.' He sat back and eyed her warily.

She spooned some of the cream off the top of her hot chocolate and licked the spoon.

'Yep. And after you had your chin on my butt all that time too.' Dear me, what had happened to her filters? They were barely present at the best of times, but lately...

His eyebrows nearly shot into his hairline. 'Excuse me?' The laughter lines disappeared.

'Sorry... sorry, stupid attempt at a joke...' She picked up the glass mug by the handle and sipped at her drink to give her mouth something else to do, trying not to wince at how hot it was and reaching hurriedly for a paper napkin to blot what she was sure was a cream moustache.

'Hmm.' He frowned at her, but she could see that generous

mouth quirking up at one corner. 'No one else has ever complained…' He lifted his cup to his mouth and took a sip. 'Yeuch. Cold. I'm not usually such a—' He shook his head and shrugged.

'—Grouch?' Flora supplied.

'Yeah. I guess.' There was a definite Down Under twang to his accent.

'It's not your job to be nice to me. And everything you said was correct, anyway. I deserved it all. It was just a bit close to the bone, today.' She looked up as her carrot cake arrived. It was an enormous portion, completely covered in custard. 'Crikey. I can't eat all that.'

'One way of filling out that wetsuit,' Jake said, staring at the brimming bowl.

'It wasn't my wetsuit.'

'I guessed that when I grabbed a handful of neoprene with nobody inside it,' Jake said, and then added in a high pitched voice that was obviously meant to be her, 'Oh no, I can manage thank you, I don't need rescuing. I'm enjoying myself out here, really. The water's lovely…'

'Oh dear. Was I really that bad? Sorry. Glad you ignored my bleatings, although I think you made that last bit up. I really am my own worst enemy sometimes.' Flora's appetite waned as she contemplated the huge dessert. 'Do you want this?' She pushed it towards him.

'I'll help you, if you like.'

'I'm not double dipping with you, I hardly know you.' She leapt up. Everything she said sounded like a double entendre. It had to be the sea air. 'I'll get another dish.'

When she returned to the table, she spooned a small portion into the new bowl, and couldn't help a chuckle at Jake's attempt not to look disappointed. 'This one's for me. I think my eyes were bigger than my belly when I ordered that lot.'

'My gran used to say that to me.' Jake pulled the bowl

of still steaming dessert towards him without hesitation. 'Thanks, er, Anna. Very kind of you.'

They ate in silence for a moment, and Flora felt the hot custard and carrot cake warming her at last. Shrugging out of her leather bike jacket, she hooked it over the back of her chair and watched him devour the rest of his bowl. 'You don't sound like you come from round here.'

'I do – sort of,' he said, between mouthfuls. 'But it's a long story.'

Flora looked out of the floor to ceiling windows, where the darkening sky had unleashed a torrent of rain, and said, 'I'm not going anywhere right now. Want another coffee?' She hurried on, 'As a thank you for rescuing me?'

'You don't need to thank me. It's my job. You're not from round here either are you? That's not a Welsh accent.'

'I know. It's not really an accent at all, is it? I'm also a "sort of". With a long story.' She could hardly believe she'd told him that. She was used to people telling her their confidences.

'I've eaten your carrot cake, so I'll get the coffee. What are you having?'

Flora gave in. 'Latte, please.'

Rain beat at the windows, and there were ragged white tips to the grey waves as golden pools of light from the café spilled across the car park. It was cosy in there, and she had nowhere else to be. Neither apparently did anyone else in the café, as it was still packed. And she had to admit to being just a tiny bit intrigued by Jake, a bronzed Antipodean anomaly amongst the dripping cagoules and winter-pale faces. He might have been gruff with her, but there was nothing threatening about him. He just looked like a man with a lot on his mind. She remembered the girl lifeguard describing him as a good egg. And who was she to judge, with her school nickname of Cactus? She could be hellish spikey when she wanted to be, couldn't she?

Chapter Five

Jake watched her from the counter as he waited to place his order. Arms folded, she glared out at the rain as if it was a personal affront. She was tiny, her sharp elbows wrapped around the knees she'd brought up to her chest, and with her glossy, cropped dark hair she reminded him of a cross fairy from one of the children's books they'd always had knocking about for the kids in the Lifeguard Station. She looked like someone trying to be tough, although he'd felt the hardness of her muscles beneath the baggy wetsuit, and despite his admonishment, he'd rather admired her spirit as she'd tried to paddle her way out of trouble.

She was a good-looking girl, like a pocket Angelina Jolie, but he preferred carefree, sun-bleached blondes in bikinis. Like his girlfriend back in Oz. Except that he didn't even know where she was any more, apart from on the other side of the world. Probably.

His order of coffees, along with a couple of extra muffins, arrived on a tray at his elbow while he was musing, and he bore it carefully past the heaps of steaming waterproofs and rucksacks.

Wrapping her small hands around the mug, she smiled a thank you at him.

'Go on then. Your story. Get it off your chest.' She fixed him with a steady gaze from pale grey eyes. Like one of those husky dogs, he found himself thinking. A bit unnerving, in a way. He spread his hands on the table. It was almost a relief to talk to a stranger.

'I was brought up here when I was a child, after my parents died,' he began in a matter-of-fact voice, staring at his fingers.

'Oh,' she murmured, and he looked up to see compassion in her face.

'Don't worry, this isn't a "poor me" story.' He smiled at her. 'I'm just giving you a bit of background. So my grandparents took over and brought me up. They ruined me, honestly. Don't feel sorry for me!' She was silent and watchful and he felt compelled to continue. 'They pretty much let me do whatever I wanted, so I did. I've travelled all over the world and I've just come back from travelling in Australia. Ended up near Sydney.' He stirred two sugars into his coffee to give himself something to do.

'What did your grandparents think?'

'They were happy if I was happy.' Even to his own ears it sounded selfish.

'And were you happy?'

God, it was like being interrogated. He nodded. 'Hell, yeah. I used to call regularly, but then my life got so busy that—'

'You didn't have time.' She finished his sentence without a trace of accusation and he grunted his agreement. He didn't want to add that Wales had faded from his day-to-day consciousness as time went on. He'd made a life for himself in Australia, and he could almost convince himself that he was truly a local. And not just the little lost boy that everyone knew him as here. He stared beyond the rain-lashed windows to the silver grey sea, the foaming waves crashing onto the sand. It was nothing like Sydney. He still couldn't decide if that was good or bad.

'So why have you come home?'

'My visa's up.'

She frowned. 'What does that mean?'

'You can get a work visa for two years before you're thirty.'

'You've been in Australia for two years?' She made it sound like a lifetime. 'The longest I've been away for is two weeks. So lack of a visa is the reason you've come back?'

He shrugged. 'Yep, I've passed the magic age.'

'Ah. Me too.'

'Oh yeah – you said something about it being your birthday…'

He watched the colour rise to her cheeks. It made her look softer, less angry. 'So, enough about me. What are you doing here?'

She shrugged. 'It's my big romantic birthday break.' She indicated the vacant chair beside her, straight-faced. 'Duh. Can't you see my hunky, virtual boyfriend here?'

Jake swivelled his eyes to the empty seat and back at her, and then raised his eyebrows in mute enquiry.

'And, no, I don't want to talk about it. It's too tragic for words. It's like something off daytime telly.'

'Like what?'

'Never mind.' She shrugged. 'Let's just say that my shithead boyfriend can't keep it in his pocket.'

'Can't keep… what?' Jake creased his brow and then understood. 'Oh. So you're here on your own.'

'Yes.' She glared at him. 'But I'm not a victim, okay? I'm fine. Totally fine. He's not spoiling my life. And neither is she.' Her mouth clamped into a thin, straight line, loosening just enough to allow one bitter word to slip through. 'Bitch.'

'Ah.' Jake looked into his mug. He had no idea what to say. This was girl territory and he was out of his depth. 'So,' he tried. 'You dump the shithead boyfriend and then go surfing. Well, you go for a drown, anyway.' He blew on his coffee. 'I can see your logic.'

She stared at him in silence for a long moment, and then pealed with laughter, revealing a whole other side to her personality. It was like seeing the sun appear suddenly from behind a dark cloud.

'It seemed like a good idea at the time,' she said, her mouth still holding the curve of her smile.

'Oh trust me, I'm not knocking it. Apart from the drowning bit, that is. Everything I told you about safety and stuff still stands.' He turned the mug round in his hands. 'But the sea is my escape. It's the only place I feel like I properly exist.'

She eyed him, nodding slowly. 'I think I got that already. You're different.' She gestured through the window towards the beach. 'Out there.'

It was his turn to sit in silence. It hadn't quite been the truth. The sea had always been his escape, and bringing Flora back to shore had proved to him that he could still do it, but it was never going to expunge the mistakes he'd made. His eyes roved over the beach, turning soft purple as a stormy dusk began to bruise the sky. She was on a roll now though.

'So. No boyfriend. And no job either. Happy Bloody Birthday to Me.' She made a sound that was probably an attempt at a self-deprecating laugh, but came out like a harsh snort, 'hah'. 'And nowhere to live, now I come to think about it.'

'You lost your job at the same time? Did you work for him?' Jake hazarded a guess.

'No, thank God. I couldn't spend all day in front of a computer screen like he does.' She sat up and drew her arms backwards across the table, leaning back in the chair with a sigh. She stared over his shoulder and shook her head. 'You don't need to know about the job thing. Another tale of woe.' She turned a bleak expression on him. 'But I had to get away. Luckily, I'd booked my mum's holiday cottage for the weekend. There's plenty of bubbly and foil wrapped hearts to feast on. I'm going to eat the lot by myself tonight. It's been one of those days.' She turned a tight smile on him that didn't reach her eyes.

'Oh.' No wonder she'd burst into tears. And his grumpy attitude hadn't helped at all, with his high and mighty proclamations. 'I think you've trumped me in the sad story stakes.'

'I'll be fine.' She lifted her chin, and met his eye, but even he knew that when women say they're fine in that tone, it meant they were falling to bits inside but too proud to tell you.

'Hang on a minute— So when exactly is your birthday?'

'Today.' He caught the tiniest wobble of her bottom lip in that fierce expression.

'Oh hell. Well, er, happy birthday! I bought you a muffin.' He pushed one towards her. She stared at it and he held his breath. What would he do if she burst into tears?

'Thank you, but... can I have the other one?' she said. 'I prefer lemon muffins.'

He laughed. 'A woman who knows her own mind. I like it.' He was pleased to see her eat the cake, as she'd barely managed more than a spoonful of the carrot cake she'd purchased earlier. 'So, you mentioned that you were "sort of" from round here. What's that about?'

She turned a naughty smile on him. 'I was conceived here.'

He coughed on a stray crumb of muffin. He hadn't been expecting that. Her smile turned to concern and she got up to bang his back.

'I'm fine!' He held up a hand, his eyes watering. 'You can stop beating me now. Thank you.'

'We used to holiday every summer here when I was little. I loved it.' Her pale eyes became soft and a smile played around her mouth. Jake leaned forward, watching her. 'Mum and Dad bought a tatty little cottage right on the beach when they were cheap, and every time we came here, they did a bit more to it. I was left to wander on the beach, do what I liked. It was paradise. Just the three of us.' He watched as her eyes roamed the sea, lost in her thoughts. She seemed oddly familiar, with that jut of her pointed chin and those upturned, fairy eyes. As if mischief was never far away. She was silent for so long, he thought she'd forgotten him. Then she heaved a sigh, and turned a brilliant, beaming smile on him. 'No point in dwelling on the past though, eh?'

He shook his head in agreement, but wasn't fooled in the slightest. This was someone very much dwelling in the past.

'So, what's your real name?' He saw her eyes widen, and knew his earlier instincts had been correct. She lifted her chin.

'It's Flora.'

'Flora? Exactly like Anna, then. I can see how the mistake was made.' He narrowed his eyes at her. 'Are you on the run, with a false name? You haven't killed your boyfriend, have you? I mean, I'm pretty sure he deserved it, but—'

'No!' She glared at him, and then huffed, rummaging in the pocket of her jacket for a business card which she handed over. He read, Kutz2Go, Ask for Flora! Along with an address and phone number. 'No point ringing for a recommendation from my pervert of a boss though. And he might sound a bit funny, seeing as he's nursing a broken nose...' she said, with a shrug of her eyebrows. 'Which he totally deserved.' Jake felt his own eyebrows rising. Broken nose? She carried on, 'Unless you speak to one of the girls, of course.' She gave him a lopsided grin and carried on as if she was advertising herself. 'I'm a hairdresser. Fully qualified. I can do colour, cuts, highlights, extensions, the lot. Fancy a makeover?'

There was a long pause and Jake thought about meeting his gran on the stairs that morning, and how unruly her usually perfect hair was.

'The makeover thing was just a joke,' Flora said, hesitantly. He stroked his chin, eyeing her.

'Sorry, I was just thinking. I think I'm beyond redemption, but I know someone who would love a bit of pampering. Gran doesn't go a week without a hairdo, and I know that she's probably hating the way she looks right now. Could you do that?' He waved a vague hand. 'Shampoo, er, blow-dry?' He'd reached the limit of his knowledge of women's hair care. 'I'll pay you, of course.'

'Surely she's got her own hairdresser? She'll think I'm bonkers just turning up.'

Jake blew out a long sigh. 'I hadn't really thought of that. I just wanted to do something nice for her.'

'Flowers? Gin? My mum loves gin. It's dead trendy right now. You can get all sorts of flavours and stuff.'

Jake frowned. 'Gin? God, I don't have a clue what Gran drinks these days.' He sipped his coffee. 'I feel like I've come back as a stranger. It's so weird. Everything looks the same as it used to, but nothing is.'

'Maybe you should take your grandparents out. Get to know them again. They might feel the same about you. You've been away for a long time.'

He felt a jolt in his stomach and tugged at his long hair. He had caught his gran staring at it, askance, several times since his return. He hadn't thought of that, either. 'What are you, some sort of therapist?' He smiled, but she'd made him look at things in a different way.

'Me? No. Yes. I'm a hairdresser!' She shrugged her little pointy shoulders. 'People tell me stuff all the time. I'm a good listener.' The colour rose in her cheeks a little as she leaned forward. 'I could do your hair though. If you like.' Her hand lifted and her small, slim fingers worked in the air as if they were combing through his head. He lifted the dry heap of hair off his head, self-conscious now. It truly hadn't occurred to him.

'Er... like what? Short back and sides?' He laughed nervously, and she rewarded him with a gentle smile, clearly in her element.

'Well, maybe, if that's what you want. Or just a tidy up. But if your gran sees you looking more like you did before you left, maybe...? And if she likes it, then maybe she'll let me do hers?'

He heard himself agreeing to her plan without quite knowing how it had happened. Was she some sort of mind reader? She'd made it sound like it was his idea to start with.

'Where?' he asked.

'I suppose you could come to the cottage. I'm not sure that's a good plan though…'

'I live in a hotel,' Jake said, guessing at her meaning. She didn't feel safe with him. He waved an arm to suggest that it wasn't far.

'Random.' She blinked. 'Okay…'

'There's plenty of room there, and lots of people about. You'll be perfectly safe. And er, obviously, I can pay you.'

'I know I'll be safe, thank you! I wasn't worried about that at all! I've done every self-defence class going. I might be short but I am tough.' Her tone was scornful. 'I am perfectly capable of looking after myself. And look, you don't have to pay me. This is a thank you for rescuing me.'

'Are you always this independent?'

A grin flashed across her face, which was all the answer he needed.

'So… are you going to try to get him back, the offending "virtual" boyfriend?' Jake wondered, as always, how it was that the blokes who behaved the worst seemed to attract the nicest girls.

'Are you having a laugh?' Flora's smile sent shivers up his spine. 'I'm working out how to kill him. Horribly. And her. Bitch.'

He hoped she was joking… maybe it was him who should be worried about his safety…

She changed the subject from herself then, asking him about his life in Australia and when they couldn't drink any more coffee, it was the signal to leave. He told her he'd meet her back at the Art Café the following morning, about eleven, and take her to the hotel.

Chapter Six

Flora hurried to the cottage in the pelting rain, her jacket over her head. Thunder clapped and rumbled, and she shut the front door behind her with relief. What a day it had been. If she was going to tackle Jake's hair, she needed some fresh clothes, and all she had was what she stood up in. She'd have to do a bit of shopping sometime. Shrugging into the bathrobe again and winding a knitted throw around her shoulders, she threw all her clothes into the washing machine, curled up on the window seat, and rang her mum.

'Happy birthday, darling! Are you having a lovely weekend?'

Staring at the unopened bottle of champagne, Flora lied through her teeth. 'Lovely! I er, arrived earlier than planned, um, yesterday actually, hope that's okay, and went surfing this morning...'

'Goodness me, isn't it a bit early for that? I didn't have Spence pegged as the surfer dude type, I must say.'

'Er... no... er...' she floundered. She'd never been any good at lying to her mum. 'Spence is, er... Has he contacted you, or anything?' She swallowed. What was she going to say? She reached out and unscrewed the bottle of red wine, carrying it across to the kitchen in search of a glass.

'No. Spence is what, darling? And you arrived yesterday? Of course, that's fine, there was no one booked in, you knew that, but was the food basket there in time and – are you sure you're okay? You sound – funny...' Her mum's tone was suspicious. Flora glugged the wine into the enormous wine glass and took a long drink. The wine was glorious, deep and blackcurrant. Perfect for two. For a romantic birthday break. On her thirtieth birthday.

'Oh, Mum…' she blurted. It wasn't long before her mum had wormed the whole story out of her. Well. Almost the whole story. Once she'd blabbed the main details she paused to self-edit. She couldn't bring herself to name the 'other woman'. She was still nowhere near processing it herself. She sniffed loudly, wandering to the bathroom and unrolling several sheets of loo paper for a prolonged nose blow.

'Why didn't you say? Oh, darling, are you okay?' Flora could hear her mum tutting to herself and adding in an undertone, 'Stupid thing to say, obviously. Of course you're not okay.' She huffed loudly. 'And that Rex. Pervert! I hope you've reported him.'

'I haven't yet. I think I might have broken his nose.'

'Good.'

'Don't! What if he has me nicked for GBH or something?'

'Were there witnesses?'

'I think the customer was too busy enjoying her head massage to notice, to be honest.' Flora's laugh slurred in her own ears. 'She said she liked it nice and hard. I should've swopped places with her.'

'I think you should take him to court. Horrible man. Hasn't he heard of "Me Too"? I've a good mind to go in there and see him myself.'

'No! Don't get involved, Mum. I'll sort it.' Flora poured herself a second glass of wine and wished her mum was sharing it here, with her. She felt pleasantly warm, snuggled into the thick robe and it was lovely to talk to her mum, who'd gone suddenly quiet. Flora could almost hear her thinking.

'Flora, darling – you may as well stay in the cottage until the end of the week. There's no one booked in until next Saturday.'

Flora swallowed the wine she had in her mouth and choked. 'Oh, Mum!' She coughed, to clear her throat.

'Are you okay?'

'Yes!' Flora wheezed mightily and wiped her eyes. 'Wine just went down the wrong way. That would be lovely, are you sure?'

'Of course! Makes total sense. You like it there, don't you?'

'I love it here.' Flora sniffed. 'Thank you.' She blew a kiss down the phone and her mother chuckled and then took a deep breath.

'Surfing, you said? You weren't, you know, er…' she hesitated, and Flora waited, a little cross-eyed from the wine.

'What?'

'You weren't going to do anything silly, were you? I mean, plenty more fish in the sea – er, the, er – oh God, you know what I mean. I never liked that Spence. What kind of man just spends all day in front of a computer? Weirdo. I never thought he was good enough for you.' Flora let her rant on, running a thumbnail along the rim of the glass. When she ran out of steam, she finally spoke.

'No, Mum. I wasn't trying to top myself in the sea. I just, stupidly, as it turned out, thought it would take my mind off everything.' Her eyes travelled towards the fridge, thinking about the runny Brie that needed to be taken out, and the crackers, all courtesy of her thoughtful Mum. It was a feast. Maybe there were grapes. 'And as it happened, I was rescued by a chisel-jawed hero. Who definitely doesn't look as if he sits in front of a computer screen all day.'

'Really?' Her mum squeaked with delight as Flora munched on her picnic food and filled her in on Jake's resemblance to Chris Hemsworth. Several googled photos had to be sent before her mum recognised him.

'And he rescued you? Is he filming there? Are they filming Thor in the Gower?' She was breathless with excitement and Flora almost choked on a cracker. 'What? They do use Wales as film locations, you know. There's been *Harry Potter* and er…' Flora stepped in as her Mum's knowledge base petered out. She knew her mum well enough to know that this stream of consciousness was an attempt to divert her from her woes.

'No, Mum,' she said, slowly, 'he's not really Thor the actor. He just looks like him! Oh, never mind, you nutter.' Flora tapped the bottle, now a lot less than half full. 'Thanks though, Mum, you've cheered me right up. Thank you for all the food and stuff. I do love you.' She swallowed, feeling suddenly lonely. Time to lay off the booze. 'So anyway, I'm going to cut his hair tomorrow.'

'Whose hair?'

'Keep up, Mum! Thor's hair!'

'Won't he lose all his strength?'

'Noooo. Step away from the gin. That's someone else. Samson! Thassit. I'm going.'

'I love you too, my darling. Take care. Ring me if you need anything. I'm always here for you, you know that.' She instructed Flora how to restock the welcome basket and reorder fresh ingredients. 'You are eating, aren't you? I know what you're like. Order anything that you want, and put it on my bill. It'll be delivered.'

'I'm fine, Mum! Really, it's an adventure,' Flora insisted. 'Night night. Love you.'

Holding on to the last moment to hang up, Flora finally allowed herself the luxury of hot tears.

She had howled her way through almost half a toilet roll when she became aware of her mobile vibrating on the table. She peered at it suspiciously. It wasn't Spence and she heaved a sigh of relief, clicking on accept.

'Dad.'

'Happy birthday, sweet pea! I've been trying to ring for ages. You been on the phone to all your mates?'

Flora narrowed her eyes. Her father seemed to think that her life was a party from morning till night. She replied, cagily, with a camouflaging cough and a surreptitious nose blow, 'Muh,' and waited.

'Your mum tells me things haven't quite gone according to plan.' His breezy voice ended on a question and Flora was on alert, trying to remember what she'd told her mum in their slightly tipsy phone call. What, exactly, had her mum told him? And did her mum always have to tell him everything? 'That boss of yours wants to watch himself. I could help you out there.'

For a hysterical moment, Flora imagined her dad, gangster cap and machine gun in hand, menacing Rex of the weak chin and wandering hands.

'Really?' she asked.

'Course. If you want to press charges.'

'Oh. I haven't decided yet. I, um, I...'

'You broke his nose, your mum said. Good for you. You always did stick up for yourself.'

'Ye-es.' Well, she'd had to, one way or another. Mostly against his other daughter.

'Anyway. I don't know what your plans are, but I was just wondering whether you fancied earning a few bob while you were down that way. A little job for me. It could tide you over while you decide. Your mum said you were staying for the week. This'll give you a bit of breathing space.'

Flora thought, reluctant to commit to anything. 'What sort of little job?' She put him onto speakerphone while she thumbed to her mobile banking app and logged in. Shit! Her half of the rent had gone that day from her account, leaving her just about broke.

It had been the last thing she'd thought about, and she wished she'd cancelled it. That would have stuffed Spence right where it hurt. She cancelled it now, hearing her father moving about on his end of the phone. He was talking about something just out of earshot. She pictured him in the glossy kitchen that he shared with her stepmother. Probably grilling steaks or lobster or something. Who else was there, listening? She asked him now, and winced as his voice, obviously closer to the microphone, suddenly increased in volume.

'Just me. The TV is on. Anyway. There's a hotel near where you are that I'm interested in. It's come up on my radar a couple of times now, and as you're there…'

Typical. This wasn't a phone call just about her then. The business came first. But she needed the money. 'What do you want me to do?'

'Just go and scope it out. General repair, how many guests, how full, whether it's functioning as a hotel or whether it's on its last legs. I'll email you a checklist.'

'A bit of industrial spying?' Flora perked up. It sounded like fun. Her father laughed.

'If you like. What do you think? Could you manage it?'

'Would I have to stay in the hotel?' Flora was beginning to see a plan emerging.

'Depends on what it's like. Not if it's a fleapit, obviously.'

Flora thought quickly, visualising that empty bank balance. 'How much?'

Her father named a figure. It was far more than the job seemed to warrant, but it really would give her some much-needed breathing space. She had never taken handouts from her father, unlike her half-sister Amber who milked him dry, in Flora's opinion. He'd been clever though, a helping hand that she had to work for. She couldn't really say no.

'I'm in.'

'Half now – half when you've submitted your report. And maybe a bonus at the end if I decide to buy it and get it at a good price. Sort of a "finder's fee". Okay?'

Flora swallowed. 'Okay.'

'Good girl. You can do it.'

'Where is the hotel?'

'It's Hotel Y Ddraig.'

'Hotel er what?' Flora attempted to repeat it.

Her father chuckled. 'It's Welsh. And hotel in Welsh is "gwesty", so think yourself lucky there's some English in the name! It means Dragon House or something.'

'Sounds cosy. Not.'

'I'll send you all the details. You take care of yourself. Keep in touch. Night night.'

He rang off, and she pictured him placing the perfectly cooked steaks and salads onto the polished dining table, along with a top quality wine, to eat with the glossy and perfect Helen. She sometimes wondered how her parents had ever made her.

She plugged her phone in to charge, and switched the television on, flicking unseeing through the channels as her mind refused to let go of the past forty-eight hours. As birthdays went, this one had been more than eventful enough for her. Her phone pinged later with a long message from her father, festooned with attachments and maps. She sat on the bed and read through the list of checks that he'd sent her.

Apparently, whatever she discovered would be more useful than anything the owners might tell him with a property agent present, when they'd probably exaggerate and make the hotel seem more profitable than it really was.

She tried to read it, but it had been a long day, and her tired eyes finally closed. She would do it tomorrow.

Chapter Seven

Flora cupped her hands on the glass doors of the Art Café and peered inside. It wasn't quite ten o'clock in the morning, and she could see people moving about inside. She tucked her hands under her armpits against the morning chill and waited. The familiar sound of a motorbike engine lifted her head and she swivelled, prairie-dog style, to follow the sound. She smiled as a 'familiar from the TV' purple Triumph Street Triple coasted into the car park, the petite rider muffled up against the cold but definitely recognisable as the famous Lucy.

Flora felt her mouth stretch wide in excitement, and tried hard not to look as fan girl as she felt. She could hardly believe that Lucy actually still worked here! Wasn't she at home, being pampered as was due a star of her standing? But no, she watched the snazzily emblazoned helmet, which she knew read, 'Ticket to Ride', as it was lifted off and she smiled as the rider ran her hand across her head, restoring height to her flattened blonde hair. Flora felt her legs quicken as she walked towards Lucy, and was almost astonished to hear her own voice say, 'Can I carry anything for you?'

Lucy turned to her with a wide smile on her pretty face.

'Ooh, yes, please, that would be fab. I'm being a bit naughty today. I should've brought the car, I've got loads to carry, but it's such a gorgeous day...' She dumped the pearlescent helmet into Flora's reverently waiting arms, and busied herself unlocking her top box and retrieving various files and boxes of what looked like jewellery. Eyeing Flora as they walked across the car park, she said, 'Do you ride?'

'Yes!' stammered Flora, feeling her face flush and pleased that she had been identified from her biker jacket. She took some deep breaths. Easy tiger. She's just a person, just like anyone else. 'Yes. I've got a Ninja.'

'Cool! I'm Lucy, by the way. I'd shake your hand but...' She raised her full arms.

'I'm Flora.'

Lucy hammered on the doors of the café and peered in just as Flora had earlier. 'I'm going to get a ticking off for being late now. And I've forgotten my keys,' she muttered to Flora, who was gawping in open astonishment now. A ticking off? Surely Lucy was a goddess, who got away with everything?

Clearly not, if the expression on the tall blond man's face was anything to go by.

'Morning! Cheers, Richard!' Lucy blew a kiss at him as he stood aside to let them in, rolling his eyes at her. There was flour in his hair. Flora scuttled in alongside Lucy, looking around her with wide eyes at the empty café. So that was Richard, Lucy's business partner. Flora felt totally overawed, as if she was in the presence of royalty. After the busy pandemonium of yesterday, the café looked like a waiting television set. She felt a frisson of excitement as the lights flickered on, casting pools of light across the promenade.

'Coffee? Tea? Hot Chocolate?' Lucy asked her over her shoulder, marching towards an alcove that Flora could see now contained a desk. She dumped the files unceremoniously and came straight back to the counter. 'Morning, Jo! Coffee, guys?' she yelled through into the kitchen.

'When have I never had a coffee?' Richard emerged with a tray of perfect muffins, beautifully decorated, which he slid with practiced ease onto the display shelves. As Lucy reached out to snaffle one, he lifted an elbow and fended her off.

'You'll get fat,' he told her, with a grin. 'And the camera adds pounds.'

'Meanie.' Lucy made a face at Flora.

'Coffee, please. A strong one.' Flora's tongue was like

sandpaper after passing the night in a coma of red wine and chocolate. But at least she'd slept.

'Good night, then?' Lucy asked, lifting mugs and tamping down the beans at the shiny steel machine.

'My birthday,' Flora said, and then carried on quickly in case she was asked to describe the amazing party that she hadn't had. 'I came in to say thank you to whoever it was who raised the alarm for me yesterday morning. I was in a bit of trouble in the sea.' She waved towards the rocks, swallowing as she tried to make light of it but remembering all too clearly how terrified she'd been.

'Oh!' Lucy turned to look at her properly. 'That was you! I rang the Lifeguard Station. The number's always on the wall here. You're not the first one, trust me. I'm so glad you're okay. That must've been scary.'

Flora gulped. Lucy had rung? Her heroine! She had an urge to throw herself around Lucy's neck and grant her ten wishes or something. If she hadn't rung, she would have... She really didn't want to think about it. 'Yeah, it was rather. But I was rescued by a guy who looks like the actor from the—'

'Thor movies?' Lucy interrupted, with a laugh. 'I know the one. Damn, he's hot. Back from Oz, apparently. So, a silver lining to every cloud, then?'

Lucy put the coffee on the counter before Flora, and carried another into the kitchen for Richard. She returned with two tiny muffins on a plate and put those on the counter.

'Sharesys,' she said with a wink.

Flora laughed. 'Thank you.' She took a small bite, feeling her mouth fill with the creamy sweetness. 'Oh my God, these are the best muffins ever.'

'Indeed they are. Richard is an alchemist in the kitchen. I talent spotted him when he was just a skinny graduate.' Lucy licked her fingers and then turned to wash them at the sink.

'I'm not skinny now?' Richard poked his head through the hatch that led to the kitchen, and Lucy laughed.

'He was – is – brilliant. He made a palette of mini cupcakes in the same colours as my paintings for a big exhibition that I had put on, and we clicked together – not romantically, of course—'

'Perish the thought!' Richard's voice floated in from the kitchen, and everyone laughed.

'We found this place, and the Art Café was born!' Lucy continued. 'It's been a good few years now, and we've had some ups and downs and some adventures along the way, but we're still here!'

Flora gaped at her. She felt as if she'd just been granted a mini interview. Lucy and Richard seemed magnificent and she was... what exactly was she? She felt her confidence seep away.

Lucy eyed her. 'So, was there something you wanted, Flora?'

Flora's nerve threatened to desert her but reliably, her mouth opened and words came out, just as they always did. 'I just wondered if there were maybe any jobs going? I'd do anything.' She burrowed into the inside pocket of her jacket and pulled out one of her business cards. 'I'm a hairdresser, really. If you need your hair doing, then I'm your woman!' She stopped herself going into her spiel, and sagged a little. 'But I'm a long way from home, and I... er... Actually, this is a ridiculous idea. I don't even live here! What am I talking about?' She scrubbed her face with her hands, mostly to stop her mouth moving.

When she looked up, Jo had come out of the kitchen and was regarding her with a sympathetic eye.

'I need a haircut,' she said. 'With my mob at home there's never any time for me. And now I come to think about it, my boys look more like shaggy dogs than people.'

Lucy was watching Flora with her head on one side. 'I'm sensing a story here, aren't you, Jo? We love a story.'

Flora heard her words spilling out. '... and so, I think I broke his nose. And then I got home, and...' She clapped a hand over her mouth as she felt the murderous rage of betrayal threaten to tip her into hysteria.

'And?'

'Caught my boyfriend in bed with... with... with...' She hiccupped. 'My... my... best friend.'

'Oh, sweetie.' Lucy's eyes brimmed with tears, and Jo passed Flora a handful of serviettes from the counter. Flora was mortified that she had to blow her nose in front of her hero TV star. A sudden draught alerted her that someone had come through the door, and she scrubbed her face with the remaining serviettes, hoping it wasn't Jake already. She shuffled along the counter with her coffee, eyes downcast as she got herself together, listening as Jo took the order. There was a laminated poster on the counter announcing 'New! Takeaway Breakfasts! Ring the Art Café...' That sounded like a great idea, Flora thought. She should let her mum know, for the cottage tenants.

Lucy appeared again at her elbow. 'I'll see if there's anything we can do for you, Flora. Is this your current mobile number?' Flora nodded.

'Th-thank you. I just need to pay for my coffee. I'm meeting Jake – Thor – to cut his hair this morning.' Flora patted the bag that went everywhere with her – it had been inside her rucksack that she'd grabbed from beside the door when she fled her home. The leather pouch contained her scissors and clippers, the tools of her trade. She'd added a tube of the hair conditioning treatment from the cottage as an afterthought, thinking about how dry Jake's hair was. He was sure to have shampoo, wasn't he?

'Wow! Take photos of the transformation so we can all enjoy it!'

Moments later, Flora heard the words exiting her mouth, as usual, unedited by her brain.

'I could do it here. Hunky Hero transformed by Rescued Hairdresser after Alert from Art Café?' She made a banner in the air as she spoke. 'How would that be for a bit of early season café promo? As a thank you for alerting the lifeguards.'

Lucy's head jerked up instantly, and cocked in Flora's direction. Her eyes narrowed and she rubbed a finger across her lips. Richard, still pollinating the counter busily with mouthwatering cakes, shrugged his thick blond eyebrows and gave a minute shrug.

'Do you think he'd go for it?' Lucy said.

'Thor? I mean, Jake?' Flora turned her palms over. She couldn't keep calling him that. 'I suppose we could ask, he should be here any minute.'

They all turned to look expectantly at the door as it opened to admit one hunky hero in need of a transformation. He stopped dead, and glanced behind him.

'What?'

'Ja-ake. You know how important sea safety is to you?' Flora began. He frowned down at her.

He grunted suspiciously. 'Mm?'

'Well, how about this for a great way to promote your message, and spread some community cheer at the same time?' She could hardly believe she was saying it. It was as if she'd been possessed. She gave him the once over. He was wearing an open necked shirt in a soft light denim with a white T-shirt beneath, and dark jeans. It wouldn't have mattered if he'd been wearing a bin bag though. He would look amazing in anything.

'Oh, she's good,' Lucy murmured to Richard and Jo, all of them stood together like an audience as Flora briefly outlined her idea to cut his hair there and video it.

'It would be great for the Lifeguard Club to share and I don't mind saying what an idiot I was, being so unprepared and all that stuff,' Flora chuntered on, warming to her theme. What the heck. He could only say no.

'I just have to sit there, yeah? I don't have to speak or anything?' He rubbed his jaw, thoughtfully.

'We could…' Flora scanned the café and said, 'do it over there, by your desk, Lucy? Away from the café part, not very hygienic really, all that hair and stuff. I can whip over and get towels and shampoo – you've got basins in the ladies, haven't you?'

'In the ladies?' Jake sounded horrified. 'Hang on a minute…'

'We can do better than that,' Lucy said. 'We've actually got gender free facilities, with a shower! Jo cycles in and she uses the—'

'It's over there,' Jo pointed, helpfully. 'It's unisex.'

'I've had a shower!' Jake sounded most affronted and stepped back as if he was expecting them to strip him off and bundle him under the shower then and there.

'Did you wash your hair?' Flora asked.

'Of course I did! I might look like a surf bum but I don't stink!'

'Then I just need to dampen it. We'll be fine. Get yourself a coffee, charge it to me. I'll be back in a tick.'

52

Chapter Eight

She raced out before he could say no, collected a hairdryer, towels and a water mister from the cottage and dashed back. Jake was more or less where she'd left him, nursing a huge mug of coffee and clearly on the outside of at least one of the full-size muffins. The café was filling up already and several customers had gathered to hear Lucy explain what was going to take place. Jake had already drawn a crowd of openly adoring old ladies, who seemed delighted to have their morning coffee ritual enlivened. Flora's hands shook suddenly. What if she messed it up? What if she made him look worse than he already did?

She took a deep breath, studying him. His head was a bird's nest. Anything she did would be an improvement. And she was good. She knew she was. She touched the soft leather tool pouch like a talisman. Lucy had cleared a space at her desk, and had swivelled the spotlights over it to give a good flood of light. She beamed as Flora appeared at her side.

'Okay, I'll video you on my phone, and then we can decide how to edit it, okay? Nothing goes anywhere without my say so though – yes?'

Flora nodded. 'Of course.' Her sprint to the cottage and back had completely cleared her head and she was on full power, mentally, any lingering wine induced brain fluff completely banished. She positioned Lucy's swivel chair, wound up as high as it would go, beneath the best light and put the water mister where she could get at it. The water mister had been a last minute addition, and Flora thanked her florist mum for having one as a matter of course under the kitchen sink.

'Ready?' she asked Jake. 'You can bring your coffee.'

He followed her like Gulliver amongst the Lilliputians, and she guided him to the swivel seat, where he sat stiffly, decidedly out of his comfort zone.

'Forget I'm here,' said Lucy, and his face flicked in horror towards her as she lifted the mobile before her. He looked as if he might bolt and Flora took charge quickly.

'So... how much are we taking off?'

'I dunno.' He shrugged and Flora had to avert her eyes from the muscles bunching under his shirt. 'What do you think?'

'Let's have a look now, see what we're dealing with.' Draping a towel around his shoulders and tucking it into his shirt, her professional identity settled over her instantly, and as she lifted and clipped his hair up, she forgot about Lucy, and the hushed crowd of women, and men, who'd gathered to watch. The hair wasn't as matted as she'd feared, and she carefully teased it out into sections, twisting it out of the way and leaning back to get the shape of his head.

He was unbelievably handsome, in a classical way, his features completely symmetrical, apart from that wide, mobile mouth with the full bottom lip that strained to get at his coffee while she tried not to tug at his head too much. She smiled at the white skin revealed at the nape of his neck and around his ears, in contrast to the deep tan and freckles elsewhere.

'How short was it when you left here?'

'Pretty short.' Jake pinched his thumb and forefinger together to leave a gap of about an inch. 'I just left it to grow.' He shrugged and Flora grabbed at the towel that his broad shoulders dislodged. Tucking it in again more firmly, she felt the heat from his muscular neck with a sudden leap in the pit of her stomach, and held one of the long ponytails that now sprouted all over his head.

'Do you want to keep your hair?'

'Huh?'

'To sell? Or as a souvenir of your travels or something? To give to your girlfriend?'

She saw his eyebrows rise in surprise.

'I don't know. Should I?'

'Keep it. You can always chuck it after. Or sell it to your fan club here.' There was a ripple of laughter and Jake coloured. She steadied her hand, checked the length and cut the first ponytail off. There was a loud intake of breath from the audience. She passed the ponytail to Jake and he waggled it about.

'Two years of Australian sunshine in there!' He chuckled and Flora watched his barrel chest vibrate with his laughter. 'No going back now, huh? Get on with it then.'

'Here we go!'

She breathed silently, focusing on getting a whole head length of decent hair that she could work on, combing as she worked her way around him. She would normally be chatting to him now, putting him at his ease, asking him about himself and what the transformation might mean to him, but she felt curiously shy about him. He radiated confidence and strength, and his previously raggedy hair had seemed to be the chink in his armour. Now, beneath her nimble fingers, he was beginning to look more god-like than ever.

She was relieved when Lucy began to chat to him.

'So, tell us what you've been doing in Australia for those two years, Jake!'

He told them about his travels across Asia, predictably working wherever he could, in bars and nightclubs, on farms and boats and shops, before he'd settled near Sydney and worked full time as a Surf Lifeguard. 'I can turn my hand to most things,' he said. 'I can lay bricks, plumbing, painting and decorating, garden maintenance, whatever.'

'Wow, you're a handy guy to have around!' said Lucy. 'So, hardly back in the UK before you're pulling damsels in distress out of our Welsh waters! It's nearly the beginning of

the summer season here and we're having a bit of a heatwave
– have you got any advice for would be surfers and swimmers
on our chillier island?'

Flora stood up straight and stretched her back, smiling as
Jake answered Lucy. As she suspected, he had plenty to say on
that matter. She raked her fingers through his hair, thinking.
Right now, he looked as if he was wearing a girl's bob and she
was glad there wasn't a mirror. He would surely run a mile.
She gave his head another all over mist, plugged the trimmers
in, placed them within reach and began to cut a shape.

She was pleased with the long top layers that flopped
forward just enough to retain that surfer dude casualness
she suspected he'd want to keep, and was trimming the sides
carefully with the electric clippers when she heard,

''Ello 'ello 'ello! Woss all this 'ere then?'

The crowd parted to admit a uniformed policeman the
size of a house, and Flora's hand skittered across Jake's head,
ploughing the metal edge of the trimmer straight into his scalp.

'Holy hell!' he yelped, clapping a hand to his skull. Flora
ripped her eyes from the policeman to see her client's head
oozing blood.

'Oh God, I'm so sorry!' Her fingers tried to move his hand
to see the damage but he flicked her off.

'Kitchen roll!' shouted Lucy, towards the kitchen. 'Right
now!'

A large roll of blue kitchen paper flew over their heads,
and Flora cringed as it hit Jake squarely in the ear.

'Jeeze, thanks, guys,' he muttered. 'You're all heart.' He
reached out a long muscular arm to retrieve the roll, which had
come to rest on the other side of the desk, holding it between
his knees as he unravelled a few sheets to stem the bleeding.
He jerked his head away from Flora's probing fingers.

'Let me have a look, Jake. I'm so, so sorry. He just made
me jump!'

'Ash! Goodness sakes, you made us all jump turning up like that!' Lucy rounded on the policeman, who waved an apologetic hand.

'Sorry, guys! I've got a first aid kit in the motor, I'll go and get it.' Ash exited the café smartly and Flora breathed again, only just realising that she'd been holding her breath. Poor Jake, that must've hurt so much. How could she have done that? It was unforgiveable. She could see blood trickling down by his ear. Ash returned with a hefty case, which opened to reveal a smorgasbord of first aid supplies, and Jake submitted to being inspected and dabbed by the big policeman.

'Just a scratch!' Ash announced, cheerfully. 'I'll take myself away now then. You'll live, young man!'

Jake probed at his head with a pained expression. 'A gouge, more like,' he grumbled. He lowered his brows at Flora and let out a long growly breath. She held her own breath, expecting him to leave right then and there. Eventually, with narrowed eyes, he said, 'Oh, go on then, finish the job. I've had worse.'

'Shark bites?' Lucy asked, sympathetically, resuming her filming and blowing a kiss to Ash as he left. Flora suppressed a sideways eye roll as she approached Jake, trying to steady her trembling hands. Shark bites? It wasn't *that* bad! She finished trimming around his ears, carefully avoiding the actually quite livid wound with a guilty lurch of her stomach, and plugged in the hairdryer.

'Nearly done!' She tried to make it sound breezy, but Jake's mouth was a straight line now, and he was back to being the lecturing grouch she'd met on the beach. Trust that policeman to turn up! Why was he here? Who was he? Why had Lucy blown a kiss at him? Something pecked at her memory and she froze suddenly as she remembered that the big policeman was in fact Lucy's fiancé. What had she told Lucy about herself? God, she could never have been a spy in the war. She was rubbish at lying or keeping secrets. Her secrets were already threatening to spill over and she'd only had them for two days.

On autopilot now, she dried the amazing haircut she'd created, that made Jake look more like a film star than ever.

'Woooow…' breathed someone in the audience.

'What?' Jake frowned, ducking his head away from her attentions. 'What has she done to me?'

'Oh, she's good,' said Lucy, for the second time that morning. 'Trust me, she's done a terrific job.' She closed in on his head with her mobile and circled him as Flora stood back, wondering whether she could just escape attention and melt away to avoid any accidental words escaping her lips. Words that a canny policeman might hear, that might drop her right in it – if Spence had reported her.

'Me next!' said a voice, followed by, 'Where do you work?'

'Er, I…' began Flora. Brooding over her recent misdeeds she was, for once, lost for words.

'I can put you in touch with Flora, our resident hairdresser,' Lucy told the crowd. 'She's new here and hasn't quite settled in. She'll be leaving some business cards here with us so you can keep her details.'

Flora blinked in surprise. Resident hairdresser? Business cards? A teeny tiny bubble of hope fizzed inside her and she nodded, recovering herself quickly and pasting a smile on. Maybe she could set herself up here in Wales! Her own salon, somewhere locally? It could be possible… couldn't it? She risked a glance at Jake, who was regarding himself with curiosity in a tiny mirror that someone had found for him. Reaching forward, she eased the towel from his shoulders to contain the hairy fallout as he rose, stretching his back muscles with an audible crack.

'What do you think? Is it okay?' She reached up to brush away some of the stray hairs that had caught on his tanned neck and he shied away from her as if she was about to inflict further injury on him. Crestfallen, she stepped back, staring at his feet. She felt him regarding her for a moment then saw him stick out a hand. After a moment, she took it. Her hand felt tiny in his great paw.

'Good job,' he said. 'Apart from the stabbing bit. I almost don't recognise myself.' He nodded, a smile just quirking the corner of his mouth as his eyes met hers. 'But my gran will.'

She returned his smile, relieved. 'I'm so sorry about the trimmers. Does it hurt?'

'Nah.'

'Maybe you should have it properly looked at…'

'I will if my head falls off.'

'Haha. Thanks for, um, everything. Being my model and all that.' She went to shake his hand again and realised she was still holding it. Lucy appeared beside them, holding her phone.

'I'll Bluetooth this video to you two, if you've got your phones on?' Her thumb was busily scrolling as she spoke. Flora watched Jake pull his mobile out of his pocket and thought quickly. Anticipating a torrent of abuse from Spence by now, she had no plans to turn hers on.

'Drat.' She patted her pockets. 'I've left mine behind. Could you send it to me, please?' Did she really want to see herself on video, gouging a lump out of the man who had saved her life? If only that policeman hadn't turned up. It was time she went.

'Sooo, I need to clear up and vamoose.' She cocked a thumb over her shoulder, suggesting that she had a busy life and things to do. She was improving at this lying thing. 'It's, um, been a pleasure. Thanks, guys.'

Jake was towed away by an admirer, by the looks of it, leaving Lucy still fiddling with her phone.

'Got a hoover? I'll get rid of the hairy carpet.' Flora gestured at the floor, a sea of blond hair.

'What? Oh, don't worry about that, I'll get someone to sort it. Great bit of filming, I'm sure we can use it.' She held her hand up, forestalling Flora's protest. 'And don't worry, we can edit out the blood. Sorry about Ash. He always does seem to make an entrance.' She dimpled pinkly, and Flora couldn't help smiling.

'It wasn't his fault. He seemed nice,' she said. It wasn't his fault either that she was a paranoid bag of nerves. She needed to get herself sorted out, and soon, before she had a meltdown. What was she so scared about anyway? Whacking Rex had only been self-defence and the theft thing hadn't been her fault. Not really. She hadn't had a choice, had she? She squared her shoulders, cross with herself now. She would tackle that particular issue right away, clear her conscience and then try to enjoy what was left of her birthday weekend. Why should she let him spoil it? Plus, she had a lucrative little spying job that could turn out to be fun, and that would give her a little financial cushion to sort herself out while she found another salon, or whatever. The response to Jake's transformation proved that she was as good as she thought she was. Apart from the bit where she'd stabbed him. She could kick herself for that, she really could.

'... so if you're in need of a chat or anything, just pop in. I'm always happy to sneak a quick cuppa!' Lucy had been talking and Flora hadn't registered a word until about ten seconds previously.

'Oh, thank you. That's really kind. I'm here for the week, so I'll be calling in for some of those amazing muffins!' Flora cleared her throat to disguise the sudden lump that had arisen at the thought of returning home. She smiled briskly. 'Bye, then. Thanks again!' Checking that she had her tools and the small mountain of equipment she'd brought over from the cottage, she scurried out of the café.

Chapter Nine

Jake had been hovering by the entrance for a while. He felt a bit mean, just mooching off like he had. She'd done a cracking job on his hair. Just a shame she'd made a hole in him. Although, clearly, she hadn't done it on purpose. It was only a small hole, in relative terms. On the verge of leaving, he was relieved to see Flora burst out like a cork from a bottle, weighed down with towels and bits and bobs.

'Want a hand with that lot?'

She looked a bit startled, and gripped her awkward burden to her until one of the towels under her arm slithered away. He caught it, and deftly scooped the rest into his own arms, resting the hairdryer on the top.

'You lead, I'll follow.' He jerked his chin, and watched her indecision transfer itself to her little pointed chin and a determined set to her body. They marched for a few minutes in silence, and he looked about him, frowning slightly at the cottages as they approached. He'd had an idea that he might recognise this tatty cottage that she'd spent all her childhood holidays at, but they had all been renovated and smartened up. She led him to the gate, and held out her hands for the towels. He looked around, holding onto his burden.

'No car?'

'Nope.'

'How did you get here then?'

'Motorbike.' She shrugged, and he saw with a fresh eye that her biker jacket was the real thing and not a fashion item. His gaze travelled down to her boots, and saw just how sturdy they were.

'What sort of bike is it?'

'It's a—' Her mouth snapped shut. 'Why do you want to know?'

He shrugged. 'I was just interested.' He narrowed his eyes at her. 'Or is it a made up bike, like your name was?'

She cocked her head on one side. 'I'm never going to live that down, am I?'

'Nope.' He shook his head with emphasis. 'So? Or is it, like, really tiny? A scooter? Or a moped, or something?' Something about her made him want to tease her. She bit instantly.

'Is it hell! It's got one hundred and sixty two of your finest, fastest Italian stallions powering it!' She clapped a hand over her mouth, her eyes darting over his shoulder.

'Sounds impressive.' He contemplated her, intrigued. 'Let's have a look then.'

She wavered and looked distinctly uncomfortable. 'Oh, er, it's… um, in the garage.' She waved a hand in a nonchalant way. 'And I… er, can't remember where the key is.'

Every other biker Jake had encountered had been only too keen to show off their machines. A sixth sense told him she was lying. He shrugged. It was nothing to do with him. She had her reasons.

'Alright, no worries, I was only making conversa—'

'Oh, for God's sake, okaaay!' She rounded on him, and he stepped back in surprise. 'It's my boyfriend's bike. You wheedled it out of me. He doesn't know I've got it. Okay? Well, he probably does by now. Happy? I've stolen my boyfriend's bike. Ex-boyfriend. There, I've said it. Out loud.' She stopped and stared at him, a smile lifting the corners of her mouth. 'God, that feels good. I couldn't have held that in for another second.' She blew out a long breath, and added, 'I'd be a crap spy.'

He stared at her for a second or two as her words sunk in and then exploded with laughter. She was bonkers, really. But she was entertaining with it. She grinned at him. 'And that bloody policeman, turning up, I thought he'd come to nick me for stealing it! Or assaulting my boss. I jumped out of my skin!'

Jake stopped laughing and fingered his wounded scalp thoughtfully. Assaulting her boss? Flora turned and marched up the little path to the front door. 'Coffee?' She threw the words over her shoulder, turning the key in the lock.

'I'm too scared to say no. You might stab me again.'

'Get in there, and grow a pair.' She held the door open with a grin. 'Wimp.'

He ducked his head with exaggerated care and followed her into the stylish kitchen, admiring the sea view. He perched against the counter, watching Flora crash about making coffee and more or less redistributing the towels and stuff he'd carried over.

She was such an anomaly. A tiny, spitting powerhouse, like a wild kitten he'd once found that had left him lacerated. He didn't mention that though. He had an idea that any comparison with cute, fluffy kittens might bring further injury to his person.

Banging two mugs on the wooden table before them, she slapped a stainless steel coffee press down, slopping coffee from the spout, plus sugar and a packet of chocolate Hobnob biscuits.

'Mm, my favourites. As my lovely mum knows.' She ripped the top off the biscuits and offered him one. 'I can't tell you how much better I feel.'

'That's good,' he said, warily, taking two biscuits, and dunking them chocolate sides together into his coffee. 'So, er, do you want to tell me the rest of it?'

'The rest of what?' She directed a sharp look his way. 'Isn't that bad enough?'

'Well, not to make light of it or anything, it's not like you've stolen the bike from a total stranger or anything. I mean, presumably, he knows you've got it.'

'We-ell. I think he does. But he might not.'

'Right.' Jake took a big breath. 'Give it to me straight. Both barrels. Do your worst. Let's have it.'

'He doesn't know that I caught him shagging.'

'What? How does that work?'

'All the noise? The porno movie noises?' Flora mimicked the gasping and made an expressive head wobble. 'They were "busy". And I just, kind of, backed out the way I came in.'

'Wow. I can't help feeling that they might have been kind of lucky.'

'Lucky?'

'That you didn't murder them there and then?'

Flora sat back, a corner of her lip caught between her teeth. 'Well…' she began.

'You didn't, did you?' He held his biscuit sandwich into his coffee for too long and a chunk fell off.

'Naaah.' Flora pushed her lips out in a rueful pout and blew a long breath from between them. 'Don't think I don't wish I had though. But I'd already given my boss a broken nose that afternoon.'

Jake touched his head. 'Sounds like I got off lightly with this, then.'

'Oh God, I'm sorry.' Flora clapped a hand to her heart. 'That was terrible of me. I'm a professional! I haven't done that since I was an apprentice!'

Jake chomped through another biscuit. 'So, the broken nose?'

'He sexually assaulted me. Pervert. He was bloody lucky to get away with a broken nose!'

Jake could feel his eyebrows rising higher and higher. 'Sounds fair to me. What happened next?'

'I got home and found the shithead boyfriend shagging.'

'Great day so far.' Jake rolled his eyes. 'And then?'

'Then?'

'There's more, isn't there?'

'Are you a priest in real life?'

'Yes.'

'Really?'

'No. But I don't need to be. You're like a bottle of pop, jigging about there. I've known you for a nanosecond and even I can see there's more. You'd be a shit poker player.'

Flora sagged into her chair, and Jake felt a rush of sympathy for her. Maybe he should go. He barely knew her, although she felt weirdly familiar to him. Was it that he'd rescued her? There was bound to be some sort of empathy there.

'There is more. But... I just can't make sense of it.' She looked suddenly bloodless and all the zing had gone out of her.

'Don't tell me then. You don't have to.'

'No. I know. I'd like to. But... um, first, I need a bit of help. And I have no right to ask you...' She slurped her coffee, pulled another biscuit from the packet and stared at it. 'So you don't have to stay. You can go, if you like. This probably all sounds completely mad to you.'

Her eyes rose over the biscuit to meet his, and to his own surprise, he said, 'What do you need help with?'

She sat up straight. 'I need to make sure I'm insured on his bike. When I took it, I didn't give a rat's arse whether I was. But today, I'm scared shitless that something will happen to it and I'll end up having to pay for it. His bike is worth a fortune. About five times as much as mine.'

'Did he usually insure you on it?'

Flora rested her chin on her cupped hands, still holding the biscuit. 'I think so.'

'Surely he won't have taken you off the insurance then. It won't be in his interest.'

'I hadn't thought of that.'

'Er... he knows you've left him, presumably?'

'I don't really know…'

Jake blinked. She was a whirling sputnik of energy. How could you not notice that she wasn't there?

'I mean,' she carried on, using her hands for emphasis, 'obviously, I'm not there. But because he doesn't know that I know, he might not realise why I've gone. Although,' she folded herself onto the chair seat, 'there is the brick thing…' She ate the biscuit she'd been waving about and gazed at him, her eyes huge.

He leaned back, watching her. 'The brick thing…'

'I put a brick through *her* car window.' She brought her pointed knees up to her chin and smiled with satisfaction. 'That stupid, soft-top Mini car thing of hers. I smashed the side window.' She demonstrated the actions and Jake followed her arm with his eyes. 'And then I threw the brick in after and watched it bounce off her "top of the range" luxury leather upholstery. Bitch.'

Jake nodded, slowly, visualising as she talked. 'Oka-ay. And so, he would know because…?'

'See, I've been thinking about that.' Flora flicked her hands out and back. Jake fully expected lightning to shoot from her fingers. 'She'd go out and find the window smashed… "oh boo hoo, I don't give a shit",' she added as a bitter and emphatic aside, 'and then she'd go mincing back to him with an: "oh, Spence, some nasty person has blah, blah, blah," she mimicked a high pitched, whiney voice and then added in her own voice, 'I wish it had been her head – and he'd say, "oh no, how awful, I'll get some plastic sheeting and duct tape to keep the rain out of your poor itsy bitsy liddle widdle Noddy car", and he'd go into the garage to get it, and lo and behold, his bike will have disappeared. Leaving mine in its place.'

She shrugged, and slurped her coffee. 'So, he'll know I've gone and so has his bike. And then, of course, I didn't come home. Not when he was expecting me too, anyway. And just maybe, maaaaybe, they might have thought, "oops, did she catch us shagging?"'

Jake caught himself, watching and listening with his mouth open. She was like a one-person entertainment troupe. Someone should sign her up for the TV, video blogs or something. The silence seemed deafening without her speaking. He closed his mouth and cleared his throat.

'So, has he been in touch since you left?'

'I have no idea. I've hardly turned my phone on.' She turned a huge pair of grey eyes in his direction, her shoulders sagging. He'd seen a bushbaby once with the same expression. 'I don't know what will be worse. Nothing at all, or a torrent of abuse about his bike.'

'Right. One thing at a time. You're not planning on keeping his bike, are you?'

'No! I only took it cos I couldn't get mine out. I did try. See, I can't turn my bike round in the garage cos there's not enough room with his bike in there. So I thought, if I take his bike out, then I could maybe turn mine round. And as I sat on it and rode it out of the garage, I kind of thought, he's riding another woman, so why don't I ride his bike-baby... so I rode it here. I wasn't going to actually keep it forever.'

'Okay. And you're not going to torch it or anything... haha...'

'Ooh, that's an idea!' Flora sat up, a smile on her face.

'No. No, it's not.' Jake rolled his eyes at her and nodded at the phone. 'Turn it on, and let's see how the land lies. And then take it from there.'

Flora pulled the phone from her jacket pocket. Her fingers fumbled with the switch and she slid it across the table as it began to emerge from its sleep state. 'I feel sick. I can't look.'

Jake picked it up. 'Deep breaths.' In a parody of her words to him, he added with a wink, 'Grow a pair, wimp. And remember, it's not your fault.'

Flora put her face in her hands.

'How come I always need to be reminded about that? Isn't it classic abuse, when they make you feel like you're the one in the wrong?'

The phone began to beep in Jake's hand as incoming messages flashed onto the screen. 'Uh-huh.' He kept his voice light to take the sting out of it. 'Ooh. He's cross with you...' He silently read the first few words of each message as they scrolled up the phone. 'He's a piece of shit, isn't he?' He looked up to see Flora with her eyes shut and her fingers in her ears. 'Flora. Flora! Unlock your phone.'

'I don't want to look at it.'

'It's only words. Come on, we can sort it out.' He slid the phone her way and she pressed her thumb onto the home button. The beeping continued. She looked down and her jaw dropped. 'Bloody git! He's got a nerve.' She read aloud, '"Bring my bike back immediately!" What was it you said about torching it?' Her fingers began to fly over the keyboard.

'What are you writing?'

'I saw you, you two-timing fucker... you and, and... her... etc, etc.' She circled her finger in a tumbling motion.

'Great idea. Diplomacy isn't your strong point, is it?'

'Pah. Why should I be the diplomatic one?' She leapt up and flung open the fridge, peering inside. 'You know what? Sod the coffee. It's wine o'clock somewhere.'

Jake twisted in his chair to look at her. 'It's not even lunchtime!'

'Whatever.'

'No. Sorry. It's not the answer.'

'You sure you're not a priest?'

'Look, you're not the one in the wrong here. He is! And it sounds like he cares more about his bike than about you! You just want to make sure that you're insured on his bike until you can get it back to him. Okay? Focus on that first.'

'Fine!' Flora rattled the wine bottle back into the fridge with a longing glance. 'I'm having chocolate though.' She rifled through another cupboard and brought out a gigantic slab of Dairy Milk. She ripped open the purple wrapper and offered it to him before breaking off a line of chocolate chunks, inserting one end into her mouth like a lollipop. 'So,' she said, indistinctly, 'what do I write?'

'I saw you with her. Bike is safe.' He grinned as Flora mimed puking, with a finger in her mouth. 'Please confirm bike insurance remains until returned.'

'Blimey. Formal.'

'Yes. Go on.'

Flora tapped out the message and pressed send. They waited. Flora made more coffee and ate more chocolate. Ping! She read out the message.

'"When are you coming back? We need to talk."' She snorted. 'I am never going back. And I've got nothing to say to him either. Nothing that doesn't contain lots of F-words, anyway.'

'It's a stalling tactic. Write, "Confirm insurance."'

There was an even longer pause, and the one word reply pinged back: 'Yes,' she read.

'That's it. Leave it now.' Jake poured them both another coffee, shaking the pot as it only filled their mugs halfway. 'That's all you needed to know. He can sweat on the rest. You could block his number now, if you like. Give yourself a break. You're not in the shit any more. Not with regard to the bike, anyway. I'll make some more coffee. Before you get the wine out again.'

'Blimey. You could set yourself up as a relationship counsellor.' Flora sat back, reading the phone again. 'Genius. What do I do about the broken nose and window?'

Jake laughed as he refilled the kettle. 'I reckon they got what they deserve. And I would never dream of telling anyone what to do. My relationships are nothing to be proud of, trust me.'

They drank coffee and polished off the biscuits and chocolate. Flora was lively company again and made him laugh with tales of her biking exploits.

'Well, I need to find myself another biking buddy to ride with now,' she said, draining her mug. 'Maybe there's a bikers' Tinder app or something. More coffee?'

'Nope, I'll never sleep if I have any more, and I've only just got myself back on UK time as it is. I must be off. Thanks though for the haircut, it's been fun. Glad to have helped.' He rose and stretched, collecting their mugs and depositing them in the sink. She followed him to the front door. He looked around him. 'This place looks stunning now. I remember this row of cottages when I was a teenager. Us surf bums used to hang around in the holidays, showing off in front of the townie teenage girls on holiday with their folks and bored out of their minds.' He laughed. 'I don't remember you, though. I'm sure I would have. Didn't you say that you used to come here every year in the holidays?'

'I did. Until I was eleven.'

'Ah. That explains it. Because now I think of it, there was a girl in this cottage who I hung out with for a while. I reckon she was about fifteen.' He sighed. 'Tall girl. Long blonde hair. I think she was the first to break my heart.' Making a fist, he banged his own chest with a rueful smile. 'I guess your folks rented it out for the holidays, if you weren't coming here.' He looked again at Flora. Her lips were compressed so tightly they'd lost their colour altogether. 'What?'

'When was this? Exactly?'

Jake thought, aware that he'd said the wrong thing somewhere, but not at all sure what. 'About fourteen, fifteen years ago, I guess. Why?'

'And it was this cottage?'

'Yes – I'm sure it was. Hah. I remember us hanging about on that gate, trying to snog without her parents catching us...' He tailed off. 'But it was a long time ago.' He opened the door, some instinct making him feel relieved as he stepped through. 'Anyway. Thanks again for the haircu—'

'I bet that was Amber.' Flora blurted the name, her voice hoarse with rage. 'My bloody, sodding sister. What the fuck was she doing down here? This was my place first! Mine!'

Jake gaped at her, puzzled. 'She was your sister?' He held his hand as high as himself, palm down. 'Tall? Legs up to—'

'Alright, don't go on! She's my half-sister. Christ. Is there anyone she hasn't had her hooks into?'

'It was years ago, Flora! She was a kid!'

'Yeah. Leopards never change their spots though, do they?' Flora's face was ashen. 'She always had to have whatever I had. She wasn't allowed here. This was my special holiday place.'

Jake retreated to the next step, putting them on the same eye level. 'You don't get on...'

'You could say that. Amber...' she took a deep, shuddering breath '... Amber is who I saw shagging my boyfriend.' She closed the door on him with a soft click.

Chapter Ten

Jake stood outside the door for a long and outraged moment. He wanted to pound on it with his clenched fists and tell Flora exactly what he thought of her and her gigantic leap to the conclusion that his teenage dalliance with Amber had anything to do with her.

God, she was bonkers. Up and down – he didn't know where he was with her. He couldn't help wondering about her relationship with this boyfriend of hers. She was hard work!

And she was right about making a terrible spy. Her thoughts wrote themselves across her features, as they made their way, unedited, to her mouth. She wasn't easy company, by any stretch of the imagination. But she was entertaining. He felt his mouth betray his earlier anger by relaxing into a smile. Or at least, she had been, until about five minutes ago.

And then he considered the terrible, awful revulsion of being betrayed in that way by your own sister, and his outrage subsided. Really, considering all this had only happened within the last few days, she was probably entitled to be a bit bananas.

Her accusations still rankled, but he retreated from the doorstep, dug his hands into his pockets and headed for home. Flora and her issues had been an engaging diversion to the more pressing problems facing him there, and the sooner he dealt with them, the quicker they'd be sorted out. He hoped.

His grandfather was nowhere to be seen, but he tracked his gran down in her office. He tapped on the open door as he entered so as not to make her jump.

'Okay, Gran, what's the most useful thing I can do for

you, right now?' She looked up from her computer screen in surprise.

'Haircut!' She assessed him for a long moment and then her pale lips stretched in a wide smile that was lovely to see. Thank you, Flora, he said, silently. 'Goodness me. It takes years off you. And you look clean.'

Jake laughed. 'Clean? Now I feel as if I'm fifteen again. Do you want to check behind my ears?'

'I don't need to.' His gran grinned, her eyes back to the screen. 'I can see behind your ears now.' She saved whatever she'd been working on and pushed herself back on the swivel chair, nodding appraisingly. 'So. You're "back in the room" then.'

'Yes. Sorry. I suppose I have been a bit absent.'

'Mmm.' She looked at him thoughtfully, and clasping her hands, rotated her thumbs in the gesture that Jake recognised of old. He waited.

'Well.' She fixed him with her bright blue eyes. 'There are so many things that need doing that I don't know where to start.'

'Shall I make a list?'

'Good idea.' She handed him paper and a pen. 'Ready?'

'Go for it, Gran.'

The list, by the time she'd finished dictating it, was long, and Jake felt a mixture of sadness that so much had gone unattended, and guilt that he hadn't noticed, and that she hadn't asked him already.

'There's a lot on here…'

She tossed her head slightly. 'Well, if it's too much for you…'

'Gran! I meant…' He paused, wondering how to phrase it. Everything he was going to say next was going to sound like criticism so he just went for it. 'I don't mind doing any of it, I want to help! I meant – why have some of these things not been attended to like you usually do?'

His gran looked away, a grim set to her mouth. 'Things are tough, darling. People want more these days, and it costs money.' She shrugged. 'It feels like a vicious circle. If I don't provide the mod cons, we don't get the guests. But we need the guests to pay for the improvements.'

'And Gramps isn't as...' he paused again, choosing his words '... up to speed as he used to be.'

'He's fine.' Her voice brooked no argument.

'I, er, don't suppose you've thought about selling up, or anything?' He said it lightly, as if he knew that it was unthinkable, really.

'Of course I haven't,' she snapped. 'Why on earth would we? This is our home!' Her brow furrowed and her lean, upright posture completely belied her years. She steamrollered on. 'And what on earth do you think I would do all day? Or maybe you think I'm past it, and should just sit and watch daytime television. Who would run the place? What about all the people who use it? Where would they go?'

Jake blinked. He didn't quite know where to start. 'Maybe we could all sit down and have a proper chat about it, you know, soon. With a glass of wine. Put some ideas on the table.'

'On the table? Is that some sort of business jargon you've picked up Down Under?'

She pulled the list she'd dictated towards her, indicating that the subject was closed. Running a finger down his writing, she tapped decisively. 'The entrance is looking a little overgrown. Could you possibly get a ladder and tackle the ivy and the honeysuckle that's gone mad there, please, darling?'

'While I'm out the front, Gran, I can keep an eye on reception. Get yourself a nice cuppa and put your feet up for an hour or so.'

'I might just do that.' He was surprised. He'd expected a

little battle after her speech. Leaning forward, he kissed her soft, papery cheek.

'It's nice to be home again,' he told her, making sure he picked up that long list as he left the office. He was going to be busy.

It was good to feel useful again, he thought, as he assembled the various tools and equipment he needed. He had always enjoyed manual labour. It gave him time to think. Did he want to do it as a career for the rest of his life though? He couldn't decide. What the hell was he going to do? He had carefully avoided any suggestion of taking over the hotel, and his gran had avoided mentioning it too. If he did take it over, it would be a very different hotel to the way it was at the moment. And he wasn't even sure whether he wanted to.

He'd always loved being there, meeting people, being involved, but he hadn't grown up with the thought that this was what he'd been born to inherit. More's the pity, as it was a wonderful old building, and should be making a mint. But Gran, although she was a formidable hotel owner and manager, was quite resistant to change. He secured the ladder against the wall, pulled on a pair of heavy gloves and clambered up, tackling the worst sections first.

He'd been up and down the ladder several times by the time the first of those 'people who use the hotel', as his gran had referred to them, began to arrive. A group of mostly women of all ages, they called a greeting up to him as they passed. He peered down, spotting their colourful and capacious bags. Some of them even had wheeled trolleys. He knew who these were. The Knit and Natter group. They were responsible for the ridiculous bits of hippy dippy woollen knick-knacks festooned everywhere he looked. All over the trees. Some of the garden seats wore woolly overcoats. Surely it made them a laughing stock. God only knew what the guests made of it.

He also knew perfectly well, that there would be cake in

those bags, and probably a few bottles of wine. His gran allowed them to colonise the smaller sitting room for a ridiculously small amount of money, in his opinion. Other places would be charging them corkage, he was sure.

He yanked viciously at an overhanging creeper and nearly fell off the ladder.

Chapter Eleven

It was tempting, Flora thought, to stay in the cottage that afternoon, and not go out at all. She could have food delivered, as her mum had said, and hibernate there. Let the world go on without her. Had her mum really let Amber and her parents stay here? Their father and his new wife? Why? It had been their special place, the three of them, until...

She marched into the kitchen and opened the fridge door, contemplating that bottle of wine again. Jake's words rang in her ears and, with an effort, she inched the door shut.

She felt bad about sounding off at him now. She really was living up to her spiky nickname lately. Anyway, there was a better solution to her mood than that bottle of wine – and Jake himself had made that possible for her.

Fifteen minutes later, she pressed the starter button on the Ducati Diavel and listened to the mighty engine roar into life, the vibrations sending a thrill through her entire body. With the garage and cottage safely locked behind her, she entered the postcode for Hotel Y Ddraig into the bike's satnav. While it loaded, she pulled on her gloves and took a deep breath to counteract the familiar butterflies of mixed anticipation and apprehension, present every single time she started a ride. She'd long ago decided that it was a bit like how an actor must feel as they were waiting in the wings, the necessary adrenaline rush which made you alert, that sent all your nerve endings tingling and pinging. If those butterflies ever stopped, it would mean that she wasn't paying attention.

The hotel was ridiculously close. It would have been quicker to walk there. She stopped at the shabby, peeling sign that said Hotel Y Ddraig, and tried the pronunciation again in her head as she peered down the short drive to the building itself. Partly obscured by overgrown trees and a huge shrub that bore the most enormous, brilliantly coloured blooms, the parts she could see appeared to be a mansion house. A car beeped, making her jump, and she realised she'd managed to block the narrow road. Raising her hand in apology, she rode away, without a plan of her final destination.

She just followed her nose, deciding that if she could see the sea, she couldn't go far wrong. She could explore, maybe find another nice café. The little hamlets and villages lining the Gower coast passed her by, largely unnoticed. Not because they didn't interest her, but because she wasn't tuned in properly to her surroundings. Just the road ahead, and how to safely negotiate the next corner on this still unfamiliar bike. She marked herself on each bend. Head up. Look round the curve.

It was amazing how quickly she'd got used to riding a completely different bike. Everything was in more or less the same place on each machine – the throttle and front brake was on the right hand, and the clutch was on the left. You changed gear with your left foot, and you used the back brake with your right foot. But because your whole body rode a bike, you got used to everything being exactly where you needed it, without thinking about it or looking.

When she'd first taken it, the Ducati had seemed completely alien. From its designer, raked back, hungry appearance to the vast wide back tyre, huge engine and scooped out seat. The sleek black tank was so much longer than her friendly little Ninja, and the riding position was just… weird. Her feet were forward instead of back and she sat upright instead of leaning forward, and it was a stretch for her short arms. The power – well, that was something else. The markers on the Ducati's digital speedo zoomed across the display with the merest twist of the throttle.

She'd screeched in her helmet as she took bends too fast,

blessing that huge wide back tyre as it stuck her and the bike to the curve, and her foot flailed in search of the gear lever that wasn't where she expected it to be. The long journey had familiarised her with it, and today, she was enjoying herself. Feeling at one with the machine, she skipped round the winding lanes wearing a beam of joy.

Eventually, she found herself at Port Eynon. Charmed by the collection of whitewashed cottages stepping downhill towards the sea, she parked up overlooking the long sandy beach and looked around her. The small row of shops hosted a café and a fish and chip restaurant, and she wandered towards the beach shop at the other end of the row.

Inside, she was transported back to her childhood, remembering the feel of her holiday money, safely tucked inside the tightly clutched holiday purse. She'd pored over these exact items, she was sure, as a child, in the wonderful throes of indecision about how to spend that holiday pocket money. Fridge magnets with thermometers on. Glass lighthouses containing sand. Cuddly toy seals and dolphins. Sunglasses with starfish and shells on the arms.

Nothing changed at the seaside, it seemed. Year after year she'd looked forward to the long school holidays by the sea in their little cottage. Her dad used to come along for some of it, then he'd go back to work as a troubleshooting hotel manager, in a different hotel each time and it had been her and her mum for the remainder.

The cottage had been a lot more basic then. There hadn't even been a proper shower – she remembered strip washes by the sink at first, and then a hose contraption that attached to the bath taps for a while, before her father had said he wasn't camping inside any longer and had paid someone to come and put a proper bathroom in before their next summer visit.

It had never occurred to her before that other people might have been using the cottage. How could she have been so naive?

Obviously, since the divorce, the cottage was her mother's business. Her income. But since it now held none of the familiar scents or items, her memory of it remained untouched, exactly how it used to be. Their summer hideaway. Hers.

She felt irrationally angry all over again at the thought of her mum being bullied into allowing her father and his new wife using the cottage. And bloody Amber. Making googly eyes at the local talent. The thought of her snogging Jake repulsed her, even though she knew she had absolutely no right to be.

The shop seemed suddenly claustrophobic and she hurried towards the door, anger throbbing in her pulse all over again. Closing the door behind her, she walked across the car park towards the sea and stared at the broad expanse of grey blue water, bounded by a long stretch of windblown sand. The scents of the familiar salty air filtered into her brain, sending clean, fresh fingers into her nausea.

There was a bench overlooking the beach and she plonked herself onto it, leaning forward with her elbows on her knees. She couldn't keep dwelling on the past all the time. It was exhausting, and it was getting her nowhere. Someone had told her once, 'If you can't change what's happening, change your thinking.' Maybe they were right.

Springing upright and spinning on her heel, she marched back into the beach shop, towards the fridge magnets, selecting the one that made her smile the most. It had a huge ice-cream at one end and sunshine icon at the other and announced in a cheesy and overblown font, 'Gower!'

'I'd like to post this, please. Have you got a little padded post bag or something?' The woman behind the counter put down her knitting and rummaged in a carton.

'How about this?' She held up a small envelope that was exactly what Flora wanted, except that it had already been used.

'Um…' she began. Perhaps she hadn't made herself very clear. Just as she was wondering how to rephrase her question, the woman smiled.

'I've got some labels – here you go! Just write the address and stick it on.' She handed over the labels and a pen, and Flora wrote her mother's address onto it.

'How much is that?'

'Don't be daft, you can have that!' The woman crinkled her eyes. 'Always trying to recycle where I can.'

Flora was taken aback. 'Oh! That's so kind, thank you! I'll have a postcard too.' She darted back and selected one with a selection of views, and asked to borrow the pen again, scrawling quickly, 'Thinking of you, Mum, Thanks again, love you lots, Flora XXXX'

'Nearest post office is Reynoldston,' the woman told her, anticipating Flora's next question as she paid. 'But it's a pretty ride. Nice bike.' She tipped her head towards the door. 'I heard you pull up.'

'Do you ride?' Flora asked.

'Me? No. My bloke does. We go out together sometimes. But it gets busy down here in the summer so I don't always have the time.'

Flora left the shop with a smile on her face. She entered the post office postcode into the bike satnav and zipping the little parcel safely into her rucksack, she waved at the lady in the beach shop, and headed for the post office.

As she rode, she looked over the hedges at the patchwork fields and bright blue strip of sea above them and thought about the hotel she was meant to be spying on. She'd have to go and have a look inside first, before she booked in to stay. She shuddered. She couldn't stay there if it was an absolute dive. There might be cockroaches. Dirty toilets. Bed bugs. Yeuch. She'd seen the reality TV programmes that showed up the seamy side of hotels. And her own father had told her enough horror stories from working in the hotel industry. He was a tough nut though, she wouldn't get paid if she didn't do the job, and she didn't expect to be, either. She had her pride. But she needed that money. Her little holiday from real life was nearly at an end, and she'd be back to the horrible reality of getting a job, and somewhere to live, and peeling her life away from Spence's.

The post office was easy to find in the little hamlet, there was no one else waiting and she handed over the small amount required to send it. A little further along was a pretty pub, and Flora's stomach rumbled as she spotted the pavement sign that announced, 'All Day Food'. Her mum's voice reminding her to eat echoed in her head.

She tucked the bike beside the grassy verge, not fancying the look of the gravelly car park, locked it and strolled into the pub. It wasn't busy, and she made for a seat by the window, so she could keep an eye on the bike.

She ordered a ham and cheese toastie with chips and salad, and gazed out of the window while she waited. It was weird having no one to talk to, and she didn't want to get sucked into telling the world her woes on Facebook.

The toastie arrived with a meagre portion of chips and salad, and she took a bite out of it. The melting cheese burned the roof of her mouth and she was glad there was nobody to watch her as she glugged down the remainder of her orange juice and soda, spilling it down her chin in her haste. She went to the bar to order another, leaving her food to cool. A man came in and went straight to the bar. When he leaned over it to look through into the adjacent bar before shouting, 'Hello? Service here!' she assumed he was a local. The sleeve of his sweatshirt rucked up and her attention was caught by the tattoo on his forearm. She wasn't a huge fan of tattoos, and this one wasn't going to make her change her mind. She thought she could make out feathers, and was that a weird cartoon pig? She felt him looking at her, and said, 'Um, nice ink.'

'It's alright, innit. I'm having it done all the way round.' He pulled his sleeve up and she gaped at the hideous images crawling round his arm. It was as if a three-year-old on hallucinogenic drugs had been let loose with a Sharpie. She couldn't stop staring.

'Oh, that's erm...' she licked her lips and managed '... interesting.'

The barman strolled in at that point, saving her from blurting anything more incriminating, and tattooed man said sharply, 'Is 'e in? Back door's locked, innit.'

Flora raised her eyebrows, about to ask for another drink, when the barman strolled back the way he'd come, returned and muttered, 'He says he'll be out there in a minute.'

Tattoo Man strode straight out, and the barman said to Flora, 'What can I get you?' as if the entire exchange hadn't taken place. He set her drink on the counter, took her cash and disappeared out of the bar again.

Flora returned to her much cooler food, munching more carefully this time. The window seat gave her a great view of the road, and Tattoo Man's hatchback car, where he stood, waiting impatiently. He stared at her bike, and her blood chilled. She was on her feet when he was joined by a burly man wearing a white apron. They both peered into the back of the hatchback, and Flora narrowed her eyes to see what they were looking at. It was intriguing. Tattoo Man was clearly selling something, not altogether legal, judging by his furtive glances up and down the (empty) lane. Flora's imagination ran amok. Contraband booze? What did they call it when you made your own vodka? Maybe it was roadkill. Didn't ponies roam loose here?

She was almost disappointed when Apron Man stood up carrying what looked like several trays of raw meat, all neatly cling wrapped and sterile looking. Flora guessed at steaks, as there seemed to be no fat on them. Tattoo Man stuffed cash into his pockets, slammed the boot shut and jumped into the driver's seat. Flora heard the gears crunching from inside the pub.

She looked down at her half finished plate of food, thoughtfully. Her appetite had waned. Maybe she was being suspicious, and Apron Man might only have been buying meat for his own barbecue at home or something, but she didn't really want to stay to find out. It was time to go.

She may as well put her current mistrustful mood to good use, she decided, as she rode along the stunning coastline back towards the cottage. She turned into the potholed drive of Hotel Y Ddraig.

Chapter Twelve

The car park was behind that vastly overgrown shrub with the brilliant and exotic blossom, and as she got closer she could see that they were in fact knitted flowers. Huge knitted roses in glorious colours. A collection of daisies garlanded around the lower boughs. It was unexpected and astonishing – and rather beautiful.

She parked well away from the several other cars there, carefully paddling the bike backwards and avoiding gravelly debris and the slippery grassy weed growing through the gaps in the tarmac. Ruffling a hand through her hair as she took off her helmet, she looked around her. The few other cars reassured her that the hotel actually was attracting guests, and she walked towards the entrance, making mental notes. Pretty architecture but windows needed cleaning. Containers and hanging baskets full of dead plants. Kerb appeal sadly lacking.

'Stand still! Stay exactly where you are.' A startled Flora looked around her for the disembodied, but horribly familiar voice. There was a ladder, resting against the wall near the entrance and her eyes travelled up it… and came to rest on Jake, dressed in navy overalls, and wielding a vicious looking pair of loppers.

'Ooh! Hello! You working here then?'

He glared down at her. 'No! Don't you come anywhere near me while I'm up here! You're a disaster zone, you are. You've already damaged me once today.' He made an audible tut and began to climb carefully down. 'Are you stalking me, woman?'

'Well. You seem to be everywhere I go – the beach…'

'… luckily for you…'

'The café…'

'… and I've got the scars to prove it…'

'… and now you're here! Maybe it's you who's stalking me!' Trying hard not to laugh, she glared at him in exasperation as he jumped lightly off the last rungs. Somehow, covered in grime, his hair sticking up and with his muscular neck exposed at the open collar of the filthy overalls, he looked even more impossibly handsome. She huffed. 'You've made a right mess of that nice haircut, I see.'

'What are you doing here?' He looked her up and down, noticing the helmet on the crook of her elbow and she watched a smile curve that wide mouth up at one side. He'd forgiven her then. 'I see you're putting that confirmed bike insurance to good use.'

'Mm. Yes. Thank you for that. And, I'm…' She rolled her eyes and wobbled her head. 'Okay! I'm sorry for having a meltdown this morning. I'm not going to keep apologising for making a hole in your head though. It was an accident and I've said sorry already so many times!'

'Okay. Apology accepted. And you were quite right. My gran said it was a huge improvement.' He gazed down at her, and she felt her legs go a bit tingly as she looked up at him. What was that all about? She was never having anything romantic to do with men ever again, after what had happened to her only a few days ago! They couldn't be trusted. She frowned at him.

'Anyway. What's this place like? Is it nice?'

'Not bad, actually.' He nodded. 'People seem to like it.'

'It's pretty tatty, isn't it?' She looked up at the charming but crumbling façade, seeing where he was clearing away the foliage. 'It's clean though, right? No bedbugs or anything?'

'Bedbugs?'

'I suppose you wouldn't know, really.' She rethought her approach. 'What are they like to work for?'

'Oh, they're very nice. The pay is pretty shit though.'

'That's terrible! Why are you working for them then?'

He winked at her. 'It's a bit of a favour.'

She headed towards the entrance and he walked alongside her. She gave him a pointed look. 'Shouldn't you be finishing your work?'

'Yep.' He shrugged without breaking his stride. The entrance opened into a wide, nicely proportioned lobby, clad in dark wood panelling.

She took in the line of wellies just inside the door, and the tall coat stand, already draped with a variety of coats. It felt a bit like walking into someone's house, and Flora half expected to be greeted by a waggy-tailed black Labrador and a bewhiskered earl with a shotgun over his shoulder. The stone flagged floor bore a worn mat that Jake rubbed his boots on and, after a moment, Flora did the same.

'Reception is just there.' Jake pointed to an area further inside, which looked as if it did double duty as the bar, and Flora marched towards it, looking for a bell or some means of summoning assistance. She was taken aback when Jake strode in front of her, lifted the bar top and reappeared facing her, behind the counter.

'Jake! You'll get into trouble! Get out of there,' she hissed, looking around her.

'How can I help you, madam? Are you looking for a room?' He reached behind him and brought out a register.

She frowned. 'Excuse me?'

'Single? Preferably one without bedbugs, I imagine?' He gave her a hard stare and somewhere in her brain, the cogs rewound to that first meeting in the Art Café.

'Oh, shit!' She clamped a hand over her mouth, and then shifted it to cover her eyes. 'You told me you lived in a hotel! Oh God.' She peered through her fingers at him. 'You live here, don't you?'

Jake raised his eyebrows at her and scratched his ear. A bit of moss dropped onto the counter.

'Uh-huh.'

There was a pause as Flora thought about what to do next.

'So,' he said. 'Room or not?'

'Can I have a look at it first?'

'To check for bugs?' He flattened his mouth, but picked up two sets of keys and lifted the bar top. 'You can leave your helmet here, if you like. It'll be perfectly safe.'

She hesitated for a moment and then handed it over, watching as he stowed it under the counter. He pushed open the wide double doors into a generous corridor, flanked by a spacious sitting room, containing big squashy sofas. 'If you'd like to follow me, madam. No bags?'

'I travel light.' She tossed her head, playing him at his game, and followed him. She could see from his body language that she'd offended him. His shoulders seemed even wider than before, and they'd been pretty wide then. She peeked into the rooms as they passed, hearing her bike boots squeaking on the floorboards until they were muffled by the worn rugs. She could smell polish.

There was a second sitting room, smaller than the first one, furnished with ancient sofas, upholstered in a blue and faded pink blown rose fabric. There was a polished dining table near the French windows, bearing a tea tray and a cake tin, and she glimpsed a garden, stretching away and bounded by more overgrown shrubs and trees, sprinkled with spring blossom. She could hear a hum of voices in there, and the clack of knitting needles. It was very homely.

She stopped. 'That's so pretty!'

He backtracked to see what she was looking at. 'Yes. This is the old part of the hotel. It's even nicer in the summer. The "tattiness" becomes charming.' His voice was flat and she put a hand on his arm.

'I'm sorry about the tatty thing. And the bedbugs.' She took a deep breath. 'I seem to spend all my time apologising to you.'

'You do.' He didn't look at her, and she removed her hand. He carried on walking and she had to run a little to catch up.

'Although. It is a bit tatty.'

He stopped and studied her. 'Do you always say exactly what's in your head?'

She hesitated. 'No! Well.' She shrugged. 'Yes. I guess. Is that so awful? At least you'd always know I wasn't lying about anything.'

'Even if it upsets people?'

'Why would people be upset by the truth?'

'Jeeze. That's a naïve way of looking at life.' Jake ran his fingers through his hair, which was probably a mistake, as bits of climber fell onto the patterned carpet.

'Okay. I'm sorry I was truthful.' Flora spread her palms. 'Can we be friends again?'

'Were we friends before?'

She looked at him, doubtfully.

'I thought so, yes...' Was he teasing her now? She didn't know him well enough to know. 'You helped me sort out my issue with the bike... and I cut your hair... yes, and your head, I know—'

'And I saved your life.' Again, that flat tone that gave nothing away. Flora decided he was teasing her.

'I fed you all my chocolate biscuits! And you ate most of my carrot cake and custard!'

'That is true.' He regarded her gravely, and she had a flashback to that ticking off at the tide's edge. 'But, you know, friendships are built on trust. It's an earned relationship. This morning, you practically accused me of shagging your sister, as if it was a personal affront to you! First of all, it had nothing whatsoever to do with you. And don't be casting me in the "shag 'em and leave 'em" mould. I was fifteen. My life was more about surfing than sex.'

He took a deep breath. Her heart pounded in her ears. 'Flora, I've seen the nicer side of you, and I liked it. But your tongue can be a harsh weapon.' He laid a finger lightly on her mouth. 'Be careful how you use it.'

Her lips tingled where his finger had momentarily been. It smelled of soap and something sharp, and tangily green, which must be the ivy and climbers he'd been pulling down. It was an incredibly intimate thing to do and it took her totally by surprise. Had she accused him of shagging Amber? She'd been so angry, she hadn't thought. Her voice, when she found it, sounded thin and remote. 'I've had to stick up for myself. When I was eleven…'

'Oh, spare me the pyscho-babble. You're thirty now. Take some responsibility for yourself.'

Flora felt her stomach clench. She felt sick. Nobody had ever spoken to her like that. And somehow, the fact that it was him made it much, much worse, and she couldn't even begin to start analysing why that was.

He strode away. She stood and watched him go. Did she want to follow him after a bollocking like that? He looked back at her, waiting, and she found her legs moving of their own accord. 'This is the newer wing. Where the bedrooms are.'

He pushed open a heavy door, and Flora saw the difference straightaway. The walls were smoothly emulsioned in a warm cream, the deep blue patterned carpet was smart and fitted. They climbed a set of stairs and Flora became thoroughly disorientated as they turned across a landing and eventually, Jake held a door open for her. She looked inside. The room was surprisingly spacious, in restful shades of creams and greys, with tasteful textiles in warm ochres and pictures on the walls. She walked in for a better look, and peeped into the en suite, spotless and tiled from top to bottom in warm stone to echo the main room.

The cups and saucers looked clean, as did the kettle, although she noticed there was no biscuit with the selection of teas and coffee. Not exactly a big deal, but did it mean there was no money for fripperies?

'It's very nice.' She tried to keep the note of surprise out of her voice and walked to the window. 'Fabulous view!' She stared out over the sweeping bay.

'Yes. Do you want to see the other room?'

'Does it have a sea view?'

Jake shook his head. 'Afraid not.'

'Then no, thank you. I'll have this one, if I may?'

'How many nights?'

'Two, maybe longer.' She was dithering. This was business. Taking a deep breath, she said, 'I'd like to check in on Saturday for two nights, please.'

'I'll reserve that for you now. We'll need to take a credit card and it would have to be charged for the full amount if you don't turn up.'

'Yes, I understand.' Her stomach lurched at his formal tone. He was still mad at her. Well, she would do her snooping and then be out of his life, and not have to give him a single thought. He would no doubt be glad to see the back of her. The thought failed to give her much pleasure. 'What time can I check in?'

'From four p.m.'

'That seems late, but thank you.' She turned for a last look at the view and marched stiffly out of the open door and then stopped, wondering which way to turn.

'Left,' he said, locking the door behind them.

'I totally knew that.'

He smiled and her stomach flipped with pleasure, to her annoyance. 'It's easy once you've done it a couple of times.'

They walked along the corridor side by side. 'It's because it's a new addition. It doesn't flow as well as the original house.' They reached the transition between old and new again.

'That was a very nice room,' Flora said, pensively. 'But I still prefer the old part. It's lovely,' she said, remembering that cosy sitting room.

'My thoughts exactly.'

Flora jumped and spun around to see that a smartly-dressed older lady had joined them, her approach masked by the thick carpet.

'Hello.' She held out a hand. 'I'm Molly. I own the hotel. I see you've already met my grandson. He does usually dress a little more smartly than this to show potential guests around.' Flora didn't miss the look of reproof she sent to Jake and tried to explain.

'Oh, I'm sorry, I think that was my fault – I stopped him working. We've already met. And I've seen him in a lot less than this!'

Molly's eyebrows rose.

Jake said, hurriedly. 'This is Flora. She means my wetsuit, I think. I rescued her in the sea yesterday.'

Molly regarded Flora with more interest. 'Aha. You are the one responsible for this!' She gestured at Jake's head.

'Oh, yes, but that, that—' Flustered, Flora whirled a finger above her own head, indicating the region of Jake's wound. 'It was a—' She bit back the word 'mistake'. Hairdressers of her standing didn't make mistakes. 'It was the shock, you see. Seeing the policeman appear like that.'

Molly's forehead puckered a little, but she was clearly too well brought up to ask what on earth Flora was talking about. Jake dipped his head towards Flora.

'Gran doesn't know about the hole in my head,' he murmured. 'She means the haircut.'

'I'm not deaf, you know,' Molly said. 'And I saw the hole. I wondered if it was some kind of pre-emptive head-piercing trend.'

Flora eyed her, finally spotting the glimmer of a smile. 'Jake is being very nice about it, but I'm sure it hurt horribly. I haven't stopped apologising. I feel terrible.'

'Well, you've made a very nice job of that terrible haystack he came home with, all things considered.'

'Gran told me that I looked clean,' Jake offered with a grimace. Flora and Molly exchanged a look and he snorted in disgust, but Flora had spotted his eyes crinkling with good humour.

'Well, I must be getting on,' Molly said. 'Are you going to be staying with us, Flora? Or were you just having a look round?'

'Oh, I'm staying.' Flora bit back an urge to curtsey. There was something terribly regal about Molly. 'I'll be here on Saturday.'

'How nice. I do hope you enjoy your stay. Would you excuse me?' She smiled and with a last thin-lipped look at Jake's overalls, headed towards the sitting rooms.

'Wow. I feel as if I've just met the queen.' Flora watched Molly's straight-backed walk. 'I'd love to see the rest of the hotel. Maybe you could show me around when I'm here?'

'No probs. But right now, I've got work to be getting on with. To make the entrance look less "tatty".'

She rolled her eyes. 'Okaaaay. I asked for that.'

They were back at the reception area more quickly than she'd thought possible, and she fished out her credit card, watching him take the details. He gave her a confirmation of her booking and then jerked his chin towards the entrance.

'So, if that's everything? I need to, er...'

'Thank you, yes. I just need my helmet, please.'

'Good thing that was hidden away when you met Gran,'

Jake said, casually, as he handed it over. 'She's got a thing about bikers.'

'A "thing"? In a good way?' Flora took the helmet carefully from him.

Jake shook his head. 'Er… no. Not in a good way at all. I'll show you where to put your bike when you arrive on Saturday.'

'What? Have I got to hide it? But I'm a paying customer!'

'Not really hiding, as such. Just, um, it might be safer there. You'll want to have it locked up nice and safe, won't you?' They'd arrived in the car park, and he stopped to admire the Ducati. 'You were right though. It's a hell of a beast.'

Flora felt a surge of pride, even though it wasn't hers. 'It is. I'll be quite sorry to see it go.' A ripple of anxiety prickled her skin at the idea of the handover with Spence. 'So where am I parking?'

Jake beckoned her around the side of the hotel to a row of Victorian outhouses, and pushed open a door. Flora peeped in. Bigger than a double garage, it contained a collection of surfboards, a few trunks, old cases and storage boxes. How would she turn the bike round in there? She straightened her shoulders, determined to worry about it later.

'I've got some spare padlocks with keys.' Jake pushed the wooden door shut. 'I'll give you one and you can lock it up. That lot is my junk. If anyone was going to nick it they would've done it by now.'

'Thanks, I appreciate that.'

As they walked back to the car park he said, 'There's a party tonight, down at the Lifeguard Clubhouse, if you fancy going?' His voice was casual. It was as if his entire personality had heaved a sigh of relief to be back in the open air again.

'What?' Flora gaped. 'You've given me a bollocking about being gobby and now you're inviting me to a party?'

'Yeah. You're not the only one who can be annoying. It's what mates do, isn't it?'

That infuriating, lopsided grin again. She let the 'mates' thing go, absurdly pleased to be back in the fold. It had been chilly out there for a little while.

'What sort of a party? Does everyone wear flowery shirts and shorts? Or wetsuits?'

'Well, you could if you wanted to, I suppose.' His cheeks lifted in a smile and she couldn't help staring at him. 'But usually, just jeans and stuff does the job. It's the "beginning of the season" do. There'll be music and a bar of sorts. Wine and beer, nothing too fancy. A bit of grub – usually it's burgers and sausages. It's informal and a bit of a laugh. A few beers. A bit of a boogie. Watch the sun go down.'

'But I won't know anyone.' She frowned, visualising herself standing alone on the edge of the party. 'You're not trying to punish me for forgetting you lived in a hotel, are you?'

'Naaaah, I'm not that much of an old grouch!'

She laughed. 'You sounded proper Aussie then.'

He laughed, showing bright white teeth. 'I'm sure that'll be wearing off pretty soon. I'll be back to being proper Welshie! Anyway, trust me, you've already made an entrance. You're the first rescue of the season. You're almost a mascot!'

'Thank you.' The pleasures of sitting in the cottage in solitary splendour had worn off very quickly and the thought of a party was enticing. And she loved to dance. 'I'd love to.'

'Great. About seven thirty? Dress warm.'

'I'm sure to find something in the extensive wardrobe I brought with me.' She smiled. 'Thanks. See ya later, cobber!'

Chapter Thirteen

Jake tugged at a thick stem of climber. Pulling as much away from the masonry as possible he severed it as far down as he could reach, allowing it to drop to the ground, narrowly missing the Knit and Natter group as they wobbled their way out, their voices a lot shriller and more giggly than they'd been on arrival. No doubt it had been a 'knit one, glug one, drop one,' type of session.

'Oops. Sorry, ladies!' he called down, insincerely.

'And gents!' called back the two men, laughing as they shouldered their rucksacks.

Jake could barely believe he'd invited Flora to the party at the beach. He hadn't even been planning to go himself, let along taking someone along. And that someone being the confusing and enigmatic Flora, of all people. What was it about her? He just couldn't figure her out. And despite him telling her he wasn't interested in what had happened when she was eleven, he was intrigued. Oh, he was so good at being pompous. He, whose life had been dictated by what had happened when he was five, and who at nearly thirty-one, wasn't any better at 'adulting' than she was. Not really.

She'd looked pretty amazing, riding away on that huge bike though, he had to admit. And pretty damn sexy too, in her leather jacket and boots.

And why exactly was she booking into their hotel? He hadn't asked, and she hadn't volunteered. It was her business, of course, but it seemed odd. He climbed down the ladder, and wheelbarrowed the cut creeper away to the compost heap.

By the time he returned, another group were arriving to use the hotel. He recognised some of them from before his travels, and nodded as they called a welcome to him.

There were a number of children with them, wearing, he couldn't help noticing, bee costumes and trainers that lit up as they walked. He grinned at their headbands of nodding pom-poms as the penny dropped. He knew who this lot were. The local drama group. No doubt this was their summer production in the making.

It was great that the drama group existed, of course. It was the fact that they used the hotel virtually free of charge that irked him. Surely, they irritated the other guests? Although he'd never heard any complaints, and certainly his grandparents had always encouraged interaction with the community.

He moved the ladder, climbed back up, and hacked away at the remaining clinging foliage. He wanted to get as much done as he could while there was still some light.

With a party in mind, Flora inspected herself critically in the cottage's full-length mirror. She was wearing exactly what she'd worn to ride down here on Thursday afternoon: jeans – which were actually motorbike jeans, lined with Kevlar and with pockets for armour at the knees and hips. They were stretchy, and she could just take the armour out and ta-daah, they looked like ordinary skinny jeans. A black T-shirt, which was her salon uniform, the thick fleece which went under her motorbike jacket, also black, and her bike boots. Black. No surprises there. She'd tell anyone who asked that she was in her Goth phase. No one would ask though. Wearing all black in the salon was a recognised kind of hairdresser's uniform, but away from the salon, it sent a strong message of aloofness. Well, whatever.

She didn't have a scrap of make-up with her, but her cheeks looked nicely pink from the fresh air she'd already inhaled during the last two days. She wouldn't be seen dead going to a party dressed like this, normally. But this wasn't a normal weekend. And more to the point, she wasn't looking to impress anyone. Not for the purposes of attracting a man, anyway. Right now, she didn't care if she never ever fell in love again. She'd please herself, explore the world on her motorbike, and never be disappointed by a man again. Her thoughts drifted towards Jake and those impressive muscles, and she censored her reflection as her mouth curved in a smile. She barely knew Jake. It had only been two days, if that. He was undoubtedly serious eye candy, but she was dead inside when it came to men, she told herself. Trust nobody, she admonished the mirror. She frowned as she recalled their conversation in the hotel about trust. What a nerve! Was he so perfect? She swung away from her reflection. To think she'd almost decided to ride into Swansea and find a late opening supermarket for some new threads. She didn't need them. They would have to take her as they found her. And in any case, some of them at the Lifeguard Station had seen her in a much worse state than she looked right now. Even though they thought her name was Anna...

When Jake knocked at seven thirty, Flora opened the door with a yawn that she had to smother with her hand.

'Boring you already, am I?'

'God, I'm so sorry, I nodded off!' She opened the door wide to let him in. 'I'm thirty now. Officially old. I'm already having nanna-naps.' She grabbed her bike jacket. 'Is it going to be outside? Is that why you said to dress warm? I've only got what I stand up in.'

'Well, no, it's inside, but the roll up shutters tend to be open and so it can be pretty chilly.'

'I'll just have to dance and keep myself warm.' Zipping the jacket up, she turned to him. 'I'm ready. Will I do?'

'Yep. Looking fine.'

She laughed, locking the door behind them and shoving

the key deep into the inside pocket of her jacket. 'I love the way blokes say that without actually looking at you.'

He grinned down at her. 'I looked! I did!'

They strolled along the narrow path together, towards the beach.

'So.' Flora cleared her throat. 'Jake.'

'Uh-oh. Sounds like the Flora truth serum again...'

'Well. You're not entirely awful looking, mostly due to that amazing haircut I've given you,' she said. 'And you're quite nice, when you're not bollocking me. So – girlfriend? Or girlfriends, plural? What I'm asking is, will I be,' she crooked her index fingers to indicate apostrophes, '"In The Way" tonight?' She looked up at his impossibly handsome profile silhouetted against the darkening sky. 'You only have to say. You don't have to babysit me. Or feel sorry for me or anything. It was nice of you to get me out of the house. But I can talk to people.'

'Do you ever stop talking to people?'

Flora pretended to consider. 'No. Although mostly, people talk to me.'

They walked in silence and Flora thought he probably wasn't going to answer her. She was almost startled when he spoke.

'My girlfriend decided to go walkabout.'

'What does that mean?'

'It's an aborigine tradition. It used to mean wandering in the bush, but apparently it can also mean sodding off for as long as you like and leaving all your responsibilities behind. In a camper van with another bloke.'

Flora glanced up at him. His face was set, and she wished, not for the first time, that she'd kept her mouth shut, and talked about the weather or something. He looked down at her and made her jump as his ocean coloured eyes met her gaze. 'So in answer to your question, you won't be cramping my style tonight.'

Flora nodded. She threaded her arm through his to his obvious surprise. 'Right then. Mates night out it is! I'll hold your hair back if you puke, okay?'

After a pause, he threw his head back and laughed, a deep, pure rumble that had Flora joining in.

Talk came easily then, and by the time they got to the Lifeguard Clubhouse, easily identified as the party venue by the sounds coming from within and the smoking barbeque, they'd agreed and argued over their musical and film tastes, finding some solid shared interests and others that were wide apart.

'Ooh, I love this song.' Flora jigged alongside him, surprised to find him keeping time with her. Spence would have made a face and gone straight to the bar by now, leaving her to dance alone. She'd never really minded, loving the music and the feeling of her body moving, but she'd always wondered what it would be like to have a boyfriend who actually liked to dance. She adjusted her rhythm to suit Jake's bigger frame, and he grinned down at her, as in tune with each other, they approached the crowd already there and Jake led them, dance-walking to the makeshift bar at the rear of the building.

'Wine or lager?' he shouted, over the music.

'Lager!' She'd had enough of wine. And she never got drunk on beer. Her stomach was full long before the effects kicked in. He gave her a thumbs up and handed her a plastic pint glass and a can of Stella. Moving away from the bar, they found a space to pour their drinks.

'Pretty good.' He nodded as she poured a perfect pint. 'Most girls pour it into a milkshake.'

'I worked behind the bar in a previous existence,' she told him, her gaze sweeping the fit, non-smoking, clean cut crowd. Just what she'd expect from a bunch of lifeguards. She thought she recognised the two girls who had helped her in the first aid room, deep in conversation with their mates. Divested of their huge fluorescent jackets and wearing skinny jeans and sparkly tops despite the evening chill, it was hard to be entirely sure. She moved her hips gently to the music, then as Beyoncé exhorted the crowd to 'put a ring on it', she handed Jake her plastic glass and felt the rest of her limbs join her hips in time to the music as she sashayed away from him a little. Her mouth stretched in a huge smile as the two girls joined her and danced, hamming it up to the words. Jake watched them with a smile on his own face, and she saw his beer slopping up and down as he joined in quietly, boy-style, in place. At the end of the song she claimed her drink.

'Good mover.' He raised his eyebrows at her.

'You too.' She eyed him over her pint. She was having fun, she realised. She'd ditched her lying cheating boyfriend, and she'd smashed her bitching sister's car window and she was, just for tonight, with the most handsome man on the planet, and doing her favourite thing in the world apart from biking – dancing. 'Thanks for asking me. It was just what I needed.'

He raised his glass at her with a smile. People came over and knuckled Jake's shoulder or shook his hand, and then hers as he introduced her. She couldn't hear their names over the music, and was content to smile back and bob happily in time to the tunes, watching everyone else dancing.

'Ooh!' She stood to alert as she spotted a familiar face. It was Lucy, dwarfed by her policeman fiancé, ruggedly handsome in a heavy navy sweater. A slight and pretty young figure stood alongside them, her mane of dark hair artfully arranged in curls that must have taken ages. Her face lit up as she was hailed by her friends.

'Hey, Daisy! You're here! Love the hair!' She was claimed, as Flora watched, by a little gaggle of youngsters, all around twelve. Daisy's face was animated and although Flora couldn't hear them over the music, she watched with a smile as their mobiles were brought out and they posed for giggling selfies. Ash, head and shoulders above most, carved his way through the crowd towards the bar, nodding and smiling at people as he went. Flora felt bad about being so scared of him earlier. She scanned for Lucy now, spotting her watching Daisy with a smile on her face, as the youngsters swayed without moving much to a tune she didn't recognise. Was thirty that old? She told herself off with a self-deprecating snort. As Lucy's eyes roved around the clubhouse, they came to rest on Flora and she waved, moving towards her. Flora felt a little bolt of pride. Lucy was coming to talk to her!

'Hi!' she mouthed, taking a half-pint glass and a wine bottle from Ash. 'Thanks, sweetie!' He grinned at them both, shoved two cans of Coke into his pockets, took the bottle from Lucy and poured a generous measure, which he handed back to her. Flora liked him even more at that moment.

'Back in a mo,' he shouted, 'taking this to Daisy!' He held up one of the cans.

'Great party!' yelled Flora.

'They always are!' Lucy yelled back. 'Except that you can't hear anyone speaking!'

Jake turned towards them. 'Shall we go outside? The barbie is on.'

They nodded and he led the way, taking her cold hand in his large, warm hand as if it was the most natural thing in the world and threading through the packed crowd. Outside, the air was crisp and the noise level much, much lower. There were several gazebos daisy-chained together and festooned with fairy lights, and alongside those were three half-drum barbeques, laden with sausages and burgers. Her stomach rumbled suddenly, as the scents of grilling meat drifted over.

'Grub?' Jake said.

'Hell, yeah.' Flora licked her lips as they joined the queue. 'I've got money! You don't have to buy everything for me.'

'Put yer money away,' Jake said. 'You're my mate-date tonight.'

'Oh. Okay.'

'And anyway. It's hardly going to break the bank here. Burgers or hot dogs, only a couple of quid each?'

'Ah. I see your logic.' Flora punched him lightly on the arm. 'So our next mate-date, will probably be hideously expensive and my turn to pay?'

'Aw, listen to you two, arranging dates,' Lucy said, behind them in the queue.

'Mate-dates,' Flora said, solemnly.

'Yeah. She's offered to hold my hair back if I puke,' Jake said, his eyes on the food.

Ash laughed. 'Not that she's left you any hair to get hold of. And sorry again about scaring you earlier.'

'That's okay, we've sorted out all Flora's misdemeanours,' Jake said, earning himself a jab in the ribs from Flora. 'What? You're legal again now!' Flora rolled her eyes.

'Lalalaa,' said Ash, putting his fingers to his ears. 'I'm not listening.'

Lucy snuggled up to him with a grin. 'Flora rides a Ninja. She's a fellow biker. Be nice to her.'

'I'm nice to everyone!' Ash protested. 'Unless they're bad guys.'

'I'm on a Ducati Diavel this weekend,' Flora said in a rush to get it out of the way. 'I've borrowed it from my shitty ex-boyfriend.'

Ash raised his eyebrows. 'He can't be that shitty. Expensive bikes, Ducatis.'

'He owes me. Big time.' Flora let out a long breath.

'How are you enjoying it?' Ash asked.

'It's fantastic,' Flora said. 'I love my little Ninja, but it's going to feel like half a bike after this beast.'

'How long are you staying?' Lucy asked. 'Maybe we could do a ride out while you're here?'

'I'd love that!' Flora beamed. 'I'm at the cottage until the end of the week but my dad has paid for me to stay at Jake's hotel for a bit longer. Late birthday pressie.'

'Jake's hotel?' Flora saw Ash and Lucy exchange glances, and wondered why. Did they think she was going there to sleep with Jake? She felt colour rush up her face and was glad it was dark. 'Oh no, don't make me pronounce it. Hotel ee Dragon something or other.' She made a face.

Cocking a single eyebrow, Jake translated for her, and she tried again, under her breath.

'Ah. Well, we'll sort a ride out soon then, before you leave,' Lucy said. 'You've got my mobile number. I sent the vid to you.'

'Fantastic.' They chatted about motorbikes until the food was in their hands, and found perches on the club trailer, loaded with various vessels that Flora didn't have a clue about.

'I don't suppose you ride, Jake?' Lucy asked.

He shook his head. 'No.'

'Ash is a brilliant teacher, if you fancied giving it a go.'

Jake shook his head again. 'As you know Gran has been absolutely anti-bike for years. Gramps used his race winnings to buy the hotel outright because it was what Gran wanted, and people came to stay just because of who he was. It was a real bike magnet at the time. Lots of pretty young girls, hanging about, evidently, the staff told me. Maybe Gran wasn't impressed by that.'

'So, I don't understand.' Flora frowned. 'Why is your gran anti-bike?'

'She told Gramps to pack it all in.' He shrugged. 'I've never really got to the bottom of it. I don't know whether he crashed, or nearly crashed, or what happened. Neither of them speak about it.'

'I always wondered why she…' murmured Ash.

'The whole anti-Art Café thing? Yeah, I can imagine.' Jake nodded.

'Yes!' Lucy said. 'I wondered what happened.'

'What's this?' Flora was lost by the shorthand language that seemed to be going on between the three of them.

Lucy faced her, her expression sombre. 'We've had a few run-ins with Hotel Y Ddraig over the years.' She pronounced the name in faultless Welsh and Flora tried to commit it to memory. 'Planning permissions blocked, complaints about bike noise, bad TripAdvisor reviews that we tracked back to Molly, Jake's gran. Rumours about stale cake. That sort of thing.'

'My turn to apologise,' said Jake, rubbing the back of his neck. 'I think Gran would prefer it if motorbikes were wiped off the planet.'

'That's why you hid my helmet...' Flora said. 'And showed me where to park my bike when I check in!'

'Uh-huh.'

'I liked your gran.'

'She would've been different to you if she'd known what you arrived on.'

'So, you're not anti-bike, then, Jake?' Ash asked.

'Me? No. Not at all. Each to his own,' Jake said. 'But it would break Gran's heart if she thought I was riding a motorbike.'

'That's tough,' said Ash.

'So I get my kicks hurling myself into towering waves instead.' Jake lifted his pint and said, 'Cheers!'

'Thank goodness you do!' Flora said, lifting her glass and knocking it against his. 'I wouldn't be here if it wasn't for you.' She said, then, 'So, er, how did your parents die? Nothing to do with motorbikes?'

'No, as it happens. They died of carbon monoxide poisoning. On a boat they were delivering.'

'Oh, God, Jake…' Flora froze, with her hot dog halfway to her mouth. The sympathetic silence spoke volumes. Lucy was the first to break it.

'Here's to our vices!' she said, not quite smiling. Her eyes met Ash's, and she got up and wound her arms around his shoulders from behind, planting a kiss on the back of his neck. Flora, trying not to stare, could only guess at what was going through her mind. She wondered what it must be like to love someone that much. Did you worry about them all the time?

Daisy emerged at that moment from the noisy throng of the clubhouse. She looked around her, and Lucy called her over. Flora saw the little girl smile as she hurried towards them.

'Do you want some food?' Lucy asked her. 'This is my daughter, Daisy,' she told Flora and Jake.

'No, it's okay, I've got my money.' Daisy patted the little sparkly bag that was slung cross-wise over her shoulders. 'I just wondered where you were.' She glanced shyly round at the little group and Lucy introduced them all to her.

'So, this big man here is your dad, his name is Ash,' she began, with a mischievous smile and Flora laughed as Daisy flicked her head and hip to opposite sides, crossing her eyes and poking out her tongue in one fluid, momentary movement. Lucy continued, 'This is Jake, who has been a member here since before he was your age. He's just come back from Australia, where he's been working as a professional lifeguard.'

'Wow!' Daisy looked impressed.

'And this is Flora, who is a hairdresser, and having a little holiday here.'

'Your hair is beautiful,' Flora said. 'Did you have it done at a hairdresser?'

'Lucy did it,' Daisy said with a beaming smile. 'It took aaaages.'

'About an hour.' Lucy nodded, twirling one of Daisy's

glossy locks round a finger. 'We've been practicing, haven't we, sweetie?'

'Well, you've done a great job of it.' Flora nodded. 'It is time consuming, I know. But totally worth it, you look stunning, Daisy.'

'Thank you,' the little girl said, shyly. 'Do you have your own salon?'

'Not yet, but I'm planning!' Flora heard her own words and found herself beginning to believe them. Daisy smiled up at her, her teeth ever so slightly gappy, her face illuminated by the fairy lights, and Flora caught a glimpse of the beautiful young woman she would become. She lifted her gaze and saw Lucy and Ash staring at his daughter with identical, thoughtful expressions.

'Shoot the first boy who comes knocking,' Flora told them, straight-faced, 'and hope the rest get the message.' They all contemplated her and then Daisy for a long moment, and Flora wavered. Ash broke into a deep chuckle, and Lucy rolled her eyes with a smile.

'It's certainly tempting,' Ash said, smiling down at Daisy, who eyed them suspiciously.

'What?' she said. 'What have I done?'

'Nothing at all, lovely girl. You enjoy yourself,' Lucy said, briskly, as Daisy's friends arrived to bustle her into the queue for the barbecue.

'They grow up so quickly, don't they?' Lucy said to Flora. 'And she was such a cute little thing when I first met her. She's Ash's daughter. But you probably worked that out.'

'She's still cute. And you obviously have a great relationship.'

Lucy nodded, and the smile of pride on her face struck at Flora. Had her stepmum ever looked at her like that? They watched the girls join the queue, the boys jostling and barging each other, the girls slightly aloof in their party outfits.

'It's a bit of a shock, seeing them all dressed up like that,' Lucy said. 'We're so used to seeing them in wetsuits, or shorts and hoodies.'

'Looks like she's got a lot of mates!' Flora tried to keep the note of envy out of her voice. 'What about you, Jake? I bet you had a ton of mates when you were their age.'

'Well,' he sipped his pint, 'I had a ton of mothers!' His mouth lifted in a lopsided smile. 'I seemed to belong to every family in the bay.'

'Aww, how sweet!' Flora grinned, trying to picture him as a little boy.

'Ye-eah. The novelty starts to wear off when you get to my age though. I only have to walk through the hotel and…' he paused, clearing his throat and adjusted his voice to a higher pitch '… ooh, look at you, you're so grown up now! I remember when you first came here, with your little chubby legs. You were so cuuuuuuuuuute!' He resumed his own, deep voice with a smile and added, 'And if I don't dodge fast enough, they do that cheek pinching thing. Why do they do that? It bloody hurts!' His audience chuckled.

'Do they try and spit wash you with an old hanky they fished out of their sleeves?' Ash asked, a glint of amusement in his blue eyes.

Jake spluttered into his pint, and Flora felt the vibrations of his deep rumble of laughter.

'No! That's disgusting,' Jake said, to laughter from all of them.

'Thank God for baby wipes,' murmured Lucy.

'I had a stepmum,' Flora said, taking a sip of her beer and disappointed to find there was only half an inch left. She barely remembered drinking it.

Lucy's eyes were on her straightaway. 'How did that go?'

'Oh, she's lovely. Very beautiful. Glossy, if you know what I mean.'

Jake's eyes were on her too, and she couldn't blame him. He was probably wondering what she was going to say, given her outburst earlier that day about her half-sister. Had it only been today? It seemed like an eternity ago. 'She and my mum get on okay together. Which is a bit weird, if you ask me.'

'Very civilised,' said Lucy. 'It must've made things easier for you?'

Flora paused before she answered. 'In respect of my parenting, I suppose, yes. But...' She stared sadly into her empty glass.

Jake said, quickly, 'I'll get another round – but I don't want to miss anything!'

Flora laughed. For all his lecturing about taking responsibility for your actions, he was as much a gossip as anyone else. 'My round,' she said. 'What are you guys having? Same again, Jake?'

He nodded, 'Cheers, Flora.'

'I'm fine with my wine, thanks,' Lucy said.

'Coke, please,' Ash said. 'My turn to drive tonight.' He rolled his eyes at Lucy with a smile to show he didn't mind and Flora made her way to the bar.

'Hey, Anna! Anna!' One of the first aid girls materialised alongside her. Flora had forgotten her false name. Should she confess? 'You're not dancing!'

'I've just scarfed down a dog,' Flora said, her mouth close to the girl's ear. 'Getting a round in now, and then, trust me, I'll be back on the floor, shaking my booty.'

'How you doing? No problems since we saw you?' the girl yelled over the music. 'I'm Karen, by the way. It was me who got your key out, you naked surfer, you!'

The music stopped just as Karen's last words hung in the air and several people turned to stare at them.

Flora stared right back and announced, straight-faced,

'Hardcore, me.' She giggled with Karen, who had a hand over her lips, her eyes alight with laughter.

'Sorry! Me and my big mouth!'

'That's usually me. By the way, my name isn't Anna. I made that up. It's Flora.'

Karen was goggle-eyed. 'Hello, Flora! So, should I ask, or are you on the run?'

'Well, if I was, I haven't got very far, have I?' Flora caught the eye of the middle-aged man dispensing cans and bottles. He didn't look like a lifeguard, but judging by the number of children of all ages here, she guessed he was a parent. 'Four lagers and two Cokes, please!' She'd doubled the order, it saved them queuing again, and the drinks were cheap as chips. Even she could afford them, since her dad had put some money in her account. 'What can I get you, Karen? For lying to you!'

'Lager, please.'

Flora ordered another two cans, and handed them both to Karen. 'Could you give the other one to the other girl, please? You were both very kind to me that day.'

'You're welcome. It's what we do.' Karen took the cans from her. 'So I see you and Jake hit it off in the end. He looks great now all that terrible hair has gone. Wonder what made him do that?'

'Ah. That was me. I'm a hairdresser. Payback for rescuing me.' Flora followed Karen's gaze through the gap in the crowd to where Jake was deep in conversation with Ash and Lucy.

'Impressive.' Karen nodded and then waggled her eyebrows with a lascivious grin. 'Is this the start of a holiday romance?' She waited.

Flora's face grew hot. She shook her head emphatically. 'Naaah. He's very nice and everything, but I just came out of one relationship. I'm not ready to jump into another one.

Anyway, if you'd like your hair done, Lucy at the Art Café has got my number. I'm looking for premises to start my own salon.' Once again, she was amazed at how easily the words came now. 'But I can come to your house, if you like.'

'Wow, you've certainly networked fast! How long are you staying then? I thought you were just on a break.'

'I used to holiday here as a kid. I can feel it pulling me in again,' Flora confessed. 'Another week, then I'm staying a few days in Jake's hotel, and then I'll work something out.' She hadn't even thought about how this salon idea was going to actually work. But now she'd said it aloud, it made sense to her. She had a secret Pinterest board, entitled, My Salon. Where to live was the least of it, wasn't it? Okay, so where to live was a pretty big deal. She couldn't live on the streets, obviously. She'd think about it later. Something would come up. And if she did a good job for her dad, she'd have a decent wedge to put towards her plans.

Her stomach lurched abruptly. To earn that wedge, she was going to have to spy on Jake's grandparents' hotel. How had that escaped her attention? She'd been so distracted by Jake himself, that the full import of her task only settled over her then and there. What would he think of her? After that ticking off about trust? Some mate she was. He rescued her and she was going to try and find all the hotel's dirty washing and tell her dad, so he could potentially buy them out at the lowest possible price.

She swallowed. How could she be so stupid? Would she ever think ahead further than what was directly before her? What was she going to do? The cold tins slipped in her hand and she gripped them tighter.

'Are you okay?' Karen's expression was concerned. 'That hot dog's not coming back, is it?'

'Er, no, no.' Flora pulled her mouth into a smile. 'I'm fine. I just thought of something I, er, need to sort out, that's all.

Er, lovely to see you again, Karen, and, um, don't forget me when you next need a haircut! Bye!' She managed to keep the fake smile stitched to her face until she turned away and pushed through the crowd. She needed some fresh air. How was she going to look Jake in the eye?

Chapter Fourteen

Jake looked over the crowd to see where Flora had got to. She didn't know anyone there, so she could hardly have got into conversation with an old mate, could she? He rapidly revised that view. This was Flora. He'd only known her a couple of days, but already he knew that she had no reservations about chatting to complete strangers. She didn't actually seem to have reservations about anything much, including biffing her boss for sexual harassment and riding a couple of hundred miles on a stolen bike.

He grinned. He wanted to know more about this tiny person with the big personality. She made him laugh, and she made him cross. She made him, what? She made him... feel. After the... the incident, he'd shut himself off. His girlfriend going walkabout hadn't surprised him. Not really. It had hurt like hell at the time, but he couldn't blame her for sodding off with someone else. In all honesty, he hadn't really been present in their relationship at the end.

He wasn't a bit surprised Flora had liked his gran. They were similar personalities. She was another who 'said it as it was'. It was almost always 'her way or the highway', he thought.

'I'll just go and see if Flora needs a hand,' he said, casually, to Lucy and Ash, not missing but choosing to ignore the knowing looks they exchanged. He met Flora as she was coming out, balancing tinnies in her arms. Her expression looked troubled.

'S'up?' He took the drinks from her. 'Did something happen? You alright?'

'Yeah. Yes! I'm fine. Fine.' She turned a beaming smile on him that he wasn't fooled by for one minute. He sighed. She really was off the wall. He shouldn't get involved. And she wouldn't even be here for long. Even while his head lectured him his stomach unaccountably see-sawed at the thought of her going. Don't be so bloody stupid, he told himself. Find yourself a nice, sensible girl, who doesn't ride a massive motorbike, doesn't wear a bike jacket and boots all the time, doesn't take chunks out of your head, doesn't say exactly what's skittering across her brain. He shepherded her back to where Ash and Lucy were waiting.

'Did you get lost?' Ash grinned, nodding a thank you for the Coke tins she handed over.

'Uh, no, I, er, bumped into one of the girls who fixed me up after Jake rescued me. We got chatting. I offered to do her hair.'

'I'll make sure I don't barge in on that one then.' Ash laughed, and Jake involuntarily fingered the sore place on his scalp. He hurriedly shoved his hand in his pocket as he saw Flora's expression of anguish.

'I can hardly feel it now,' he told her. 'I think the bruise from the flying kitchen roll has taken over.'

Lucy made a face. 'Filming never goes to plan, in my experience!'

'I'd love to hear some stories about that,' Flora said, quickly, pouring her beer into another perfect pint.

'I thought we were going to hear some stories about your childhood, Flora,' Jake said, seeing that Lucy was reluctant to divulge. He knew that she'd made a series about biking from social media, and guessed that she'd probably signed a contract preventing her from talking about it.

'My childhood?' Flora's mouth tightened into a pout, and even while he acknowledged that this was not going to be a happy tale, he couldn't help noticing that her lips were pink and soft and that he had an urge to plant his own on them. It must be the beer. Even though he'd only had one. He focused on her as she spoke.

'We used to come here every summer, since I was little. It

was the highlight of my year. I'd always have my birthdays here, and Mum and Dad eventually bought the cottage when it came up for sale. I remember it always being sunny.'

'April and May are often the best months of the year here.' Lucy nodded, lifting an expressive hand up at the cloudless, clear dusk.

'Then in the six weeks holiday, we'd come back down. Dad would go back to work during the week, Mum and I would be here for the whole holiday, and he'd come for weekends when he could. It was no different to our usual lives, just in a different place.'

'Sounds lovely,' murmured Lucy.

'Yeah.' Flora nodded, slowly. 'It was. Until, the year I was eleven, my dad told me that I had a sister.' She took a long swallow of her lager, and Jake watched her, realising he was holding his breath at what might be coming next. 'I thought he meant that Mum was having a baby.' She laughed. 'I thought that was bad enough. I didn't want to think about them having sex, ewww!' Jake saw Ash and Lucy exchange glances. 'But he said, the little girl who came to your birthday party? And I remembered, the tall, pretty lady who had come along with her tall, pretty daughter, a year or so younger than me. She had blonde hair in a swingy ponytail that I was really envious of because my hair never did anything I wanted. She'd been okay. I quite liked her, actually. I just accepted her as someone my parents knew.' She shrugged. 'And it turned out, she was my sister. My half-sister.' She stopped to sip from her plastic glass and looked at them all.

'Shi-it,' Lucy was the first to speak, on a long breath. 'So, your dad had been…'

'Yep. Got it in one. He had another family going on. Weekends with us, weekdays with them. I'm surprised he found the time to go to work.'

'And he just expected you to accept this girl?'

Flora nodded. 'What was really weird, and is still weird, is that Mum just accepted the whole situation like it was normal. She's always got on with Dad's other woman. She never fought for him. I've never understood it.'

Jake watched her, beginning to understand her prickly defensiveness, and just why she'd been so furious with him earlier that day. She stood upright, shoulders back, chin lifted, and he felt an urge to catch her up in a hug and protect her from all her hurts. She'd probably stab him with something though, so he didn't.

'Your mum *accepted* the other woman?' Lucy turned to Ash. 'Don't get any ideas. I would *not* be that nice.' A puzzled frown crossed Ash's face and Jake wondered briefly how it must feel to have found your soul mate.

'I know. It *is* weird, isn't it?' Flora chewed her lip. 'Look, I don't want to bore you, talking about myself all the time. This wasn't meant to be confession time.'

'It's not boring,' Lucy assured her quickly. 'I'm terribly nosey, really. I think it's why I wanted a café. You hear all sorts of bits of people's lives. Why did they wait until you were eleven before telling you? I mean, families are pieced together in all sorts of ways these days, aren't they? Ours is.' She shrugged.

'Mine too,' Jake said, slowly.

'Yeah, I know. Apparently, just before my eleventh birthday, Helen told my dad she was pregnant and he decided he needed to make more of a commitment to her and the new baby.' Flora swallowed her beer. 'Dad found a shop for Mum to start her floristry business, with an apartment over it, and he bought it for her and we moved there. Mum adored it, although I made a hell of a fuss about everything. I was probably a real pain in the arse. Mum loves flowers more than anything, and there's a balcony and a garden at the back.'

'It sounds glorious. And your dad bought it for her?'

'Yes. He and Mum agreed to a quick divorce and he moved in with Helen and Amber. We've never had any of that terrible rowing over children and maintenance. I never heard any of it anyway. Mum still lives there, and she still runs the florists. With her business partner Heather. They've been friends for years.' Flora shrugged and continued, 'Dad lived on the other side of town and used to pop over a lot. I probably saw more of him than I had before, which was probably the idea.'

Lucy said, 'Okay, I'm almost scared to ask – did you continue to get on okay with the half-sister and new baby?'

Flora made a rueful face. 'Helen had a miscarriage at five months, just after she and dad got married. As for Amber, well, it started off okay. Occasionally I stayed over at Dad's. Me and Amber shared a room. God knows why they thought that was a good idea. Aversion therapy or something? Anyway, one night Amber cut my fringe off with paper scissors while I was asleep and she Sharpied my eyebrows into a mono-brow.'

'Oops. Kids are horrible, aren't they?' Ash made a face.

'Yep. What made it worse was it was the day of my school photo. Her mum was furious with her, and she used everything off her dressing table to remove most of the Sharpie, but there wasn't much she could do about my missing fringe. Amber had left about half an inch, right across my forehead... really tatty, and at an angle...'

'Oh my God, that's terrible!' Lucy's eyes were full of sympathy. 'Did you both go to the same school?'

'No, thank God. And that was the end of shared rooms, so she was happy. I was too, to be fair. Dad came over to see me instead and I got him all to myself. Even when she got to comp, it was surprising how many times we bumped into each other. Sports events were a nightmare because she was better than me at everything, even though she was younger.

Of course, having the same surname didn't help. People always comparing her long legs against my stumpy useless…' She shook her legs to make them laugh, but now that she'd started on her revelations, she couldn't seem to stop.

'That wasn't all. While I was still staying over, she took all my Barbie dolls – I had loads, and I was far too old for them, but I loved those dolls, they were like my little family, and Mum always packed some up to take with me. Silly really.' Flora shrugged her skinny shoulders inside the bulky jacket. 'Anyway, Amber and her mate arranged them all on the road outside, and let the cars run over them.'

Nobody said anything, but their expressions were enough.

'Didn't her mother punish her?' Lucy looked horrified.

'Oh yes. But it didn't stop her. She just got more sneaky. She cut holes in my school tights, and I had to go to school in socks, and everyone laughed at me.' Her lager was going down fast. 'Course, I'd try and get my own back. But I was a short-arse with a mean line in backchats, and she was tall and beautiful and everyone loved her, and no one believed me when I said she was a bitch to me. And she was younger than me, so I was supposed to be more mature about it. The only weapon I had was my tongue.' She glanced up at Jake and he felt a stab of guilt about his sweeping accusation that day. 'And that just earned me the nickname, Cactus.'

'So, um, do you get on with her now? I mean, kids can be cruel, but you know, as you grew up…' Lucy asked.

'I thought we'd managed to be mates, to be honest, after all this time. She's cooked her goose with me now though. Good and proper.' Flora paused for a moment, and looked over their heads, her eyes shining brightly. 'It was her I caught shagging my boyfriend a couple of days ago. What a cliché. My sister shagged my boyfriend.' Her eyes met Jake's and he desperately wanted to take back his mean censorship of her in the hotel, as she dashed the unshed tears from her eyes with the back of her hand. He wondered what on earth was coming next. 'I told Lucy it was my "best friend" and I've got Jake to thank for me being even able to say it was Amber. I haven't told my parents and I couldn't even say it in my own head yesterday.'

He blinked with surprise. He hadn't realised that he'd been of any use at all.

'Jeeze. Well, I think you're holding it together pretty well, if you ask me,' Ash said. 'Unless you've murdered them both and stashed them in a trunk.' He laughed and then stopped, peering at her solemn face. 'You haven't, have you?'

'Why does everyone ask me that? Do I really look like the sort of person who murders people?' She looked around at their thoughtful expressions before adding, 'Gee, thanks. Don't think I didn't consider it.'

'Anyhoo. Enough about me! Great music, anyone for a wiggle?' Flora lifted her glass to them and then added, in a slightly slurry and surprised voice, 'My beer keeps evaporating.'

'We'll just go and have a chat to those people over there, and then we'll be in,' Lucy said, with a smile.

Jake took the opportunity to steer Flora back into the clubhouse, just in case the alcohol provoked a rush of confessions about planning to kill them both that she might regret later. In complete contrast to his earlier pronouncement that she needed to take some responsibility for herself, he found himself wanting to look after her, shelter her from anyone who might run over her dolls again.

She waved now at two young women, who danced in their direction, and he smiled at them without having a clue who they were. How was it that Flora already knew members of his own club and he didn't? People warmed to her, despite the fact that she was often completely random. She'd already got Lucy intrigued – and Lucy was a TV star! She probably had a whole crowd of people dying to talk to her, and yet she'd been hanging out with them.

'What are you doing tomorrow?' he asked her now, an idea forming in his head.

'Having a lie-in,' she mouthed, her entire body moving to the music.

'Boring. Do you fancy having an adventure?'

She looked intrigued. 'Always.'

'Want to come out on a double ski with me?'

'I can't ski! Wait, what are you talking about? There's no snow here! Artificial ski slope? That sounds cool.'

'Not that kind of ski. This is a surf ski. Kind of a kayak. For lifeguards.'

As the words sank in, Flora backed away, holding up a hand. 'Oh no. You're not getting me out on that sea again. No. Did I say no? I totally meant no.'

'You won't drown, I'll be…' he began, and then stalled. What if something happened, and he couldn't save her? What had he been thinking? He shook his head and held his hands up, palms forward. 'Yeah. You're right. Stupid idea. Forget I said it.'

She frowned at him, her eyes narrowed. 'Oh. Now you've dared me, so I have to do it. I can swim. But I'm gonna need a wetsuit that fits me.' She thought for a second and said, 'I haven't even got a swimsuit.'

He blinked. So, that meant… he couldn't help himself picturing her neat body…

'Woss hapnin?' Karen's eyes switched from one to the other as Flora filled her in. 'I can lend you a cozzie. I've got loads. I'll find you a small one, if you can come a bit before eleven? And a wetsuit, yes,' as Flora's mouth opened. 'Can I come too? My shift doesn't start till the evening.'

'What do you do?' Flora asked.

'I'm a paramedic.' She smiled. 'Yeah, I know, it's a bit samey doing this too, but it's what I know.'

'Well, if I'm going with a paramedic and a pro Aussi Lifeguard, I couldn't be in better hands. Count me in.' Flora gave a loud and nervous laugh and Jake felt a bit light-headed. She'd made him as impulsive as she was.

'I'll see who else fancies it, shall I?' Karen danced away from them and Jake, with mixed feelings, watched her chatting to the groups of young men standing around the walls.

'It's like bikers, isn't it?' Flora said, following his gaze. 'One person decides to go out, and before you know it, there's a dozen of you and you've got a ride out.'

'Uh huh.' Jake nodded but he wasn't really listening. He was thinking about clubhouse keys, how he was going to get in and lock up now he didn't have them and which double ski was the most stable, and how far they would go, and whether the cafés would be open on the beach he was planning to paddle round to. Karen returned.

'There's about eight of us. Maybe more. Gethin, over there, he has a key to the clubhouse. About eleven? By that time we should've cleared this place up.'

'Won't they want a long paddle? I wasn't planning to go that far...'

'It'll be fine. I said you were taking a newbie out. They're treating it as a pre-season warm up.'

'Okay. Eleven it is.'

'I better not drink any more then,' Flora said.

'Me neither,' said Jake, glumly. He'd been looking forward to a relaxing few beers tonight. Flora's tendency to speak without thinking seemed to have rubbed off on him. 'Let's exchange mobile numbers in case you change your mind.' He didn't know whether he'd be relieved or disappointed if she cancelled.

'I'm on Coke now anyway. I can't dance and drink.' Karen beamed at them and bobbed away in time to the music. 'See ya tomorrow!'

121

Chapter Fifteen

Flora was awake, nursing a huge mug of coffee as the sun rose. At least, she thought, there was a sun. Would it be cancelled if it was raining? She had an idea, having met quite a lot of lifeguards last night, that it probably wouldn't be. That they'd see it as a challenge. She straightened up a little. Well, she wouldn't cancel a ride on her motorbike if it was raining, would she? It would be something different today. A new experience.

She liked an adventure, she told herself, and then sagged in the chair, trying to stop her mind reliving the grey, murky sea as it sucked her down... and anyway, Jake would be there. He wouldn't let anything happen to her. And all the other people who'd said they were coming along, they looked like adverts for some fitness magazine. She'd be fine. Fine! The sleepless night had just been because her body was over stimulated from the music.

She felt the now familiar churning sensation about the task her father had set her, but consoled herself that she wouldn't be there for long. A bigger wave of disquiet swept over her at that thought. Was it the thought of going back to Coventry? The thought of not setting up a salon here, in the seaside town that she already had such a connection to? Or the thought of upsetting Jake?

She couldn't keep thinking about Jake all the time. It was just a silly rebound thing. A desperate need to be found attractive, after the massive blow Spence had dealt to her self-confidence. She could count the length of time she'd known him in hours, for goodness' sake. He was nice, and he'd walked her back to the cottage the previous night after the party. And, she swallowed, recalling it, she'd put her face up to be kissed, like you would, wouldn't you? After a lovely night out? A sort of date? Her face heated with shame at the memory. It wasn't even like she'd been drunk! And he'd bent over her, and he'd kissed… her cheek. And turned to go, with a 'See ya tomorrow,' and a wave.

She'd felt a complete idiot. And today, she had to sit in some sort of 'kayak for two' with him. She could cancel. Say the food last night had made her sick.

No, she couldn't. She never lied, and she had her pride, and she was more than a bit curious about what lay ahead.

She yawned, staring at the clock. She could get another couple of hours sleep, surely. She took her mug back to bed and drained the last inch or so, put her head on the pillow and was fast asleep in seconds.

When the alarm sounded on her phone, she couldn't think what on earth the noise was. Knuckling eyes still asleep, she blundered into the shower, more to wake herself up than to be clean.

'What am I doing?' she said aloud to her reflection. 'I'm going to be in the sea in twenty minutes!' Dragging her clothes on, she got herself organised and rode to the Lifeguard Station with mixed feelings about whether she might be too late and whether they'd wait for her or not. Oh dear, they might go without her, and she could have a lovely breakfast at the Art Café and read the Sunday papers or something, and then go out on the Ducati and explore a bit more of Gower. No such luck. They were all there, and looking busy.

'That's one hell of a funky looking bike!' Karen said, approvingly, walking over to her as she parked. 'Good morning! You nearly missed the best bit.'

'What's that?' Flora strolled back with her, eyeing with apprehension the huge multi-layered trailer on the forecourt, which she now realised held what seemed to be dozens of brightly coloured, glossy kayak type things. They looked impossibly narrow and long, and each one trailed a rudder at the narrowest end. She could be wrong, but she'd never seen a kayak with a rudder before. And surely, these things were over five metres long!

She paced alongside as Karen still chatted on. The seats were just shaped dips. There wasn't a spray deck. They were basically just a really, really long bit of coloured plastic that you sat on and paddled. She was never going to balance on one of those. It didn't look much wider than her hips. How did the blokes manage on them? Hang on. She could ride a huge motorbike. She sure as hell could manage one of these.

'The Big After Party Clear Up! Here you go.' Karen broke into her musings, handing over a pair of rubber gloves and a bin liner. 'Rubbish goes into this, cans and bottles in the recycling.' She nodded at the wheelie bins, appropriately marked. 'There's coffee and bacon butties on the go in the kitchen. You look knackered, girl. Didn't you get any sleep?'

'Not really,' Flora said, with a shrug. 'Did you remember the cozzie and wetsuit for me?'

'Yes.' Karen nodded, hefting a full black bin liner with apparent ease to the huge black wheelie bin. 'I dug out a few. They're in the ladies changing room. Take your pick.'

'Thanks. Right, I'd better go and earn my place on this, er, ski thing!' Flora gritted her teeth, mouth breathing against the smell of spilled, stale beer, and marched with determination into the building, which last night looked like a nightclub, and in the cold light of day, looked like a tip.

'Yo, Flora!' Jake hailed her from the depths of the building, wielding an enormously wide broom, and pushing before him a heap of discarded tins and crisp packets. 'Look at this lot, bloody bums,' he grumbled, cheerfully.

Flora set to work picking out the cans and looking around her for something to transport them in. As she worked, she realised she was part of a team of people, some of whom she recognised from the previous night, most of the men with stubble and sticky up hair and cheery expressions. Everyone wished her a good morning, and passed comment on the perfect sea conditions, and how they were looking forward to a great paddle. Her stomach was in a free fall of nerves, but having a job to do helped.

The scent of bacon was mouth-watering, and prompted them all into rapid action. It wasn't long before the building was as clean as it was going to get, and she trooped upstairs to the kitchen to claim her coffee and bacon roll.

'Come downstairs, I'll show you what we're going out to play on,' Jake said, indicating with his head and sloshing coffee over the floor, to cries of mock despair from the assembled crowd. 'Sorry, sorry, give me a bit of cloth, I'll clean it up!'

Someone darted forward with a bit of kitchen roll and mopped the spill with a loudly muttered, 'Bloody Ozzies...'

'Cheers, ya Pommie!' Jake said, with a disarming smile.

Flora laughed with all the others. She liked the camaraderie there. It was very similar to the groups she'd biked with, when she was out with Spence. Spence... The bacon roll stuck in her throat and she coughed, earning herself a whack between the shoulder blades that threatened to dislodge her teeth, never mind the bit of food.

'Getting your own back?' she wheezed at Jake, tears in her eyes.

'That'll teach you to put holes in me,' he said. 'I hope I'm still waterproof. Come on, we haven't got all day.' He led her back into the room that had been the disco. 'This is the boathouse. All these,' he waved an arm that included the laden trailer, 'are called boats. Even though they're not actually boats. Okay?'

Flora shrugged. 'Okay.'

Jake tugged away a tarpaulin. 'Ta-daaah! This is our ride.'

Flora stared down at the hulking beast. Covered in repairs, it was hard to tell what colour it had originally been, but it was double the width of the vessels on the trailer, and for that she was grateful.

'Oh,' she murmured. 'It's, er...'

'She's not pretty, and she's heavy, but much more stable than the ones on the trailer, so we'll have a ball.' Jake nodded, and Flora tried out a smile, but her jaw was wobbly and so were her legs. 'Go and get changed, and we'll see you back here to sort out paddles.'

Karen was already in the changing room, tugging a wetsuit over her tall, Amazonian frame. Flora felt like a hobbit, by comparison. 'Try this lot.' Karen nodded at the heap of swimming costumes and brightly coloured neoprene on the slatted bench alongside her. 'I've had some of them for years. I should've had a clear out ages ago. There must be something there to fit you.'

They picked through them together, and after a few false starts with wetsuits that barely went over her feet, they found one that fitted. More or less. By the time Flora had shoved her arms into the sleeves, she was panting and hot, and Karen was doubled over in hysterics.

'I can't get my arms down! It's too tight!' Flora's tongue hung out as Karen zipped her up, which made her laugh even more. 'Stop laughing, you rotten bitch. How am I supposed to row a boat in this?'

'You don't row it, you paddle it.' Karen sniggered. 'Once the water gets into the suit, it'll ease up, I promise you. It's perfect. If it's too loose, the water just keeps gushing through and you freeze.'

'Yeah. I've already experienced that.' Flora rolled her eyes. 'But, really? I can hardly walk! Look!' Attempting a few steps, she swung her legs stiffly from the hips, and Karen doubled over with mirth. Flora tried to glare at her, but her amusement was infectious. 'How am I supposed to sit down in it?'

'Trust me,' Karen hiccuped, fanning her face. 'Walk into the sea, and all will become clear.' She cleared her throat with an effort. 'Hopefully. Or the seams will burst.'

'Oh, great. Cheers. What do I wear on my feet?'

'I've even brought you booties along!' Karen wiped her eyes and stared thoughtfully at Flora's feet. 'Although, I don't think my feet have ever been that small... I think we've got some of the kids' ones in the lost property.'

She went into the corridor that linked the male and female changing rooms, leaving the door casually open, and Flora caught a glimpse of Jake strolling out with his wetsuit pulled up only to his waist, his muscular torso on display. Her throat dried. He was utterly, utterly sensational. Her mouth was still open when Karen returned with a selection of neoprene boots.

'You'll have to do this. I can't bend down that far,' Flora said, and rolled her eyes as Karen once again shook with laughter.

'It fits, Cinderella!' she announced, tugging the boots on as Flora winced. 'You shall go to the ball!'

'I'm so glad you're having fun,' Flora said, hobbling straight-legged towards the door, listening to Karen's helpless giggles behind her.

'Love you!' Karen gasped, catching her up, and holding the door open. 'OMG, you are such a good sport, Flora.'

Flora experienced a tiny glow of pride alongside her discomfort. Spence had more than once levelled the accusation that she was boring, despite the fact that he seemed to spend all his time on the computer.

Jake, that jaw-dropping torso now beneath sober black neoprene, blinked when he saw her, and she steeled herself for more mickey-taking. His solemn gaze taking in her no doubt red and sweaty face, and Karen's tears of laughter, he nodded, but said nothing. Uncomfortably restricted, she turned her entire body to look around her, appeased a little as she watched some of the men struggling to zip up their suits, complaining that they must have 'shrunk over the winter', to jeers and jokes.

Checking the size against her arm, which she held up with difficulty, Jake found a paddle and then zipped her into a buoyancy vest, both items apparently from the kids' section. She twirled the double-ended paddle experimentally and several people nearby ducked.

'Try not to decapitate anyone,' Jake said. 'You might need them to pull you out of the water later.' There wasn't a trace of a smile. He was back to Mr Grouchy, the one who'd ticked her off at the water's edge. Was he regretting having asked her? Did he think she'd be a liability?

Yet again, she thought, she'd dived in feet first. Having already nearly drowned, she'd agreed to go out on this ancient patched up vessel, with a bunch of people she barely knew, without a clue of what she was meant to be doing. She couldn't even take a deep breath, with this stupid wetsuit corsetting her ribs. But even as she stood there alone, holding the paddle, amongst all these super-fit people who seemed to know exactly what they were doing, excitement about the prospect of adventure overtook her trepidation. You only lived once, after all.

The sea seemed an agonisingly long way, in the tight wetsuit, and Flora was actually relieved to wade in, she was so hot by then. Several of the men ran into the sea with shouts, diving head first under the waves and stretching their arms afterwards.

It was a weird sensation. Despite the water lapping around her knees, she was completely dry, impervious to the cold and wet, and as she watched the men, she realised with reluctance that the water had to go in at her neck. Taking a deep breath, she ducked down, trying not to get her hair wet, and squealed as the icy water trickled down the suit. After a few moments, the suit released its suffocating grip and she whirled her arms, scooping the water to get it past the tight cuffs.

'Oh my goodness, that's so much better,' she told Jake, who was holding the boat steady and viewing her with a perplexed expression. 'I thought Karen was having me on. I am toasty warm! Where do I sit?'

'You're at the back this time. I steer, you do all the paddling.' He grinned at her and she realised her disbelief was written all over her face. 'Go on, get in.' She plopped her bottom into the open, sculpted seat, and he handed her the paddle. 'This way up, okay? Put your feet under those straps.'

The boat wobbled alarmingly beneath her. It was so low in the water, and her heart thudded with fear. 'Copy what I do, so your paddle goes in the water on the same side as mine does, at the same time.' She nodded. What on earth had she agreed to?

She squeaked as Jake lowered himself into the front seat, feeling the boat rocking. He had a leg in the water on each side of the boat, and as she looked at the others, she could see them doing the same. She lifted her knees and stretched them out to the sides. Her feet went nowhere near the water, and she hurriedly tucked them back under the straps. God. What she wouldn't give for legs as long as Karen's.

She saw Jake's vast shoulders rotate, his paddle blades rising and dipping into the water at the same time as his legs smoothly returned to the pedals before him. The boat surged forward. Rotating her own paddle, she experimentally plunged it into the sea, squealing as the force of the water almost took it from her hands.

'Just put the blade in halfway,' Jake called over his shoulder.

'Now you tell me.'

'You'll get the hang of it.'

She did. She managed ten matched strokes before the muscles in her arms protested. There were huge waves before them, and Jake leaned forward, digging his paddle in with rapid strokes, pulling them up and over the surf. Her fear was replaced with excitement, despite having what felt like a full bucket of seawater flung in her face. It was like the acceleration on the Ducati.

'This is brilliant!' she yelled, seeing briefly the profile of Jake's cheeks creasing in a smile as he concentrated on climbing the next wave on the boat, which even she could see probably weighed at least double the other vessels, not including his passenger. As the boat slapped heavily down and over the foamy crest, she laughed aloud with pure exhilaration.

'Amaaaazing!'

'Keep paddling!' he yelled back at her, as the final wave approached. From her position so close to the water's surface, it looked huge, and she tried her hardest to mimic Jake's rhythmic arm swings.

In her peripheral vision, she saw one of the boats, now riderless, bob into the air, high of the tumbling surf, and she closed her eyes as their vessel rose vertically and hung in the air for a moment along with her stomach, before crashing down on the other side of the huge wave.

'Holy shit,' she breathed, still holding her paddle in the air. She looked around at the calm sea now they were beyond the waves. To her relief, the rider who had fallen off was clambering back onto his ski, flicking the hair out of his face. 'That was scary.'

'Okay?' Jake twisted to look at her. She nodded. 'You did good. That's the hardest bit. It's all easy from now on.' She doubted his confidence, but as they bobbed on the placid water, she watched the long bows of the other boats rise over the waves like Viking longboats before joining them, some of the riders wet haired and grinning. Karen paddled close to them, holding her ski balanced with one paddle in the sea.

'How are you getting on?'

'It's brilliant!' Flora yelled back.

'You're a natural.' Karen smiled. 'You've got really good balance. It's probably the biking.'

Once everyone was together, they paddled along the coastline, keeping to the smooth waters away from the breaking surf. Flora paddled for a few strokes and rested for more, which seemed to make no difference whatsoever to the speed of the boat. And she'd always thought she was fit!

As Jake paddled in an apparently tireless rhythm, his powerful, triangular back and muscular butt only inches from her toes, she watched the coast slide past them. The pink stratified cliffs pushed granite fingers into the lacy surf, and she inhaled the fresh salty and unmistakeable scent of the seaside. Seagulls bobbed on the glassy surface, and craning her neck, she peered down into the clear waters, terrified and exhilarated simultaneously by how deep it was.

Her back was starting to ache from the unaccustomed position with her legs stuck straight out before her. Peeping at the others, she saw that they all had their knees bent, but she was too short to do that. The muscles in her hips were cramping and she tried to stretch without rocking the boat. It was a small price to pay though, for the tour of the beautiful coastline. It was so quiet too. Only their own shouts across the water, and the natural sounds of wind and waves and bird calls. The sky was blue and the sea reflected it in the dips and troughs. She'd never realised there was so much colour before. It was mesmerising.

They turned towards the coast slightly, and Flora could see a long golden strip of beach. Much as she'd enjoyed her trip, she was relieved to be heading for solid ground now. Her shoulders ached, along with her back, and now she was doing a full body inventory, there was a blister beginning in the space between her thumbs and forefingers, her neck hurt and her bottom seemed to be made only of pointy bones.

'As we go down the waves,' Jake said over his shoulder, pausing in his paddling, 'lean back and let me steer, okay? If we fall out, hang on to your paddle, and keep me in your vision. I'll tell you what to do.'

'Okay.' Unease stirred her stomach. Falling out wasn't part of her plan. Glancing sideways at the other riders, all of them lined up parallel to Jake, she flicked back the hair that was now in her eyes and had to snatch at her paddle as it slid away. How easy was it going to be to hold onto it if they were floundering around in the water with this boat bobbing about all over the place? And, hang on, the biggest waves were the furthest from the beach, weren't they? So that meant, this one coming up behind them now, would be...

She glanced over her shoulder and glimpsed the monster wave gaining on them. She had no time to think about it, as Jake lined them up squarely to the wave and she saw his paddling rate speed up – then he leaned right back with the paddle in the water like a rudder.

Frozen with terror, she looked down the boat over his head into the dark foamy sea beneath them, registering that she was now about ten feet in the air in a slippery craft that had a mind of its own and seemed now to be intent on slewing sideways back into the wave.

There was nothing to hold onto.

Chapter Sixteen

Fighting with the ancient boat, Jake swore violently as it ignored his attempts at steering and skewed left. Bloody thing! The waves weren't particularly big, but the balance was a bit off on this old tub, what with a non-paddling passenger plus all the fibreglass repairs. If they fell off now, the ski would hurtle in without them, and probably arrive in bits on the beach, and they'd have to swim in with their paddles. He guessed that Flora probably wouldn't enjoy that.

Upping his work rate, and using his body weight, he made a superhuman effort and straightened the old bitch up, and she rewarded him by surfing down the wave a treat.

'Are you still there?' he shouted over his shoulder, concentrating on keeping the boat square for the next one.

'Just about!' she shouted back.

The next wave was smaller but made life difficult as another bigger wave followed on its heels, and once again Jake fought the boat's desire to tumble broadside. He was definitely getting a workout on this thing. He could feel his back muscles burning as he dug in and counterbalanced. Whose stupid idea was this again? Oh, that would be his.

They bounced over the tumult of messy swells and just as Jake thought they were more or less home and dry, they were sideswiped by another double wave. He whipped his paddle from one side to the other but in those split seconds, their balance was lost and he heard Flora's small shriek as she slid off. Twisting to look for her unseated him too, and he clawed for the boat's slippery sides, managing to grip one of the webbing straps that had thankfully been rivetted onto this older model.

'Flora!' he yelled, treading water and hanging onto the boat as it bucked against him. 'Flora!' He looked wildly around him. Oh God, this was such a stupid idea. What had he been thinking? As he called out again, he could see the others in the group paddling towards him, looking around them.

Where the hell was she? She was wearing a buoyancy aid. She couldn't drown. Had she banged her head when she fell out? Was she underneath this bloody awful boat and trapped? He held his paddle and the boat together, ducked his head beneath its war-torn sides and could see nothing but murky bubbles. As he brought his head back up, she was there, beside him. With her paddle.

'It's... bloody impossible... to swim...' she gasped, a grin on her wet face, 'holding this bloody thing!'

'Flora! You *star!*' He almost went to kiss her with relief, and settled at the last minute for a matey, 'Alright? Ready to surf this beast in for the last bit?'

'Yeah,' she said, mimicking a bad Australian accent. 'All good, mate!'

He grinned at her. She was game for anything. Steadying the boat for her to climb in, he hauled himself in after her, settling quickly and getting into his paddling rhythm straightaway.

You couldn't just sit there, in between the waves. Even these smallish ones could roll you up like a carpet and spew you onto the sand. And he had a reputation to uphold, as the pro Lifey. He lined himself up with the shore and willed the craft forward.

To his surprise, he felt Flora adding her strength to his, and between them, they surfed straight through the shallows onto the sandy beach. He leapt off and held out a hand to Flora. She climbed off unsteadily, still gripping her paddle, he couldn't help noticing.

'Hello, beach!' she said, rubbing her back and looking around her as the last of the group surfed in. 'Am I glad to see you!'

Carrying the craft in pairs, one on each shoulder, the group parked them a hundred metres or so up the beach. Except for their ancient and weighty tub, which needed two of them to carry it. Flora carried their paddles.

Satisfied that the skis were safely out of the way of the tide, Jake announced, 'Café, everyone?'

There were cheers all round, and they began to walk up the beach, deserted except for a few dog walkers who regarded them with curiosity.

'Coffee! Totally! Women and child—' Flora stopped, then grinned and said, 'Women first!'

'First in line buys the round,' someone said, to laughter.

'I'm buying for my engine,' Jake said, some of his earlier tension seeping away now that they'd completed the first leg and she hadn't drowned. She'd been a lot better than he'd expected. 'Well done, Flora. I could feel you paddling on that last stretch. Really made a difference.'

'I couldn't wait to get onto dry land!' Flora stretched her arms. 'It wasn't as bad as I'd thought, and I'm glad I did it, but I'm equally glad it's over. It was a good adventure, though! Thanks!'

Jake gaped at her as her words sank in. 'Um, it's not over yet... How did you think you were going to get back?'

'You've got that trailer thingy, haven't you? Isn't it here, waiting for us?' She looked around her as if she expected to see it, rumbling down the beach towards them.

Someone said, 'That's a good idea. We should do that next time.'

Jake could see the dawning realisation on Flora's face, and her head whipped round to stare at the sea. He felt bad for her. She looked devastated. Had it really been that bad?

'You mean,' she said, her voice grim, 'there's no trailer? I have to get back in that thing? No, thank you. I'll walk back.'

Jake swallowed. That was a yes to the 'had it really been that bad' question then.

'Have a coffee and warm up,' said Karen, obviously overhearing her. 'You'll feel different after that. Come on.' She linked her arm through Flora's and practically towed her up the beach, to Jake's relief. He was clearly not her favourite person right now.

After hot drinks, and a variety of snacks, they were heading back to the beach. Flora was very quiet during the usual banter and tales of other ski trips, each more epic than the last.

'How come,' Flora wanted to know, 'you risk your life out there,' she nodded at the sea, 'but won't get on a motorbike? That thing,' she pointed at their double ski, 'is a lot more scary than my bike, I'm telling you.'

'Yeah,' he said, 'but if you fall off, you don't get gravel rash.'

They carried the boats down to the sea, and he held the boat steady as Flora heaved herself reluctantly into her seat.

'Stop wobbling the boat!' he yelled, as he paddled over the choppy waters towards the lines of surf rolling towards them.

'I'm not wobbling it!' Her voice sounded quavery. 'I'm scared!'

If this was Jake's idea of a 'mate-date', it was the date from hell. It was a good thing, Flora decided, that she was going to be leaving soon. She'd spent far too long in the sea this weekend, and not enough time on the bike, as far as she was concerned. She watched the coastline again, but somehow couldn't muster the pleasure of the outward journey. The sky had greyed over, and the sea seemed lumpy and colourless and she was cold. And tired. And achey. Her biceps burned after only a few strokes now, her thigh muscles were cramping, and she was too miserable to join in the banter amongst the group as they paddled alongside.

Even if she wanted a boyfriend – and her resolve wavered, gazing at that phenomenal body as the paddle blades dipped in and out before her – even if she did, which she didn't, not so soon after shithead Spence, Jake wouldn't be right for her.

He wasn't a biker, for starters. And she wasn't a lifeguard. How would that work? Their hobbies were chalk and cheese. Plus, given the chance, his gran would kick her bike over.

And anyway, he clearly didn't fancy her. He'd had the perfect opportunity to give her a proper snogging the previous night, and he'd kissed her cheek! She snorted with irritation at herself. Why would it matter that he hadn't snogged her, if she didn't fancy him anyway?

She huffed. It wasn't that she didn't fancy him, she told herself. He was lovely. It was that he wasn't right for her, so what would be the point? It was typical that she should stumble over such a handsome guy. And he was single. Yay. And not into bikes at all. Boo. In fact, his family were properly anti-bike. It was so frustrating. She blew over her bottom lip, making it vibrate noisily.

'Lot of puffing going on behind,' Jake yelled over his shoulder. 'You okay?'

Lost in her thoughts, Flora was startled by his voice. 'Oh, yeah, I'm fine. Bit knackered, that's all.'

His paddle paused for a moment, one end stabilising them in the water. 'Just enjoy the ride. It's quicker going back, the tide is pulling us along.'

He was right. As Flora watched, the cliffs rushed by, and he wasn't doing anything. She couldn't just sit there any longer though. She'd freeze. She picked up her paddle, and timing it with Jake, swung it to one side, then the other. The blades only just skimmed the water, but the action warmed her muscles.

It didn't seem long before they were at their beach again. Flora could see the Art Café perched on the prom, and was surprised, as she surveyed the beach, to see that the Hotel y Ddraig was just behind it, on a higher vantage point. Thinking about what they'd been discussing the previous night, she thought it was possible that Molly could see the Art Café from her hotel. She determined to check it out. Maybe she could help Lucy in some way.

Karen hailed them. 'The rest of us are carrying on to the next bay and back. Take the key off Gethin there, and then drop it into the Art Café when you lock up, okay?'

Flora regarded them with respect. Every bit of her body was longing for a hot shower, and they were all off for another marathon paddle! Gethin steered alongside and handed the key in its flotation bubble to Jake and with yelled goodbyes, they were on their own.

The surf, although big to Flora's eyes, was better behaved this time, or perhaps she knew better now what she was supposed to do. Jake helped her up, and then pulled the boat out of the water.

'Ah. Forgot this bit. You and me have to carry this old tub up the beach.' He sent her an apologetic look.

'Never mind. The exercise will warm me up.' Flora bent to lift her end of the boat. She groaned. 'Oh my God! This thing weighs a ton!'

'Yeah, sorry! I've got the heaviest end, if that helps.'

It didn't. With him being so much taller, all the weight seemed to be resting in Flora's blistered hands. Her legs were bowing beneath the weight, and she staggered up the beach, gasping for frequent breaks.

'Oops. I suppose I should've checked to see if it's taken water on,' Jake said, as they were almost outside the clubhouse. He didn't meet her eye as he unscrewed the bung, and lifted the opposite end of the long vessel above his head.

'You have to be joking.' Flora watched in dismay, her hands resting on her knees, as several buckets worth of seawater gushed onto the sand. 'I've carried that lot all this way! You're in big trouble, matey.'

'Sorry.' Jake lifted the boat higher and they watched it weeing copiously and seemingly endlessly. 'How about dinner tonight, at the hotel?'

'Hmm. That's if I've got the energy to eat it.' Flora waggled her arms about to get the blood flowing. 'You might have to cut it up for me.' She flexed her hands, inspecting the blisters. 'And spoon-feed me. It's a good thing I'm staying for a few more days. I couldn't have ridden my motorbike back. Look at my hands!'

'Holding the paddle too tight,' Jake pronounced, looking as directed.

'Oh. Thanks for the sympathy.' Flora glared at him. 'So – you can manage this ancient old barge by yourself, now it's empty, can't you?'

Jake looked at her with a stricken expression and she clamped her lips over her laughter. It seemed an endless logistical operation, getting that boat into the boathouse. It had to be hosed down to remove the salt, and then manhandled into position.

Flora climbed the short staircase to the changing rooms almost on her hands and knees. Switching the shower on and hoping it was hot, she reached round to unzip the wetsuit, her hands hunting for the tail that was always attached to the zip-pull. Aghast, she twisted to peer at her reflection in the rapidly misting mirror. There was no way to unzip the wretched thing. She'd have to wear her bike jacket and her boots over it and ride it back. Sort it out later. No. That was ridiculous. She'd still need help even then.

'Jake! Ja-ake!' Steam clouded the corridor as she pushed the changing room door open. With a hand over her eyes, she yelled, 'Jake? I need a hand, please, if you could.'

'S'up?' He lifted a finger from the hand clamped over her

face and she scanned him with one eye. 'I'm decent. What's the problem?'

'Oh.' She couldn't help her up and down glance through her fingers. He was wearing a towel tucked round his slim waist. That was all. Just a towel. Not even a very big towel. His upper body, pumped by the morning's exercise, was ripped, each muscle outlined. Aware that she was staring and hoping she didn't have her tongue hanging out, she glued her eyes to his and explained her predicament.

'Easily sorted. And you can put your hand down now, Flora. You've seen me.' She couldn't stop seeing him, even with her eyes closed. His proximity as she felt his warm hand at the nape of her neck locating the zip pull, made her shiver. He gave her a little nudge. 'You'll freeze. Hurry up and get in that shower.'

'I'm going.' She didn't move. Her limbs refused.

'Can you get this thing off okay?'

'I'm sure I can.' Finding her legs at last, she ducked into her changing room and hoped she could get it off. She tugged at the sleeves, rotating her shoulders. If he came in here dressed, correction, undressed, like that and had to help her out of this wetsuit, she'd ravish him where he stood. She paused in her efforts and considered calling for help before having a stern word with herself.

He was by far the nicest and hunkiest bloke she'd met for ages. Maybe even ever. What had his girlfriend been thinking, going off with another bloke in a camper van? Why couldn't he be a biker? Did it matter? She could try harder with this paddling malarkey. Could she get him on a motorbike?

She had one arm out. It was bright pink from the cold. Almost neon. Much grunting and groaning popped the other arm free. The legs were another matter. Goosepimpled and shivering she glared down at them. She'd have to cut them off. The neoprene ones, anyway. Not her actual legs.

She giggled. Remembering Karen's words about the water loosening the neoprene, she stood under the hot shower. It was bliss. But it didn't seem to help with the wetsuit removal.

'I'm getting old out here,' Jake's voice floated in. 'Either you've fallen asleep, or you're stuck in that ancient wetsuit.'

'I think I need some technical assistance,' Flora called back. 'Maybe a hacksaw, or something.'

Jake laughed. 'I'm coming in. I promise not to look.' He ambled straight in with his hand loosely over his eyes. 'Okay, I lied about the not looking bit, but I knew you'd still have your swimsuit on and I can't help you if I can't see what I'm doing, can I?'

'How did you know I was even wearing a swimsuit?' Flora eyed him. He was dressed already, which was a shame from the point of view of lusting shamelessly, but a relief at the same time as there was no accidental chance of her following through her intention of molesting him. She must not. Theirs would be a business relationship very soon, and her father always maintained that business and emotions shouldn't mix. Which was exactly why she had never worked for him before.

'I could see it through the neoprene.' Jake peered between his fingers. 'You can't hide anything in a wetsuit.'

Flora swallowed, remembering how she'd been observing his back muscles rippling. It hadn't occurred to her that he might have been assessing her.

'I can't get this thing over my arse!' She wrenched downwards with all her strength, the suit yielding only slightly and pinching her hips. 'Ow. Bloody thing. I am never, ever going out on one of your adventures again. Ever!'

'Come and sit down a minute. Let's get these boots off. Hm. I've got déjà vu...'

'Ha ha. Those were flippers. And this time, I have all the gear on.'

'This is true. Right, there's a knack to this. You have to roll it down, and pull it off inside out. Ready?'

'What?' She held up a hand. 'I can do that.' Jake's arched eyebrow and knowing expression didn't help at all. She tugged and she heaved and she swore, and the wetsuit refused to relinquish its grip. 'I give up.'

'I won't look. I promise.' Flora sent him a murderous look. 'I won't! It's a knack. I can do it with my eyes closed. Stand up a minute.'

Stepping close to her, he took hold of the wetsuit, obediently closed his eyes, and carefully rolled it down her hips. She grasped his shoulders to stop herself falling over, and their upper bodies touched for a long moment, leaving a long wet imprint on his T-shirt. He smelled nice. Shower-fresh clean. He turned his face towards her.

'Are you sniffing me?'

'No,' she lied.

She could feel her nipples standing to attention and tried to will them flat. It's the cold, she told herself. It was not. It was quite possibly the most erotic thing in the world. His warm hands were moving against her essentially naked body, and he was undressing her.

'Sit.' She held his arms and lowered herself to the slatted bench, staring at his corded forearms. He still had his eyes closed. 'Let go of me, or I can't do the last bit.'

'Sorry,' she muttered. He may have had his eyes closed, but the feel of his warm hands as they slowly travelled down her cold, bare thighs was intoxicating. She wanted to grab his head and pull it towards hers. He managed to remove the suit with a minimum of yanking. Until he got to her feet.

'Karen must have been about seven when she wore this last!' He heaved at the material, overbalancing as it finally freed one foot, and ending up sitting on the damp floor.

Flora laughed and held her hand out to him. 'Thanks! You're saying I have the body of a seven-year-old child?'

His eyes raked her. He bent his head over her other ankle. 'Oh no. I'm not saying that at all.'

'You're cheating! You looked!' Feeling very hot, despite hardly wearing anything, Flora reached for a towel and realised something else. 'I don't have a towel!'

'You'll just have to come out like that.' Jake waggled his eyebrows and she hurled one of the booties at him. 'Mine's a bit damp, but it's better than nothing.' He strode into his changing room and returned with a frayed and worn towel. 'Sorry, it's pretty ancient, but it was clean this morning, honest.'

'Thanks. Better than nothing!' Flora took it, and rubbed her hair dry. She looked up at him. 'Yes, thank you, you can go now.'

'Sorry!' He hurried out, yelling from the corridor, 'See you outside.'

Quickly wriggling out of the borrowed swimsuit, she threw it into the sink to give it a rinse out, wrapping Jake's towel around her. If the Goddess of Fate had wanted her to have a fling with Jake, then she was certainly making it easy for them. Flora fought the urge to sniff the towel for his scent. What was it about smells? Using his towel was such an intimate thing to do. It was almost on a par with using his toothbrush.

She was in such a quandary. She needed her father's payment to fund her next step. And she just knew that Jake was not going to be happy with her when he knew. She'd already seen him in grouchy mode, and she wasn't at all keen to be on the receiving end of it again.

She didn't have to set up business here. She could go anywhere. Couldn't she?

Of course she could, her brain said. Her heart wasn't at all sure.

Chapter Seventeen

Jake jumped downstairs two at a time and checked round the clubhouse. Anything to distract himself from the half-naked pocket goddess in the changing rooms. Closing his eyes had made it so much worse. It focused his mind on the smooth skin that had been beneath his fingers. He'd had to think about rugby scores and the hotel boiler that needed looking at. Anything not to be thinking about her hips, bottom and firm thighs.

The old, borrowed swimsuit was transparent where the material was stretched. Flora would no doubt be appalled to realise how see through it was. A snapshot memory of her breasts, perfectly outlined, floated across his brain. When she'd pressed herself against him, he thought he was going to burst through his jeans. His groin twitched again, and he flung the door open and marched around the building, ending up staring at the weeds growing in profusion at the fire escape back door. Another job to add to his list.

He was light-headed with relief that today's paddle had gone off without mishap. Apart from Flora's little dip. And she'd not been at all happy on the way back. It had been too far, he realised that now, berating his stupidity. He couldn't remember the last time he'd taken a girl newbie out. And certainly not in Wales. He should've just gone in and out of the bay a few times, playing on the waves. In and out... his breath caught, his imagination way ahead of him. God, man. Get a grip of yourself. That made him laugh aloud. He was behaving like a teenage boy!

She'd be gone soon. Just a few more days. There was no point in pursuing this. A quick holiday shag, that's all it would be. And even though he'd only known her for a few days, she was worth more than that.

She was intriguing, and funny, and brave, and beautiful – but she wasn't part of his world. He was all about the sea, and inevitably, the hotel. She didn't fit into that at all. It was a shame. He'd enjoy her company, but not let himself get involved, while she was staying. That would be very unprofessional, and his gran would not approve of him bed hopping around the guests, and certainly not with a biker chick.

So, better to just have a bit of fun and not get involved. His poor, tattered heart was still in bits over his walkabout girlfriend. She would have screamed with laughter over those waves and paddled almost as hard as him, her long blonde hair whipped by the wind and sea. But she'd sneered at his worries, his anxieties, after 'the incident'. She'd said he should just get over it. Accused him of being dreary and gloomy. Instructed him to 'Move on.' And when he couldn't, she had.

Flora had boosted his confidence, although she didn't have any idea. Successfully rescuing her the other day, and getting her out on today's ski paddle had terrified him, but little by little, reminded him that he could still do it.

It was a shame about the motorbike. And that she wasn't that keen on the sea. And the complicated family and boyfriend concerns. He didn't need all those issues, he tried to convince himself. Just for once, it would be good to have someone uncomplicated. Wouldn't it?

'What have those nettles ever done to you?'

He looked up with a start, to see Flora, hair only a little damp, his towel over her shoulder, her rucksack and helmet in her hands.

'You were glaring at them. Pretty ferociously, actually.' She handed the towel back, neatly folded, and he stuffed it into his holdall. 'Thanks for that. I hung Karen's wetsuit and booties up on the pegs to dry. Will that be okay? Will she get them?'

'Yes. What did you say? Oh. Yes! Karen's in here all the time. She paddles pretty much daily. Or she used to.' He hunted for the clubhouse key. 'Have you got everything? I'd better lock up.' He pulled the door closed and turned the key. There was nothing he'd like better than a hot chocolate with Flora, but really, he had jobs to do, and he'd just decided that he shouldn't encourage her. So no one was more surprised than him when his voice said, 'Fancy a quick hot chocolate at the Art Café while I'm dropping the key off?'

'Love to. I'm freezing.' Flora didn't even hesitate. 'I'm going to ride over and park in their car park, so I can keep an eye on the bike.' Flora pulled her helmet on. 'See you in a bit.'

Jake watched her go, jiggling the key in his pocket, then ambled thoughtfully over to the café.

'Two hot chocolates, please. Two muffins, one lemon and one salted caramel, please.'

The blond guy, who he knew was Lucy's sidekick, served him, as Flora burst through the door, taking her helmet off and ruffling her hair.

'Hi, Richard!' She hailed the blond guy breezily, and Jake marvelled at how she already seemed to know so many people in the short time she'd been there. 'Ooh, thanks, Jake, you remembered my favourite – salted caramel, mmm!' She licked her lips.

'But... you said lemon was your favourite!'

'Did I?' She shrugged. 'I can't decide any more. Every single one of these is gorgeous, to be honest. I'll have the lemon one, then.'

Richard held up a knife. 'I can't bear to see people fighting over cakes. How about I cut these in half for you, and you can have half each?'

Flora nodded enthusiastically, like a child, and Jake chuckled at her.

'What have you two been up to?' Richard asked.

'Jake thinks he's on *Hawaii Five-O*, and made me paddle up ten foot waves.' Flora's face was solemn. He was surprised that she even knew about the ancient but iconic TV programme. Neither of them had been even born when that came out. 'Or *Baywatch*. I don't think I'm tall enough to be Pamela Anderson though.'

'Really?' Richard eyed Jake steadily. 'Ten foot waves? Goodness me.' He watched as Jake swiped his card in the machine. 'Then you should totally repay his kindness by taking him out on the back of that fabulous bike of yours.'

Jake noted the thoughtful expression lingering on Flora's face, and said, hurriedly, 'Oh, er, no. She doesn't have a spare helmet.'

Richard retreated along the counter to serve another customer, but not before he'd said, 'Don't worry about that. I've got a spare helmet, and gear to fit you.'

'Ah. Thanks!' Jake smiled, weakly. He couldn't possibly say, no thanks, my gran wouldn't like it, could he? Very manly. Not. He carried their tray to a table near the window.

'Richard is just teasing you.' Flora nibbled a bit off each half muffin, in turn. 'You don't have to pillion me.'

'I knew that.' Jake stared out of the window, wondering what it might be like, and how he'd feel being in what was historically considered to be the woman's seat. He shrugged. It wouldn't bother him. He had the greatest respect for Flora on that bike, and he suspected, as Karen had already pointed out, that her balancing ability on the surf-ski today was due in no small part to her ability to balance that bike.

His reluctance was more to do with how his gran would react. Until now, it hadn't really been an issue. Her pronouncements had pretty much gone over his head, and although he knew about her obsession to spoil the Art Café's reputation, it had never stopped him using the café. In fact, he felt it was his communal duty to maintain at least some sort of peaceful relationship there and it was a tribute to the café staff that they still served him, he'd always thought. Although he couldn't ignore the fact that his visits often made him feel guilty, and he never told his gran that he went there.

He felt enormous appreciation for the upbringing his grandparents had given him. He smiled.

'What?'

'Oh, I was just thinking about being a kid at the hotel. I used to get away with murder.' She leaned forward, her chin in her hand, her curious eyes on his. He grinned at her. 'I had a den, up on top of the linen cupboards. I used to take my comics and sweets and a drink and my CD collection for my Walkman, and hide up there all day. Especially when it was raining.'

'So. Every day then.' Flora looked out of the window. 'I seem to remember that it rains a lot more here than it does back home. You must have practically grown up on top of that linen cupboard.'

Jake laughed at her mischievous expression.

'I used to think I was being so clever, and naughty, and that no one knew where I was.' He spooned the last of the hot chocolate from the bottom of his tall mug. 'But I think that they were actually very pleased that I was out of the way. Now I come to think about it, there was always the latest comic up there, and a fresh pack of biscuits. My favourites.'

'What were your favourites?'

'Wagon Wheels!' they said together and laughed. 'They're so much smaller now!' they said, simultaneously. Flora sat back.

'I bet you weren't really a nuisance. I bet they loved having you around.'

'Looking back on it now, it must have been really tough for my grandparents. They were grieving for their daughter and her husband. And apparently, I looked very like my mum the whole time I was growing up. She was blue eyed and had these long eyelashes, so that must have been pretty tortuous, in its own way. And, of course, they could only guess at what was going on in my head.'

Flora's eyes filled with tears, and she reached out to hold his wrist, briefly. The lightest touch of sympathy, and yet more than his previous girlfriend had managed during their entire time together.

'What *was* going on in your head?'

Jake drew in a long breath, a bit shocked. Nobody had ever asked him that, or as directly as that. 'I can't really remember. At least, not in actual words. I've often thought about it, and I do remember crying a lot and asking where my mum was...' His throat closed over. The past telescoped into the present. The details were fuzzy, but the feelings, the pain of losing his mummy and daddy were still sharp. The bewilderment of nothing being as it had been, nothing. Not breakfast, not bedtime, his toys, his bedtime story, the train set in his bedroom and the bunk bed with the slide. The way Daddy used to tip him upside down and make him laugh and piggyback him round the garden, all those hazy pictures still existed even though they were submerged in his memories. He reached for a napkin and gave his nose a vigorous blow.

'You don't have to...' Flora whispered. 'It must've been awful for you.'

'No, I'm fine. I was, er, just thinking about something else...' He opened his mouth to tell her – and then clamped it shut. It wasn't fair to load his horrors onto her, even if she was a good listener. He supposed it was the years of paying attention to her customers' rambles.

'So, anyway, I learned to roller skate in the hall. The staff used to send me on errands to collect things and off I'd go on my skates to get a towel, or soaps or something. I could even do the stairs, after a few mishaps.' He laughed. 'The guests were very patient. I expect I was explained away as the resident orphan, and they all felt sorry for me.'

Flora remained silent, and he time travelled in his head, seeing the hotel through his child's eye. 'Having to go to a new school was probably the worst part. I was quite scared. And apparently I was the thinnest child in the world.' He laughed at Flora's expression. 'I was, really! I'll get Gran to dig out some old photos. I was almost transparent, despite eating like a horse, and spending so much time in my den, scoffing biscuits.' He raked a hand through his hair. 'But I was lucky really, because I was only five, and the kids in my class were still quite new to each other, so they just accepted me. And their parents totally ruined me, having me over to play.'

'I remember you telling me you'd been adopted by every family in the bay.'

'Uh-huh. When it was my turn to return the play dates, the other kids were blown away that I lived in a hotel. It was the ultimate Get Out of Jail Free card. We camped in the gardens. Had a treehouse, made dens, had barbecues – all under supervision, of course. My Gramps loved all that. It was proper *Swallows and Amazons*, *Famous Five* stuff.' He felt his face smiling as the memories floated back to him.

'Your childhood sounds very different to mine.'

'Yes.' He eyed her, thoughtfully. 'Maybe. Although I wonder if that sense of not quite belonging anywhere is the same? As if you're dragging your anchor.'

'Ooh. That's deep.' Flora sat back and restlessly twirled the long spoon inside her mug. 'You could be right. I don't know if I've ever thought about it like that.' She was silent for a moment or two, and Jake became lost in his own thoughts. When she spoke again, he'd lost the thread of their earlier conversation. 'Are you still in touch with the mates you went to school with?'

'Yes, sort of. Instagram, that sort of thing. If you grow up here, you either play rugby, or join the Lifeguard Club, or both. I did both. It served me well in my travels. I could get a job almost everywhere via one or the other. I've had an incredible time, met amazing people, done things I would never have dreamed of.' He chewed his lip. 'And now, I've come home, and it feels like almost everyone has moved on.' He opened his hands and rested his chin on them. 'I feel like a cat that's always on the wrong side of the cat flap. I missed here while I was away, and I miss there, now I'm here. When you're away, you never think of things changing at home. And then you get home, and although things look the same, mostly, the people have altered.' He stared out of the window, rubbing his chin. 'Oh, look, this is a bit maudlin, isn't it? After our exciting morning? I should be getting back – the jobs will have mounted up.'

'God, yes, sorry, I didn't mean to keep you from your responsibilities. We seem to talk for Wales once we get oing, don't we?' Flora collected their mugs and plates and returned them to the counter. She yawned, shrugging into her jacket.

They ambled towards the door, and Flora called out a goodbye. Richard leaned out of the kitchen.

'We're doing a Chippy Run to Port Eynon tomorrow evening, if you fancy it?' He sent a sidelong glance at Jake. 'I can bring some extra gear, if you like. Ash and Lucy are in, and Nic, my wife, is coming too.'

Jake saw Flora's face light up. 'Count me in, please!' she said. 'What does Nic ride?'

'Ancient red Firestorm. She'll never get rid of that bike.' Richard grinned at Jake. 'So, you in?'

Jake's stomach was gripped with tension. 'Er—' He cleared his throat, and was horrified as his attempted laugh turned into a strangled yelp. 'I think I'm washing my hair...'

'No worries.' Richard nodded. 'See you in the car park tomorrow, Flora, five thirty.'

'Okay!' Flora's voice was a squeak of excitement and Jake registered a sense of, what was that? It couldn't be jealousy. That would just be ridiculous. He'd only known her a couple of days. Was it really only a few days? He pulled his jacket round him and strolled out, trying for a casual 'I really don't care' look.

'I could pillion you just that tiny bit...' She grinned up at him, buckling her helmet strap.

'Oh yeah, and have Ash spot me with no helmet on. Sounds like a plan.' He rolled his eyes. 'I'll run. Bet I beatcha.' He set off at top speed, his holdall containing his heavy, sodden wetsuit and towel banging on his back. Behind him, he heard the Ducati's engine roar into life, and wondered again what it might feel like to ride that beast. It felt good to run, to feel the long muscles of his thighs working. He used to run every day back in Sydney. Everybody did. Although the muffins and hot chocolate were jiggling around in his belly now...

Chapter Eighteen

Flora twisted the throttle, revelling in the roar of the big engine. She was going to miss this bike. She rode out of the car park, spotting Jake pounding the pavements ahead of her. Of course he was going to beat her. She didn't mind. She was rather enjoying watching his long legs pumping like pistons. Plus, there was no room on these tiny roads to open it up.

A Chippy Run tomorrow though! That was exciting – riding out with Lucy and her friends! It was like a lottery win. Maybe better. She'd seen Jake's expression though. A mixture of horror and indecision. She wondered if he'd change his mind and come along.

She turned towards the hotel drive and switched off the barely warm engine, noticing as she did so, that the top-most scrolls on the wrought iron gates were now sporting multicoloured knitted apparel. Interesting. And rather pretty, in an unexpected way.

Jake rested his hands on his knees and sucked air into his heaving lungs.

'Don't bother congratulating yourself.' Flora rolled her eyes. 'Why do blokes have to be so competitive?'

'See you around, then.' Jake coughed.

'I guess so.' Neither of them moved.

'Although,' Jake said.

'No more adventures today, thank you.'

'Have you forgotten that I owe you dinner at the hotel, tonight, seven o'clock?'

Flora considered him thoughtfully. She'd thought he was joking about that, earlier. Dinner with him would be rather wonderful, actually. And, cringing inwardly as she thought it, she could have a bit of a look round the hotel.

'Thank you. That would be lovely.'

'Shall I knock for you?'

They both laughed at the childish absurdity of the phrase.

'Naah. It's only up the road. Thanks.'

Flora watched him jogging up the drive, feeling the sea salt on her skin, drying and a bit itchy. She needed to get herself some fresh clothing. At the very least, underwear! Hers was in danger of falling into tatters with the constant wash, dry, wear cycle of the last few days. She googled the nearest big supermarket for some inexpensive gear, and tapped it into the satnav. The passing of time dawned on her. It was Sunday, and the shops closed at four. She needed to get a move on if she was going to go shopping.

Much later, wearing new jeans, a top, and blissfully fresh new underwear, Flora strolled towards the hotel, turning back often to watch the sun painting the sea and sky pink and orange. It was so beautiful here. Tantalisingly close to a big city, and yet, out here, it felt like a world apart. No surprise that her parents had loved it so much.

Turning back to the hotel she cast a critical eye over the façade and wondered what her father's plans for it might be. It was still tatty, but she could see the fruits of Jake's labour, where the overgrown foliage had been hacked back and the creeper tidied.

In the reception, she looked around her more carefully than last time. The coat hooks just inside the wide front doors now sported colourful crocheted coverings. She smiled as Jake arrived. He followed her gaze.

'Oh, for goodness' sake. This place is being taken over by hippies. I never even catch them doing it!'

'The yarn bombing?'

'The what?' Jake frowned.

'Yarn bombing. It's sort of street art. Knitted grafitti. It's big in London and Paris. I think its fab. So unexpected, and a great way to add some colour when nature isn't giving us much.'

'I bet I know who's behind all this.' Jake made a noise that was a cross between a snort and laugh, clearly not impressed. 'It's the Knit and Natter bunch. Knit one, drop one, glug one.'

'Glug one?' Flora stifled a laugh at his expression. He looked, and sounded, like a grumpy old man.

'I can hear the bottles clanking away in their bags when they turn up. I'm sure they're just sitting in there getting sloshed. And not even buying our wine!'

'Mm, really? Maybe I should take up knitting…'

'And they're not the only bunch who turn up here and use the place like it was theirs – and hardly pay a penny.' Jake's face was set in a grimace, and Flora stored the info away in her head to explore later.

'Who else comes here?'

'Hah!' That snorting laugh again. 'There's a drama group. An art group. A writing group and a book club.' He shrugged. 'I can't tell the difference. They just seem to turn up with books and drink wine. There's meditation or mindfulness, or whatever the current buzzword is, and a mother and baby group that sings the "Wheels on the Bus" over and over and over and over again.' He looked glum. 'When they're not singing "Wind the bloody Bobbin Up".'

Flora giggled. 'It sounds fun.'

'Pah. They're just taking advantage of Gran, as far as I'm concerned.'

There was a long silence as Flora thought about that.

He shook his head and huffed, his face breaking into a slow smile that made her ears ring. 'Sorry. Just ignore me. Anyway, hello! You look very lovely. I haven't seen you in aaaages!'

Flora laughed, following him along a threadbare carpet

through a door marked, Dining Room, on a brass plaque. Polished tables were set with white linen. It was like stepping back in time. He pulled a chair out for her at a table near the tall windows, curtained in a deep crimson velvet. The chandeliers cast a sparkling light, catching the evening sunshine. Apart from them, the room was empty. She couldn't help feeling surprised. It was obvious the hotel wasn't very busy, but she would have expected a few other diners.

Jake stood alongside the table, a white cloth over his arm.

'I should have asked this before, but, are you vegetarian?'

Flora narrowed her eyes at him. 'No, but what are you…?'

'Phew.' Jake looked relieved. 'I can only cook steak. Do you like steak?'

'I do, but…'

'No buts! I asked you for dinner at the hotel, and you shall have it. Especially after making you paddle up ten foot waves.'

Flora giggled. 'But why are *you* cooking it? Why isn't anyone else here?'

'Ah. Well. There's a really good reason for that.' He smiled down at her, his eyes turquoise and fathomless.

'Is there?'

'Yes.'

'What is it then?' She lifted her eyebrows, enjoying his embarrassment. He looked as if he was thinking of a good reason but then, after a moment or two he clapped a hand over his eyes.

'I didn't know that the kitchen was closed on a Sunday night as we now offer a Sunday lunch service only apparently.'

'You've only got one chef then? And tonight is his night off?'

Jake nodded. Shaking out the snowy white cloth he held it up to cover his crimson face and peered round it at her. 'Did I mention that I've been away? We never usually eat down here, with the guests, unless we've brought our own guests, if you see what I mean, and I've sort of lost track.'

'Where are your grandparents eating?'

'They've got their own kitchen upstairs but I think they've already had theirs.'

'Okay. No worries. What can I do to help? I can't just sit here, I'll be bored to death.'

'Really?' Jake eyed her. 'But I'm supposed to be feeding you.'

'Oh, bollocks to that. It's not a date, is it?' She stood up. 'Come on. Show me to your kitchen. I'm starving.'

After only a small hesitation, he led her through the door marked Private, into a huge stainless steel kitchen.

'My goodness. This is colossal. Did your grandparents used to feed the whole village?'

Jake looked around him. 'It is big, isn't it? The hotel used to be so much busier than it is now. There were no days when the kitchen was closed that I can remember. Times have changed.' He opened the enormous fridge and scanned the contents. Then prowled around, opening other doors and cupboards. 'That's weird.'

'What is?' Flora had found herself a little stool in a corner and was perched on it.

'There were trays full of steak in the fridge yesterday morning. It can't all have gone last night.'

'Never mind. We can have something else. I'm not fussy.' She watched him open and close cupboards and made a decision. 'I'm still starving,' she told him. 'Want to come over to mine? It'll be pasta. Sauce out of a jar. Garlic bread. Nothing fancy, but plenty of it.'

Jake stared at her for fully a count of ten. He didn't even try to convince her that he could cook something else.

'Red or white?' His hand was poised over the wine rack.

'One of each? Or red, for preference?'

Two bottles of red accompanied them as they left the hotel. Flora noticed the vintage Land Rover parked on the drive.

'That's an oldie,' she said. It sat, timeless, square and uncompromising.

'Yep. Almost the first thing I did when I got home was to start her up and tinker about. It's ancient and about as sophisticated as a lawn mower and it's probably destroying the planet every time I start it up, but I bloody love this old bus.'

'How long have you had it?'

Jake laughed. 'Gramps taught me to drive in it. I used to sit on his lap and turn the steering wheel. Just down the drive though,' he added, hastily. 'Not on the road.'

'Hah! I'm not exactly one for upholding the rules!' She tipped her head up to look at him. He was easily a foot taller than her. 'What's your grandad like?'

'Gramps? He's a legend.' Jake chuckled.

'How?'

'Gramps always used to say, every single time we were out in the Landy, that we were hurtling along, being overtaken by cyclists and old ladies in electric wheelchairs.' He laughed again. 'Every. Single. Time.' He shook his head. 'It drove Gran mad.'

'Used to say? Doesn't he drive any more?'

'I suppose he must do. I seem to be missing an awful lot, don't I?'

Flora was silent, and he continued, 'I haven't seen much of him since I've been back. He seems to spend all his time in front of the telly, watching sport. That's not like him.'

'Maybe he doesn't feel very well.'

'I've tried talking to Gran about him, but she just brushes me off.'

'Maybe you just need to make a bigger gesture. Take him out. In the Landy, maybe?'

'A trip out in the Landy is a terrific idea. Why didn't I think of that?'

'Because you're not brilliant like me?'

'Or as modest.' He chuckled.

'Where would you take him?'

'He likes Rhossili. And there used to be a cute café there. I can check that. There's a nice breezy walk to the headland and back, if he can't manage the cliff path.'

Flora tried to feel pleased and instead was rattled to find that she was, well, she was jealous. That she'd like to be going to Rhossili to the cute café, with Jake. In the silence that followed as her brain wrestled with her conscience, the idea of having lunch, in a café, or a country pub connected with Jake's kitchen dilemma. She stopped dead and turned to face him.

'Jake. What does your chef look like?'

'Pete? Um…' Jake scratched his short beard like a cartoon thinking character. 'Forties, buzz cut, looks like he's been crayoned over by a five-year-old.'

'You mean, really bad tattoo?'

'Yeah. Why?'

'Does he buy and sell wholesale meat?'

'I have no idea. I don't know anything about him. He's not been here that long as far as I know.'

'Um, look, this might be absolutely nothing, but I was in this pub yesterday and a man with the worst tattoos I've ever seen came in. Bit aggressive.'

'Pig tattoo?'

'Is that what it's meant to be? I wondered if it was.'

'So?'

'Erm, yes, bit hostile, argumentative. He wanted someone from out the back, and a big guy in a white apron came out to his car, and there was a lot of pantomime bad guy stuff, you know—' She mimed creeping about, looking over her shoulder. 'And the big guy in the apron gave him cash and took off with some trays of red meat. Tattoo Man was eyeing up my bike, parked opposite his car. That's what made me watch them.'

Jake listened to her intently. Which made a nice change from Spence, she couldn't help noticing, who never listened to her at all.

'We have to check this out. Right now.' He about-turned, and headed back the way they'd come.

'Now? Bloody hell,' Flora grumbled, hurrying after him. 'I'm starving.'

'You can have some crisps, if you're good.' Jake told her, his long legs stretching ahead of her. He looked back then, and held out a hand. To her surprise, she took it, and they jogged back to the hotel together, and into the kitchen.

Jake checked everywhere thoroughly this time to be completely sure the steak hadn't materialised before he made any further decisions.

Chapter Nineteen

'I can't see anywhere else where he would have put steak.' Jake frowned. 'Time to get Molly and Bryn involved. Would you mind coming and telling them what you saw?'

Flora nodded, and followed him. The passage wound along and up a flight of wide stairs, and Jake tapped on a polished door.

'Gran? It's Jake.'

Molly opened the door. 'You don't have to knock, darling. Oh, hello.' Her expression went into polite mode as she registered Flora's presence, and Flora was glad that she was wearing her new, clean clothes.

Jake lost no time bringing them up to speed, and Flora added her story to it, even as she surreptitiously took in her surroundings. The apartment was comfortable, but quietly shabby, just what she'd expect from a couple in their seventies. Polished wood and faded blown rose fabrics, just like the hotel. Lots of side lamps casting a warm glow over the room. Quite cosy, she decided, trying to imagine a five-year-old boy rampaging through this room, and actually visualising it quite well. The idea of a sad and bewildered child crying here pricked at her eyes. It was harder to imagine this towering giant beside her as a skinny kid. But she remembered his stories of having a den on top of the linen cupboard. The business was an extension of their home. No wonder they regarded it so possessively. Flora swallowed. She, who prided herself on the truth, was trashing her loyalties all over the place just by standing here. Shouldn't she just have let Pete bleed them dry, causing further ruin, so that her dad made a better deal? Even as the words flitted across her brain, she dismissed them. She couldn't ever stand by and watch injustice happen right in front of her. Dad could sort it all out later. This was a priority. Jake was a friend.

They all trooped into another room, where Bryn sat before a huge computer screen. This room had made the leap into the twenty-first century. There were pinboards and calendars and filing cabinets and everything was shiny.

Bryn activated the screen, and he and Molly tracked the orders. This tall, lean man with the shock of white hair didn't fit Flora's idea of the old man Jake had led her to imagine. Also, there was no mistaking the family likeness. As a hairdresser, she spent a lot of time assessing people's heads. There was the wide mouth with the lopsided smile, and the same shaped eyes and forehead, although his eyes were paler. He was, like his grandson, a bit of a looker, even at his age. So the family resemblance had held strong across the generations. Jake would probably make beautiful babies, with his bone structure and smooth skin. She wondered what his girlfriend in Australia had looked like and felt irrationally jealous of her relationship with Jake before reminding herself that *she* wasn't Jake's actual girlfriend. Just his friend. She had a word with herself and tuned into the discussion before her.

'There. I *did* make the order, and here...' they followed Bryn's finger on the screen '... here's when it was delivered.' He made the same huffing noise that Flora had heard Jake make. 'And he's tried to make *me* look as if I'm going a bit...' He stopped, pursing his lips. 'You're sure you've looked everywhere in the kitchen?' His eyes narrowed. 'I don't want to be accusing him of something if—'

'Shall we all go and check again?' Molly's voice was smooth but assertive, and Flora wasn't a bit surprised that they all rose as one and trooped down to the kitchen. She didn't know where to look, so she sat on the little stool again and watched them hunting through every cupboard and fridge and freezer and bin. They checked the orders, and the wastage, and even the wheelie bins in the yard.

'Nothing,' Bryn declared. Molly and Jake shook their heads. 'We only had two orders for steak at dinner last night and today was a carvery.'

'Well,' Molly said, after a moment. 'It's obvious that we need to have a chat with Pete. I suggest we do it in the morning.'

'I can stand as witness,' Flora said, her heart hammering with apprehension. All the moisture seemed to have shrivelled from her mouth.

'Thank you,' Molly said. 'That would be very much appreciated. Although we'll try to keep you out of it.'

'I can't wait,' Bryn said. His mouth was a thin line. 'He's made my life a misery, that man. He made me think I was going gaga...' He looked up at the ceiling, clearly restraining his emotions.

'Oh, darling, why didn't you say?' Molly's brow creased as she looked up at him. Flora saw Jake stare at the tiled floor, his mouth compressed. There was a long silence.

'I should go,' she began. This was a family moment and she was intruding. Jake's head jerked up.

'Oh, but... I haven't fed you!'

'Well, I was about to feed you...'

'We haven't eaten yet, either,' Molly said. Flora's stomach rumbled loudly, and Bryn laughed.

'That sounds like a yes to me.'

'Are you sure?' Flora looked from one to the other. 'Jake thought you'd already eaten. I was going to just knock up a pasta and some sauce out of a jar...' Her voice faded at Molly's shocked expression.

'Out of a jar? I think we can do better than that.' She chuckled at Flora. 'How do you think Jake got to this size? Are you vegetarian, Flora?'

'No. I eat anything. Thank you. And let me help, please!'

Molly bustled off around the kitchen, switching on the vast oven. To Flora's astonishment, she brought out several flat packs and put them on the counter.

'Pizza?' Her eyes twinkled as they met Flora's.

'God, yes, please! I'm as hungry as a horse!'

'Better put some chips in too.' Switching on the deep fat fryer, she directed Jake to pull out an enormous bag of frozen chips. 'Real ones. Not those terrible oven things.'

Flora laughed. 'I thought you were, er…'

'Going to cook it all myself?' Molly winked. 'You don't have a dog and bark yourself, do you?'

'Fair point. What can I do to help?'

'Open that wine.' Molly nodded at the two bottles they'd taken and brought back. 'And pour me a big one. I'm going to need it after tonight's news!'

They sat in the dining room at two tables that Jake pulled together, sharing pizza and chips and wine. Flora thought she'd never laughed so much in her life. Molly's sharp observations were set off by Bryn's dry asides – they were truly a comedy duo.

Flora wanted to know about Jake as a little boy, despite him putting his head in his hands. 'Don't tell her, Gran!'

Molly eyed him, her expression mischievous. 'Jake was a perfect child, of course. You wouldn't really expect me to tell you anything less, would you?' She reached over and patted his vast shoulder. 'It's lovely to have him home again.'

Flora watched them smile at each other and saw the love there. What a story these three had. Her throat squeezed and she swallowed hard to batter down her emotions.

Bryn broke into her thoughts. 'What about you, Flora? What brings you here?'

She was startled, wondering where to start and how much information she wanted to impart. Also, she'd had several glasses of wine, and she was inclined to be blurty at the best of times.

'Have you visited Gower before?' Molly asked, leaning forward.

'Yes – in fact, my parents bought a cottage here, many years ago. It's a holiday let now.'

'How interesting. So, did you come here as a child?'

'I did. Every year, several weekends, and for the whole summer holidays. I used to love it here.'

'But you haven't been for a long time.' It was a statement more than a question and Flora frowned, wondering how the old lady knew.

'I haven't, no. How did you know?'

Molly smiled, her eyes still bright and deep blue despite her age. Her hair, Flora couldn't help noticing, was tucked behind her ears, but the cut had grown out and made her look older than she probably was, and a bit tired. She itched for her scissors.

'Oh, I guessed. From your use of the past tense.' Flora blinked, and Molly carried on, 'You said, "I used to love it." I'm so sorry. I don't mean to sound as if I'm interrogating you. I always try to listen to people. It's important to get to know them, especially when they're only here for such a short time.'

Flora was silent and suddenly on alert. She'd have to think very carefully before she spoke, which wasn't her best thing.

'I *used* to love coming here when I was little.' She twirled her glass with her fingers, willing herself not to drink out of it. Avoiding Jake's eye she added, 'Then they split up and Mum lets the cottage out now.' Brightly, she carried on in a rush, 'She's just had it properly renovated, so I thought it was time to revisit and it was a big birthday for me and I'd planned a lovely romantic weekend.'

She took an impulsive swallow of wine. 'What I hadn't

planned on was catching my sister... erm, in-flagra... with her leg over...' she gave up on the euphemisms and settled for a fierce '... shagging my boyfriend. So I came on my own.'

'Oh dear, poor you!' Molly's eyes were sympathetic.

'But Jake has been cheering me up!' Flora smiled. 'He's pulled me out of the sea and then, er, thrown me back into it—'

'You forgot the bit about the ten foot waves,' Jake interrupted.

'He's eaten my muffins, danced with me and made me laugh. If I wanted a temporary replacement boyfriend, he'd be perfect.' She grinned at him, and their eyes met for a long moment. Flora thought, sod the 'temporary' bit. He really was gorgeous. She was 'in lust'. And surely, she was allowed to be, after what Spence and Amber had done, wasn't she?

'So, how long will you be staying?' Molly asked.

'The world is my oyster!' Flora said, gaily, avoiding answering.

'Flora whacked her boss for "improper sexual advances", and left her job,' Jake added on her behalf. 'So when her stay at her mum's cottage ends, she's homeless.'

Flora glared at him. Did he have to tell them that? It made her sound sad, hopeless, argumentative, unloveable... She sighed. Nothing like telling it as it was, she realised, sagging in her seat.

'And you're a hairdresser.' Molly was silent. 'I'm sure you could find customers for a mobile service if you wanted to do that.'

'I would like to do that.' Flora hesitated. 'But what I'd really like, is to have my own salon. I don't ever want to be pushed around again.'

'I can't imagine anyone pushing you around,' Bryn said, admiration written across his face.

'No. Well, I wish you well, Flora. And if you have a spare

hour, I'd love you to have a crack at my hair. It's looking terribly "mumsy" lately.' Molly's face creased into a dimply smile. 'I can do without the "pre-emptive piercing" treatment, though, thank you.'

Flora said, over the sound of Jake guffawing, 'I'd love to, thank you. I don't have any real plans this week – Jake has my number, so just ring or text me to let me know when you are free.'

It seemed like a good time to leave, and after helping to clear away, Flora announced that she was going.

'Oh, you don't fancy a little nightcap, do you?' Molly looked at her expectantly. Flora flashed her a grin.

'Usually, I'd've said yes, but tomorrow, I want to get out on my bi—' She bit her lip over the word 'bike' and ended, lamely, 'Birthday treat. I'm hoping to book afternoon tea.'

'Oh, how lovely. Whereabouts?'

'At the Art Café,' said Flora, remembering too late, as she watched a steely expression wipe away the smile on Molly's face.

'Hmm.'

Chapter Twenty

The text alert pinged, and Jake scrabbled for his mobile, peeling his eyes open to decipher it.

I'm up. What time? It was six thirty, and it was Flora. He scratched at his stubble, working his lips together to try to find some moisture.

Last night had been great, and, at last, he'd felt as if he was home again, but he cringed now as he remembered Flora so nearly dropping herself in it with his gran. It was good of her to even think of volunteering to come back over this morning. He'd walked her home, dropping another chaste peck on her cheek, even though it had nearly killed him not to kiss her soft mouth, and then walked back into a glass of whisky. Or two. He seriously needed a coffee and some toast now, and he did not want to bump into Pete while he was having it. He'd just have to suffer.

He rang his grandparents on the hotel phone. 'What time?' His voice sounded as if he'd eaten gravel, but Bryn sounded worse. He handed the phone to Molly, who, predictably, sounded as chirpy as always. 'As soon as possible, so he doesn't get the chance to have anything else away. Fifteen minutes?'

Come now he texted Flora.

'Bloody hell,' Jake heard his grandfather say. He echoed that sentiment a moment later, scrubbing himself beneath a barely warm shower. That useless boiler was top of his To Do list. Shivering, he pulled on his jeans and a warm sweater, combing his hair with his fingers and brushing his teeth.

Flora was already at the hotel reception when he arrived, looking fresh and bright-eyed.

He blinked. 'Were you teleported?'

'I ran,' she replied. 'I didn't want to miss anything.'

They walked into the dining room. There were no guests breakfasting this early, to Jake's relief, and in any case, very early breakfasters were only offered a continental breakfast, left out for them by arrangement, not the Full English.

His grandparents arrived at the same time. Bryn looked a bit crusty round the edges, and Jake worried about him. Molly though, was in full warrior woman mode. Nobody got one over Molly.

'We'll wait just here, outside the door until you call us,' Jake said. 'No point in being mob handed at this point.'

'Yeah, except I need to make sure we're talking about the same person before you accuse him of anything,' Flora pointed out.

Molly nodded, her lips pursed. 'You'd better come in then.'

She pushed the door open, with Bryn and Flora close behind and Jake heard her begin, 'Good morning, Pete. There are some things we need to talk to you about.' As the door closed, her voice faded. He couldn't wait out there, whatever he'd said. He couldn't just leave his aged grandparents and a small woman in there, no matter how scary Flora could be. And Molly, come to think of it. He might need to referee.

He followed them in.

Pete surveyed them all, his eyes narrowed.

'What's up?'

Molly began without preamble. 'We were looking for the steak order last night. It's not in the kitchen. Do you have any idea where it is?'

'What has he lost now?' Pete gestured at Bryn, his expression sneering. 'I don't mean to be rude, I mean, he is getting on, but, y'know…' Shrugging, he whirled his finger near his ear in the universal sign that indicated madness. 'He's probably not even ordered it. Or "accidentally" binned it.'

Angry at the man's casual inference that his grandfather was mad, Jake stepped forward but with admirable calm, Bryn said, 'This one isn't down to me, Pete. I might occasionally misplace a table number, but not three dozen steaks.'

Pete blustered and banged a frying pan onto the stainless steel counter. The noise echoed horribly. 'I have no idea what you're talking about.'

'Have you set up a wholesale meat business?' Molly asked him, her voice like a steel trap. 'Or have you been collecting meat for other pubs?'

'What are you going on about? No, of course I'm not.'

'You were seen delivering our steaks to a local pub.'

Pete's eyes narrowed. He licked his lips. 'Bloody rubbish. Who is supposed to have seen that?'

Jake said, 'We've got a witness.'

'To what? I haven't seen those steaks. I bet he forgot to order them. He forgets everything, him. Can't get the table orders right. If he tells them once, he tells them a million times how to use the bloody cafetière. He's a bloody liability. It ain't me.'

Jake had also heard his gramps doing that exact thing, and he hesitated.

Into the prolonged silence, Flora said in a clear voice, 'I saw you. Handing meat over from the back of your hatchback, outside the pub near Reynoldston. In broad daylight.'

Pete's head swung towards her and Jake watched him frown in recognition.

'You! I can't imagine why you're taking her side.' He jerked his head towards Molly.

Flora's expression froze, and Pete sneered at her. 'Oh yeah, I spotted that bike helmet straight off.'

Jake's eyes swivelled in alarm towards his gran. She looked perplexed.

Pete, perhaps detecting a chink of doubt, pressed on. 'She's getting back at you!' he said to Molly. 'For all that anti-bike stuff. It's obvious! She's setting you up.'

'Riding a motorbike,' Flora said, clearly, 'doesn't make me blind.' She stood tall. 'Or less truthful.'

Jake stared at her. She was awesome. He wanted to kiss her, right then and there.

'And I know it was you. I know your car, and no one else could possibly have those tattoos,' Flora said, steadily. 'And if you need any more proof, I videoed you too.' She pulled her phone out of her back pocket and began to thumb across the screen.

Momentarily, Pete looked proudly at his arms, before realising he'd been well and truly stitched up. He stared at them.

'Fuck you lot. This place is totally on the skids. It's only been me keeping it going. Taking a bit of steak is just a perk of the job. Everyone knows that. And if you paid me properly, I wouldn't have to do it.'

'A *bit* of steak would be okay,' Molly said, evenly. 'You have completely overstepped the mark. Your attitude stinks. It was only ever going to be a matter of time.'

'I don't have to listen to this.' He unbuttoned his white jacket and tore it off, flinging it at them. 'This place can't stay open for much longer. It's a joke. You'll never manage without me, I'm telling you now.' He pointed a finger at Flora. 'And you better watch out if I see you on the road.'

Jake wanted to hit him. How dare he threaten Flora?

'Jake, if you could escort Pete to collect his belongings, please? I believe we've dispensed with his services.' Molly waved an imperious arm, and Jake moved towards him. 'You'll be paid up to today. Which is more than generous. I should be deducting the cost of the steak order.' She turned away, and Jake herded Pete to his locker, wondering now what drama would unfold behind his back between Molly and Flora. Flora held her ground, and her breath, as Jake left with Pete.

'So,' Bryn said. He looked a bit pale, and leaned against the counter. 'That went well, except that now we don't have a chef.'

Molly said, briskly, 'We can hire a temporary chef. No one is indispensable.' She scanned the kitchen. 'And it's not rocket science. I'm sure we can manage a few cooked breakfasts between us.'

Jake returned at that point, and caught the tail end of Molly's announcement.

'No, Gran. It's too much for you.' He raised his eyebrows at Flora as he said, firmly, 'Flora and I, and er, Gramps can do it, can't we?'

Flora found herself nodding, even while her stomach boiled with apprehension. She could make the occasional bacon buttie, but she wasn't up to cooked breakfasts for twenty or so guests! And she had no idea where anything was in the kitchen. Jake ushered a protesting Molly away.

'May as well make myself useful,' Bryn said, giving her a long and thoughtful look. 'I'll sort out the cereals and juices, pastries, bread for toast, jams and marmalades and fresh fruits.'

'I can help with that.' Flora bustled in and out under Bryn's direction until Jake returned.

'Thanks, Flora. But this is above and beyond, really. You've been a huge help. You don't have to stay, honestly.'

'Can you cook?' Flora asked him.

Jake didn't meet her eye. 'I, er, um, I could manage. How difficult can it be? A bit of bacon and eggs...'

'I've got an idea...' she said, reaching for her phone and making a call. 'Hi, is that Richard? It's Flora – the hairdresser, yes.' She nodded, and carried on. 'Your takeaway breakfasts, could I have, um, ten? Maybe fifteen?' She pulled the phone away from her ear as Richard's voice rose. Out of the corner of her eye she saw Jake's mouth open in shock.

'What the hell?' Richard yelled. 'Is this a joke?'

'No, really, please, listen.' Flora recited succinctly the preceding events. There was a long huffing noise.

'Flora. You can't serve hotel guests takeaway breakfasts! They'll just have to say that the kitchen is closed, and cold food available only.'

'Oh. Yes. Of course. You're right. What do I know?' Flora took a deep breath and before she could decide against it, added, 'I just thought it might be an opportunity to, um, y'know, heal the rift?' There was a long silence. Flora pressed the phone to her ear, thinking they must have been cut off. Then she heard Richard's muffled voice as he spoke to someone else.

'You still there, Flora?'

'Yes…'

'I'll be there in half an hour.' He hung up, and Flora stared at Jake. She squealed, and did a little jig.

'Oh my gosh! Richard is coming over to cook the breakfasts!' Jake's face was a picture.

'Richard?'

'From the Art Café!'

'How do you do that?' He blinked at her. 'You clever girl. Is there anything you can't do?'

'Keep my job and my boyfriend?' Flora caught her lip over her teeth and shrugged. 'Come on, show me where everything is. I'll waitress.'

Chapter Twenty-One

Richard was silent as he scanned the hotel kitchen.

'I'd kill for a kitchen this size,' he said, finally, and Jake let go of the breath he hadn't realised he'd been holding.

'Okay, Flora and I are your untrained but willing staff,' Jake said. 'Just tell us what you want doing.'

Richard buttoned up his jacket, emblazoned with 'Art Café', and grinned at them. 'I've never done this either. I'm a patisserie chef! We'll work it out between us, I'm sure.'

'But – the takeaway breakfast poster?' Flora frowned. 'I saw it, on the counter – that's why I rang you!'

'Well, yes,' Richard said, opening the fridge and scanning the contents. 'We're planning to trial the idea, see what kind of response we get. So far, not much. People want to come to us and have breakfast, not have it at home.'

'But,' Flora said again, 'you are cooking breakfasts, aren't you?'

'Smashed avocado, poached eggs, sourdough toast, that sort of thing. Not yer actual fat-boy brekkie.' He looked at the deep fat fryer and turned to Jake. 'Hash browns, deep fried, presumably? And do you use a buffet system or is it individual ordering?'

Jake blinked. He opened his mouth, but it was his grandfather's voice that told Richard what he needed to know.

'We used to do buffet, but the hot counter broke and we, er, never got round to, um, replacing it.' He shrugged. 'The hotel isn't as big as it used to be, so we manage on individual ordering these days,' he added, 'and deep fried hash browns.' As he went on to explain temperatures and timings, Jake watched him. He couldn't help feeling perplexed. It was like an alien world.

He peeped into the dining room. There were a few guests filtering in.

'Incoming!'

'Come with me, Flora,' Bryn said, picking up his order pad.

Jake's heart sank. 'That's okay, Gramps. I can—' he began.

'You'd better let them know that the kitchen is closed tonight, so they need to make alternative arrangements for dinner,' Richard told them.

'We've got a whiteboard somewhere,' Bryn said, rubbing his chin.

'I'll go and have a look for it.' Jake darted towards the kitchen door.

'Oi!' Richard called, laying sausages in rows. 'Don't all of you sod off out there. Who's my pot washer?'

Jake stopped in his headlong dash to escape and raised his hand. 'That'll be me, then.'

'Right. Pay attention. I'm training you so you can do this tomorrow, if you need to okay? First, hygiene!'

Tying an apron on, Jake washed his hands. He stood to attention. 'Ready, Chef!'

By ten o'clock, breakfast was over, and the kitchen was beginning to look as clean and shiny as it had that morning.

Richard leaned against a counter, arms folded, his jacket spattered with grease.

'Well done, team! How do you think that went?'

Jake raised his hand. 'To my surprise, I really enjoyed it. No one has ever shown me what to do in a kitchen. I've learned so much this morning. Thanks, Richard.'

'Harder than I thought,' Flora said. 'I nearly dropped an entire breakfast over that woman, the moaning Minnie.' She put her hand over her eyes. 'Bryn leaned over just at the last minute and straightened it. And those fried eggs are a liability, aren't they? They just want to go off the edge, slippery little suckers!'

Richard smiled at her. 'I thought you all communicated well as a team. The orders went out fine, to the right tables, didn't they?'

Jake held his breath, trying not to stare at Bryn. To his complete surprise, Flora said, 'Yes, no problems. We had a few issues with people changing their minds about English Breakfast tea or Earl Grey or Green tea, but that was soon dealt with.'

'So, you all okay to do this again tomorrow morning?'

Jake and his grandfather nodded, and after some hesitation, so did Flora. She shrugged, meeting his gaze.

'What else have I got to do? It's more fun than being on my own.'

'Very, very much appreciated, Richard. Send us your invoice.' Jake shook his hand.

Richard grinned around at them all. 'If you get into difficulties tomorrow, give me a ring. I'm not coming over again though. I've got my own business to run! Bye now!'

The kitchen door opened into the chorus of their goodbyes and Molly stood in the doorway.

Jake moved towards her. 'Gran, this is Richard. He's a friend. He came over at short, well, *instant* notice to help us out.'

Molly held out a hand to Richard, her round face smiling. 'Goodness me, that was rather wonderful of you. Thank you so much. I don't suppose you want a job, do you?'

Richard, to his credit, smiled back, shaking her hand. 'Thank you, Mrs Thomas, but I already have a job.'

Jake saw Molly's eyes scanning his jacket, reading the logo emblazoned there. He also registered that Richard held her hand and continued to smile at her even as her smile stiffened. Molly lifted her gaze, and Jake held his breath as her mouth opened. But Richard didn't give her an opportunity for a barbed remark.

'The next time you are passing, you'd be most welcome to pop into the café for a cuppa and a piece of cake.' He looked straight at her, still smiling.

'Thank you,' Molly said, tightly. Richard made an old-fashioned nod and released her hand.

'See you, guys.'

He waved, and Jake said, 'I'll show you how to get out. This place is a warren.' Flora trailed along with them, and Jake guessed that she didn't want to be left behind with Molly's possible wrath. She looked as if she might explode.

'So, you coming out on the Chippy Run tonight, Flora?' Richard asked.

'Hell, yeah.' Flora had to trot every few paces to keep up with them and Jake slowed his pace a little.

'How about you, Jake?' Richard sent a sidelong glance.

'I'm probably going to have to be here to fend off the hungry guests for the evening meal. We can't feed them all pizza and chips.' He paused. 'I could drive them to the nearest pub, I suppose.'

'Hm. It's a nice touch, but you don't want to make it too easy for them to go elsewhere, mate. They'll start expecting it, and before you know it, you're driving them to your own competition.'

'Yeah. Good point. Gran has probably been ringing round the agencies for a replacement chef anyway.' Jake hitched up his jeans. 'I'm bloody starving. I suppose I should've had some of that breakfast.'

'Use it as a practice run for tomorrow.' Richard walked out of the entrance, and added, over his shoulder, 'Or you could always pop over to the café, y'know. They do a decent breakfast, I hear...' They waved him out of sight.

'What a nice guy,' Jake said. 'I'm going to face the music

with Gran. You probably want to be getting off. Thank you so much for your help today.'

Flora looked up at him, frowning. 'Do you want me tomorrow?'

'Erm, I have no idea.' Jake lifted his hands. 'Talk about feeling like a spare part. I feel more like a guest here than the guests do.'

'Okay. Well, ring me if you do.' She lifted a hand in a wave and Jake impulsively dipped his head and left a fleeting kiss on her cheek. Her confused expression meant that he regretted it instantly.

'Well, thanks, again. I, er, bye then,' he muttered, and headed towards the kitchen.

'Dad...' Flora sat at the big scrubbed table back at Sea-Spray Cottage, looking over the pale sea, sparkling with early sunshine, her mobile at her ear. 'I don't think I'm cut out to be a spy.'

'Good morning, sweet pea! What's up?'

'Well...' Flora told him everything. About the chef and her part in his dismissal, and how she'd saved the day and stepped in to waitress, and how now that Molly knew that she was a biker, she probably couldn't really stay there as a guest. Not very comfortably, anyway.

Her father listened without comment, and Flora thought how different her mum's response would have been. Finally, he said, 'Okay. So what's the problem?'

'I thought the idea was that you wanted the hotel to fail, so you could buy it at a lower price?'

'I asked you to "spy" for me, as you put it, because I knew you'd be honest. And that honesty is what prompted you to help them. Don't be sorry about it. What else have you found out?'

'The hotel is in a brilliant location, on the main through

road and set just a little back overlooking the sea with pretty gardens that need attention, but it's shabby. It must have been stunning, back in the day, but it really does need some TLC. It should be rammed with guests, but because it's a bit, well, antiquated – except for the kitchen, which is bang on smart—'

'That'll be because of the health and safety regs,' her father murmured. 'Go on…'

'Er, where was I? There are quite a few local groups that use it. There's, um, a drama group, a French group, art and a book club, er, knitting groups – oh, and they've yarn bombed all over the place. It looks so pretty! Although Jake thinks they're a bunch of scrounging hippies…'

'Yarn what-ed?'

Flora rolled her eyes. 'It's a sort of knitted street art. Started in the States apparently but everywhere in the world now. Groups get together and knit pieces that fit around urban street signs, that sort of thing, ironic and witty, but anything goes, really.'

'I see. And who is Jake?'

'He's the owners' grandson.' She felt her cheek, where that impromptu kiss had landed. 'He's the guy who pulled me out of the sea.'

'You really have got in there, haven't you? Are you sure you don't want to come and work for me?'

Flora sighed. 'And I still don't know whether the owner actually wants to sell or not.'

'Well, someone registered the hotel with a property agent. Twice! People do, and then they change their minds. But the seed is there. It's my job to germinate it.'

Flora wondered what he was up to. Was he planning to turn the whole place into posh, trendy apartments? He'd done it before.

She took a deep breath, and said in a rush, 'I wanted your

money to start up my own salon. But I haven't done the job, and so I don't feel right taking it.' She felt a rush of relief.

'Hmm.' He was silent for a long time and Flora checked to see if she still had a signal. Eventually, he said, 'Don't worry about that. Keep doing what you're doing, and leave the rest to me.'

They said goodbye, and Flora's stomach rumbled loudly. It must be around lunchtime. Too early for afternoon tea, which she suspected she probably had to book in any case, but not too late for a big pot of tea and a panini, with melting cheese and…

Her stomach growled again, and she snatched her jacket off the back of the chair, locked the door behind her and headed for the Art Café.

Molly was still waiting in the kitchen, as Jake knew she would be, and he tried not to sidle in. Her mouth was a thin line. Bryn was perched on a stool. He looked tired.

'Any joy getting a temporary chef?' Jake asked them. 'I can hold the fort in terms of breakfasts, but evening meals are out of my league.'

Bryn mumbled something that Jake couldn't catch, mainly as Molly talked right over him.

'So you brought that, that… biker caff…' She almost spat the words. 'That biker caff man… in here to spy on us… with your little biker girlfriend.' Her face was dark and Jake was scared for her. She shouldn't be this angry at her age. 'Was this intended as some sort of rebuke?'

'For what, Gran?' Jake tried for a note of reason. He perched against a counter, his arms deliberately loose at his side.

'You know perfectly well why.'

Jake frowned. He didn't have a clue why, and he said so. Of course, he knew about Gran's anti-bike stance. Up till now, it hadn't mattered. It was one of Gran's little eccentricities, and they had all tolerated it. He didn't have any biker friends, and when his own mates had bikes, he was more interested in surfing and, besides, he'd always had the Land Rover. You couldn't get a surfboard on a bike. He wondered now, if that had been deliberate. A way of keeping him off two wheels.

'I don't know why. And what is it you think Richard was spying on? He was a rock this morning. He abandoned his own business to come and help. This is your issue, not mine, and I just don't understand it. Is it anything to do with my mum and dad?' The words sounded strange in his mouth, and, after all this time, still made him sad. Molly looked stricken. 'They died on a boat, didn't they? You don't stop me getting onto boats!'

'Molly, love...' Bryn said, softly, crossing the kitchen towards her. Molly's head swivelled towards him, but her expression was still tight. She was silent.

Jake pressed on, his pulse roaring in his ears with the injustice of her comments. 'So Flora rides a bike. You liked her last night, well enough to ask her to stay on for a nightcap. She stood up to that tattooed oik, she stated very clearly that she was a biker and you didn't tell her to go then, did you? You used her and she has helped us. For no reason at all!' Jake tried hard not to shout.

'Yes. Why is that? She hardly knows you.'

'I suppose, because I pulled her out of the sea?' Jake shrugged. It sounded melodramatic to say he'd saved her life, and besides, he wasn't sure he deserved that accolade.

'And the haircut? What's all that about?'

'That was a thank you for rescuing her. Is that so bad?'

'Doesn't she have any of her own friends? She just seems to be hanging around you a lot.'

'I guess, she's on her own after the thing with her boyfriend, and I'm on my own, so I'm...'

'... her "temporary boyfriend"?'

Jake frowned at her, keeping a tight rein on his temper. 'Why does that bother you?'

There was a pause, and then Molly said, in a defiant voice, 'She could just be a gold-digger.'

Jake stared at her incredulously.

'She had no idea that I even lived here! She actually thought I worked here as the handyman!'

Molly sniffed, but said nothing.

'Gran, *I* don't even know what my place is here.' He spread his hands. 'I don't know whether you want me to be part of the hotel, or whether I just live here between jobs. I've never had a role here.'

'Well, if you'd wanted to be part of the hotel, maybe you shouldn't have disappeared to the other side of the world…'

Blood pounded in his ears. His gran looked defiant, but unrepentant. Bryn put a warning hand on her arm.

'I don't have to stay…' Jake tried not to say the words, but they came anyway.

'Jake, lad, of course you're staying. This is your home. It's entirely up to you what you do with your life.' Bryn spoke up at last. 'Isn't it, Molly?'

Molly muttered, 'Of course.'

Pushing himself away from the counter, Jake said, between gritted teeth, 'Well. I'm starving. I haven't had any breakfast. So, you know what? I'm going over to have it at the Art Café. I'll probably even meet Flora over there. Maybe we'll go for a ride on her bike.' Feeling sick, he marched out.

He'd never rowed with his grandparents. There'd been the usual teenage tantrums, but on the whole he loved and respected them, and arguments had been few. He felt furious and frustrated now, as he grabbed his coat. Flora and Richard had selflessly given up their time to help, and Molly was throwing it all in their faces over some stupid prejudice that she wouldn't even talk to him about. It made no sense at all.

He'd never felt more like going back to Australia than he did at that moment. He stomped across the road and stopped at the door of the Art Café. He couldn't sit down yet. He was fizzing with anger that had begun to churn up layer after layer of emotions and unanswered questions.

Pulling out his mobile, he texted Flora. Have you had breakfast/coffee/hot choc etc? Am at the AC and I'm buying. He walked towards her cottage as he sent it, then stopped and realised it might make him look like a stalker, and she might even have gone back to bed after her late night and early start, so he circled back.

His whole life was a circle.

He liked the hotel. Did he want to work in the hotel? What would he work as? Would he ever get to make his own decisions or would he only ever be a puppet for Molly and Bryn?

He growled, pulling a hand through his hair in frustration.

Chapter Twenty-Two

'Growly *and* Spikey,' Flora said behind him. He whirled round.

'Hello! I just texted you!'

Flora checked her phone as it pinged, smiling as his message appeared. 'The answer is no and yes.'

'No, you haven't had breakfast, and—'

'Yes, to coffee or hot chocolate or whatever.' She fell into step with him, crossing the car park to the café. 'I'm guessing by the state of your hair that it didn't go well after I left?'

'Hmmm.' Jake held the door open for her, raking his fingers through his hair. 'You could say that.'

Settled on a table as close to the window as they could find, they nursed their hot drinks and waited for their food. Jake said, quietly, 'Apparently, Richard is spying on the hotel.'

Flora jumped. 'Wh-what?'

Jake rolled his eyes. 'That's what Gran thinks,' he said, glumly. 'He's working on a takeover bid.' He smiled without humour and his eyes looked sad. 'And you're a gold-digger.'

'Are you a catch, then?' Flora's tone was light-hearted, but at the back of her mind, she was still thinking of her father's task. If anyone was a spy, it was her.

'Apart from my muscles and amazing haircut, you mean?' Jake's eyes creased in the corners, and then he looked serious. 'I'd say that only the tax man will be making money when Molly and Bryn go.' He rubbed a hand over his eyes and yawned. 'I should really get some advice about it. I just never actually think about them dying.'

Flora watched the muscles in his throat as he swallowed. It felt as if all the major upheavals of her life lately had taken place with him, sitting in this café.

'Go with this now.' She poured her tea. 'I feel as if I've known you for ever.'

'Don't.' Jake groaned. 'You know what that is, don't you?'

'What?'

'It's the *Speed* thing. The film. You know.'

'Huh?' They sat back to allow the waitress to put the tray of food on the table, and thanked her.

Picking up his knife and fork, Jake grinned. 'Keanu Reeves says to Sandra Bullock in *Speed*, "Relationships based on tense experiences never work."'

'Okay. We'll have to base it on sex then,' Flora replied, without missing a beat.

'Oh my God, I loved that film!'

'Me too!'

They laughed.

'But,' Flora said, blowing on her panini to cool it down, 'I really do feel as if I know you already.'

'Naaah.' Jake grinned. 'I'm just the hunky hero who saved your skin.' His smile faded. 'Actually, I wish I could unsay that. I'm not that person at all.'

There was a long pause. Jake stared into his mug. Flora waited for him to carry on, and after a while, she said, 'You've said something like that a few times, now, and then stopped. What happened?'

Jake stared over her head, and swallowed. She could see him wrestling with his conscience. His eyes rested on hers. 'I don't think you'd think of me as the hunky hero if I told you.'

'Did you kill someone?' Flora said, lightly, and then wished she could turn back time as the colour drained out of his face. She'd said it as a joke, as he'd asked her whether she'd murdered Spence and Amber, and she'd wisecracked that she was planning to. How long ago that seemed now. Cold fingers walked between her shoulder blades and she tried not to shiver. She put her hands round her teacup.

'I didn't *kill* them. I… er, it was, uh…' He ran his tongue around his mouth.

'Start from the beginning, Jake, if it helps.'

'There are thousands of people on the beach and in the sea, back in…' He jerked his head.

'Back in Australia? When you were lifeguarding?'

He nodded. 'Your eyes are everywhere. You have to watch all the time. There are people who can't swim, and they go out with a little bodyboard in bloody huge waves…'

'Oops. Sounds familiar…'

'Yeah… although you can swim. And those were not bloody huge waves, trust me.' A glimmer of a smile crossed his face, as she pretended to pout, but he carried on. 'There was a whole family of them, on this day. Kids, grans, aunts and uncles and all. On holiday. Non-swimmers, most of them. I don't know what people think! Or if they think at all…' He shook his head. 'Anyway, us lifeys, we're on the beach as usual, this day. You're watching the sea, and people come over and ask you stuff like you're just staring out to sea for nothing, or they need first aid or something which is fair enough and sometimes they're just plain bloody distracting.'

Flora's stomach churned, visualising his story. She stopped eating. He carried on, his eyes far away.

'There were these women. A bunch of them on a hen weekend or something. Course, there's an alcohol ban on the beaches in Oz…'

'I didn't know that.'

Jake nodded. 'So they weren't drunk, but they were being a pain in the arse, hanging round, wanting photos with us, would we take our T-shirts off, could they rub sun tan lotion on us, could we rub it onto them, all that stuff. And y'know, it goes with the territory. They all think we're actors from *Baywatch*, and usually, we just politely tell them we're working, you know, good natured, bit of humour, not rude or anything.'

'Okaaay.' Flora watched him as he scraped a hand over his stubbly chin.

'I keep wondering whether to shave this off,' Jake said. 'I must look a mess.'

'It suits you. You should keep it. Really close, like that. Not that it's anything to do with me, of course.'

He smiled faintly. 'So, basically, the radio goes, to tell us that this family have got into trouble, and this bloody woman grabs at my radio and she's hamming around, pretending to answer it... and I'm trying to get her off and so – and so, I'm late, getting into the water.' His jaw set. Flora felt helpless, guessing at what happened next.

'And the little boy...' Jake gulped, his mouth twisting. He stared out of the window. 'I've seen death before. But that little boy...' He shook his head. 'And I should have been able to...' He shrugged, his expression bleak. 'I tried. I tried so hard to get there...'

Flora's tears plopped onto the tabletop. She hardly dared to ask. 'And the rest of the family?'

'They all survived. We got all of them, except for...'

Flora's brain whirled. 'But... that wasn't your fault, Jake! It was the family! Who takes their children into the sea if they can't even swim themselves?'

'That's what people said. But I can't get it out of my head. It was my job.'

'What about the other lifeguard who was with you?'

'He was quicker off the mark than me.'

'And he didn't have women hanging off him?' Flora guessed, and Jake nodded.

A memory flashed across Flora's brain. 'Oh shit. So, when I fell off my board and landed with my face in your crotch, and said something really crass like—'

'—oops, but it is my birthday?' Jake said, his eyes on hers.

Flora felt heat rushing to her cheeks. 'Ye-es... and that reminded you of those women, and so you—'

'I gave you a bollocking. Yeah. Got it in one.'

Flora caught her bottom lip with her teeth. 'That explains the personality transplant then.' She sipped her tea, now cold, and made a face. 'Surely though, you had counselling? Isn't that something they do?'

'Yep. But this time, I couldn't get past it. It's why my girlfriend left me. I can't really blame her. I suppose I wasn't much fun.'

'Jeeze.' Flora let out a long sigh. She watched him pick up the salt and pepper set in his big hands and inspect it minutely, his expression set.

'And it's why I came home. There wasn't any point in staying. It was the only thing I knew how to do really well.'

'And you felt like a failure?' Flora's eyes filled with tears again. After a long pause, she said, 'Oh, Jake. You don't think you're being really hard on yourself?'

Jake's silence spoke volumes.

'Ah – and a couple of days after you got home, you found yourself pulling me out of the sea...' Flora slumped in her seat. 'I'm so sorry.'

'You weren't to know!' Jake smiled at her, the creases at his cheeks somehow more visible than usual. His face looked hollow. 'I was bricking it. I thought you were another child! If they'd known how rubbery my legs were with fear, they'd have thought I was useless. They all look up to me, and I don't deserve it...'

'I think they'd have thought you were incredibly brave, if you ask me,' Flora said. 'I can't believe how lucky I was that you overcame that to rescue me. You were incredible, out there. You made it look so easy.'

'Well, to be honest, you made it easy for me, because you're pretty fit, and you were determined.' He smiled at her and her stomach did a little somersault.

'Have you told your grandparents any of this?'

Jake shook his head, with emphasis. 'No. And I won't. They wouldn't understand. And they'd think I was a failure, too. I don't think Gran thinks much of me at the moment as it is. '

Flora thought about everything he'd told her. 'You and me, we're a couple of lost souls, aren't we?'

He shrugged his eyebrows. 'Uhuh. Do you have plans, Flora?'

'I want my own salon.' Flora didn't want to have to answer questions like, where, and how… so she turned the conversation back to him. 'Have you thought about what you're going to do, career-wise?'

Jake ran a large hand through his hair.

'I should have, shouldn't I? I suppose I always assumed that I'd inherit the hotel, or some of it, or something.' He rotated his hands, palm up, and then rubbed his chin. 'But I still don't know if it's what I want to do.' He chewed, thoughtfully. 'I know that I wouldn't want to run the hotel the way that it's being run at the moment.' He eyed her and blew out a long breath. 'You were quite right. It is tatty. Nothing like the truth to make you angry, is there?'

'Oh, but it's also charming…' Flora petered out as Jake raised an eyebrow at her.

'I believe Gran and Gramps should sell up and retire,' he carried on, 'so they can relax and enjoy themselves, and they won't even think of it.' He sighed. 'I actually asked Gran about it the other day. She nearly chewed my head off! I understand that this is their home. But, I mean, they can't go on for ever!'

He rested his green-blue eyes on her, and she had to fight not to look away. Lying was so difficult! How did people do it?

'I don't know if it means they don't trust me with the

hotel, or whether they really want to live there.' He shrugged expressively, his eyes searching hers, and Flora again had the impression that he'd thought better of telling her something. She hunted about for a way to change the subject, feeling guilty. Was her father, with her help, about to deprive Jake of his inheritance? She gulped, and after a prolonged silence, changed the subject.

'I'm hoping to book an afternoon tea at the Art Café some time. I couldn't do justice to it today. It was always meant to be my birthday treat, and I don't see why I should miss out.'

'That sounds nice. Enjoy yourself.' He looked far away. Should she ask him too?

'So, will my astonishing waitressing skills be required tomorrow?'

'I still don't even know that! I think I'm still a kid to them.' Jake huffed. 'Although, if I was in charge, I would have asked the dinner waitresses if one of them could come in early. I was on the verge of moving out this morning, but I can ask for you, if you wanted to come in. I don't even know what the pay is.'

'I was doing it as a favour to you, really, not as a full-time job. I think I'll stick to hairdressing. No danger of dropping eggs on the customers.' She smiled, and was pleased when he did too.

'We might go out for another paddle in the week. Fancy another crack at it?'

'Um, will it be warm and sunny?' Was she flirting with him? No, she told herself. Not at any stage had he given her the slightest inclination that he found her attractive. If she found him attractive, well, who wouldn't? It was a rebound thing. Everyone knew that's what happened after being dumped. Because that's what Spence had done, hadn't he? She was fooling herself, saying that she'd left him. He'd already made that decision for her.

'This is Wales!' Jake said, pointing to the window, where she could see the sky lowering over a colourless sea. 'I can't guarantee the weather! I'll let you know when we're going. If you fancy it, drop me a text. No pressure.'

'Well,' she said, slowly. 'Me pillioning you in the sea might depend on you pillioning me on the bike...'

To her surprise, he tipped his head at her. 'You never know.'

Relaxing in the cottage, later, Flora was surprised to open a text from Jake:

Gran asks if you are able to do her hair (!) Are you free later?

She stared at the text. How very odd. After being labelled a gold-digger! After much editing, she returned a text that said:

I'm free this afternoon, until 4.30. Will that do? (Chippy Run is at 5.30. Probably better not to tell her that?)

His reply pinged not long afterwards.

Two thirty? She says Thank You.

It was odd not to see an X at the end of his texts, but Flora was relieved by it, and left it off her texts too. It meant they were still just 'mates', with no romantic complications. They had both been badly hurt by the ones they thought they loved, and Flora, although enjoying Jake's company, sensed his 'temporariness'. He'd openly said that he didn't know where he was going next.

Pulling Pinterest from the apps on her phone, Flora searched for 'Hairstyles for over 60' and saved them to show Molly.

191

Chapter Twenty-Three

'Jake tells me you are very truthful.' Molly sat opposite Flora, her hands folded on her lap.

'I try to be…'

'What do you think of my hair?'

'Too long on the sides, flat on top. It's like a mullet, from the seventies,' Flora said, promptly. 'Totally the wrong shape for your face.'

'Ouch.' Molly fixed her with a piercing stare. 'There's the truth, and then there's being brutal!' Then she laughed, and Flora saw the Molly whose company she'd enjoyed so much at dinner the night before. She relaxed a little. 'But you're exactly right. Which is why I haven't been back to my hairdresser for the last six months. I think the girl has stopped seeing me.' Molly lifted her shoulders. 'I watched every old woman come out with the same haircut. So I stopped going. I kept meaning to find another hairdresser, but…' She waved an expressive hand.

'Do you know how you'd like it?' Flora asked her, gently. It was a story she'd heard before. It was as if some hairdressers had one style per age group and you got it whatever else you'd asked for, whether it suited you or not.

'I don't look in the mirror much these days. I don't recognise myself as the person I am inside.'

Flora felt sad. It was such a poignant statement. Briskly, she pulled her phone out. 'What do you think of these? I had a look at some styles that I thought would suit your bone structure and your lifestyle.' She got up, and sat beside the older woman, feeling her hold herself away for a moment before curiosity got the better of her.

'Pass me my glasses, if you would, please.' Molly took the phone in her elegant hands, and peered at the pictures. 'I like these.' She pointed, jabbing the screen and losing the picture. 'Oh, sorry, I hope I haven't deleted it!'

Flora chuckled. 'Nope, here it is.' She handed the phone back. 'I think that one would look great, and this one. They're quite similar – how much time do you spend on your hair?'

Molly eyed her. 'I don't. I'm a wash and go kind of girl. And my hair has a kink, so I usually keep it much shorter. This is driving me mad. I've already hacked some bits off it.'

'Do you want to wash your hair now or would you like me to do it for you?'

'I can do it, thank you.' The prickly Molly was back, and Flora watched her walk stiffly away from the sofa, trying hard to hide her aching knees. She'd seen enough older ladies to recognise it.

She waited, looking round the room. There were a few photos on display. An image of a smiling young couple, with a baby between them caught her eye. The woman had Jake's eyes and hair colour, and she focused on the man, trying to see any likeness to Jake. There was something around the forehead, the nose and chin that was familiar, and certainly, the broad shoulders.

'They were a beautiful family, weren't they?' Molly said, behind her.

'Sorry... I wasn't—' Flora began and then edited herself. 'Actually, I was. I was being nosey. I love family resemblances. I used to get whole families coming in to have their haircuts, and I absolutely adored doing the toddler's first cut, and then having them coming in for their prom do when they go up to comp.'

'You must miss your customers,' Molly said, as she settled into a hard-backed chair in the tiled kitchen area that was clearly hardly used, apart from a coffee maker and a kettle.

'I do.' Flora sighed. 'And I feel really bad that I've just walked out. They must feel abandoned.'

'So. You biffed your boss.'

Flora chuckled without opening her mouth, combing and sectioning Molly's fine but voluminous silver hair. 'I suppose you could say that. All of us girls let it go on for too long. He just thought he could get away with it.'

'Even in this day and age, it still goes on.'

Flora missed having a mirror before the client. She couldn't see Molly's expression, only the back of her head. Something in the way she spoke made her think that she knew about these things. She couldn't for one minute imagine Bryn behaving like Rex, though. And Molly would surely have put a stop to it at the very first opportunity.

'How do you like it round your ears?' she asked. 'Behind, or cut round?'

'What do you think?'

'I think a cut round the ear can be a bit severe. I'll leave it a bit softer. I can always cut it if you don't like it.'

Molly held up a thumb, and Flora smothered a grin. It was a gesture that belonged to a younger person. She concentrated on her task, bending often to check the balance of the cut.

'So, you're going to open your own salon.'

'That's the plan, yes.'

'"A goal without a plan is just a wish,"' Molly said. 'I read that somewhere, and it's true, I believe.'

Flora ran her hand through the cut, assessing how the hair fell. 'I believe it too. And I've been guilty of having a complete holiday from reality here. Somewhere to live has to be my first priority.'

'Your parents' cottage?'

'I can't stay there. It's Mum's income.' Flora shook her head, even though Molly couldn't see her. 'I was just lucky enough that the cottage was empty this early in the season.'

'I don't suppose luck came into it, my dear,' Molly said. 'It's what you do for your children.'

'Oh, Molly.' Flora straightened and cuffed the tear that ran down her cheek. 'I can't begin to imagine what it must have been like for you. And Jake, being so little. Excuse me, I need to blow my nose. Bit of hair, I think…'

'Kitchen roll, there.' Molly gestured over her shoulder, and Flora took a mighty blow.

Straightening her shoulders, she eyed the haircut. It looked good so far. She couldn't wait to see it dried. She said, 'Do you have hair products?'

'I do. What do you need?'

'It's nearly finished. I'm just checking it now. Then we'll need a blow dry spray, or some texturiser, or paste? Anything like that?'

'Come with me,' Molly said. She stretched her shoulders and led the way into a spacious en suite, opening a cabinet to reveal rows of salon style products. 'Take your pick!'

Flora clapped a hand over her mouth. 'Oh!'

'Well, yes, a bit self-indulgent,' Molly said, with a little laugh, 'but you know how it is. You end up buying a different one every time you go to the salon, in the hope that it's the magic remedy for bad hair days.'

Flora scanned the contents, her professional head selecting exactly what she needed.

'My cabinet is the same, don't worry about that. But, um, that little watercolour sketch.' She pointed. 'It's lovely. Did you buy it?'

'It's nice, isn't it? I bought it from a lady at a local art show, years ago. I always think of it as Jake jumping the waves at the beach. He was about eight or nine, then.' As she spoke, Flora squinted at the signature.

'You're not going to believe this,' she said. 'But my mum painted that. Look.' She pointed to the corner. 'It's faded, but you can just see her signature. Rosie Bexton.'

Molly put on her glasses and peered at it. 'Well, I never.'

'Mum has a bigger version of that in her apartment. Only there are two of us in it. Me and the little boy.'

Molly looked at the sketch again. 'Your mother is very clever. You must have inherited your creative talents from her.'

'Mum is a florist. She doesn't paint as much these days. I remember her always having a sketchbook on her knee when we came here for holidays.' She laughed. 'I remember it always being sunny. I'm sure it never rained at all!'

'Our memories play tricks on us.' Molly smiled.

Flora nodded, slowly. 'Jake must feel quite strange, being back. He's been away for quite a long time, hasn't he?' Molly nodded, and Flora carried on, 'I don't think Australia was quite everything he'd hoped for.'

Molly was silent. Flora collected the sprays and containers she needed and said briskly, 'Right. Let's complete your transformation!'

After Flora had dried and snipped her creation to her satisfaction, she said, 'Have you got a handheld mirror so you can see the back?'

'Sod the back,' Molly said, unexpectedly. 'That's what other people see. I want to see the front!'

Flora laughed, following her into the bathroom again, her fingers crossed that it met with her approval.

Molly glared at herself, turning her head from side to side.

'Yes,' she announced, finally. 'Very good. How much?'

Flora opened her mouth and closed it again. 'I don't know.'

'You're going to open your own salon and you don't know how much to charge?' Molly's mouth pursed, and Flora winced.

'I know how much my salon cuts are, but don't people expect to pay a lot less when you come to them?'

'They do, but I've always thought that smacked of colonialism.'

'Does it?' Flora didn't have a clue what Molly was talking about.

'Expecting the professional to come to you and then paying them less. It's all wrong.' Molly sniffed. 'But you're right, it is what happens. How much is your salon cut?'

Flora recited automatically, 'Reshape and blow-dry, forty-eight pounds.'

'I'm happy to pay you that,' Molly said. 'It's a better job than my last place and that was about seventy pounds, with one of those terrible head massages that make you feel as if you're in a porn film.'

'Oh,' Flora said, faintly, smothering a laugh. 'Thank you very much.'

'And if you're going to open a salon, put your prices up, girl. That's way too cheap in my opinion.' Molly nodded. 'So, where are you planning to open? Have you looked for premises? Because you can't leave now.' She admired herself in the mirror again. 'You're my hairdresser!'

Flora did laugh then.

'I could carry on as a mobile hairdresser while I'm looking for premises,' she mused, aloud.

'And you have the transport...' Molly eyed her, and Flora's mouth dried, but she held her head high.

'I do.'

'There you are then.' Molly left and returned with a vacuum cleaner.

'Oh, let me do that!' Flora dashed forward and Molly relinquished the machine with easy grace. Flora made sure there wasn't a strand of hair remaining, and stacked the product bottles on the counter.

'Oh, by the way, I meant to ask, did you want me again at breakfast?'

Molly frowned at her, and Flora added hurriedly, 'Just to tide you over. I'm not asking for a job, or anything.'

'Thank you. That's very kind. Can I let you know a little later? I'm still waiting on a phone call from the agency. I've got your number now. I'll ring you.'

'Oh yes, of course, that's fine.' Flora stopped talking, hearing herself gabbling. 'Well, I'll be off.'

Molly paid her in cash, adding a generous tip, despite Flora's protests.

'Look on it as a bribe,' Molly said, with a twinkle in her eye. 'So that I can queue jump when you have your salon.' She showed Flora out, clearly noticing when she pulled on her bike jacket but saying nothing. Flora left feeling more confused than ever.

Chapter Twenty-Four

Arriving at the Art Café in plenty of time for the Chippy Run, with a full fuel tank and an empty bladder, as directed by every bike group she'd ever ridden with, Flora reverse parked, ready to ride out. Her stomach knotted with apprehension. What if she dropped her bike onto one of theirs? Did something stupid on the ride? Couldn't keep up? She patted the big bike, shouldered her rucksack and pushed open the café door.

'This place is home from home for you, isn't it?' It was the tall, dark-haired girl who had served her on her first visit. Jo.

'It does feel like that.' Flora smiled, glancing about to see if any other biker types were there. 'I'm going out to play on my bike with everyone tonight.'

'I've drawn the short straw for the late lock up, while you lot all go out and have fun.' Jo nodded with a smile.

'Oh. I'm sorry. Do you ride too?'

'I do, but we have vintage bikes.' Jo was a whirlwind of industry, tidying and stacking mugs and cups behind the counter. 'And I still prefer my eBike.' She flashed a broad grin at Flora. 'But don't tell the boss.'

'Don't tell the boss what?' Lucy breezed through from her office, balancing her helmet, gloves and jacket in her arms. 'Not that eBike thing again?' She tipped her head. 'I suppose that'll be how you can eat like a horse and still stay thin while the rest of us have to exist on salads.'

'Welsh salad…' Jo said, with a slow smile.

'Yes.' Lucy laughed, and told Flora, 'That's chips, in Wales.'

Flora watched their banter, comparing it to the Kutz salon. If she, *when* she, set up her own salon, she wanted this same ambience. Same loyalty. It was an achievement to be on good terms with your staff as a boss and not have them taking advantage of your good nature. Lucy and Richard had managed it. She reflected on Molly and Bryn.

The ride to Port Eynon on the far west coast of Gower was stunning in the late afternoon sunshine, although the route, following narrow lanes, was unfamiliar, and she couldn't orient herself. The six of them, Ash leading, pillioned by his daughter Daisy, then Lucy, Flora, and Richard and his wife Nicola brought up the rear. They rode through narrow muddy lanes bounded either side by terrifyingly steep ditches, and Flora's bum had twitched with fear. Then over open moorland, creeping quietly past wild ponies and their shy, long-legged foals.

It was a Gower she'd never seen, or at least, didn't remember. Opening her visor a little, she breathed in the fresh air and tried to memorise the landscapes they passed, the enticing bright slivers of blue sea and colourful patchwork fields.

They parked exactly where she'd parked before. There were tables and chairs outside the fish and chip shop, and they left their helmets on the tables and queued for their food. The evening, whilst not exactly balmy, was just warm enough to sit outside with the hot chips and cardboard cups of tea warming their hands.

'There's nothing quite like it, is there?' Richard blew on a hot chip before popping it into his mouth.

A big blue pickup truck pulled up, to a chorus of cheers from their little group, and Flora watched as a sturdy little boy climbed nimbly out of the open back. He ran across to them all, followed by a tall, handsome man with a shock of dark hair, and Jo from the café.

'Riding in the back, huh, Liam?' Ash high-fived the little boy and sent raised eyebrows to the tall man. 'Ed?'

Ed raised his hands, palm up. 'It was only the last couple of hundred yards. I went slow!'

'Flora, this is Ed, and this is Liam.' Jo introduced them with a wave of her hand, and Flora waved back, fanning the hot chip burning her mouth.

'Nice to meet you all,' she said, when she could speak again. 'It was so good of you to invite me along.'

'We didn't,' Richard said. 'That was Lucy. A couple of glasses of wine and she'd invite anyone along.'

'Shut up, Rich.' Lucy threw a chip at him. 'He's teasing you, Flora. Take no notice.' Richard ducked.

'At least this one can ride.' He winked at Flora. 'Remember that couple on the scooters she invited?' There was laughter all round.

'You ride well,' Ash said. Flora glowed. Praise indeed.

'My dad taught me,' she said. 'He used to balance me in front of him, and I'd help him steer.' She glanced at Ash. 'We had a lot of space, then. This wasn't on the road, of course.'

Daisy, listening to them, said, 'I've got my own bike.'

'Wow!' Flora registered the neat, protective outfit that fitted her properly. 'What have you got?'

'It's a fifty cc. I do a bit of mini-moto.' Daisy smiled, shyly. 'And I like dirt biking.'

'You're a lucky girl.'

'I know.' Daisy ate her way up a long, dangling chip, to Liam's admiration.

'I've got hundreds of bikes,' Liam told them.

'We have *many* bikes.' Ed put the paper wrapped parcels down, and unwrapped the little boy's portion, breaking off some of his own fish to add to it. '*We*,' he inclined his head pointedly at Liam, 'buy, sell and renovate vintage bikes. That's quite a beast you're riding.' He nodded at Flora.

'It's borrowed, unfortunately. It'll have to go back soon.' Flora's gut churned as she thought about it and she stared over the sea. Perhaps it was a sixth sense, or perhaps she recognised the familiar engine note. The hair on the back of her neck prickled and her eyes darted towards the road where it left the cover of the cottages and emerged into the car park. And there it was. A bright green Ninja motorbike. A half-eaten chip dropped from her nerveless fingers as she stared at the tall, leather clad rider. She recognised the helmet. It was Spence. Spence! Here! But how? The rider stretched his back in some apparent pain as he got off and she felt a surge of vicious satisfaction.

'Are you okay, Flora?' Lucy and Jo asked almost the same question at the same time.

She said, without taking her eyes off Spence. 'It's my ex. The sister shagger.'

'I hardly know you, Flora, but I don't like him,' Nicola said, sending a fierce glare into the car park.

'Sister? You never said it was your sister!' Jo glared at the rider too.

'She told us at the lifeguard party, Jo,' Lucy said, following Flora's gaze. 'Bastard! Sorry, Daisy.' Daisy shrugged.

It was like hearing a radio play, Flora thought, seeing and hearing her friends in some other compartment in her head.

Jo hissed, 'Bastard! Sorry, Liam.' She went to stand and Flora shook her head, putting a hand on her arm. She opened her mouth to say, 'I'll go and see what he wants,' but nothing at all came out. She watched Spence recognise his bike, and she forced herself to walk towards him, over the grass. It was the longest fifty steps she'd ever taken.

'We're just here, Flora!' Lucy called, and she felt a tiny warm glow in the frozen pit of her stomach. There were people who cared about her.

'Flora.' He had the decency to take his helmet off to speak to her, but as his face was revealed she felt her hands twitch with the instant desire to slap it. With a rock.

'How did you know I was here?'

'Find My Friends app.' He waved his phone.

'I am not your friend.' Flora reached out to snatch his phone and stamp on it, and he yanked it out of her reach. 'Obviously you didn't have it on last Thursday or you might have seen me coming home early!'

Rage rose into her mouth, and her words were unstoppable, relentless. 'But I fucking saw you, you two timing fucker.' It was a bit short on variety, but it got the message across. Fury sent tears to her eyes and when she blinked, they fell out and ran down her cheeks. He scrubbed his face with the heel of his hand, and she saw the indentations of his helmet there. It had probably taken hours and hours to get here on her little bike. She was glad. She hoped it had hurt like hell.

'I'm sorry.' He lifted his hands and dropped them again. 'I never meant it to be like this.' He rubbed the back of his neck with a grimace. 'I brought your bike. The keys are in it still. I can see the Diavel. Give me the keys, please, and I'll be gone.'

'You're *sorry*? You've only fucking come down for your bastard bike, haven't you?' Flora had an urge to fling his keys into the sand. 'With my sister – of all the people you could have shagged! And just as I thought we'd started to get along. Bitch.' A horrible thought flashed across her mind. 'Or was that all part of it? Did you think I wouldn't find out? Whose idea was it? Hers?'

'What do you want me to say?' His voice rose to match hers and Flora was aware in the corner of her eye of Ash and Richard and Ed standing and walking to the front of their little group. Tears streamed down her face and she ignored them.

'I want you to tell me the truth! Why did you do it? With her? Why? How long has it been going on?'

Spence looked over her shoulder and lifted his chin. 'Is that your bodyguard detail?'

Flora didn't have to follow his gaze. 'Do you really think I need one?' She glared at him. 'You haven't answered my questions. I think I have a right to know.'

He blew out a sigh. 'She made it easy for me.' He closed his eyes and opened them into the sky and she wanted to slap him all over again. 'I'm not proud of myself. But you know what she's like—'

'I *do* know what she's like! But no one ever believes me and it doesn't excuse you!' Flora interrupted bitterly, and Spence carried on in a monotone as if she hadn't spoken.

'She just told me what to do. She played me like a fish. She reeled me in and I was stupid enough to fall for it.' He lowered his gaze to her. 'You and me, though, we lived separate lives really, didn't we?'

'What? Are you blaming me? Really? So did you think the way to get closer to me was to sleep with my sister?' Flora was astonished. 'Separate lives?' She shook her head, trying to see the sense of it. 'Did she tell you that too? Well, it sounds like *you* were living a separate life, but I wasn't! So was this sex or are you in love with her? Because I sure as fuck ain't coming to your wedding.'

'I don't know what it is.' Spence turned a pair of sad, weak eyes on her and she was revolted by him. 'I think she's probably dumped me now she's had what she wants. She hates you.'

'And *I* hate *you*. Now – *fuck off*!' She screamed the last part. 'Take your bike and fucking look after it because I have loved it *so* much more than I ever *EVER* loved you.' The truth of her words hit her like a punch. Openly sobbing, she fished in her pocket for the bike keys and threw them at him with as much force as she could muster. They missed him altogether and sailed over his shoulder. As he turned and bent to retrieve them, she pulled her leg back to land a massive kick on his arse.

'Flora, no!' Ash was alongside her, with Richard and Ed a little way behind.

She turned to look at their concerned faces, these people

whom she had known for such a short time, but who already meant more to her than this snivelling wimp who she'd wasted years on.

'Don't waste any more energy on him,' Ash murmured to her, his bulk comforting as he turned her away. 'He's got what he came for, and, hopefully, that's the last you'll see of him.'

She heard the big Ducati start up, and wept all over again. She really had loved that bike. She wished Jake was there right now. Although in a way she was glad he hadn't been. She was sure she'd sounded dreadful. Potty-mouth, her mum would have said with a tut.

'Why didn't you let her kick his arse?' Lucy demanded of Ash and Richard as they led her back to the table. 'Ooh, Flora, me and Jo were ready to kick it if you weren't!' She lifted her fists in a fighter stance and glowered.

Jo emerged from the café and handed Flora a napkin and a glass of water. 'Are you okay, sweetie?'

Ash put one big hand over Lucy's pointed little fists with a smile at Daisy who had snuggled up under his arm. 'If Flora had injured him he'd be here for longer. And she'd have been the one in the wrong for assault.'

Flora nodded, sadly. 'Yeah. You're right. Thanks. Sorry about all the swearing, especially in front of the kids.' She drew in a great shuddering breath and blew her nose. 'I'm so sorry. I've ruined your chip run.'

'You have not. Daisy's heard it all before now,' Lucy said.

'And Liam went into the chippy to play on the machine which he's hardly ever allowed to do so he was oblivious. Don't worry about it.' Jo sat at the table facing the café.

'Was I really awful?' Her appetite gone, Flora pushed her chips into the middle of the table, where the men lost no time dipping in.

'No,' Lucy said, firmly. 'You were magnificent.' She reached over and squeezed Flora's arm. 'Don't start beating yourself up now. I tell you, every one of us here has had a drama in our lives and they were every bit as emotional as that was. Right, guys?' She glanced round the table, and Flora saw them nod at her.

'Hell, yeah,' Jo said, with a rueful smile. 'At least you didn't have a whole beach full of people listening in to yours.' Flora lifted her face to her. Jo, quiet as she was, clearly had hidden depths.

'Wow.' Flora felt the corners of her mouth lift in a wobbly smile. 'I really need to get to know you lot better.'

'So that means you're staying for a bit longer?' Nicola asked. 'Only I feel like I've missed out on a shedload of gossip here.' She reached a hand out. 'I'm Nic. I keep the Art Café crew in order. Well, their money, anyway. Bunch of spendthrifts!' They all laughed as Flora shook her hand.

'You're the accountant?' Flora was thoughtful. 'I'm planning to set up a hairdressing salon. I'll be needing an accountant. I probably won't be able to afford you though.'

'Good, reliable accountants are worth their weight in gold,' Lucy said. 'Trust me.'

'So, properties in Gower aren't cheap. Are you thinking of starting from scratch or buying an existing business? Have you started looking?' Nicola asked her. 'If you do decide to stay and start your own business, then I'd be happy to give you a quote.'

'Thanks.' Flora nodded. 'I'm a bit up in the air, really. I don't even have anywhere to live once I leave mum's cottage this weekend. Setting up a business seems like pie in the sky right now!' She clamped her bottom lip between her teeth to stop it quivering from self-pity. 'My customers are back in the Midlands. I suppose I ought to go back there.'

'Naaah.' Lucy picked up a piece of batter and put it down again. 'Never go back. Always go forward. That's my motto.'

Flora drained the cup of water that Jo had given her. Go forward. 'You're right. Even if I have to live in a caravan or something, I can make it work. And for now, I could do mobile hairdressing and start getting a clientele.'

'Liam and I lived in a caravan for a while and my hair definitely needs a trim,' Jo said, flicking the ends of her long dark hair with a grimace. 'I never have time to go to a hairdressers.'

'I'll do it now,' Flora said, with a grin. 'I've always got my stuff with me.'

Jo laughed, but eyed her thoughtfully. 'You did a cracking job of the surfer dude...'

'And his gran.'

'Really?' All eyes swivelled towards her. She nodded.

'Yep. This afternoon. She looks awesome. Ten years younger.'

'And she knows you're a biker?' Richard's blond eyebrows raised.

'Yep.' Flora looked around at them. 'She even mentioned it when I talked about mobile hairdressing.'

'I'm staggered.' Richard eyed her, thoughtfully. 'After the look on her face this morning, too. I thought I was going to be turned to stone.'

'You were brilliant this morning,' Flora said. 'Thanks for not chewing my head off on the phone!'

'Two hundred and fifty million takeaway breakfasts, please!' Richard mimicked a high-pitched voice and laughed. 'I enjoyed it, actually. It's good to challenge yourself, try something new. Fabulous kitchen. And if it improves relationships between us, then it's been worth it. We're too small a place to have rifts like that. Are you waitressing tomorrow morning?'

Flora shrugged. 'I'm waiting for a phone call. I'm only doing it as a favour to Jake, really. I'm not looking for a job there. Hairdressing is my thing!'

'All three of us could do with a trim,' Jo said. 'As you can see.'

Affecting a model stance, Ed ran a hand through his tousled black locks and everyone laughed. Flora assessed him with a professional eye. Both he and Liam would be brilliant models for publicity when the time came, if they'd let her.

'Yes, thank you, Ed. I think we got the picture.' Jo rolled her eyes with a broad grin. 'So, could you come over to us, Flora? I've got tomorrow afternoon free.'

'Oh, that would be brilliant!' Nicola turned to Flora. 'Jo has the most amazing farmhouse. The kitchen is enormous. You could do *everyone's* hair in there.' She tugged at her hair, thoughtfully.

'I'm free tomorrow. Can I send you my mobile number?' Flora pulled out her phone and then hesitated. 'You're not doing this because you feel sorry for me, are you?'

'Oh, yes, I'd totally abandon my child to your clutches if I thought you were rubbish.' Jo snorted and for a moment, Flora saw the steel within the softly-spoken girl.

'What about me?' Ed pouted.

Jo reached out a long arm and ruffled his curls. 'You'd look handsome bald, my love.'

'Well! This is a momentous occasion, I think. We've gained a group hairdresser, and a new bike! Shall we have a selfie?' Lucy brought her phone out. 'We can compare before and after hairstyles. I'll send it to you all. You'll get it when there's a signal.'

'Ooh. No pressure there then.' Flora widened her eyes and grimaced, lifting her face into a grin as they laughed, all of them snuggling together to be in the shot.

Lucy jumped up and angled her phone to get them all in, leaving just the top half of her face in the foreground. She held the photo out to everyone for approval, and then looked at it herself. Flora saw how the setting sun illuminated their faces. It looked like a lifestyle Instagram image.

'That's a great shot. It's going to look faaaabulous on the wall of my new salon!'

There was laughter, and they dispersed for trips to the loo and a wander along the beach. Kicking the soft, pale sand with her boots, Flora watched Liam and Daisy playing tag, and thought she'd never forget this evening.

Would it have happened with Spence there, if they'd still been together? She thought not. He wouldn't have fitted in, despite being a biker. He would have dominated the conversation and somehow made everything about him. She wondered what she'd seen in him for so long. Did it just get to be a habit? They'd had good times together, hadn't they? She trawled through her memories, but failed to recall anything that really made an impact. While by contrast, the last few days were already full of memories and laughter.

Would Jake fit in? Definitely, yes. His slow smile was the only thing missing in that selfie. And look, Ed and Jo had turned up in their truck and were still part of the group. Jake could have come along in the Landy.

Ed wandered over to her. 'Are you going to be okay to ride back, Flora? If you're feeling a bit wobbly, I can put your bike in the back of the truck and we'll give you a lift home. Or Rich can pillion you. We've just had a chat about it.'

'Oh, that's so kind of you all, Ed!' Flora looked up at his handsome face. 'I'm fine though, honestly. In a way, it's been a relief, getting it over and done with. And I know my Ninja inside out. Although she's going to feel like half a bike after riding the other beastie.'

'We'll all ride together to where we meet the main road, and then everyone makes their own way,' Ash told them. The sun was setting and there was a chill in the air. 'Is that okay? Do you know where you are, Flora?'

'Not a clue.' Flora grinned. 'The satnav went that way

along with about a hundred and fifty more horsepower.' She pointed towards the only road out of the village.

Ash's eyebrows lifted as he swept his eyes over her bike. 'What's this then?'

'It's a 300cc Kawasaki Ninja.'

'300cc? It looks much bigger than that!' He burst out laughing. 'So he rode it all the way from... where did you say again?'

'Coventry.' Flora chuckled.

'Tonight?'

'I guess so, judging by the state of him. Hope he's left some fuel in it for me.' She eyed Ash thoughtfully. 'He'll be a whole lot quicker going back though... if you get my drift, and I know the reg number.'

'Maybe you should be applying for the police instead of being a hairdresser,' Ash's eyes twinkled. 'We'll go back your way, don't worry.'

'Thanks, Ash.' She climbed onto the bike she'd had for years, expecting it to feel alien, and for the length of the homeward journey it did. She missed the phenomenal acceleration of the Ducati. But by the time she'd turned off towards the cottage, waving her escorts farewell, her muscle memory had kicked back in and it felt like a friend again.

She locked the bike away after giving it a welcome home pat and wandered round the cottage, feeling a bit lost and aimless after the dramas of the last few hours. Her phone pinged.

Hello Flora, this is Molly.

Could you spare the time to waitress again tomorrow morning, 7.30? You will be paid, of course.

Flora blinked. She replied instantly:

Hi Molly, yes, I can come tomorrow. Flora

Pouring herself a glass of chilled white wine, she rang her mum for a long chatty catch up, and sank into bed, setting two alarms on her phone, just in case.

Chapter Twenty-Five

Jake felt a huge sense of satisfaction after that morning's breakfasts. There was no doubt that it was physically hard work, but the amount of mental concentration required had surprised him. He had never considered that juggling orders for cooked breakfasts, especially the eggs – fried, poached or scrambled – would be such hard work and he guiltily avoided noticing the larger than usual quantity of eggshells which indicated his failure rate.

Flora had been speedy and efficient and hadn't dropped food on anyone. She had a quick mind and could remember orders and names, too. Jake presumed it was her hairdressing background, but he couldn't help being surprised when she came into the kitchen with, 'Mrs Brown said her bacon was just right, thank you.'

His grandfather contented himself with making the teas and coffees in a quiet corner, happy to leave Flora to it.

'She's faster than me,' he confided to Jake. 'And she gets the tables in the right order.' He and Bryn were getting on so much better now. Yesterday afternoon, he'd driven them to Rhossili in the Land Rover and they'd sat having tea and scones overlooking the bay. Bryn had opened up that Grumpy Pete the ex-chef had gone out of his way to confuse him, changing the numbers on the orders and making it seem as if he was going senile.

'I realise now that it was a way of hiding what he was doing. I really did think I was losing it.'

'Oh, Gramps.' Jake pulled his ear, staring out of the window. He didn't want to say that he'd thought the old man was losing it too. 'I can't tell you how relieved I am to have you back.'

'She's a bit of a marvel, that girl of yours.'

'Flora?' Jake asked as much to give himself time to think, as actually confirming that she was who Bryn was referring to.

'Of course Flora. Has Pete been working on you too?' Bryn's tone was waspish. 'Don't think I haven't noticed the way you look at her. She's fantastic. I'd hire her permanently right now.'

'You should tell her that, although I know she has her heart set on her own salon. I think she's lost a bit of confidence about herself right now, what with the boyfriend thing and whacking her boss.'

Bryn had been silent for a moment, stirring his tea. A slow smile lit his face. 'I'd like to have seen that.'

'Me too. I reckon he was lucky to get away with just the broken nose.' They chuckled, and Jake added, 'I'm glad to be home, Gramps. There's no place like home.'

'I thought you'd stay in Oz, to be honest, lad.'

Jake stared over the expanse of sunlit turquoise sea, and the bright crescent of sand that met the surging breakers. 'I need to tell you about what happened over there, Gramps.'

Since that conversation, and for pretty much the first time in his life, Jake felt that he was useful in the hotel. It was a good feeling and he knew that, by and large, it was because Flora had made everything seem possible. By ten o'clock, they were clearing down, after breakfasting themselves on one of Jake's creations. Molly came down, as they scrubbed and polished and Jake thought how much brighter she seemed. She handed an envelope to Flora. He watched her open it and inspect the contents with a smile.

'Thank you, Molly, and Bryn.'

'Thank you for this morning.'

'You're welcome,' Flora said. 'I enjoyed it.'

'We're a good team.' Jake gave the counter a final whisk with the cloth.

'You *are* a good team.' Molly pressed her lips together in what Jake recognised as her thinking face, and then said, 'I've got a dinner chef sorted for next Monday and I have a proposal for you, starting tomorrow.'

Jake eyed her warily. 'What's that, Gran?'

'If you'd like to extend your cooking skills, Jake, I've ordered a truckload of meals that can be cooked from frozen. It's a local firm, I've been looking at them for a while. They arrive tomorrow. We can schedule a temporary menu for this week, and big up the new chef for his arrival on Monday.'

Jake gaped. He knew he was gaping because his gran pulled her glasses down and regarded him over them. 'I can't, I mean, I don't know how to—'

'You worked the chip fryer, didn't you? When we had pizza on Sunday night?' Molly's direct blue eyes staked him to the spot. 'Nothing more complicated than that. Only if you think you can cope with it, of course.' She waved an airy hand. 'Everything with chips. Or pasta. You'll get the hang of it.'

Jake glanced at Flora, trying not to look pleading. She obviously read his mind though.

'I'm game if you are?' She held up a hand and he high-fived her. 'I reckon we can hold the fort for a few days, between us. It's just a bigger version of the kitchen at home. For more people…'

With his grandparents sorting out her casual rate wages, Jake was delighted to have Flora alongside him in the kitchen. By the time she left on Saturday, he'd have it all sorted. He flicked a glance out of the side of his eye at her and felt his spirits sag at the thought of her leaving.

Jo and Ed's house was beautiful. And as Nicola had said, the kitchen was vast, a wonderful mix of the old and new. A huge antique dresser loaded with a variety of mugs and Liam's drawings stood to one side, and there was still plenty of room to walk around the enormous scrubbed pine table in the centre. There was a dressing table mirror on a stand on the table, with a hairdryer and an extension lead. A pine rocking chair was in a corner next to a glorious, buttercup yellow Aga cooker. Jo saw her looking at it.

'It's gorgeous, isn't it? Beryl found it, and I fell in love with it. It's such a bright, welcoming colour!'

'It certainly is. I didn't even know they made them in colours like that!' Flora looked around her, as Jo made them a coffee. 'Sorry, I'm being terribly nosey! This is stunning – I think I'd just live in the kitchen!'

'We pretty much do, especially in the winter.'

'And who is Beryl?'

'Beryl was my neighbour when I met Ed. She was more of a mother to me than my own mother. When Ed and I moved in here, she came with us. She has her own "granny flat", and a super-busy social life, so I actually see less of her than I used to! She's collecting Liam and Daisy from school, and bringing them here to have their hair cut, and hers too. You're going to be busy.'

'Fantastic, thank you so much!'

'I'm going first, if that's okay, otherwise I'll end up doing the food and my hair won't be done – which is what usually happens, and why it's such a mess!'

'It's not a mess, but it's curly and that makes your haircuts last longer than other people's, so you're lucky!'

Jo sat obediently at the big table as Flora put a towel round her shoulders, combed through her hair, and asked her how she wanted it.

'Easy to care for,' Jo said. 'I have to split my time between the Art Café, and The Vintage Bike Palace, and Liam.'

'Okay. So basically, you want to be able to tie it back and not fanny about with it.'

Jo pealed with laughter. 'You speak my language! I'd love

to have glossy waves, and a fringe, but it's just not going to happen. I'd settle for no scraggy bits at the bottom and some sort of shape.'

Having ascertained that Jo had washed her hair that morning, Flora sprayed her curls with a mister, and combed it out.

'Your hair is beautiful. Lovely and thick,' she said. 'I'm going to take about two or three inches off, to reshape and get rid of these split ends. Is that okay?'

'Yes, that's fine. You can go even shorter than that, actually. It's so heavy, and it takes ages to dry.'

Flora pulled her phone out and showed her some photos she'd saved, and Jo pointed to a style with hair just below the shoulder.

'Will Ed be okay with that?'

'Ed?'

Flora nodded. 'You'd be amazed how attached men get to their wife's long hair. I don't want to be responsible for a domestic.'

Jo considered that. 'I don't think he'd mind, but thank you for thinking about it. I'd actually like to go shorter than that, but I need to be able to tie it back for work.'

'Let's go for this one. I can always cut some more off. I can't stick it back on.'

When, an hour or so later, an older woman clattered through the door with Liam and Daisy, Jo was looking extremely glamorous. She stared at herself in the mirror, watching the curls swing as she shook them back. Flora showed her how it would look up high on her head, pulling some tendrils out or simply tied back for the café.

'You're hired. Don't even think about moving or anything.'

Flora laughed.

'You look like a princess, Mummy.' Liam stared at her. 'Am I next?'

'I think that would be a very good idea,' Jo said, kissing his cheek. 'Tidy up for this young man, please, Flora.'

Flora settled Liam on several cushions to raise him up to her level, thankful that she wasn't very tall. He was a chatty little boy, and she had to straighten his head up numerous times, despite Jo's murmured reminders to him to keep still.

'He's fine. I prefer them talkative to terrified.' Flora grinned, finishing him off with the clippers, and passing him the mirror so he could admire himself.

Daisy said, 'Mum says, just a trim.'

Over Daisy's head, Jo mouthed, 'Mum!' to Flora, and put her hand on her chest in a silent, 'Awww, sweet.'

As Flora had suspected, Daisy's hair was in excellent condition and seemed to have been trimmed quite recently so she'd probably just come along out of curiosity, which was fair enough. Flora snipped a tiny bit off all over, careful to follow the original shape, and Daisy pronounced herself satisfied, thank you very much, posing for selfies on her phone, as the three women exchanged quietly amused glances.

Beryl submitted to a trim on her also neatly shaped hair, after watching the children, and by the time Ed came home, Flora's scissors were properly warmed up.

'You will stay for dinner, won't you? It's only a pasta thing, but Lucy and Ash are coming over too. You can invite Jake, if you'd like to?'

Flora felt the deep blush on her face. 'Oh, I, er…'

Quickly Jo said, 'It's just that I see you two together all the time in the café, and I thought you must be an item?'

'I'd love to invite him, if you're sure that's okay?' That would mean nine of them for dinner. Jo didn't seem a bit fazed. Flora texted Jake, giving him the address and a time.

He replied with a thumbs up and Flora had to force herself

to concentrate on Ed's hair, after he'd emerged from the shower. Luckily, it was such a thatch, that anything she did to it would be an improvement. It turned out that Jo gave him an occasional once over with a set of clippers. Which was fine, but did nothing for his double crown, which made his hair go in all directions. He was so tall that Flora had to ask for a lower stool so she could cut his hair. Liam thought it was hilarious to see Ed on a stool from his bedroom, his long legs folded up with his knees under his chin.

Flora only just had time to dry his hair and tidy up after herself before Ash and Lucy arrived, closely followed by Jake, carrying a bottle of wine which Beryl seemed happy to relieve him of.

Flora felt her cheeks heat as she saw Jake ducking beneath the door frame. He winked at her and she glowed.

'I didn't see your bike outside, Flora. Did you get a lift?'

'Oh I meant to tell you – but it was really busy this morning, wasn't it, and you shot off to sort the boiler out? Spence came down.' She looked up at him happily, and frowned a little as his face set. She hesitated and continued, 'And I sent him away with a—'

'Ooh, ooh, let me tell him this bit.' Lucy whirled around, beaming at them. Flora blinked, wondering what she was going to say. 'Flora was fantastic. She wiped the floor with him and tried to kick his butt but Ash stopped her and now he's gone, taking his bike with him.' There were murmurs of assent from everyone in the kitchen.

'Flora is a pocket rocket!' Liam piped up. 'Dad said! He did!'

'This was on your chip run last night?' Jake grinned. 'Sounds like I missed a good party!'

'Me too,' Beryl said. 'Am I too old to ride a motorbike?'

'See me later, Beryl,' Ash said with a wink.

'Ooh,' said Beryl, exploring every syllable. Flora loved the

Welsh and their language. 'You had me at – well, okay, I'll have a think about it.'

While the banter was going on, Flora watched Jake out of the corner of her eye. His face had relaxed and the corners of his generous mouth were lifted. She jumped a little as he bent and spoke in her ear.

'Well, I was about to try and tell you sincerely that I was pleased if being back with Spence was what you wanted, because I haven't known you very long.' He paused and her heart banged. 'But, being selfish, that's really very good news that you kicked his butt, as far as I'm concerned. So, you're staying?'

'I'm staying.'

He grinned hugely and in the crowd around the table, his large hand felt for hers and he squeezed it. Her insides melted.

'What a smart crew!' Lucy admired them all, setting wine and a box of cakes on the table. 'Cakes are from Richard. He said, could they be next on your list to throw a hair party, and do you do toddlers? Jack is two and a bit, and has taken a dislike to the barber. Apparently, he bit him. Jack bit the barber. Not the other way round.'

'Of course. I like babies.' Flora looked round, in the tiny but awkward silence that followed her words, as it dawned on her that both Liam and Daisy were stepchildren, and that no babies had followed belonging to both parents.

Jo was the first to recover, putting a heap of cutlery on the table for Liam to arrange. She asked Daisy to fill the water jugs and to put tumblers out. Daisy sang quietly as she worked, a clear, pretty voice.

'That's lovely, Daisy, what is it?' Lucy asked her.

'We're doing it in school. It's "Calon Lân",' Daisy said, importantly.

'Sing some more,' Jo said, and Daisy, unfazed by being

centre stage, obliged. Flora was astonished to hear the deep voices of Ash, Jake and Ed quietly accompanying her, and Beryl joining in with the notes she could reach.

'That is so beautiful.' Flora recognised that it wasn't English, and guessed that it was Welsh. She dabbed her eyes. 'What does it mean?'

'It means, "Pure heart",' Ash said. 'It's something about only a pure heart can sing it.'

'Does everyone know it in Wales?' They all looked at each other.

'Pretty much,' Ed said. 'It's sung at rugby clubs, pubs, male voice choirs, schools, churches...' He shrugged, as if it was the most normal thing in the world, to spontaneously burst into communal song, and brought out two steaming dishes of pasta, bubbling with golden cheese. Four baguettes wrapped in foil joined the pasta, and Beryl put out a couple of bowls of salad, and some dressing.

'Beryl and I did most of this yesterday,' Jo said, in answer to Flora's question. Once the children had eaten their fill, they were allowed to leave the table, and play on the Xbox in the lounge as the adults chatted.

'Get in line for hairdressing, young Jake,' Ed said, eyeing Flora and Jake perceptively. 'She already has a fan club.' There was laughter around the table.

Taking hold of Jake's hand again, Flora leaned forward. 'But Jake was the first. He'll always be my special customer.'

'Yes, and I've got the scars to prove it,' Jake said laconically, holding her gaze with eyes that crinkled at the edges. Flora heard the laughter, saw the knowing glances travelling round the table and smiled. Sitting beside Jake, listening and looking round at their animated faces, Flora felt as if she'd finally found her tribe.

Chapter Twenty-Six

Jake looked forward to seeing Flora at breakfast. As he tied his apron on, he qualified that. There hadn't yet been a time when he wasn't looking forward to seeing Flora. She was always surprising.

When she'd told him the previous evening that Spence had come down, he had jumped straight to the assumption that she was going back with him. It didn't register in that moment of madness that she was still there, in Wales. He'd felt a bit stupid when he'd thought it through, but in that instant, his mind had processed that *he* would have come after her and wanted her back. *He* would have fought to have her back, grovelled, whatever it took, and so why wouldn't Spence? What on earth had possessed the man to have gone behind her back with her sister, of all people?

He'd be the first to admit that he hardly knew Flora, and undoubtedly she probably had faults. Everyone had faults. Some you could live with and some you couldn't. But she had energy. And courage. And she made him laugh. And he'd wanted so much to scoop her into his arms after dinner last night and bear her away to his castle. Except that his bed needed changing and his room was a pigsty and at the end of the day she'd just kicked her bloke into touch and he didn't want her on the rebound. He could be patient. He was good at patience.

After breakfast had been cooked and served, he was surprised when she refused her own breakfast.

'I'm saving myself for later. I've finally booked my afternoon tea!' She peeped around her and lowered her voice. 'At the Art Café. Do you fancy it?' Her face, upturned to his and slightly pink from rushing about all morning, looked soft and kissable. What was it she'd asked him?

'Yes! Er, afternoon tea, yes. What time would that be?'

'Two o'clock. This afternoon.' She flicked him with a tea towel. 'Jake. Are you in there? Flora to Jake, come in Jake, over.'

'Oh! Sorry, I was just organising myself.' He caught the tea towel as she was aiming for a second flick and she dodged away as he menaced her with a return match. 'A wardrobe door is hanging off its hinges in room ten, and a chest of drawers seems to have collapsed in room two. What on earth do people do in their rooms? I'm still working my way round the ivy – although I'm starting to think that's what's holding the entire building together. And I've got some other stuff to do later.'

'It sounds busy.' Flora regarded him with a smile, her head on one side. She shrugged. 'All the more for me then. It was a short notice invite, to be fair.'

'I'm sorry. What are your plans for today?'

'I'm going to have a look round Mumbles at some potential properties for salons. Find out what the prices are, register with some estate agents, that sort of thing.'

'So, this means you're staying longer then?'

'I'd really like to. Having it out with Spence made my mind up. I feel like I have a fresh page now. So, somewhere to live has to be a priority, of course. But I'll live in a caravan if I have to. I've seen some advertised, and if I'm going to stay, I need to sort myself out.'

Jake folded the tea towel she'd whacked him with earlier, and dropped it in the laundry. 'You, Flora, are one determined woman. Have a fab day. I look forward to hearing all about it at the dinner shift!'

She untied her pinny, flinging it after the tea towel into the laundry. 'See you later.' With a grin, she blew a kiss at him and was gone. Jake watched the door swinging behind her for a while, as his brain whirred, and then went in search of his grandparents.

* * *

Flora, on her familiar Ninja, felt a bubble of excitement and marvelled that her life had turned around in such a short time. Although nothing physical had happened, just feeling positive about being in charge of her own future made her realise how unhappy she'd been for such a long time. As she turned right to head down Mumbles main street, her breath caught in her throat at the sight of the sea, a brilliant and mesmerising patch of sunlight caught between the far coast and the narrow Victorian buildings. The high street was already busy with traffic and she negotiated it carefully, finding a car park at the bottom, overlooking the bay. She'd spotted a couple of estate agents at the very top of the hill, but it had been impossible to see any empty shops as she'd navigated her way past random shoppers and cars pulling out.

The tide was out and as she removed her helmet she had to shade her eyes, dazzled by the sunlight reflecting in wet pools on the expanse of beach. She leaned on the short wall, taking it all in as the sun warmed her shoulders. Breathing in the indefinable scents of sea and blossom took her back to her childhood. It was a shame her mum hadn't moved here and lived in the cottage after the divorce. She could have grown up here.

It felt like worlds away from home. Much more than the hundred and fifty miles or so that it actually was. She wondered briefly if Spence had got home okay, and was surprised to find she still cared. His words rolled round her brain. Had they lived separate lives? It wasn't possible to live in each other's pockets all the time. You'd drive each other mad, wouldn't you? She hadn't minded that he worked at home, and he'd never apparently minded that she had regular nights out with the girls from work. She must remember to ring Karlie for a chat. As her brain randomly threw distractions at her, she struggled to unravel what had gone wrong with her and Spence's relationship.

They'd met through biking, and hung out in a big group of other bikers. As time had gone on, he'd replaced his bike with increasingly powerful versions and on rides together he'd roar off and then wait for her in a layby, some miles on. She had stopped finding it fun, and so had he. She hadn't wanted to be in debt to a more expensive bike when they were still living in a rented house, and she'd pushed away the nagging doubt that he wanted the same goals as her. She'd wanted security – and in a shard of self-illumination, she realised that she was happier here, homeless and jobless, than she'd been in the last few years with Spence. She was steering her own boat, at last, and far from feeling lonely, she felt a wonderful sense of peace and belonging. She stretched, lifting her face to the sun, and strolled towards the high street.

It was a thoughtful Flora who pushed open the door to the sunny Art Café later that afternoon. Jo greeted her with a smile.

'Hi, Flora! Ready for your afternoon tea?'

'I certainly am. I've been exploring Mumbles for a potential salon.'

'Any luck?' Jo placed a tray on the counter along with a chunky lime green teapot that held loose-leaf tea in an infuser.

'Ooh! I love this teapot. I would've had tea before now if I'd known about these.' Flora bent and sniffed the contents appreciatively. 'There's something about tea in the afternoon, isn't there? It sort of grounds you.'

'Uh-oh.' Jo placed the cup and saucer along with a tiny milk churn of milk alongside the teapot. 'Do you need grounding?'

'My head is spinning with ideas, yes. I can't afford any of the properties for the moment. But now I've made some baby steps towards making it a reality. So it's all good.'

Jo's eyes flicked over Flora's shoulder indicating another

customer, and she said hurriedly, 'If you want to talk your ideas over any time, you've got my number.' She raised her voice slightly. 'I'll bring your sandwiches and cake over as soon as it's ready.' She turned her professional smile on the customer behind and Flora bore her tray to one of the tables by the window, so she could indulge herself in what was becoming one of her favourite pastimes, staring over the beach.

It was half term, and there were many families taking advantage of the sunshine, kicking a ball about and having picnics. Jo brought over her afternoon tea and placed it on the table.

'Wow! Oh my goodness, this is stunning! I have to take a photo.' There was a variety of tiny muffins, and finger slices of chocolate cake, lemon drizzle and scones, alongside cute triangles of sandwiches with the crusts cut off, all served on the most beautiful stand. 'Is this hand painted?' Flora turned it to see better. It was decorated with swirls of colour. One tier bore sea colours, and the top tier looked as if it had been inspired by a seaside garden.

'It is!' Jo nodded. 'We're testing them and hoping to sell them here too.' She looked over the beach. 'Is that your Jake down there?'

Flora felt her face heat at Jo's expression. 'My Jake?' She followed Jo's pointing finger, and saw his unmistakeable figure on the sand by the Lifeguard Clubhouse, amongst a group of youngsters. 'It is! He said he had something to do this afternoon, or he'd be helping me eat this lot. I wonder why he didn't mention it.'

Jo laughed. 'Well, there's your entertainment while you enjoy your tea! He's certainly good to look at.'

Flora watched Jake as she enjoyed choosing which sandwich to munch. They'd all gone into the clubhouse, emerging in wetsuits and carrying surfboards. There was another adult there, and she recognised the tall, willowy figure of Karen, who'd loaned her wetsuit to Flora. She dismissed the sharp pang of jealousy as ridiculous. She didn't own Jake. Although she'd very much liked the sound of 'your Jake'. She counted the children. Six? Was that a reasonable ratio if they were going in the sea? She could see that Jake was talking to them, and the children's faces turned upwards, clearly listening. Another adult joined them, and she was annoyed with herself that she relaxed. She watched as Jake had the children lying on their boards and then springing upright to a crouched position. They looked as if they were all having fun. By the time she needed another pot of tea to drink with the cakes, they were all trotting towards the water's edge, and she had to crane her neck to see them. She thought she understood why Jake hadn't mentioned it. It was therapy. She silently applauded him and her stomach tightened. It was a brave move. She hoped it was going well.

She spent the rest of the afternoon back at the cottage, chatting over her ideas to her mum. Then she rang Karlie, who had news about Rex.

'He's going!'

'You are kidding me.' Flora felt her jaw drop. 'Where?"

Karlie's laughter gurgled down the phone. 'After you'd gone, we all got together, like we should've done months ago, confronted him and said we were sick of his pawing, and that we'd prosecute him for sexual assault if he didn't change his ways. And we'd name and shame him on Facebook if we had to.' Flora felt her eyebrows lift to the roots of her hair. So, if they'd all done this sooner, maybe she'd still be working there... but then she wouldn't have found Jake, and everyone at the Art Café...

'What's happening to the lease? Who's paying for that?'

'We've still got to put it to the landlord, but it looks like we can have the lease reassigned. So, young Flora...' She paused and Flora's brain windmilled. 'Are you interested?

Want to come in with us? You've always wanted your own salon. What do you think?'

'Oh God, Karlie... I've just spent the whole day walking up and down Mumbles High Street looking for premises and enjoying the sunshine and the sea.' She paused. She could almost hear Karlie's disapproval.

'Mumbles? What kind of place name is that?'

'It's lovely! There's a castle, and a huuuge beach, and boats and a pier and—'

'It's a "no" from Flora then.'

'Oh, Karlie.' Flora chewed the inside of her mouth. 'It's so sudden!'

'What, and you swanning off down there to the land of weird names isn't sudden?'

'I've met... someone.'

'Already?' Karlie yelled down the phone. 'You've only just dumped that dickhead Spence!'

'Yeah. I know. And I don't know where this is going, and I don't even have anywhere to live when I leave the cottage, but—' She paused, gazing out of the window over the cobalt sea, gilded by the setting sun. 'I'm not ready to leave here. It's been decades since I left, and I... I love it here. I've always loved it. Please don't be angry with me. I need to try and follow my dreams.'

'I'm sorry. I'm being selfish. I miss you!'

'Awww. I've only been gone a week. Barely.'

'Yeah. But...' Karlie had huffed down the phone, and then said, 'I get it. I do. Live your best life, Flora Bexton. Maybe I'll come and visit you when you've got yourself sorted.'

They chatted some more and blew kisses at each other before hanging up, and Flora readied herself for the dinner shift at Hotel yr Ddraig.

Her first question to Jake was, 'How was the surf class?'

'You saw then?' He went a bit pink beneath his white cap, which she thought was quite endearing. 'I only realised that you'd see it through the windows of the café when I was there.'

'So?'

He nodded. 'It was good.' His face split into a broad grin. 'It was better than good. I did it as a one off, for the club kids, and, of course, most of them know me, or know of me, so they were good as gold. And I had Karen and Geoff as responsible adults.'

'I couldn't really see you once you were in the sea. Did they get on okay?'

'Yes! They can all swim like fish – but most of them managed to get to their feet, even if it was only for a second.'

'Well done, Jake! I bet they loved you.'

Their eyes met for the briefest moment, and Flora felt her mouth go dry. The dinner waitress bustled in with the first lot of orders and they were too busy to say anything other than 'More chips needed!' and 'Do you think that's cooked properly?'

Luckily there weren't too many diners, and Flora felt exhausted by the time everyone had been served.

'We're going to need a system, I think.' She stared at the washing-up that had piled up around them. The young dinner waitress, Amy, swung in with the last lot of cleared plates.

'Well done you two. I know it wasn't exactly top cuisine tonight, but there were no complaints from anyone. I think people have realised we've got a bit of a crisis and they're just happy not to have to go out somewhere else.' She looked around the kitchen. 'Bloody hell. Is there a pot you didn't use?'

Jake rubbed a hand over his face and laughed. He blew out a long breath. 'Don't worry. I'll sort it out. You girls get off home.'

Flora and Amy exchanged glances. 'Many hands make

light work!' Amy said, pulling on a pair of gloves. 'Let's have some music though, huh?' She switched the radio on, and the three of them worked companionably and efficiently until the kitchen was once again spotless.

'See you tomorrow!' Amy sang out, disappearing through the swing door.

'It's dark now. Let me walk you home.' Jake threw his jacket and apron into the laundry basket. Flora opened her mouth to say she'd be fine and then closed it again. That short walk back to the cottage together was exactly the right way to finish off the day. And his quick hug, and kiss on the cheek, along with his soft, 'Thank you, see you in the morning,' left her feeling gooey inside and looking forward to doing it all over again the next day.

Flora and Jake had just finished the breakfast service the following morning, when Molly and Bryn came into the kitchen.

'Good morning!' Flora beamed at them both.

Without preamble, Molly said, 'Flora, I don't know what you might think of this. We can't afford to give you one of our paying guest rooms, but we have some little rooms in our wing that used to be for the servants, back in the day. They're rather sweet, I've always thought, but... well, anyway, you can have a look for yourself. If you're interested, then you could either pay a peppercorn rent,' she took a breath, and continued, 'Or you can work here for board and lodgings.'

Flora's mouth closed slowly. Her eyes flicked towards Jake and she saw him smother a grin.

'Did you know about this?'

He shrugged. 'Maybe.'

Flora focused on Molly. 'That's so kind of you. All of you.' She knuckled her eyes and reached for a roll of kitchen paper. 'Could I have a look at the rooms, please?'

'I'll just finish up here and then I'll join you,' Jake said.

Flora followed Molly and Bryn, her eyes wide, through the narrow corridors and up some winding old wooden stairs. The corridor became more worn as they progressed, carpet became flagstones, the centre shiny from more than a hundred years of foot traffic and wallpaper had long given way to cream painted walls, yellowed with age. There was a faint smell that reminded her of her grandparents, a certain soap, although she couldn't remember exactly what it was.

'Here's the first one.' Molly pushed open a door, and Flora peeped in, her heart thumping in anticipation of whatever ancient horror might lie within.

A bare, cream enamelled antique metal bedstead stood on a dusky pink, patterned rug, on a sea of polished dark floorboards. There was a chest of drawers and a desk in the same dark wood with a pretty, antique brass lamp, a wheelback chair and a wardrobe opposite. A few old and rather pretty paintings were lit by a beautiful chandelier. Charmed already, Flora walked towards the casement window, draped with faded cream and blue flowered curtains and a pelmet and gasped as she looked out over the trees and shrubs of the garden and a panoramic view of the sea.

'I love it. But surely this wasn't a servant's room? It's so pretty! Look at the fireplace and the chandelier!' She bent to inspect the fireplace further. A cream painted wooden surround framed curved crimson tiles within which sat snugly a black hearth. She felt as if she'd stepped back in time and if she looked out of the window now, she'd see ladies in long dresses and parasols and gentlemen courting them from a distance.

'It was probably the housekeeper,' Molly said. 'There are some really tiny rooms right under the eaves, but we use them mostly for storage. These have had a bit of an upgrade since their servant days anyway, hence the chandelier. Can you believe, we used to be so full that we let these out too. If you're sure you like it, we'll sort out a mattress, and your fresh bed linen and towels will be part of the deal.'

'Could I see the bathroom, please?' Flora asked. 'Is it on this floor?'

'It's next door,' Molly said, leading the way as Jake joined them. 'We designed these rooms as singles. It made better sense to have them sharing a bathroom than to go to the expense of en suite.'

The bathroom was dated but working and there was a shower over the bath.

'I love that bedroom. Should I look at the other one?'

Bryn laughed. 'Choices, choices,' he said, leading the way along the passage a little further. He opened a door and stood back to let her look.

It was quite similar to the first one, but a smaller window and the bathroom was further away. Flora made her decision there and then.

'Thank you. The first one is my favourite. But first, I need to know how much you'd want, or what sort of work I'd need to do for it. I mean, I'm completely unskilled for hotel work. And I want to be able to build up my hairdressing business, so I can't work all day and evening.' She put her hand over her mouth as she saw Molly blink rapidly. 'Sorry, I'm gabbling, and I probably sound terribly ungrateful...'

'But you are at least honest, and we are coming to appreciate that about you,' Molly said with a smile. 'Could we count on you for the breakfast service and this week's temporary dinner menu? And then helping out with the cleaning, chambermaiding and reception as required. I'm sure there will be other areas in which you can be useful. We can be flexible. We'll draw up some hours, a kind of contract, that sort of thing, and perhaps if your hairdressing takes off then you could pay rent instead. But keep us posted and we can sort that out before it becomes an issue. Two weeks notice on either side?'

Flora thought for a moment. It represented security for the time being, an opportunity to learn some new skills. It didn't escape her notice that it also meant seeing more of Jake…

'Yes, please. I'd love to take it on. Thank you. I feel so lucky. Thank you. Don't you need references or something? You don't really know me…'

'From what we have seen we think we know enough and trust our judgment.'

'Oh.' There was a lump in Flora's throat.

'When are you leaving your mother's cottage?'

'Saturday. Will that be okay?'

Molly nodded. 'Saturday will be perfect.' She left with Bryn, and Jake and Flora stayed for a little longer, while Flora clicked off a few photos to send her mum.

'You're a dark horse.' She gently knuckled his solid bicep and he flexed it, cocking his eyebrow in a mock bodybuilder stance.

'I am. What are your plans today?'

'I'm vegging out and sunbathing on the beach while we still have this amazing weather.'

'I might come by and kick sand over you later, if I'm free.'

'Pah. You could try.' She leaned out of the window for one last look and then left. This time she paid more attention to where she was going as they wound down the ancient stairs.

'I'll have to buy some chalk and put arrows so I can find my way to my room!'

'You wouldn't be the first!' They parted at the bottom. 'See ya later!'

Flora jogged back to the cottage on springy legs. She had somewhere to live! Molly liked her! She might see Jake later! She was a step closer to having her salon! She was – oh crap – she was still spying on the hotel… she walked the remaining few steps to the cottage, deep in guilt.

She rang her dad and brought him up to date.

'That's great news, sweet pea. Well done. Were there more rooms up there?' She began to tell him and then stuttered to a stop. 'Dad, you're not planning to just knock it into apartments, are you?'

There was a pause. 'Why do you ask?'

Flora saw her reflection in the polished glass oven door, waving her arm about and glaring. 'Because it's their home! And it's a hub for the community! And... and... it's beautiful. It's a piece of history.'

'Even history needs a helping hand occasionally, sweet pea.'

'I just feel guilty, taking their kindness and repaying them by passing their secrets on.'

'First of all, you're working for them, so they're not just being kind. And knowing you, they'll be getting their money's worth and more. And second, you haven't told me anything I hadn't guessed. You're just confirming a few things. And they might not even accept my offer anyway. So stop feeling guilty. Okay?'

'Okay.' They chatted a little longer, and Flora hung up, feeling better. She decided to go and enjoy the sunshine while she could.

A few hours later, in the scorching heat on the strip of beach at the front of the cottage, a sudden shadow made her shiver. Shading her eyes, she squinted up – and leapt to her feet with a shriek as she saw Jake holding a bucket of water over her. A Jake wearing a pair of board shorts and a loose white T-shirt that made his tan look mahogany. His teeth, bared in a wicked grin, looked fluorescent.

'I wouldn't have,' he said, lowering the bucket and looking her up and down. She determined not to follow his gaze. Her visit to the supermarket for additions to her meagre wardrobe had included an impulse buy bikini, and today was its first airing outside the changing room. 'I'm only here in my capacity as lifeguard to check that you're wearing sun tan lotion, ma'am.'

'Oh, I am, yes.' She looked down at herself and screamed as sunlight glittered off the water from the bucket a second before it splashed over her hot skin.

'Gotcha!' He sprinted towards the sea, and she pursued him, laughing as he looked over his shoulder and realised how close she was. At the water's edge she flung herself full length at him and he toppled forward into the shallows.

'You rat!' she panted, flopping to her knees beside him. He didn't move. 'Jake?' She pushed his shoulder. 'Jake! Don't mess about. Jake! Oh God, Jake!' She heaved at his shoulder to turn him over but he was so heavy and then with a groan, his great arm lifted and he rolled onto his back, pulling her with him. She saw his lazy grin and pummelled his chest with relief. 'You're a shit, Jake. I thought I'd...' She stopped as their eyes met.

For a long moment their faces were inches apart, before the next wave crashed into them, knocking her over and dousing them both in cold seawater.

He set her on her feet and said, 'Can you body surf? Just do what I do. Last one in buys the ice creams.' He held her prone and gave her a mighty shove beachwards as the next wave approached. She held her body straight, spluttering with mock rage as he surged effortlessly past her. He turned and waded back towards her, drawing her upright.

'Sorry, another surf class. See you later!' He turned and jogged back up the beach, and she watched his toned body until he was out of sight.

Flora kicked the water in frustration, her body thoroughly awoken. She turned and ran back into the waves with a smile. At least now she had somewhere to live she could practise some body surfing.

Chapter Twenty-Seven

On Saturday morning after her waitressing stint, she locked the cottage and garage with a lump in her throat. She'd enjoyed the previous day to herself in the sunshine, between her kitchen shifts.

Jake had said she could leave her bike in his shed, behind the hotel. Her pulse thundered in her chest as she rode there, trying not to look at the gravel and potholes. If you look at it, you hit it, the mantra repeated itself in her head, so she focused on Jake instead, timing her revs to tackle the upward slope into the cleared space. A little sweaty with relief, she put the side stand down.

'Are you going to turn it round, ready to go out?' Jake tipped his head to one side. 'Only there isn't another bike to steal in here when you want to go out for your next chip run...'

Flora huffed. She eyed the space. Not quite enough room to push it in a U-turn. She'd have to manoeuvre it. She squared her shoulders. She'd managed it in the cottage garage, although that had been completely empty. She could do it here. She could. Totally. She climbed off, feeling clammy with nerves.

She leaned the bike into her and pushed it tentatively, squealing as she felt the bike dropping away from her. Jake was alongside the bike in a flash.

'What do I do?'

'Just stop it falling on the floor!' Flora puffed and grunted and pushed the bike a tiny bit forward and a tiny bit back and stopped to take her jacket off because she was so hot. 'Gah!' She glared at the bike. 'Why is this so difficult? I see women my size pushing bikes about in the dealers without any effort at all! Why can't I do it?' She fell short of stamping her foot, but she did it in her head. Jake was silent. It was a welcome alternative to the pompous mansplaining she'd always got from Spence. He'd spent ages showing her how easy it was to manoeuvre a bike, and then every time she did it, he'd leapt towards her in a panic that she was going to drop it. Consequently she didn't have an ounce of confidence in herself. And she knew that no one would believe that about her, but dropping a twenty-five stone bike was a pretty big deal. And her Ninja was so much lighter than the big Ducati.

'You can do this,' Jake murmured. 'I'll just stand here so you don't strain yourself trying to hold it up if it goes.'

Flora flicked her eyes towards him and nodded her thanks. She was quite sure that he could tuck this bike under his arm and carry it round the garage. She had never felt so feeble. It wasn't about strength though, was it? It was technique. And determination. And she had one, even if she didn't yet possess the other.

Hours passed as she continued to push and pull, or at least, that's how it felt.

'I can't do it.'

'Yes you can.' Now he was being kind, and that was worse.

'I need to keep it upright and let it roll.' She rotated her shoulders, noticing them round her ears and forced herself to relax. 'Right, come on, you bitch. I'm in charge here.' Lifting the bike to vertical off the side stand, she tightened her core and pushed forward. Maybe the bike sensed that she really meant it this time, because it rolled forward.

'Ooh!' She squeaked. 'Sorry I called you a "bitch", bike!'

Turning the bars, she rolled backwards, and then forwards, and as sweat from her forehead threatened to drip into her eyes, she finally got the bike facing outwards. She tipped it carefully onto the side stand and then threw her arms in the air and did a little silent dance.

'I bloody did it!' She stopped mid-jig and eyed him. 'You didn't help me, did you?'

'Me?' Jake raised his eyebrows. 'After you threatened that poor defenceless machine I stayed well out of it. That was all you.'

'Thank you.'

'I told you. I didn't do anything!' His protests stopped as she impulsively stretched up and planted her lips on his.

'What was that?' he said, his green-blue eyes on hers, unblinking.

Pink faced, she said, 'That was for not bossing me about and "telling" me how to do it and then doing it yourself. I feel like I could do anything now.' Feeling silly beneath his unwavering gaze, she went into a jokey wrestling pose, and added a 'grr,' for better effect.

Mid 'grr', he reached out and pulled her towards him. She was on tiptoe, her mouth millimetres from his.

'What I meant was…' He dipped his head and she closed her eyes as his lips rested softly on hers. 'That wasn't a kiss. *This*, is a kiss…' One hand cradled the nape of her neck and the other wrapped right around her, pulling her into him. Her body melted into his and her hands slipped around his firm, slim waist, feeling the smooth, long muscles of his back working beneath her fingers. He smelled nice. He always smelled nice. Her mouth opened and his tongue gently licked her lips and then it was inside her mouth and it was as if they were one person and she was aware of every part of him, the feel of his soft stubbly beard, his ribs moving as he breathed, the hardening of his groin against her, his shifting weight as he gathered her up more tightly.

They might have stayed there all morning if Jake hadn't given her a regretful hug, holding her slightly away. She whimpered, shamelessly, holding her arms high towards his neck, and he bent to kiss her again.

'I'm sorry, lovely girl. I've got a list of jobs as long as your—'

'This long?' she interrupted, pushing her hips provocatively against his and waggling her eyebrows suggestively. 'Aw, Jake. Can't I be on your list?'

'Later. I promise. Later.' He chuckled, folding her back into his arms for a moment and then releasing her with a groan. 'Right, come on, let's get you into your room.'

'That's "later", isn't it? I mean, only five minutes, but it's still later...' She peeped up at him out of the corners of her eyes, fluttering her eyelashes.

'What? No, you shameless hussy.' He laughed. 'I mean, much later. Oh, you know what I mean! Let me get your rucksack.'

'So you let me push a twenty stone motorbike about, but I can't carry my own rucksack?' She laughed, but handed it to him anyway. It felt nice to be looked after, for a change.

Her attic room had been cleaned and made up with fresh bed linen and towels. There was a small television on the chest of drawers. It was so homely and welcoming now.

She stared at the bed, and then up at him, her eyes travelling the broad shoulders and muscular arms and visualising herself held within them.

'Where is your room?'

'Not far, it's—' He stopped and looked at her, his eyes narrowed. 'Oh no. You're a bad girl.' He seized her and planted a kiss on her mouth, lifting her up onto ballet points. She nuzzled into his neck.

'Please don't leave me,' she bleated pitifully. 'I'm all alone...' She felt his chuckle vibrate through his chest.

'If there's one thing I know about you, Flora, it's that you won't be alone for very long. Go and explore. There are always people here, doing something. Join in! They're sure to love you.' He paused, his eyes dark, and then said, with a sigh, 'I have to go. Ancient boilers and old plumbing wait for no man. Room Sixteen has a blockage. God knows what that is. But I'll be back.' His expression sent a wave of lust through her entire body, despite the thought of a blockage, which sounded revolting.

'Go! Be useful!' Flora waved him off and then set to work, arranging her few possessions. She bounced on the bed, her body still tingling from Jake's touch. Her emotions crashed about like the sea she could see from the window, and she felt a bit lost and disorientated. She'd do what he suggested and go and explore.

Wandering down the stairs, she found herself in the smallest sitting room, amongst a group of about a dozen people, all of whom seemed to be draped in knitting, brightly coloured balls of wool clashing with the faded rug.

'Hello.' The speaker was a small, elderly woman. Only her head seemed visible over a mound of wool. 'Are you a knitter?'

'Not really. Well, actually, no. My gran tried to teach me, but...'

'Crochet?'

Flora shook her head with regret.

'Would you like to learn?'

'We have tea.' Another voice piped up from a corner of the room.

'And cake,' said another.

Flora's eyes travelled around the gathering. She took in the intricate pieces and the different flower shapes. 'Are you the yarn bombers?'

The busy needles stopped and they all looked at each other.

'What have you heard?' This was a man. His eyes slid from side to side.

'Oh, Brian. Stop being such a drama queen. King.

Whatever.' The group laughed and Brian subsided. 'So, how long have you got, young lady?'

Flora checked her watch and said, slightly guarded, 'A couple of hours, I suppose.'

The grey-haired lady delved into a capacious bag and brought out a crochet hook, and two vibrant balls of yarn. 'Magenta or turquoise?'

'Um... magenta, please. What glorious colours!'

'I'm Anwen. We've got fifteen minutes before tea and cake, and you can learn to cast on by then. Come along and sit down.'

Flora did as she was told, once again feeling as if she'd blundered into a bygone age, as she held the hook, wound the soft, brilliant pink yarn round her fingers and listened intently to Anwen's instructions. By teatime she'd produced a long, wavy length of chain, and couldn't have been more proud of herself. She also had a much bigger appreciation of the complex motifs that hung from the trees.

'Can I help?' she asked Anwen, as the older lady announced, 'Teatime!', pushing herself out of the armchair.

'Of course you can! We always need young blood.'

Flora followed Anwen, wondering how this was going to work.

Anwen led them into another room that seemed to belong to the back part of the hotel, like her bedroom. A sort of un-modernised secret room, long and thin, with a single glazed door that led out to the garden, and was simply kitted out with a painted dresser bearing cups and plates, an ancient stone sink and counter, a kettle, and several large cake tins.

'Could you fill the kettle... um?' Anwen paused, eyebrows raised, head tipped.

'Flora.'

'That's a pretty name.' Anwen put three trays out and assembled the cups on them. 'Not a name you hear these days.'

'Mum loves flowers. She's a florist.' As Flora filled the kettle to the top, she watched as Anwen brought out spoons and big knives from the deep drawers of the dresser. 'This is a handy room.'

'Yes. It's the Residents' Kitchen.'

'Are you all residents, then?'

'Goodness me, no.' Anwen laughed. 'But we've been coming here for so long, we may as well be.'

'Do you remember Jake coming here?' Flora poured the boiling water into an array of china teapots, turning to refill the kettle.

'Aah, yes. We all do. Poor little mite.' Anwen folded her arms, and stared out of the door. 'Such sad times for the family. I remember them getting married.'

'Who?'

'The daughter!' Anwen said in a, 'Keep up!', voice.

'Is Jake like her?'

'He was. She was a stunner. But I tell you who he is the absolute spit of at his age now.'

'Who?'

'Bryn. His grandad.' Anwen leaned forward. 'Now, he was a looker, I tell you. Just like young Jake. But goodness me.' Her voice lowered. 'Him on that bike! Used to race, so he did. Big, in his time. Marvellous, he was.' She sighed. 'Shame, really.'

The kettle boiled, and as if Anwen had completely forgotten what they were talking about, she instructed Flora how to make the tea, and then sailed into the sitting room with the cake tins, leaving Flora with three trays laden with heavy teapots and cups. Her mind whirled. Maybe she could find out exactly what had prompted Molly to stop Bryn racing.

Flora learned a lot in the next hour, but none of it was to do with Jake or his grandad.

She was inordinately thrilled, however, with her crochet achievements, and when the group packed up and left, she remained in the sitting room, concentrating on the hook dipping in and out of the bright yarn.

Staring out over the gardens, she imagined what it must have been like there, fifty or sixty years ago. Before central heating. When the motorbikes were Nortons and BSAs, Triumphs and Royal Enfields.

Carefully winding her crochet up, and stabbing the borrowed hook through it, she took herself for a walk around the hotel gardens

She was entranced by the rambling grounds, the creaking wishing gates that led from one garden to the next, each bounded by borders waiting to burst into bloom. There were garden seats positioned to best catch the views, and Flora wandered over the too long grass to inspect the yarn bombed benches. With a much better appreciation, born of her afternoon's tuition, she marvelled at the clever stitching. The grounds rose up behind the hotel, as she'd suspected from her marathon paddle with Jake, and she walked to the highest point and turned to look over the sea.

She caught her breath. It was magical. The late afternoon sunlight threw apricot rays over the turquoise waves, their lacy fringes fanned out across the bay. Just as she'd thought, she could see the Art Café dead ahead, see the people inside eating and drinking. She pulled her phone out and took some shots, winging them off to her dad.

There was a message from her mum, thanking her for the postcard, and was she okay? Lots of kisses.

She sent back a jolly text with the photo that she'd just taken, and added a little face with rolling eyes. What her mum always called an 'emomi' and in her head now, so did Flora.

A reply pinged from her dad, Take care X.

She wished she'd made another cup of tea, and that it was a big mug, not a cup, so that she could bring it out here and sip it on one of those colourful benches and just listen to the roaring sea, with the sun on her face. It was the most relaxed she'd felt in a very long time. She thought how lovely it would be to be able to paint this, like her mum. Or to bring a novel out and just sit, enjoying the sounds of the gulls overhead. Or, she remembered, maybe some wool, and a hook...

She and Jake weren't doing the carvery on Sunday. From Monday, it would be all be down to the new chef, and she probably wouldn't be needed at all. Tonight would be her last evening shift.

She pulled the bright wool out of her pocket, and sat in the sunshine, crocheting, for all the world like an Edwardian lady, and as her fingers worked, so did her brain.

In the kitchen that evening, Jake crossed the space between them in a couple of long strides and wrapped her into his arms. He hadn't seen her since the morning, and he'd driven himself mad thinking about her. She lifted her pointed little chin to him and he kissed her thoroughly. Cupping her firm bottom with one hand, he was eyeing the worktop with a lascivious eye when she pushed him away a little.

'Aprons on and handwashing.'

'Ooh,' he said, putting his arms around her to tie her apron, as she giggled helplessly. 'I love it when you're bossy.'

The food must have cooked itself as they stopped just sort of actually having sex throughout the entire preparation. Not being able to touch each other simply made it more erotic, and by the time the service was over, he was ready to burst.

He untied the apron he'd tied earlier and she leaned into him.

'Are we supposed to lock up?' she said, ever practical. He chuckled.

'Yes. Front door is shut at ten, but guests have a key.' He looked down at her. 'Why? Does that worry you?'

'Me? No.' She shook her head emphatically. 'Noooo.' She frowned at him. 'Yes! I've never lived somewhere that doesn't lock the front door!'

'We used to have a twenty-four hour reception, when we were full all the time,' Jake said.

'I know the answer to this before I ask – but no electronic keys or anything?'

'Nope. Just old-fashioned lock and key type keys.'

'What if someone loses their entrance key?'

'If they ring the bell to get one of us up to let them in, we charge them and we pelt them with Danish pastries at breakfast the following morning.'

She frowned at him and regretting his flippancy, he said, 'I lied about the Danish pastries. That would be a waste. And we make a judgement about the charge, it depends on their attitude.' He took her hand. 'I already locked up. Come on, I'll show you how our bit locks too.' And then I can take you to bed and no baddies will be able to get to you, he added in his head. He was touched that she'd momentarily shown her fear. If he'd suggested she was scared, she'd probably have whacked him with something and stamped up the stairs, protesting loudly that she was scared of absolutely nothing.

He kissed her, led her through the fire door that led to their wing, locked it and kissed her again. They squeezed awkwardly side by side along the narrow passage until Jake did what he'd been wanting to do all day and swept her into his arms and carried her up the stairs, their lips fused. At her door, he set her gently down while she fumbled for the key and unlocked it. She stepped inside.

'Goodnight,' she said, shutting the door. He blinked. What? The door opened a nanosecond later. 'Just kidding,' she said, grabbing the front of his belt and flipping the buckle open. 'Get in here.'

'What would you have done,' he said, much later, into her sleepy ear, as they lay with their arms wrapped around each other, 'if you'd opened that door, and I'd gone?'

'I would have come after you,' Flora murmured. She stroked his chest and he trapped her small hand with his much larger one.

'You don't know where my room is.'

'I'd find you. I'm very resourceful.' She threaded her fingers through his and draped her knee across his hips.

'Ouch. Mini me can only take so much of a bashing, y'know.' He reached down to rearrange her and she lifted herself onto him, her mouth on his. 'And you've given him a proper work out, you little minx.'

'Oh, dear.' She slithered down a little, her tongue following, and he felt his groin respond. 'I'll just have to kiss it better then...'

Flora woke first the following morning, as the sun beamed through the curtains that they hadn't bothered to draw. She felt her skin against his and revelled in it, pushing her bottom into his lap. He tightened his grip and she grinned.

He growled softly into her ear, 'You are not having me this morning. You're a sex pest.'

'Ooh, a challenge! I like a challenge.' She wriggled round in his arms to face him, planting kisses on his handsome, sleep softened, adorable face. His eyes remained resolutely shut. He was... unbelievable. She couldn't believe how lucky she was.

'If we don't get up, your gran will come looking for us.'

He was still, and even with his eyes closed, she saw his brain working.

'Okaaaay.' Levering himself up, he threw the covers back and clambered out of the bed, and then opened his eyes.

'Mini-Jake is awake…' She grinned at him, watching his gaze follow hers.

'I don't fancy you,' he said. 'It's just biology.'

'Yeah, right,' she said, wrapping her arms around his waist as he yawned mightily.

'Unhand me, woman,' he said, without conviction. They showered together, to save time. It didn't. They emerged into the kitchen dazed and giggly.

'I want you later, in that apron,' he whispered into her ear when she returned with the first breakfast order. 'And nothing else.'

She left an order, straight-faced, in the grab bar that was simply a very rude drawing. At the end of service, she felt exhausted.

'I need a nap,' she told him, as they scrubbed and wiped the kitchen clean.

'Me too,' he said, the lascivious glint in his eye indicating anything but.

'You'll have to carry me up to bed again. I'm wrecked.'

He waggled his eyebrows at her, and swept her up, pulling at her apron strings with his teeth and making her giggle.

It turned out, neither of them were as tired as they thought, but Flora had set the alarm on her phone this time, and they awoke refreshed and yawning a few hours later, rain beating against the window, and adding to the feeling of cosy intimacy. His smooth, muscular shoulder was beneath her head and she turned her head and bit it, gently.

'Ouch,' he said, not meaning it. She opened her mouth for another bite and then said, 'We have a night off tonight. Shall we cook something that's not "prick and ping" for your folks?'

'I just want to eat you.'

'Oh, sir,' she simpered. 'I'm just a lowly kitchen maid!'

'And very insubordinate too – I saw that drawing!'

She giggled and wriggled against him impatiently. She didn't have to wait long.

Only hunger drove them from the room, later in the afternoon. Scampering down the stairs, they ran into the cool, damp, salty air and onto the beach. Holding hands, they pushed open the door of the Art Café and stepped into the warm, welcoming fug of drying waterproofs.

Chapter Twenty-Eight

Jake and Flora had arranged to meet in the hotel kitchen that Sunday at half past five. She was already there, frowning a little at the ingredients she'd laid out on the worktop, after chatting with Richard about what they could cook. He sort of wished she hadn't invited his grandparents. He just wanted her to himself. And then in his bed. Or hers. He didn't mind which.

She brought the remaining ingredients out of the fridge from their earlier shopping trip and set them on the worktop.

He poked them. 'What's this for?'

'It's a tin of pineapple. Surely, even in your sheltered life travelling the world, you've seen a tin of pineapple.' She put her hands on her hips. 'How have you managed to travel like you have and not learned to cook?'

He shrugged. 'No one ever showed me. And,' he smiled apologetically, 'there never seemed to be a shortage of people wanting to feed me.'

'You're a disgrace, man.' Flora dimpled at him, and turned away to fetch the chopping board. 'It's time you learned how to look after a woman.'

She squealed as he grazed his lips against the back of her neck, and whispered, 'Don't worry. I know how to look after a woman.'

Molly and Bryn were already in the dining room, and there were two bottles of wine on the table, one already opened and poured. He hoped they hadn't heard the squeaks and laughter coming from the kitchen, as he and Flora brought out the dish of sweet and sour chicken, with rice and crunchy baby vegetables, and set it on the table.

'Well,' Molly said. 'You've obviously worked very hard in

there.' She lifted her glass, and with a smile playing round her lips, said, 'Cheers!'

Jake glanced at Flora and she returned a wide-eyed, guileless look that sent lust waves to his groin. He wondered how on earth they were going to get through this meal.

'I'm sorry, I think the rice is a bit stodgy,' Flora said. Jake looked at his almost empty plate in astonishment. He'd thought it was perfect. The entire meal was perfect. It had tasted wonderful, as far as he was concerned.

'I thought it was very nice,' his grandmother said. 'There is a rice cooker.'

'I wouldn't know how to use it,' Flora said. 'I only know how to do it in a saucepan. It's usually perfect, but I was a bit distracted this time.'

'Strange kitchen, I expect,' Bryn said, with a twinkle in his eye. 'It's delicious. Did you learn to cook?'

'Mum taught me. I was a picky eater when I was little, and the slightest thing would put me off my food.' Flora smiled. 'I think Mum thought that learning to cook might keep me more interested.'

'And did it?' Molly asked.

'I still can't eat when I'm really upset,' Flora said. 'But it never stops me cooking!'

'And now you're teaching Jake.' Molly eyed him and Jake couldn't get a sense of what she was thinking. He felt that whatever he said next, she would take as a slight of her parenting skills.

'Thanks so much for my room,' Flora said, into the tiny moment of silence. 'It's so pretty. I bought some freesias to put on the windowsill.'

'I adore freesias. They're one of my favourites. The scent is delicious,' Molly said. 'Do you want a vase?'

'That would be lovely, thank you.' Flora blushed. 'I couldn't resist them when I saw them. I didn't think about how I was going to display them. In the end, I cut the top off a plastic water bottle and used that.'

'Very innovative.' Bryn nodded with a wise smile.

Jake listened in astonishment. He didn't know his gran loved freesias. Was that what they'd bought at the supermarket that afternoon? And how had Flora turned that slightly awkward conversation round like that? He fidgeted in his seat. He'd enjoyed cooking the food and eating it, and now he wanted it all gone so he could get on with the bit he was really looking forward to. Her bed or his?

'Oh no, I totally forgot about a dessert!' Flora clapped a hand over her mouth as the last bits of the sweet and sour were scraped up and eaten. 'Sorry everyone.'

'There's always ice cream in the freezer, and frozen desserts, if anyone wants it.' Molly looked around the table. Nobody answered. Jake would definitely have said yes, at any other time. 'Or we could just have coffee,' she continued. 'And perhaps, a little nightcap to round off a lovely meal?'

'Coffee it is,' Flora said, standing to collect the plates. Jake leapt to his feet, stacking the plates and bearing them away to the sink. The pans were already soaking, and he turned on the potwasher. He took the dirty dishes off Flora as she brought them through, squirting them vigorously with the bendy tap.

'It's gone well, hasn't it?' Flora smiled and hugged him from behind as he worked. 'Well done us. I'll do coffee.'

He turned to return her embrace. She was right, it had gone well. He couldn't believe that he'd never done this for his grandparents. There'd always been a chef, and whilst he'd been tolerated in the kitchen, he'd never been encouraged. The kitchen was a hot, noisy and dangerous place, not for children. He'd learned to scramble some eggs from a mate while he was travelling and that was about it.

She'd made a difference to his life already. He could be patient, and wait for the evening to come to a natural close.

Molly plus a couple of brandies was hilarious and wonderfully indiscreet. She had a fund of stories about the hotel over the years, and Jake watched Flora wiping tears of laughter from her eyes.

He was so glad Flora had crashed into his life. Her energy was intoxicating.

'I shall be sorry when the new chef starts tomorrow. I have so enjoyed this evening,' Molly said and Bryn agreed. 'We won't be able to do this again.'

Flora's head tilted. 'There's no reason why not. You have a perfectly nice kitchen. If you don't mind, maybe Jake and I could do this once a week or maybe once a month in your kitchen, and...' She paused in mid-flow. 'That's if you don't mind, Molly?'

Jake held his breath. Apart from tea and coffee, he didn't remember his grandparents cooking for themselves. They'd always sent down for something to be brought up. Even if the chef made it for them specially.

'It sounds like a wonderful idea,' Molly said. 'Thank you! We'll have to sort out some dates.' She stood, a little unsteady on her feet, and Jake moved smoothly and unobtrusively to offer her an arm. Molly hugged him and kissed his cheek. 'Lovely evening, darling,' she said. 'Goodnight everyone.'

Escorting his gran back to their apartment, Jake felt as if he was actually, properly home, at last.

Days turned into weeks. There were more parties on the beach, progressively long ski paddles, more chip runs and long walks along the coast. Their family cooking evening at Molly and Bryn's apartment became a regular, much enjoyed and increasingly ambitious, event.

Flora got used to her duties, meeting the team of chambermaids who came every day and left her stunned by their hard work. She learned how to make beds and clean, and teamed up with Jake daily to provide breakfasts, as Josh, the new chef, was a single dad and was only available for the dinner shifts. Flora suspected that it was Molly and Bryn's way of including their grandson in the hotel and certainly he seemed to have found new purpose. She made him laugh by writing silly messages on the orders that went into the grab bar, and he saved her the best bits of bacon for bacon butties.

They made Spotify tracks and played them in the kitchen, dancing together when the orders were slow. Flora sang along and Jake was astonished by her pure, clear voice.

'Why aren't you on the stage with that voice?'

She considered him, and couldn't say that she didn't have the confidence because he made her feel as if she could do anything she wanted to.

Jo, Nicola and Lucy were as good as their words and recommended Flora's hairdressing skills far and wide, and soon she had the beginnings of a round that was growing steadily. As the days lengthened, she joined the Art Café for evening rides when she could.

One Sunday, she and Jake wandered onto the beach after their breakfast stint, and she spotted the Lifeguard Club setting out the warning flags and the yellow rescue vessel that Jake had saved her on.

'That's a patrol,' Jake explained. 'See the two red and yellow flags over there? It's safe to swim between them. Paid lifeguards are hired to work, usually during the school holidays, and the volunteers generally do a Sunday, the rest of the time.'

'So, isn't that something you should be doing today, then?'

Jake was silent. He surveyed the sea, and the beach, and the clubhouse, and Flora felt his longing to be part of it. She gave him a little push.

'Go on, Jake. It's a part of you, all this. Like motorbiking is a part of me.'

'Yes, but...' He swallowed, still watching the club members. 'Apart from the odd surfing class, I haven't exactly been a model member.'

'They'll be delighted to have you. I'd lay money on it.'

'What will you be doing?'

'Sunbathing, or going out for a bike ride with Lucy or her mates from that ladies only bike club she belongs to.'

'You just want to get rid of me, don't you?' Jake's smile was slow, and she grinned back as she nodded.

'Totally. Go, my hunky hero.' She blew him a kiss and watched him jog into the clubhouse.

She sat on the sand, watching them for a while, and then she retrieved her motorbike and went shopping in Swansea to buy a wetsuit that fitted her, and some Factor 50 sunscreen.

She showed Jake her purchases later, as they were about to go to bed. He made her try the wetsuit on.

'Very nice.' He nodded, approvingly as she shimmied out of it. 'I prefer the suit you're wearing now though.' He reached out for her and nuzzled her neck. 'Have you ever been skinny-dipping?'

'No...'

'We'll go – when the sea warms up a bit more...'

They didn't have too long to wait. Wales was about to have a summer that neither of them would forget.

Chapter Twenty-Nine

'There is not a scrap of air.' Pushing the orders into the grabber, Flora fanned her face with a menu. Even with the windows open, it was a furnace in there. There had been a few short-lived bursts of rain, but not enough to fill the reservoirs or clear the air. Everyone longed for a proper thunderstorm.

'It can't last. This is Wales.' Jake's dark blond hair was stuck to his head beneath his hat. He turned the sausages over with one hand and flipped the eggs with the other. Flora smiled at his dexterity. The days of a food waste bin overflowing with eggshells were few and far between these days.

'I am so ready for that swim,' she said, picking up the tray of hot food. It amazed her that people wanted cooked breakfasts in weather as stifling as this. They had an hour to themselves before her other duties, and the morning swim had become a ritual for them. The silky feel of the seawater on her skin invigorated her, and she rejoiced in her improved fitness and water skills as she dived beneath the waves, taught by Jake.

'Sounds perfect,' he said. 'I can't wait.'

She ran to the beach, kicking her heels up high behind her, laughing as he caught her easily, picking her up like a rugby ball and continuing to run before hurling her, fully dressed, into the sea, and then launching himself in after her.

Floating on her back, she looked over at him as he sneaked up on her like a hippopotamus, only the top of his head visible.

'I've never been so happy,' she told him, wrapping her arms and legs around him, and letting him swim her out to sea.

Later as they walked back along the drive, she exclaimed, 'Dad!' He was wearing a smart suit, getting out of a car she didn't recognise, but he changed his cars all the time.

'Hello, sweet pea!' he called back, stretching his shoulders. 'How's that for timing?'

'This is a surprise.' Flora went to hug him, and then stopped, assessing herself. He smelled expensive, as always, and his suit was unwrinkled. Unlike her. Standing back, she rubbed her hand over her hair. 'Sorry, I'm a complete mess. We've been swimming. In the sea! It's glorious, we—'

'We?'

'This is Jake. Jake, this is my dad.'

'Hi, Jake. I'm Davi— Dai.'

'Good to meet you, Dai.'

They shook hands, and her father took a deep breath. 'It's good to be back in Wales.'

'You've picked the best weather, for sure,' Jake said, giving him a hand with his suitcase. 'Flora, you okay to book your father in? I'm heading off to do my jobs.' He bent his head to kiss her lightly on the lips, shook Dai's hand again and left.

Flora made sure he was booked into the new wing, and led the way. What was he doing there? A surge of apprehension rolled in her stomach.

'Have you come check the place out for yourself, Dad?' She watched him inspecting the room as she spoke. He looked out of the window.

'Great view.' He leaned his elbows on the sill and Flora joined him.

'It is, isn't it. That's the Art Café, there.' She pointed. 'I've told you about them.'

'The bikers?' He nodded.

'Yep. Best cakes ever. I'll take you over there.' She paused. 'How long are you staying for?'

'A few days,' her dad said. 'Right, I have some work to do—'

'Me too,' Flora said. 'And I need to change. I'm free about two thirty though…'

'I'll meet you at the reception at half two, then. We should do this afternoon tea you keep telling me about.'

He appeared in casual fawn chinos, a short-sleeved check shirt and sunglasses pushed into his neatly-trimmed grey hair, managing to still look like the businessman he was. Flora had showered and changed into shorts, which were her daily non-hotel wear. Her flip-flops marked her out as a beach bum. Her hair had grown out of its short pixie cut, and she rather liked it, catching it up in a little ponytail which Jake enjoyed tugging.

She was sure that Amber would have showed up in a delightful and feminine sun dress and heels, and her heart sank a little as she compared her appearance unfavourably with her absent sister's. Then she straightened up. Jake liked her exactly like this. He'd never asked her to change into a dress.

The beach was busy, and so, inevitably, was the Art Café. Flora regarded the long queue with dismay as it wound out of the door.

'Shall we just go for a walk, and maybe get an ice cream to tide us over?' She couldn't imagine him eating an ice cream, somehow. He was too smart. Too city.

'Why not,' her father said, allowing himself to be steered along the promenade.

'Has it changed much since you were here?'

He looked around him. 'No, not really. A few new houses and lots of these little cottages done up. The beach huts are still the same. I bet they go for a fortune now.'

'Ever the property tycoon!' She rolled her eyes and smiled

at him, watching the frown on his face smooth away. He looked great, she acknowledged, for a man in his fifties. Hair greying at the sides, still lean and fit. The fact that her mum maintained a good relationship with him meant that she had found it easier to forgive him, and his new wife, who had always been kind to her. It was only Amber that she couldn't forgive him for.

'How is the cottage looking?'

Flora said, 'It's gorgeous. I've loved staying in it. Mum has done a great job of doing it up. It's so classy.'

'Pleased to hear it.' Her father chuckled quietly. She almost missed it.

'What?' she asked, suspiciously. She frowned, thinking about her mum's flat, overloaded with floral wallpaper and knick-knacks. Then she thought about her dad's uncluttered house, with its clean and sleek lines. 'Oh. That was you?'

'Let's say it was a joint effort.'

Flora was silent. 'Did you bring Amber here when she was about fifteen or so?'

'Amber has never been here.' He shook his head, emphatically. 'To be honest, it wouldn't have been her thing. She's always preferred the bright lights. She would've been bored to death here. Why do you ask?'

Flora jammed her hands into her pockets. 'Just something Jake said. He thought he'd met her.'

'And?'

'Nothing.' She lifted one shoulder in a shrug and tried to hide it but he spotted it.

'Oh. So you got arsey because she was in your "special place" and you didn't know about it?'

Flora's head sank onto her chest. 'Might have,' she muttered. 'It was a reasonable assumption.'

'It was a paranoid assumption!' He glanced down at her. 'Isn't it time you girls learned to get along?'

'After what she did?'

He stopped walking. 'Flora. What *are* you talking about?'

Flora spread her hands. 'Dad.' She took a deep breath and said in a rush, 'It was Amber who Spence was over the side with. I saw them both. Together. In our bed.'

He glanced at her sharply and then drew in a long and silent breath. 'I didn't know that.' His lips compressed, and he put an arm out to draw her in for a hug. 'I'm sorry, sweet pea. That was unforgiveable.' His pronouncement made her lips wobble.

By the time they returned to the Art Café, the queues had died down, and Flora towed him inside, proudly introducing him as her father.

'Just a little break,' he said, in answer to their friendly queries. 'And to catch up with my daughter, see what she's up to.' He winked at her. 'Not trying to drown herself or anything silly.'

'Da-ad.' Flora sent him a look, carrying the tray to a table. 'I'm thirty now, y'know. I can crochet. And knit. I'm a grown-up!'

'I wish I was.' He laughed. 'Tell me about this Jake of yours. He's certainly a healthy looking specimen.'

'Yeah. He is. He's incredible.' Flora stared out of the window, thinking about all the times she'd sat in this café, talking non-stop with Jake. Her life was so different now. 'I'm really happy here, Dad.'

'Really happy?' Her dad sat back. 'Who are you, and what have you done with my favourite daughter?'

'Am I really your favourite daughter?'

One side of his face lifted in the lopsided grin that she remembered when he was joshing with her, and she laughed.

'We work together every single morning. We've been out on a double ski loads of times... we've—'

'Double ski?' His brow wrinkled, and she explained. 'Uh-huh. Sounds like fun. Is it?'

'Yes! Once you get used to it. I was rubbish in the beginning, and scared, and my arms hurt, but now, I've got muscles, look!' She curled her bicep, and he looked as directed. Her heart sang. Even at her age, it was lovely to have her dad to herself.

'Marvellous. And you both go out on this – thing – together?' She nodded.

'Oh, sweetheart.' He put his hand over hers and gave it a squeeze. 'This place has done you good. You look tanned and healthy and happy. You've always loved it here. Like me. Which is why we bought the cottage.' He looked a little sad. 'I miss it.'

'Really? You jet all over the world!'

'I do. But this place is special.'

'Jake says that too.' She toyed with her cold drink. 'And he's been in Australia for a few years.' She stared again out of the window at the busy beach and when she looked back, her dad was eyeing her thoughtfully.

'Enjoy that friendship, sweet pea. Don't take it for granted, because the best friendships can last longer than a marriage.'

It was Flora's turn to feel sad, then. Was he talking about her mum? Certainly, their friendship seemed to have survived his betrayal and subsequent remarriage.

'So... I'm almost scared to ask this, but, what are you doing here, Dad? What are your plans for the hotel?'

He was silent for a long time, and she watched him gazing over the crowded beach. He turned to her.

'Right at this moment, I don't really know. It started off as just a casual enquiry. But your phone calls and your photos have intrigued me, and—' He shrugged. 'I miss the place. I've got some time owing to me, so I thought I'd just trundle down and have a look for myself.'

Flora gulped. Had she brought about the hotel's downfall, with her own enthusiasm? He refused to be drawn on anything further, and changed the subject. As she spoke, her brain whirled.

Should she play down the hotel's charms so he'd lose interest, or play them up, so he'd offer a better price? Should she let Jake know? Or Molly? What could she even tell them?

Chapter Thirty

Flora's dad had decided to stay longer, and so had the sun. Day after day, the cloudless cobalt sky paled towards the hazy horizon and became the sparkling turquoise sea, barely ruffled by a breeze.

Nobody wanted cooked breakfasts any more, and Jake and Flora made sure the stocks of fresh fruits, yoghurts and pastries were sufficient for their guests, who surreptitiously wrapped them in serviettes and took them onto the beach.

'Your dad seems to be enjoying himself,' Jake said, as they cleaned down the kitchen. The slightest movement made beads of sweat stand out on their skin.

'He does.' Flora smiled. 'I can't believe he's been here for over a week. He spends ages chatting to Bryn about motorbikes, did you know that?'

Jake shook his head. 'I didn't know that.' Flora saw everything, it seemed to him.

'The smart suit has gone, it's all shorts, casual shirts and flip-flops. He still spends all day on his laptop and mobile, but at least he gets out in the sunshine to do it. He's got a tan!' She laughed. 'In Wales. In a week. If we could only rely on this weather every summer, nobody would go abroad, he says. Ready for your swim?'

'I may have to jump in wearing this lot. I am boiling.' Jake gave the kitchen a critical once over, filling in the fridge and freezer temperature logbook. He took his responsibilities seriously, and his Food Hygiene Certificate had left him wanting to know more. He'd started checking out catering qualifications, but he didn't want his grandparents to think he was abandoning them. They relied on him now for so much, and he enjoyed his increased involvement. Maybe he could do some kind of part-time courses. He'd have to do some more research. Maybe have a chat with Josh, the evening chef, who was affable enough.

Clouds of mosquitoes dive-bombed them on the short walk to the beach.

'I reckon there's going to be a storm.' Jake swatted them away with a tut. 'Maybe we'll get some surf at last. I'm bored with this flat water.'

'I don't think I've been bored once since I arrived,' Flora said. 'I love it here.'

'Naaah. It's having me as the main attraction, that's what it is.' He caught her to him and kissed the freckles that made her face even more lovable.

'So modest.' Wriggling away, she flicked her towel at him with a grin and then fanned herself with it. 'Phew. I feel as if I'm trying to breath underwater.'

They stood together for a moment, contemplating the pale duck egg blue sea against a horizon that was the deep blue black of a mussel shell. Somehow, the sun illuminated the beach brilliantly. It looked unearthly. Definitely storm weather.

'Don't complain. This is probably all the summer we'll get. It'll rain until Christmas when this breaks.'

'Christmas...' She sighed. 'Log fires, and snow...'

He chuckled. 'Log fires, yes. But we never get snow.' His expression became serious, and he glanced at her.

Where would they both be at Christmas? There wouldn't be guests, so what would he be doing?

The sudden sharp gust of wind took with it the propped parasols and bright towels, and then was gone, leaving the grumbling sunbathers gathering their scattered possessions. The air seemed charged with electricity and they looked up at the sky, waiting for the rain.

Nothing. It seemed hotter than ever, and he felt the cool

water close over him as he swam with a head up front crawl over the oily-smooth sea, Flora not far behind.

It was an effort to get out, and he felt sticky and unrefreshed by his dip.

'Listen to those busy bees!' Flora stopped to admire the trimmed lawns and weed free car park as they wandered slowly home. 'You've worked so hard on this garden, Jake. And look how well the knitted flowers blend in with the real thing. Really clever. I'm trying to make one, but it's taking me ages. I have to keep unpicking it.'

He watched the bees and their bright yellow saddlebags of pollen. He'd never even given them more than a passing thought before Flora. That knitted flower thing, though... he tried not to roll his eyes where Flora could see him. He knew how much she liked them.

'Oh, and I meant to tell you,' she said, 'how this knitted graffiti thing started here.'

'Go on...'

'It was to cheer your gran up, when you left to go travelling.'

He was startled, and stared again at the fake blooms. Another mischievous little gust made them dance and bob before it died away again, followed by a smatter of refreshing, fat raindrops. It hadn't even occurred to him that his grandparents would miss him. It had just been, well, his right to travel, hadn't it? They'd waved him off, fussing about whether he had enough money and was his passport and visa correct and he'd just assumed... that they were relieved to get him out of their hair. His voice was croaky when he answered.

'Oh,' he said. He swallowed. 'I... I... it never...' He stared at the woollen blossoms more closely. 'They are rather pretty, aren't they?' He reached for her hand and lifted it to his mouth, kissing her tanned skin. She was amazing, the way she found out these things. 'Thanks for letting me know.'

The raindrops turned into a freezing torrent and hand in hand, they ran into the cool, dark entrance hall. It always took a while for your eyes to adjust, so it was a moment before Flora's hand dropped suddenly from his and she gasped... 'Amber!'

The girl leaning against the reception was stunning. She'd been perfectly named, for her smooth hair and body undulated in shades of toffee and caramel. She wore a white sleeveless dress that stopped at her knee, and heels that had to be at least six inches high, which put her at his eye level. She lifted an eyebrow in his direction and he could have sworn that she purred at him.

There was nothing of Flora in that face. Or that body, for that matter. It was hard to imagine that they were related at all, let alone as sisters.

'Amber. Why are you here?' Dai arrived at the same time, air kissing her on the offered smooth cheek.

'Daddy.' She pouted. 'You say it like you don't want me here.'

Dai eyed her, and then met Jake's eyes. Jake put his arm around Flora, feeling how tight her shoulder muscles were. Everything about her said she was spoiling for a fight.

Amber was the first to light the blue touch paper. Maybe she assumed a level of safety, with her dad present.

'Oh. It's you, shortarse, spoiling everything as usual.' She scowled. 'You smashed my car window, didn't you?'

Flora twisted from beneath his arm. 'I did! And I wish I'd done it with your head, you rancid, skanky bitch!'

Amber swept a glance over Jake. 'I see you've already found a replacement.'

'Yeah, you can keep your hands off him!'

Amber snorted. 'Oh, he clearly has no taste. He wouldn't appreciate me.'

Dai stepped towards her. 'Amber.' His tone was sharp. 'There's nothing for you here. Off you go. We'll speak later.'

Jake found his voice then. 'Yes, please leave. I know all about you.'

'Really? What has the hobbit told you about me?'

Jake hesitated, uncertain what, if anything to divulge. He saw Flora stiffen at the insult.

'Everything!' She spat the word at her sister. 'I've told him everything about you. Like I should've told Spence.'

'Don't believe her.' Amber's tone was dismissive. 'She's a liar.'

'Amber…' Dai's voice carried a warning note.

'I haven't known Flora long, but I know she always tells the truth,' Jake said. 'Whether it's something you want to hear or not.'

'How did you know I was here anyway?' Flora rounded on her sister. 'Have you been spying on me?'

Amber laughed, a forced, short laugh. 'You've got a bloody nerve, calling *me* a spy.'

Jake saw Flora blanche as if she'd been struck and he frowned.

'You're not welcome here,' he snapped at Amber. 'There are other places to stay. Go to one of them.'

Amber stood her ground. She inspected her fingernails before drawling, 'Oh. So, your ever so truthful little girlfriend hasn't told you that our daddy has been paying her to spy on your hotel?'

Jake's stomach went into free fall as his brain absorbed her words.

'It wasn't like that!' Flora stared up at him, her face stricken.

'What *was* it like then?' Amber said. 'Do tell us.'

'Dad can explain it better than me.' Flora shot an arm towards him.

'Look, I knew Flora was on her uppers but she would never take any money from me,' Dai began slowly, 'and I gave her a little job to do, so that I could pay her.'

'Well. You've just repeated what I said. In more words.' Amber smirked.

'Shut up, Amber!' Dai roared. 'You're stirring up trouble, as always!'

'A little job? So this was charity, Dad? And I've been feeling really guilty about it but—'

'—but never stopped doing it in case the cash dried up?' Amber interjected smoothly.

Jake's reaching fingers just missed a raging Flora as she shot past him. She snatched up the vase of flowers on the reception desk and flung the contents at her sister. They all stared for one shocked moment as the stinking khaki stain spread down the snowy white dress.

With an animal howl, Amber launched herself at Flora, her arms outstretched, connecting with a thud. On autopilot, Jake waded into the screaming, snarling frenzy, and was aware of their father also trying to pull them apart.

He lifted Flora bodily. Amber screamed even harder until he noticed that Flora had one of her hands wrapped in a handful of her sister's hair.

'Leave it!' he yelled in her ear. 'Let go!' He settled her onto her feet. She had a cut lip and tears poured down her face and he stared at her as if he'd never seen her before.

'What on earth is going on here?' Molly appeared at the reception, her words echoing his thoughts. Several guests were gathered behind her, their faces a mixture of concern and avid glee at the drama.

'Molly,' Dai panted, gripping Amber by the arm. Her stained sundress was crushed and torn at the neck, and she had lost a shoe. 'I do apologise. This is my other daughter. She's not staying.' He gave her a little shake. 'Are you?'

Amber looked sulky. 'Apparently not.'

Jake relaxed his grip of Flora, and she darted out of the entrance, still sobbing. Throwing a furious glance at Dai and Amber, he followed.

Chapter Thirty-One

Flora blundered towards the shelter of the big trees. She could hardly see through the torrential rain and her own tears. The wind ran icy fingers over her skin and she huddled, her arms wrapped around her shivering body, under the swaying branches. She'd lied and she'd been punished. It was what she deserved. She was going to lose everything. Everyone. Jake caught at her arm.

'Flora. What was that about?' His voice, close to her ear, was hoarse and she leaned forward, longing to put her face close to his, nestle into his broad shoulder. He shrank away from her and she burst into helpless sobs. She'd ruined everything.

'I n-need to tell you... but I c-can't go back in there.' She caught her lip between her teeth to stop the trembling, wincing as she tasted blood. What the hell was she going to say? She couldn't deny what she'd done. Her face felt raw and bruised and her scalp stung. She could hardly believe that it had been barely hours ago that they were complaining about the heat. That they'd been so happy. Her body shook uncontrollably. Just like it had when Jake had rescued her from the teeth of the sea, months ago. He wasn't going to rescue her this time.

'Wait there, under the tree.' Jake could hardly look at her. 'I'll be back.' He returned with two ancient raincoats, and draped one over Flora's shoulders. She threaded her arms into it and it dwarfed her. 'Let's walk down to the sea.'

She nodded, her heart already breaking. He didn't offer his hand to hold. Her belly curdled with self-loathing and fear.

As they reached the end of the drive, the wind nearly took them off their feet and they clutched each other to regain their balance. Flora stared at the bay, pushing her own anguish away. It was unrecognisable from the calm tranquillity of only a couple of hours ago.

The sea had become a boiling cauldron. The tide surged up the beach, higher than she'd ever seen it. Slate dark waves rose in peaks, smashed together and gathered speed before dashing their fury against the prom. The surf rose ten, fifteen feet, more, into the air and hung there for a frozen moment before spilling across the road.

They hung onto the railings as the wind howled and lashed their faces with salt spray. Beach brollies and abandoned picnics skittered across the pavements, eddying in mad circles before rising into the air. A wheelie bin trundled crazily past them, ricocheting off a parked car. Struggling to open her eyes into the blast, Flora scanned the beach and prom to see if anyone was there.

Jake pointed at the Art Café, dwarfed by the towering spray. Only the tail end of his shout, whipped away by the wind, reached her. '... someone in there?'

She squinted, shielding her eyes with her hands. It was hard to see who it was, but there were definitely people in there. She gulped. Those huge floor to ceiling glass windows, exposed to the brute force of the sea... And it wasn't even high tide yet.

Jake yelled at her. 'They can't stay in there! You go back to the hotel, I'm going to help!'

'No!' Flora shouted. She couldn't leave him there, alone. 'We'll do it together!' A violent crack of thunder made them both jump. Hand in hand, they staggered along the prom to the café, and Jake wrenched the door open. The wind shrieked in with them like a live creature, whirling chairs and tossing racks of postcards and menus.

'Richard!' Jake shouted, dashing into the kitchen as Flora stared, transfixed in horror at the floor to ceiling windows that now seemed submerged in the sea.

She wrenched herself away, and spotted the small figure of Lucy pushing boxes of what looked like jewellery stock into metal cabinets. 'Leave it, Lucy! You have to come now. It's too dangerous!' Lucy stared up at her, her eyes streaming with tears.

'I can't lose everything. I can't!' They both screamed as spume beat against the big window and thunder splintered the air.

'Leave it, Lucy! It's not worth it!'

With a terrified glance at the vibrating windows, Lucy shouted, 'Where's Richard?' She stared wildly around the café. The storm noise was deafening.

'I think Jake is—' At that moment, Jake joined them, holding Jo's arm. Flora gaped at them. 'Where's Richard?'

'You go! Richard is outside, trying to put the shutters down!' Jake bellowed. 'I'll go and find him!'

Flora was gripped by pure, reflexive fear as Jake plunged into the mouth of hell through the front door, which flailed and crashed. Tears of terror sprang to her eyes. Surely no one could survive out there! But if anyone could do it, Jake could.

Gripping Lucy with one hand and Jo with the other, Flora grimly spearheaded towards the door, only for it to be filled with a soaking wet and burly figure.

'Ash! Oh my God, Ash!' Lucy was in his arms in a moment, and Flora was relieved to see him.

'Jake has gone to help Richard!' Her voice was whipped away and she indicated with a straining arm. Ash pulled the three of them towards the door, pointing them to safety as he turned towards the two men.

'No! Ash!' Lucy screamed after him. Seawater cascaded over them, and the three women fought for their footing on the slippery decking. Flora shook the water from her eyes and squinted.

'I can see them!' She saw Jake and Ash pulling Richard

away from the shutters and screamed as they were swept off their feet. 'No!' she wailed, struggling to get to them and slipping, thudding painfully onto her knees. She sobbed, clawing to her feet, searching for Jake. Grey figures advanced in the nightmarish murk, but she couldn't see who was who. Let it be Jake, let it be Jake...

'It's going! Go! Go.' Ash reached out and she felt rather than saw another pair of hands pull her forward as they stumbled into the wind, hammered by the combined savagery of sea and rain.

'Jake!' Squeezing her eyes together she turned her head from side to side.

'I'm here! Go!'

There was a horrible, animal, groaning noise, and the ground shook.

Flora recognised Richard's stricken voice as they slipped and lurched towards the safety of the road. 'No! Oh God. Oh God! It's going...'

Reacting as one, they turned, gaping, their safety forgotten. Sheet lightning blinded them. The promenade sagged slowly to one side, and the big glass windows of the Art Café finally gave way...

'Noooo!' Lucy buried her head in Ash's chest. Jake's hand still gripped Flora's. Nobody could tear their eyes away from the horror of the scene.

'There's nothing we can do!' Jake turned, herding them away from danger. 'Come into the hotel. You can make phone calls and get dried, at least.'

As they straggled sadly along the drive, Flora noticed that the knitted flowers she'd only admired that morning had torn away, lying in tattered threads in the mud.

Shocked, silent, and sodden, they trudged into the hotel entrance, shivering uncontrollably, and everyone jumped at another deafening crack of thunder. A flash of lightning illuminated them even in the gloomy lobby. Molly rushed towards them.

'Oh, my dears! Richard! Goodness me, whatever has happened? Come in, come in, we'll get you some towels. The fire is on in the main sitting room, Jake.' Molly herded them in and Flora desperate for distraction, followed her to the linen cupboard along the corridor.

She couldn't face Amber if she was in that sitting room. She just couldn't. Her world was collapsing around her. Molly gave her a shrewd look, as they pulled out a pile of towels and blankets, but said nothing.

'The prom has gone,' Flora told her, trying hard not to cry. 'Into the sea.' Her lips trembled.

Molly looked shocked, but said, ever practical, 'Is everybody accounted for?'

Flora nodded. 'They are. Shall I make some hot chocolate and coffee?'

'If you think you can... and bring the brandy. You've all had a shock.'

'Has my sister gone?'

Molly shook her head. 'Unfortunately, no. But I think your father has her under control.'

'Some hope,' Flora muttered. She followed Molly into the sitting room and distributed the towels. Jake was banking the log fire up. She didn't look for her sister, but her dad appeared at her side as she headed for the kitchen.

'Are you okay, sweet pea?' He put his arm across her shoulders, and once again, Flora fought not to burst into tears. Her throat hurt. 'Not really. I still haven't spoken to Jake about... what Amber said. I could fucking kill her.'

'Yeah.' Her father compressed his lips in a sad smile and exhaled. 'Me too. I'm sorry. This is my fault too.'

She tipped her head into his shoulder. 'And the prom has

gone. Gone! Into the sea. The café... it's... just... gone! I can't believe it! Poor Lucy! Poor Richard!' She did cry then, and her father turned her towards him and let her sob. She straightened her shoulders. 'I'm supposed to be making hot drinks.' She blew her nose on a paper napkin and pushed open the kitchen doors. The rain drummed at the windows. She still hadn't spoken to Jake and every instinct shrank from doing so. But the elephant was in the room, and although he'd held her hand as they'd fought their way off the promenade, that had been survival. It hadn't been the easy, fingers entwined, 'there's no other way of walking' type of handholding.

'I can help with those.' It was Bryn. 'The road is flooded, apparently.'

Carrying the hot drinks on a tray, she saw Jo, Lucy and Ash huddled round the phone in reception, blankets around their shoulders. She placed three mugs of hot chocolate on the counter, and bit back her tears as she heard Ash saying, 'Don't cry, Daisy, everyone is fine. Yes, Lucy is here—' He passed the phone to Lucy, who rubbed her face and composed herself to speak.

'Hello, darling, are you okay? We're fine. Drying off now, and Flora has brought us some hot chocolate to warm us up. It's only a building...' Her voice broke and she handed the phone back to Ash.

'No, Lucy's fine. She's upset, yes. Yes, I'll tell her you love her. We'll be home soon. Give my love to Nanny and Bampy. Love you, sweetheart.' He blew a kiss down the phone and hung up, looking shaken. Tears poured, unheeded, down Lucy's cheeks.

'Ed thinks he can get to us in his truck.' Jo still had her mobile phone. She turned to Ash. 'We'll all fit in the cab if your car won't make it.'

'Good old Ed and his big boy toys. Tell him thanks, Jo.' Ash nodded at her.

'Thanks, Jo. I still can't believe it.' Richard slumped on a chair alongside, his head in his hands. He looked up at Flora and muttered his thanks as she passed him a mug.

'I wish I could do more,' she said.

'We wouldn't be here if it hadn't been for you two,' he said. 'I've told Nic we're safe. I'm just so glad she wasn't there. It all happened so quickly! By the time we'd realised, we were in the middle of it! It's never been that bad. Never.' He raked his hands through his hair, his expression bleak. 'But… it's only bricks and mortar. Nobody died. Thank God. Molly has been great, by the way. She told us we could stay over, if we needed to. No charge.' He smiled faintly at her. 'I think you've defrosted her, Flora.'

Flora blinked. She thought that Molly would ice over very quickly when she heard what she was going to say. 'The sitting room is really cosy. Come in whenever you want and get yourselves warm.'

She saw Bryn carrying a coffee pot, and her father with the other tray, and followed them into the lounge. Pairs of eyes turned as one to stare at her curiously and she backed straight out. It was the last place she wanted to be. She went to her room. The little room that had felt so homely. The rain pounded against the rattling window, and she stared out over the angry sea, bursting into tears again as she saw the roof of the Art Café gaping open and destroyed by surf. A few minutes later, there was a tap at the door, and she struggled into jeans that stuck to her cold thighs.

'Coming!' Scrubbing any signs of her tears off her face, she opened the door. It was Jake.

'Are you okay?' He put his hand out and rested it on her shoulder and then withdrew it as if he was burned. He shifted his gaze somewhere over her left shoulder and she felt sick. For that tiny moment she'd thought it was all going to be okay. 'I'm not going to drag this out.' He sat on the only chair, and she perched on the bed, her hands shaking. 'What was Amber talking about?'

Flora's teeth chattered. 'As she said, Dad asked me... to... to... do a job for him... to f-f-find out about the hotel... because it had come up for sale a couple of times recently, and each time it had been cancelled. He's always liked the hotel... I... I don't know what he wants to do with it. He hasn't told me.' She fixed her gaze on him. 'But I never told him anything terrible about the hotel! I said it was lovely, and charming, and yes, a bit tatty, but only the truth!'

'Oh yes. Flora and her famous truths.' He stared at her, his sea blue eyes brilliant against his tan. 'When were you going to tell me? Or my grandparents? They took you under their wing, because I told them you could be trusted. You've made me look like a fool, Flora.' He stared out of the window. 'And what exactly is your father doing here?'

'I don't know!' Flora held her hands out, palms up. 'I really don't! He doesn't tell me anything!'

'Maybe he doesn't trust you either,' Jake said, bitterly. 'I told you, not long after I met you, that friendship is an earned relationship, built on trust.'

'I know. I know you did.' Tears poured, unchecked, down Flora's cheeks. She wanted to run away from his blistering appraisal, but her own view of herself was a thousand times more caustic. 'I'm sorry.'

'Do you know what the worst bit is? You went on and on about how your sister betrayed you. About how your father betrayed you and your mum.' He breathed in, silently, a pulse beating in his forehead. 'And you... you betrayed me. Us.'

'I'm sorry! I just wanted... I wanted it all. I'm so, so sorry.' She put her face in her hands, and wept. She heard the door open and close quietly. She was alone.

Chapter Thirty-Two

Jake got up at first light to see how much damage had been done to the hotel. He'd lain awake, listening to the roof tiles skidding off the roofs, waiting for the tall chimneys to be next. The garden was littered with smashed tiles and clothing, he presumed from nearby gardens. His gran's carefully tended planters were either overturned or overflowing with debris. The patio had been damaged by falling masonry, and he looked up to see where it had fallen from. A split had opened up on one wall. He'd need to have a proper inspection of all this with his grandparents, so they could call the insurers and get the ball rolling.

He was astonished to see a very pale Flora in the dining room. He'd really thought he was going to have to man the breakfasts by himself, somehow. Her eyes were red and raw, she had a whopping shiner and a split lip from her punch up with Amber... She didn't look at him, as she took the orders and collected the food. She spoke only when it was absolutely necessary, with no eye contact, and then when he looked round for her at the end of service, she'd gone, leaving her apron hanging on the hook.

He felt dull and heavy. Should he go and find her? He didn't even know what he'd say to her. Nothing had changed during the sleepless night. A part of him wanted to gather her up and say he didn't care what she'd done. Every bone of his body had missed her last night. After the dramas of the day, he'd wanted her small body curled against his, the rain drumming on the windows, and them together, safe.

Another, more insistent part was dismayed by her. Disillusioned. Saddened. As if his feet were sliding in all directions. He *did* care about what she'd done. She might have been able to lie, but he couldn't. Then he thought about how she'd changed things in his life. How she'd brought him closer to his grandparents after his absence. How she'd encouraged him to turn up for his lifesaving shifts on the beach. How she'd got him interested in cooking, and how, under her patient tuition, they'd learned together, and how he'd attempted and become quite adept at more complicated dishes. He sighed, his stomach tight and knotted. It was her who had got him doing what he was doing now, a role in the hotel, feeling useful.

He scrubbed and cleaned the kitchen and dining room. Switching on the radio for news, he heard only Flora's singing in his head. He had no appetite for his own breakfast, and thought about all those breakfasts they'd eaten together, here in this kitchen. Drying his hands, he filled in his logbook, and sat on a stool, not knowing what to do first.

Molly pushed the kitchen door open, interrupting his thoughts.

'Hi, Gran. Did you sleep okay? I've started to have a look at the damage—'

'We're going to need a new breakfast waitress,' Molly said straightaway. 'Unless Bryn goes back to doing it.'

'Wha— why? Has Flora gone?'

'Yes.' Molly didn't try to dress it up, and she didn't start criticising her, for which he was grateful.

'You just let her go? Couldn't you have stopped her?' His pulse pounded in his head.

'She's a determined young lady. I don't think anyone could have stopped her.' Molly's gaze lingered on him.

'I could have.' He ran his fingers through his hair. Did he want to? Would it change how he felt? He knuckled his chin. 'How is she getting home?'

'On her bike, I imagine.'

Jake glanced out of the window, at the trees blowing. 'In this?'

'She's always seemed a capable person.'

Impulsively he sprinted through the back door – just in time to see her bike disappearing down the drive, and he bellowed after her, 'Flo-raaa!'

She had gone. And he knew her well enough to know that she wouldn't be turning round to come back. He cursed having helped her learn how to turn her bike around. She hadn't made that mistake again.

Molly had gone and he walked numbly into the reception. Dai and Amber waited there. Jake's brows drew together in a deep frown. This had all been their doing.

Dai had reverted back to his smart suit, and Amber was wearing fresh clothes, as if nothing had happened yesterday. Feeling completely wrong-footed now, Jake resorted to a businesslike veneer of civility.

'We're checking out, Jake,' Dai said. 'I just want to say that, up until yesterday, I have never enjoyed a stay so much, and I apologise again for the fracas yesterday.' He turned to give Amber a piercing glare.

'I apologise too.' Amber raised her head a little and he felt a curious sense of satisfaction to see her bruised cheekbones and ragged hair.

'Did you have breakfast this morning?'

'We did, and very nice it was too, thank you.'

Jake blinked. Flora had served her sister, and hadn't said a word. It was more than he could have done.

'When you see Flora,' he said to Dai, as he handed over his receipt, 'please say goodbye from me.' The older man gaped at him, and Jake realised that she had left without telling him, either. 'You just missed her.'

Dai glared at Amber. 'This is down to you.'

Amber dropped her head, the bravado of yesterday gone. There had clearly been discussions during the night.

Jake eyed Dai thoughtfully. Maybe if Amber hadn't been there, he might have asked the man what his plans were.

After all, he was ultimately at the bottom of all this. Phrases came and went in his head and he settled for, 'We had some words last night too.'

Dai's clear grey eyes, so like his daughter's, rested on him silently for a long moment as if he was weighing up his words. He said, 'I'm not leaving the area, just checking out here. I don't want to embarrass your grandparents by staying on after that disgraceful event yesterday.' Amber, staring at the carpet, said nothing. Bringing out a thick business card, Dai placed it on the reception. 'I need to check to see if Sea-Spray Cottage has sustained any damage first, but I would very much like to speak to you at a later date.' His eyes flicked towards Amber and back to Jake. 'You and your folks, that is, if that would be okay.'

Jake picked up the card, and read it quickly. It felt expensive but told him nothing, other than that it had to do with property investment. He needed to know what was going on. He nodded, and looked around the desk for a card from the hotel. There wasn't one. He couldn't even remember when there had been one. He sighed, giving a small shrug, 'I'm sorry, I don't seem to have a…'

'Don't worry, I've got all your details.' Dai smiled and held out his hand, which Jake refused to take. 'I'll be in touch.'

He marched briskly out of the hotel, Amber trailing and limping slightly, he was pleased to see. Jake fingered the card, and googled the details before delivering it to Molly in their apartment. She was on the phone, and he waited until she'd finished.

'Insurance company,' she began, looking up at him with her eyebrows lifted in mute query.

'Why do you hate motorcyclists so much?' He was more astonished than she was at his words.

'I don't *hate* motorcyclists! I helped Richard and that other couple, last night, didn't I?'

'You've only declared an amnesty since Flora arrived. But you've had a hate vendetta for years.' He thought, how was it that they'd talked about nothing but Flora all morning, and she wasn't even there? 'I need to know, Gran. Richard and Lucy and Ash, they're our,' he corrected himself, '*my* friends. And their business has just been smashed to bits. We need to support them. In the same way that they supported us, when Pete the chef walked out.'

Molly pressed her lips together, and looked away. He sighed. She wasn't going to tell him. Then she said, 'It was so long ago.' She sat down. His grandfather came out of their bedroom, his hair brushed flat. He looked tired and sat beside Molly, patting her hand.

'Has that awful girl gone?'

'Amber?' Jake said. 'Yes, just now. With her father. I checked them out.' He handed them Dai's card and then looked at Bryn. 'Flora's gone too. But not with them.'

Bryn's forehead puckered. 'Our little Flora? Why has she gone? To escape the dreadful sister?' He made it sound like a fairy story.

Jake rubbed his hands over his face. If only it was.

'Personal reasons, Gramps,' he said. He swallowed. 'Gran was just about to tell me what started her off on her biker-hate campaign.'

'Goodness me. Were you?' Bryn gazed at Molly. 'Best thing, probably. Get it off your chest. I'll make some coffee.'

Molly seemed to have dried up, after Bryn's meandering. She said, in a daze, 'Your grandfather was the best biker the world had seen.' She looked towards Bryn, and Jake saw the mutual affection there. It was lovely, but it made him feel lonely for Flora. She smiled. 'I was his brolly dolly.'

'His what?'

'You must have seen the glamorous girls on the starting grid for races? In bikinis and heels, they hold an umbrella over the driver or rider in their leathers, to keep them cool.' A smile played around her lips. 'That was me. I know it's hard to believe now, but I was a stunner.'

'She was indeed.' Bryn put the cafetière carefully on the coffee table and went back for mugs.

Molly smiled up at him and Jake suddenly caught an echo of the woman she'd been. 'I spent ages on my appearance. I did sit-ups for hours to keep my figure, and I ate next to nothing. It was what you did in those days.' Her eyes drifted around the room as she recalled. 'We were so happy. We went all over the world, racing. It was a truly glamorous lifestyle.

'I'd always wanted a classy, luxury hotel, and I was thrilled when we bought this. Well, his winnings bought it. Bikers came from everywhere, just to catch a glimpse of our Bryn.' She sighed. 'It was *the* place to go. Bikes packed into the car park. Parties every weekend. Film stars. Starlets. Anyone who wanted to be seen with the right crowd. Thank God there was no social media then.' Her mouth creased in a smile. 'There were always bonfires on the beach, champagne parties and skinny-dipping.'

Jake felt his cheeks grow hot as he remembered skinny-dipping with Flora in the dark, warm sea, the feel of her taut skin, smooth and warm, her legs wrapped around his hips. He couldn't imagine Molly and Bryn doing the same thing.

Molly glanced at Bryn. 'And then I discovered I was pregnant. It was marvellous, such wonderful news.' She ran her tongue over her lips.

'I'll get some water.' Jake went to the kitchen and ran the tap until it was cold, filling a glass and adding ice and a slice of lemon and handing it to his gran. The kitchen that he and Flora had served Beef Wellington from, and paella from the huge flat pan they'd bought especially. It had always been such a party. Flora had always made it fun. He swallowed, angry and with a primitive urge to kick or smash something.

'It wasn't the wonderful pregnancy I'd hoped for. I was sick, all the time. And I put on so much weight! I looked as if someone had inflated me.' She placed the glass carefully on the coffee table. 'It all sounds so petty now. So selfish. I was probably just like Flora's awful sister.' She smiled at Jake, a wavery, thin smile, and he perched forward on the edge of the chair and hugged her.

'No. She really is awful. She's destructive.'

'Maybe,' Molly continued. 'Everyone has their story. So, obviously, I couldn't be Bryn's brolly dolly, looking like a python that had swallowed a beach ball. My best friend, Clara, said she'd do it instead. We all looked after ourselves in those days, and she would've looked fine on the grid. I didn't want anything to spoil Bryn's photos. I even went along in the beginning, and gave her tips. *Tips!*' She shook her head, pursing her lips. 'And if she'd just stayed on the grid, things would probably have been okay…

'But Bryn raced overseas at times, and she went with him because I couldn't travel in my condition. Women had been throwing themselves at him since I'd known him, and of course I used to wonder, but he was always so attentive, and I trusted him. But then, I wasn't there to fend them off! I was here, in the hotel, like a…' she described an enormous circle with her hands '… huge walrus, waddling about.'

'Darling, you were beautiful. I always said so,' Bryn told her.

Jake had a sudden vision of Flora, pregnant with their child… smiling up at him. He rubbed his face hard to expunge the idea.

Molly continued, 'But Clara, she wasn't content with just being with him at the races, she'd be here too, wanting him to pillion her to places, and posing alongside him. I was relegated to the sitting room, while everyone went off and partied.'

'I wish you'd told me,' Bryn murmured, his veined hand on her shoulder. 'None of this should have happened.'

'Hindsight is such an exact science, isn't it?' Molly patted his arm. 'I was a jealous woman. I still am.'

'So?' Jake prompted.

'Well, inevitably, I caught her, that bloody Clara, draped all over him. And I said, well actually, I screamed, "Me or the bikes. You choose."' Tears trickled down her cheeks. 'And luckily, he chose me. Me and your unborn mother. And by the time that beautiful baby girl was born, Bryn had retired from racing.'

Jake was silent as his brain processed her words.

'I never saw Clara again,' Molly said, 'and I was heartbroken because she'd been my best friend for so long. I packed away all the photos, and the press releases and the certificates. I didn't want to be reminded of it. Any of it. And the people stopped coming here. They came for Bryn, and the motorbikes, you see, and none of it was here. I'd thought that I was part of the attraction, and it made me mad to realise that I was a nobody.' Bryn made a little sound of dissidence, and she sent him a small smile. 'Of course, that meant the money stopped coming in too. I didn't really notice, in the beginning, because I had my beautiful baby girl. It's amazing how time-consuming they are.' She sipped her coffee. 'I'm being very long-winded, aren't I? I'm sorry. It's doing me good to tell it all. I've held it inside for so long.'

'Take your time, Gran. There's no rush.'

'We would have liked another baby, but nature had decided no. We were sad, but we had Jennie, and that's more than many couples get. We had the most splendid wedding for them, and I was there when she had you. You looked just like she had, my darling.' She tightened her lips, and her eyes brimmed with tears that balanced on her lids.

'And then we lost her.' She dabbed her eyes with a paper napkin and then said, 'But we got you. A precious little life to cherish. I didn't really care about the bike thing by then.

Until the Art Café showed up, and they reminded me of all the things I'd thrown away.' Her face was bitter. 'I can see them from my bedroom window you know. I watched all those bikers in the car park, and I remembered what it used to be like here. I felt as if they were rubbing my nose in it. Laughing at our hotel, that's got smaller and shabbier, while they were in the papers and on the TV and everyone was talking about them and how lovely they were.' Her head dropped and Jake had to crane his neck to hear her. 'And they made me realise how stupid and jealous I'd been. I hated them. But I hated myself more.'

'Oh, Gran.' Jake bent over her and kissed her. 'You both gave me a wonderful childhood here. No one could have asked for better parents.'

Bryn got up to make more coffee. When he sat down again, Molly said, 'Your Flora. She had decisions to make, you know. No home, no job, and she needed the money. This was only ever a temporary position, and she knew that. Women need stability in their lives, and her father's money would have given her that.'

Jake said nothing, his heart rate quickening just at the mention of her name. The hollow in the pit of his stomach echoed again. He bent to listen harder.

'I gave her a hard time when she told me, and, on reflection, I admire her coming to tell me. She could have just gone,' Molly continued.

'She did the breakfasts...' Jake said, quietly. 'She even served her sister. I think I would've tipped it over her.'

'She was good fun,' Bryn said. 'I liked her. And her father. We used to have some great chats about bikes.'

'Flora told me.'

'Well, Jake, my darling, I stopped telling you what to do a long time ago. You have to make up your own mind,' Molly said. 'But try and remember – we all live some kind of a lie.'

Chapter Thirty-Three

'You can't watch television forever.' Flora didn't even look at her mum, standing before her with her hands on her hips.

'I can.' Flora reached her arm out to point the remote control round her mum. It was forty-six hours and thirty-nine minutes since she'd left the hotel. She had felt duty bound to turn up to do the breakfasts the day after the terrible storm, had endured Jake's cold shoulder and had then gone straight to see Molly. She could have asked her dad to go with her, but it was her mess, not his. It had been the hardest thing in the world to do. She'd stammered and stuttered her way through her confession, and Molly's face had remained expressionless.

'I'm disappointed in you,' she'd said, and Flora's knees had buckled. Disappointed? It was the worst reproof of all.

'I'll leave today.' She'd gulped back her tears.

'I think that's probably best.'

And that was that. She'd rung her mum, packed her few clothes back in the old rucksack, rather more than she'd arrived with, and left her wetsuit hanging in the wardrobe. There wasn't much opportunity to wear a wetsuit in the Midlands. She shut the wardrobe door quickly.

Leaving her key in the door, she'd sneaked out the back way.

The rain-lashed ride to her mother's apartment on her little Ninja had felt like punishment. She missed the power of the big Ducati, its presence on the road.

The storm hadn't blown itself out and gusts swept her across the road more than once. It had been so scary, and she was so busy concentrating that she hadn't even cried in her helmet. Hollowed out from weeping, she'd gone way past that anyway.

She'd fallen exhausted into her mum's arms, poured out her woes, and then slept solidly for twelve hours, in her queen-sized bed. When she'd woken, she'd lain still, her eyes travelling around the bedroom, until they came to rest on a painting. Of two children holding hands, jumping the waves. Her and Jake. The lump in her throat refused to be swallowed and she wept silently, the tears soaking into the pillow.

'Catch up with some of your friends!' Her mum suggested now. 'Go for a walk. You can't hide forever.' She snatched up the remote control and switched the set off. 'Stuff happens. You have to deal with it. This isn't dealing with it. This is hiding.'

Flora looked up at her. She was sick of the television, but it stopped her thinking of what a mess she'd made of things. Her mind went round and round in circles trying to work out how things could have ended happily ever after, but they always reached the same conclusion. It had been the salon, or Jake. She should have told her father that she wasn't playing his game any more, but then she would have carried on being a breakfast waitress/chambermaid/general minion, with a few home hairdressing customers. She had enjoyed it, but that was because of Jake.

Could she have done it forever? Would it have been enough for her? She didn't know. It was that very indecision which had kept her onside with her dad. Kept her dreaming of that salon. And now, that dream was tarnished and worthless. The cost had been too high.

'Mum, how did you cope so well when Dad left you? And you still seem to be such good friends, even though he, y'know…'

'Do you know, that's the first time you've asked me that?' Her mum wandered into the kitchen. Flora got up and followed her. 'Cuppa?'

Her mum filled the kettle and flicked the switch. Flora

brought down two mugs from the cupboard. In common with everything else in the apartment, they were floral, and brightly coloured. The cool, chalky tones of the cottage came to her, and she swallowed the sadness that she felt, that she was never going to go back there.

'Did Dad help you with the cottage?'

'Of course! He has all the contacts – and impeccable taste. We did discuss it, but he knew how it would look best. It's gorgeous, isn't it?'

Flora nodded. 'Yes, it is. It's really classy. A good job. I wonder what his plans are for the hotel?' She held her hands up at the look on her mum's face. 'Sorry! Sorry, I know it's like Groundhog Day. I'll change the subject.' She stirred her tea. 'I interrupted you. You were telling me how you've stayed such good friends with Dad.'

'Because we were good friends before we were married.'

'Hmm. That's weird. Dad said something about that when we were chatting once. About Jake. We were good friends.' She sipped her tea. 'And I managed to trash that. But... Dad wasn't exactly a saint, was he? For *years*!'

Her mum busied herself at the sink. 'Ah, well. I knew about all that.'

'You *what*?'

'Not all of it. I didn't know about Amber until quite a lot later.' Flora snorted, but said nothing, not wanting to interrupt her mum's flow. 'I think your father guessed before I did.'

'Mum, I'm lost.' Flora frowned, trying to think where she'd not listened properly.

'Darling. I had you – and you are the most precious thing in the world to me – and I went right off sex.'

'Ew,' Flora said, faintly.

'And that's not unusual, for most women, straight after childbirth,' her mum carried on, ignoring her daughter's prudish expression at the idea that her parents had actually had sex. 'But I just didn't want to. And I knew... someone, but I didn't know how she felt about me. So, I didn't say anything to her, and she didn't know how *I* felt about *her*. I carried on, being married to your dad... even though, it was a bit of a lie, really.' She shrugged. 'But he knew. He knew when he saw me with this... um, somebody, that I loved her. The trouble was, I loved him too. But not in the way he wanted. And he found somebody else who loved him in the right way. He found Helen.'

Flora listened, slack jawed, her mind racing. 'So... you're gay. That's why you and Helen always got on so well?'

'Yes.' Her mum nodded. Then sat up straight. 'Oh – no! I like Helen – but I don't fancy her! We weren't a threesome! Per-lease! I was just glad that your dad had someone.'

'So... I don't get it. Who did you have?' She ran her mind over all her mum's friends, of which there were a great many.

Her mum eyed her, over her empty cup. 'More tea?'

'No, thanks. Mum, you don't have to tell me. I'm not judging. I'm just shocked that... that I didn't know. That you didn't feel you could tell me. For all these years.'

Her mum fingered the cuts on her thumbs. She was always pricking herself on thorny stems. Her business partner, Heather, was always nagging her to wear gloves. Nagging, like a... Flora slapped her forehead.

'God, I am so stupid. It's Heather, isn't it?' Her mother's face told her everything she needed to know. Heather, who had encouraged her to follow her hairdressing dreams. Heather, who helped her with her homework and had always been available for lifts to Brownies when her dad was away. How had she been so blind?

'I've loved Heather since forever. She's so kind! Oh, Mum. I'm so sorry you didn't feel you could tell me.' She got up and wound her arms around her mother, kissing her cheek. Her mum stroked her arms.

'You were always a bit – outspoken, judgemental. It's hard enough to come out. So, I just didn't.'

Flora thought of something else. 'Oh no, and all the time I've been here, Heather isn't? Because I'm sleeping in your bed? I'm so sorry. I'll find somewhere to live. I will.'

'You're fine where you are, for now. Heather has her own place. We couldn't have managed all these years any other way. But it's time now for you to get off that sofa, sweetheart. Your dad has put money in your account, hasn't he? Maybe you need to start looking for that salon premises.'

'It doesn't seem so important now.' Flora heeled the brimming tears from her eyes. She had enjoyed her relaxed, bantering relationship with Jake without ever analysing it. They had fun together. He'd made her feel secure, emotionally. Neither of them had ever used the 'L word' on each other, but she had known she loved him, and she had felt sure he loved her. Had she taken him for granted? The thought made her uncomfortable. 'If I hadn't wanted the salon so much, I'd still have Jake. I was greedy. I wanted to have it all.'

'There are plenty more fish in the sea,' her mother said, gently. 'You found Jake, after Spence, and you never thought that would happen.'

'I was angrier about Amber than about Spence, I think. I stopped being in love with him quite a long time ago, if I'm really honest with myself.' Flora heaved a sigh. 'How long did you wait for Heather?'

Her mother was silent.

Flora shrugged, minutely, and sighed. 'Yeah. When you know, you know. How am I going to fix this?'

Jake put the knitted blossoms into a carrier bag. He'd collected them after the storm, and handed them over to Anwen at one of their Knit and Natter sessions.

'Can they be salvaged? Gran loves them.'

Her surprised expression was quickly recovered. 'Aw, I thought they'd been blown away! Yes, of course, we can sort them out. A bit of a wash and refurb, and they'll be good as new.'

'That would be great. Perhaps you could show me how to fix them back onto the trees and I'll do that for you.'

'Er, of course. Any… er, news about Flora?'

He shook his head. 'Sorry.'

'Oh dear, dear. My hair is in dire need of a trim. Never mind. Well, tell her we miss her, won't you?'

He nodded. He hadn't been able to tell anyone why she'd gone. He'd said it was family issues. Only his grandparents knew the real truth, and he believed they missed her almost as much as he did.

After the knitting group, his next stop was the big supermarket on the way to Swansea, and he stopped dead in the entrance, assailed by memories of he and Flora shopping together. He could hear her in his head now, as he wandered along the spirits aisle:

'Taking my advice about gin for your gran, huh?'

He had no idea there were so many varieties. He wished she were here now. Should he stick to traditional or go for something trendy? What would Flora have done?

He picked up one with a brightly coloured label which said 'grapefruit' and then looked at one in a sophisticated, heavy black bottle and remembered what Gran had said about how smart the hotel used to be. Putting the colourful one back, he went in search of tonic waters. He remembered Flora telling him that there were so many different types. The array was baffling. He picked up a pack of assorted flavours and turned towards the checkout, adding a huge bouquet of lilies.

At the last minute, he veered away from the manned checkout, and went to the self-service, remembering how Flora, when he'd confessed that he didn't know how to use it, had grinned and shown him, and how they'd used it every time, how he'd raced to find the bar codes before her. As he waited for the member of staff to verify his age before he could purchase the bottle of gin, he thought of how she would have laughed.

By the time he'd paid, and had to buy a shameful single use plastic bag because, without Flora, he'd forgotten the reusable bag, he'd decided.

He could live without Flora. But he didn't want to. He was going to get her back.

Chapter Thirty-Four

One hundred and eighty-seven hours and forty-six minutes since she'd left the hotel, but who was counting?

She'd had a text from her dad.

If you're still thinking about that salon, let me know before you look at anything. I've got contacts, I can get you the best price. Let me help you. I'm sorry it all went pear-shaped for you. X

Thnx Dad. Not thinking about anything yet but will let you know if I do.

Flora sighed. It was time. Swinging a leg over her Ninja, she rode to the salon she'd worked at for so long, and pushed open the door.

'Flora!' Abandoning their clients briefly, the girls crowded round her, hugging and talking at once.

'You're so brown!'

'And fit!'

'Are you back now?'

Grinning, Flora returned their hugs and looked round the salon. 'So who do I have to beg to hire a chair?' Her heart shrivelled a little, but she kept that smiling face on. She had no one to blame but herself.

'Well,' said Karlie, 'it was you who started the revolt. Although Rex was pretty revolting already...' She laughed. 'You're hired. Yes, girls?' There was a chorus of agreement all round. 'We're business owners now. And we owe that to you.'

Flora started the following day, texting her old customers and taking walk-ins with a smile, just to get her client base started again. Between times, she had her own hair cut by Karlie, keeping it just that little bit longer than she used to. She lurked in the salon tea room, trying not to check the social media updates for Jake and the Art Café, and failing.

Jake had posted nothing new since she'd left, which wasn't a surprise, but the Art Café had posted hundreds of photos of the crippled promenade and the café. The prom had been declared irretrievably damaged and there were no plans to rebuild. The Art Café had gone forever. The memories of that day rushed back, and she was overwhelmed with sadness all over again. She hadn't even said goodbye to them. Would they know about her and what she'd done? Her friends must hate her now.

A week after she'd started back at the salon, she came out of the staff tea room, to see a familiar face in her chair.

Flora plugged the clippers in, switched them on and gathered Amber's caramel coloured hair in a rough ponytail on top of her head, and held the buzzing trimmers close to the root of it. 'You have got a bloody nerve, coming here.'

Several customers' heads swivelled to stare at her, horror on their faces.

'It's okay. She's my sister. I'm allowed.' The heads swivelled back, but Flora saw all the watchful eyes in the mirrors. She lowered her mouth close to Amber's ear.

'What do you want?'

'To say I'm sorry.' Amber's eyes met hers in the glass.

'Okay. You've said it. Now fuck off.'

Amber's reflection glared at her. Flora glared back, holding her ponytail to ransom with the clippers. After a long, charged moment, Amber murmured, without moving a muscle, 'Bitch.'

'Ratbag.'

Flora switched the clippers off. Amber still didn't move, but she said, 'Coffee?'

Her stomach lurching, Flora mouthed to Karlie, 'ten minutes?' and she nodded back in a 'you okay?' gesture. Flora made a face and crossed her fingers before collecting her bag and heading with Amber to the nearest coffee shop. They sat at a table that hadn't been cleared and kicked a carton of orange juice and a sandwich pack out of the way. Neither of them drank the coffee. Flora was the first to speak.

'Why, Amber? Why did you do it? Jake and Spence? Why? What have I done to you?'

'I'm jealous.' She shrugged. Flora gaped. It was the most honest response she'd heard from her sister since she'd met her.

'Of what? You're the one with the legs up to your armpits, and the perfect hair, and the classy looks – and Dad actually employs you!'

'Yes.' Amber stirred her coffee. 'But he does that to keep an eye on me. He told me that the day you left the hotel. You're the one he talks about all the time. I'm a liability, apparently. You manage to tell people things they don't want to hear and they still like you. How do you do that?'

'What?' Flora was confused. Turning each sentence over in her mind and examining it, she was already behind, struggling to keep up as Amber continued.

'You were born first. You've always been the favourite. He calls you "sweet pea" and he calls me Amber.'

'Oh. I always thought he just couldn't remember my name.' Flora blinked.

'Can you imagine how it was, thinking I was the only one, then finding out I had a sister, and I wasn't even the eldest?' Amber shook her head and her expensive lowlights rippled. 'I feel like I've spent my whole life playing catch up with you.'

Flora was stunned. 'But... but... your mum treated us both the same!'

'That made it worse. I thought she'd be on my side.'

'You hacked my fringe off! On school photo day!'

Amber fidgeted. 'Ye-es. You were always going on about being a hairdresser when you grew up and I thought I'd give it a try too. But it went a bit wrong, and I had to keep cutting bits off to even it up and it wasn't my fault really. I couldn't even do that right.'

'And you let the cars drive over my dolls!'

'I did. Yes. I did do that.' Amber's head dipped. She stopped stirring and sat with her hands gripped together and her shoulders hunched.

'I loved those dolls.'

'Yeah. That's why I did it. You had everything. You had Dad first.'

'And you shagged Spence... Although he was a bit of a twat, really.' Flora stared at her. 'You really are a total bitch, you know.'

'I know. I'm sorry. Anyway, I did you a favour, getting rid of Spence for you. His replacement was—'

'Don't push your luck, Amber.' Flora frowned. 'I appreciate what it must've taken for you to come here and say all this. But I can't forgive you just like that. Not after everything,' she gulped, 'and all these years. You bullied me because you could get away with it.'

Amber hung her head, and her voice, when she spoke, was barely audible. 'Sorry. I really am sorry. If I could turn the clock back, I'd—'

'—you'd do it all over again, I expect.' They stared at each other, and Flora felt that strange bond between sisters that was always going to exist, even if they hated each other enough to do physical harm.

'So, you haven't seen Jake since?'

Flora felt the familiar lump in her throat at the mention of his name. She shook her head. 'No. No thanks to you. I was going to tell him myself. Somehow.'

'Well,' said Amber, her expression for once sincere, 'I hope it works out for you. He seems genuine.'

They stood to leave and there was the strangest moment of

reconciliation as they turned to give each other an awkward, stiff fingered hug that lasted only a second.

'So,' Flora said, as they left the coffee shop. 'How did you want your hair cut?'

'You didn't really think I'd trust you with my hair, did you?' Amber was back in familiar territory, except for the faintest glimmer of a smile. 'It's only just started growing back after you pulled chunks of it out!'

Chapter Thirty-Five

It was a few weeks later that Dai rang, although it might have been longer. Flora had lost track of time.

'Sweet pea – I've got something I'd like you to have a look at with me. Would you mind?' Her father's voice on the phone took her straight back to the hotel when he'd stayed there, to their long walks along the prom – which didn't even exist now. When would everything stop reminding her of Jake?

She wondered if her dad had found her possible salon premises, and tried to feel some excitement. He arranged to collect her from the salon the following evening, and she made sure she looked smart for him. Since their meeting, she and Amber had communicated a bit more, and Flora, although suspicious still, was a little kinder towards her, a little more understanding of her behaviour.

Amber in her turn, sowed several seeds in her head, and one was that Flora could make a bit more of her appearance, start to at least look like the successful salon owner that in her dreams, she could be. She ditched the endless black T-shirts, and tentatively tried a few items in a palette of sea colours that to her surprise enhanced her eyes. She wondered what Jake would have said, if he could see her now, wearing a subtle sheen of make-up, her hair stylishly cut again instead of the messy ponytail.

Her father's sleek car was waiting for her, and she leaned back in the luxurious leather seats after he'd kissed her cheek.

'How are you doing, lovely girl? You look very nice!'

'You're not going to believe this. This,' she indicated her smart outfit and heeled sandals, 'is Amber's doing.'

He shook his head. 'Wonders will never cease.' He smiled,

his eyes crinkling, and she saw that he still had a tan from his time in the Welsh sunshine. Would it ever stop making her cry to think of Wales?

'Where are you taking me?'

'To the office first. I've had plans drawn up. I want your honest response to them.' He stretched his neck, and Flora realised that he was nervous. She was intrigued, watching his fingers drumming on the steering wheel.

'Me and my famous honesty...' She pressed her lips together in a rueful smile and he glanced at her briefly.

'Yes. Exactly that. I want you to be absolutely truthful. Okay?'

She nodded, feeling a flutter of apprehension. Her father's offices were quietly tasteful, and brought to mind Sea-Spray Cottage. He led her to a room with a vast, polished table, topped with several large format drawings. He spread them out, and rotated them for her to see.

She frowned, trying to make sense of them. It was a huge building, not at all what she'd expected.

'This is the entrance.' His finger tapped the spot. Gradually, she orientated herself. It was strangely familiar.

'Oh no! Dad – is it Hotel Y Ddraig? Are these,' she peered at the drawing again, 'are they apartments? Oh no. No, no, no, no, what about Molly and Bryn? And Jake? You can't do this to them...' She pushed the drawings away, stricken. 'Why are you making me look at this?'

'Look again, sweetheart.' Her dad's tone was patient. 'See here? This is the café...'

'God. It's huge!' She backtracked. 'This café... with floor to ceiling windows...'

'Yes. That will be the new Art Café.'

'Wow.' Emotion threatened to overwhelm her as she remembered that terrible day in the storm. She put a hand over her mouth, gazing at the drawings. Tears dripped through her fingers and onto the paper. It was like a rebirth, and she was having trouble taking it all in.

'These are the community rooms, that can be rented out...' He straightened up, rubbing his lower back. 'And here, this is where the guest rooms will be, all en suite.'

The plans swam before her eyes. 'Dad, it looks... well, it looks amazing. But I don't understand why you're telling me.' She sat down suddenly, confused and dry mouthed. There was a buzzing in her ears.

'Well, I wondered if you might be interested in this bit.' He pulled out another set of drawings. The elevations looked like glazed Victorian railway arches. They were at the rear of the hotel. Where she used to store her bike. 'I thought,' he said, diffidently, 'that this might make a great salon. If it was something you were still interested in...'

Flora stared at the drawings. She visualised her sign in that archway, by the sea, part of something exciting, progressive.

'I can see that it would be wonderful.' She chewed her lip, pensive. 'So it's a kind of Art Hotel, is it? With space for exhibitions, and a stage, and community groups. And that huge café – that could be cooking workshops, and taster evenings. And residential courses, art holidays, as well as ordinary guests. It'll be fantastic. A real crowd puller, and great for tourism.'

Her dad nodded, enthusiastically. 'That's what I thought. So.' He tapped the second set of drawings. 'Would you like to be part of it?'

'Of course!' Flora shook her head, sadly. 'It's really kind of you, Dad, but truly? Anywhere else but there. I couldn't set up my business, knowing that I'd had a part in Jake and his folks selling up. It would feel so wrong. I'd be reminded of them every single day, and I'd miss them terribly. I miss them every day as it is, and they're miles away. It wouldn't be any good, without Jake to share it with. I can't believe you've even asked me.' She blinked back the tears that settled on her lashes. They fell anyway, dripping onto her smart jeans.

Her dad poured a tumbler of water from the cooler. Handing it to her, he said,

'Before you say no, perhaps you'd like to meet my new business partners.'

She looked at him sharply, her stomach full of ping-pong balls. And she hoped she knew, with all her heart she hoped, as he opened the connecting door, who was going to be in there.

Jake wore a pale blue shirt, open at the neck, and a smart mid-blue jacket over dark jeans. Already on his feet, he took a step towards her. She drank him in, seeing that his hair needed cutting and feeling absurdly pleased that it did.

The buzzing in her ears increased. She stared warily at the hand he held out, and he dropped it slowly. Her eyes bored into his.

'You couldn't have told me about all this before?' She was aware of other people in the room, but she spoke directly to Jake. 'I've been torturing myself all these weeks, and *this* has been going on!'

'Flora,' he said. 'I wanted to tell you.' She watched the muscles of his exposed throat as he swallowed. 'And every time I played the scene out in my head, I got as far as, I love you, Flora, please come back, and then I realised that I had nothing to offer you. We had an amazing summer, but I didn't have a proper job. I was the one who wanted to help you set up your salon, and I couldn't.'

Flora opened her mouth to protest. 'But—'

Jake shook his head, and continued, 'Sorry, I have to tell you this. Your father has rescued us. Hotel y Ddraig was failing fast, and even I didn't know how bad things were. None of this,' he waved his hand at the drawings, 'would have happened without you. It's only just fallen into place, and only now do I feel that I have something to give you, after all that you gave me. Please forgive me.'

'What am I forgiving you for?' Her voice was husky.

'For being an arse?' He took a deep breath. 'And for not coming after you straightaway. I ran down the drive after your bike. And I have missed every single bit of you, every single minute you've been gone. You made me see what I had, that was right under my nose. I didn't have to go to the other side of the world to find happiness.'

He held his hand out again.

'I love you, Flora. Please, please come back.' This time she took it, and almost wept at the warm familiarity of his skin against hers. She was never, ever going to let him go again. 'And just to show you how serious I am, I brought this for you.' He handed her a sheet of printed paper. She scanned the words, looking up and around the room. Molly and Bryn and her mum smiled back at her. They were all in on it!

'I can't believe you did this,' she whispered, reading the words again.

'Ash put me through my paces.'

'What is it?' her dad asked, craning his neck to see.

'It's his CBT certificate.' Flora handed him the sheet, her other hand still firmly in Jake's. 'The basic bike training test. Earning your "L" plates.' She laughed at his mystified expression. 'I know, they didn't have them in your day. But it's the first step towards passing your proper bike test. And Jake knows exactly how much it means to me.' She grinned at Jake. 'I'd better start training for my lifesaving qualification.'

'So does this mean you're in?' Dai asked.

'What's it going to cost me?' Flora said.

He grinned. 'I can tell you've been spending time with Amber!'

Flora laughed at Jake's stunned expression, and went to hug Molly and Bryn and her mum.

'Lucy and Richard wanted to be here too,' her father said, 'but I said we'd go to them, once we knew what was happening with you two.'

'Oh!' Flora's hand flew to her trembling mouth. 'They wanted to be here?'

The four of them discussed the new plans, and Flora tried hard to concentrate, but all she could think about was Jake, and her salon, and when was she going back to Wales.

'I can't believe you met my mum without me knowing.'

Jake nodded, his eyes never leaving hers.

'I went with Dai and Gran and Gramps… she showed us her painting. The one of you and me in the waves that Gran has a sketch of?'

Flora nodded. 'I know the one.'

'And then I remembered. When you said, in that terrible storm? "We'll do it together."'

Flora looked puzzled. 'Erm… Did I?'

'You used to say that to me, when we were little, and I was scared of the waves. You used to grab my hand and say, "We'll do it together."'

'I was so bossy, even then.' Flora looked shyly up at him. She couldn't imagine him being scared of the waves, or anything, ever. A thought struck her, and she blurted, interrupting her father explaining his plans for the new driveway. She smacked her forehead. 'So Amber knew too! It's been a conspiracy, hasn't it?' She pretended to pout at their faces. 'And you had a nerve to tell *me* off for spying!'

'I think we did it better than you, as it happens,' Jake said, straight-faced. 'You always said you'd be a rubbish spy.'

Chapter Thirty-Six

The brand new Art Hotel celebrated their opening with a huge party. Flora had marvelled daily as it evolved before her eyes. She'd selected the best of the before, during and after photos, and had framed them for her salon.

Her salon! She had to pinch herself that it was really happening. It was so beautiful, better than she'd ever imagined, inspired by the seaside location, in driftwood textures and natural shades of teal and sand.

Her dad had gifted her a long lease, and she used the money he'd paid her for 'spying' for her fixtures and fittings, knowing perfectly well that he was behind many of the purchases at excellent prices. She wouldn't let him down. She'd built up a good client list on her mobile round and her dream team of beauticians and other part-time hairdressers, renting a chair from her just as she'd done, were as excited about the new business as she was.

Even more exciting was the thought of her mum and Heather, living together in Sea-Spray Cottage. They'd sold their florists business and rented out their own properties, and were renting a unit in the row adjacent to Flora.

'It's called "HeathRose". It's our pre-retirement plan,' they'd told her, as she'd hugged them so tightly that they'd laughed for mercy.

'We're all together. Back in Wales. I couldn't ask for anything better.'

Molly and Bryn were partners and had a garden flat within the hotel.

'It will be wonderful to sit out in my very own garden,' Molly told Flora. 'And Anwen has been teaching me to crochet!'

'I'll see you at the Knit and Natter group!' Flora said.

'Also the book club and the writers' group. I have so much to write about.'

'You won't have time to retire.' Flora hugged her impulsively, and said, for the billionth time since she'd come back, 'I'm so, so pleased to be here.'

Jake was on his way to becoming a fully-fledged chef. He, Richard and Josh, the hotel chef who had joined them after Pete had been sacked, with Amy the dinner waitress who'd been so supportive in their early days, and all the staff from the Art Café had teamed up to become the catering team for the Art Hotel.

The drive and entrance gates had been refurbished with spectacular dragons either side and the shrubs that had hidden the building for so long had gone, which Molly was sad about, but there was now a wonderful view of the hotel. Flora remembered the brave, knitted blooms that had festooned the dark, glossy leaves and arranged delivery of an array of camellias and dwarf azaleas to be delivered to Molly's new garden. One of the building team obligingly planted them according to Molly's imperious directions.

Flora's salon sign was one of the last jobs to be done. As the builders took away the ladders with a flourish, Flora was there to record the moment with the remote-control tripod she'd bought for her phone. She turned to arrange everyone for the photo.

'Bryn and Molly, in the middle, here, Dad and Helen on one side with Amber, Mum and Heather on the other, my bike in front, and me and Jake on each side? Or...'

'Get on with it!' they chorused at her. So she did. The photos, printed in sequence and framed like a cartoon strip, later hung over the salon desk, showed her on each one as a blur, running to and fro, and everyone laughing. The salon bore its new name proudly: 'Waves'.

The huge function room, with its ability to be split into smaller rooms with floor to ceiling dividing doors, was set up for a live band on the stage and a disco alongside for later. The spacious restaurant housed in its new orangery extension and panoramic windows with sea views was the main focus of the launch party.

Display shelving showcased a fabulous variety of designer crafts and jewellery, and spotlights lit the exhibition of paintings in the dedicated gallery that gave the hotel its name. Fairy lights twinkled over everything and there were snowy white tablecloths and trays of sparkling champagne glasses. The hired waiting staff would be handing out drinks and canapés. Press packs and screens bearing photos of the epic reconstruction were set out in the sitting room.

Flora had spent the entire day doing everyone's hair for the party. Except Amber's. Some things never changed.

'They all look stunning, and I'm going to look like I've been dragged through a hedge,' she grumbled to Jake, towelling dry after her speedy shower. He kissed her, and her insides melted, just as they did every single time.

'You always look stunning. Go like that, and cause a stir.' He waggled his eyebrows at her and she laughed, her gaze travelling over him.

'You look incredible.' He wore a crisp white shirt with the top two buttons undone, under a dark charcoal suit. Flora wiggled into the teal, body hugging dress she had shopped for with Lucy. She, along with Ash and Daisy, Richard and Nicola, Ed, Jo, Liam and Beryl were all staying over in the hotel, as were her parents, Heather and Helen, Flora's 'mums'. And Amber.

'No punch-ups tonight,' Jake warned her.

'Oh, we're *so* over that.' Flora waved an airy hand after applying mascara to her fake lashes. 'Mostly. It's what sisters do.' She slipped her feet into the heeled party shoes and picked up her sparkling, dainty bag, stuffed with 'Waves' business cards.

Molly and Bryn were already at the party, both looking elegant and smiling, and posing beneath Bryn's race bike, suspended from the ceiling in the café restaurant. The motorbike press were there in force, taking photos and asking for interviews.

The bike had been unearthed from its hiding place in one of the outhouses – Molly said she knew it had been there all along – and Ed had done a wonderful job of restoring its looks, although not its engine. Bryn had creakily thrown his leg over it, and wondered aloud how on earth he'd ever folded himself onto it to race at high speed.

'If you get it going, I'll want to ride it. And I don't think that's a good idea,' he'd said, sadly. His birthday surprise had been a pillion ride on a racetrack with Superbike rider, Carl Fogarty, who'd been only too happy to oblige. Bryn had declared himself satisfied with that. Until the next one…

When it seemed that the hotel could hold no more people, Flora's father commandeered the microphone and welcomed everybody.

'Thank you all for coming, some of you from a considerable distance,' he began, picking out and naming people, some of whom Flora recognised as their investors, sponsors and friends, and many who she didn't. 'We are delighted to have created a dream team with Molly, Bryn and Jake from Hotel Y Ddraig, and Richard and Lucy with their staff from the Art Café,' he paused for effect, 'and we are proud to present – The Art Hotel!' There was applause. He was a brief but entertaining speaker and he wound up with, 'I'm not going to hold up the fun any longer – enjoy the evening!' as he introduced the band and female singer.

Jake held his hand out and led Flora on to the floor, where they were quickly joined by many others.

'I love this song!' She smiled up at him.

'Is there a song you don't like?' He grinned, twirling her away and then towards him. The dance floor was full, and Flora smiled and waved at lifeguards she knew, and clients, and then spotted Amber, dancing with a good-looking man. She steered Jake towards Lucy and Jo and signposted with her eyes.

'TV Tom and Amber! Of course! Match made in heaven,' Lucy said with a grin. 'I think you might be seeing a lot more of your sister...'

'Oh, joy!' Flora pretended to look dismayed, but she knew people did change. When they wanted to.

As the band's first set came to an end, they stopped playing and in the silence a petite figure climbed up on the stage, with no introduction. It was Daisy.

'What's Daisy doing up there?' Flora whispered to Jake.

Lifting her clear young voice, Daisy sang the first two lines of the haunting Welsh love song that Flora now knew. Projected on the wall behind her, were the welsh lyrics of 'Calon Lân', and the crowd's heads turned to read them.

Deeper voices joined Daisy's from each corner of the room, and one by one, singers added their more powerful voices and walked through the crowd to form a choir. Their beautiful vocals filled the room, and with a lump in her throat, Flora blotted at the tears that balanced on her lashes. The singers arranged themselves gradually in a horseshoe around Flora and Jake.

As the music died away, Jake lowered himself onto one knee before her. Her tears fell before he even spoke.

'Flora, you may be small, but you have the biggest, purest heart. Will you marry me?' He opened the velvet box and Flora gasped as the perfect rock twinkled back at her. She threw her arms around him.

'Oh, Jake. I love you so much. Yes. Yes!'

There was deafening applause all round, and the band started up again as their families and friends enveloped them in hugs and kisses. Amber towed TV Tom with her to congratulate them both.

'I'm glad for you, sis,' she said. 'I always said he was a genuine guy, didn't I? And if I hadn't... well, you know, you wouldn't have... y'know. So I did you a favour, really. You should be grateful to me.'

'Amber...' Jake's grip tightened on her, but it wasn't necessary. Flora raised her eyebrows at her sister and said, mildly, 'You do enjoy living dangerously, don't you?' She held out a hand to TV Tom. 'Hi, Tom, thanks for coming – I hope you're enjoying yourself!'

Jake collected a bottle of champagne a little later and steered them both outside to cool off from their dancing exertions. The chairs and tables were empty out here, while everyone tucked in to the food that was being served.

'Happy?' He tipped his head towards her as he poured her glass and then his own.

'Totally.' She tipped her diamond ring so it winked in the lights. 'I have never been happier.'

'Can we join you two lovebirds?' Lucy and Ash waited for them to answer before sitting at their table. 'This place is stunning, isn't it? And we've got some news too, but we want to keep it quiet for the time being. Daisy knows, and our parents, and that's all.' Lucy looked at them and her face broke into a huge grin. 'I'm pregnant! At last! We've been trying for so long... and anyway, we decided we really ought to make an effort and actually get married. And we thought, let's strike while the iron's hot, and book our reception here, before anyone else snaps it up. What do you think?'

'Oh, my goodness, that's just lovely news. I'm so pleased for you both.' Flora leapt up and threw her arms around Lucy, while Jake pumped Ash's hand. 'I'll go and find Dad and you can book the date.' She ran inside and located her father, telling him the news quickly. He followed her back outside.

'I've just realised, I don't know who the hotel manager is.' Flora put a hand to her mouth.

'Yes, you do,' her father said.

'Who?'

'Me!' He smiled at them. 'I had such a lovely time here last year, and Helen has been asking me to slow down for a while... so I'm stepping back from the property market, and managing this hotel while it gets up and running. There are bound to be teething problems, and I'd like to nip them in the bud before they get a hold. And then, my plan is to retire down here, and relax. Take up biking again. Whatever.' He shrugged. 'So, name your date, guys. Let's go and ink it in to the calendar! We've already submitted an application for permission to hold weddings.' The three of them headed for the office, leaving Flora and Jake alone.

'Weddings! I could do the hair... Mum and Heather could do the flowers...' She looked at Jake, who was eyeing her, speculatively. 'What?'

'Would you like children?' he asked.

Flora eyed him. 'Should we have discussed this before you asked me to marry you?'

'Well, it's not a deal-breaker,' Jake said, hurriedly. 'As long as I have you...'

'What if I want a whole brood of them?'

'Do you?'

'I might...'

Jake pondered for a moment. 'I'll have to teach them all to swim...'

'And ride motorbikes. Like Daisy does...'

'I think we ought to get our names on that calendar too.' Jake took her hand. 'Come on, Flora Bexton. Let's start planning for when we're going to be Mr and Mrs Foley.'

Flora stopped dead. 'Hang on. Mrs Flora Foley? I think hyphenated will be the way to go.'

Jake laughed, and carried on walking.

Trotting beside him, Flora mused. 'What if we have a Felicity? Or a Frederick? Philomena? Frankie? Ffion? I like Ffion. But Ffion Foley? Ffion Bexton-Foley has a much better ring to it...' She came to a halt again. 'Oh God, look at the width of your shoulders... Ouch... Ja-ake!' She hurried after him. 'I might be having second thoughts...'

Thank You

Dear Reader,

Thank you for reading my third novel, *Escape to the Art Café*. I do hope you enjoyed meeting my characters and following their story.

Flora and Jake were both born from areas of my life. I, like Jake, was very involved with the local Surf Life Saving Club and I'm delighted that my family are still committed and active members. And I'm rubbish at pushing my thirty-stone motorbike about, just like Flora, which is how her story began.

As with the other characters in the Art Café novels, I fully expect to see them all together in real life, sitting around a picnic bench overlooking the beach, blowing on their chips after an evening rideout. I like to think they'd invite me over to share their chat!

It's exciting and terrifying in equal measure to share them with the world. I would be thrilled if you took the time to leave a review on the retail site where you made your purchase. Reviews really do help to improve a book's profile and sales and are very much appreciated.

My contact details are given at the end of my author profile, and if I've encouraged you to learn to ride a motorbike, or to become a member of a Surf Life Saving Club, details of how to do that are there too!

Much love,

Sue x

About the Author

 Sue McDonagh's career as a policewoman for Essex Police was cut short when she was diagnosed at the age of twenty-four with ovarian cancer. After a successful recovery and a stint working as a Press Officer she moved to Wales.

In Wales her love of art evolved into a full-time occupation and she made a living teaching and sketching portraits at shows. In 2014 she was a regional finalist for the Sky Arts Portrait Artist of the Year. She now works exclusively to commissions from her art gallery.

In 2009 she learned to ride a motorbike, and now helps run Curvy Riders, a national, women only, motorbike club. Her joy of motorbikes and her love of writing inspired her to write the Art Café series.

Sue is a proud mum and granny in the gloriously blended family she is honoured to be part of. She lives a mile from the sea in Wales and can often be found with her border terrier, Scribble, at her art gallery. Scribble thinks the customers only come in to see him. Sometimes, Sue thinks that too.

When she's not painting, she's writing or on her motorbike. She belongs to a local writing group and the Cariad Chapter.

For more information on Sue visit:
https://twitter.com/SueMcDonaghLit
https://www.facebook.com/SueMcDonaghWriter/

More Choc Lit

From Sue McDonagh

Summer at the Art Café

From watercolours and cupcakes to leather jackets and freedom …

If you won a gorgeous purple motorbike, and your domineering husband said you were too fat for leathers and should sell it, would you do as you were told – or learn to ride it in secret?

Artist and café owner Lucy Daumier intends to do just that – but learning to ride is far from easy, especially under the critical eye of prickly motorcycle instructor, Ash Connor.

But gradually she gets the hang of it, and in the process re-discovers the girl she used to be. So starts an exciting summer of new friendship and fun – as well as a realisation that there is more to Ash than meets the eye when she is introduced to his seven-year-old daughter, Daisy.

But can Lucy's new-found happiness last when a spiteful family member wants to see her fail?

Visit www.choc-lit.com for details.

Meet Me at the Art Café

Would you take a chance on a bad boy with a leather jacket and a vintage motorbike?

That's the question single mum Jo Morris has to ask herself when she collides with local bike mechanic Ed Griffiths on a rainy Welsh hillside. Working at the Art Café, Jo hears the gossip and is all too aware of Ed's reputation.

But whilst he's certainly no angel, there is something about Ed's daredevil antics that Jo can't ignore. And as she gets to know him better and watches the kind way he deals with her young son Liam, she begins to wonder – is there more to this 'bad boy' than meets the eye?

Visit www.choc-lit.com for details.

Introducing Choc Lit